PRAISE FOR OLIVIA CUNNING'S RED-HOT SINNERS ON TOUR SERIES

"The chemistry is palpable, and their sexual encounters page-searing…Cunning has me hooked."

—*Love Romance Passion*

"Extremely well-written…I honestly fell in love with each of the band members. Oh, the glorious plot! So good, so yummy, so hot!"

—*Sexy Women Read*

"Entirely irresistible—the only two words needed to describe the captivating characters…unique and entertaining."

—Suite101.com

"What caught me by surprise was the laugh-out-loud humor and the intense relationships…the romance was sweet, sexy, and had my heart racing."

—*Fiction Vixen*

"A super smokin', hot and kinky story that pushes the bounds and left me weak in the knees. Seriously!!!"

—*Seriously Reviewed*

"Erotic decadence from the first word, and I couldn't get enough of it. [Cunning] nailed the rock and roll scene for me."

—*Leontine's Book Realm*

"Wicked, naughty, arousing, and you'll be craving the next page of this book as if you were living it for yourself!"

—*Dark Divas Reviews*

"Readers will love the characters and enjoy their scorching love scenes and passionate fights."

—*RT Book Reviews*, 4 stars

"The sex is incredible and the love is even better. Each rocker has a piece of my heart…An excellent read."

—*Night Owl Romance*, 5 Stars, Reviewer Top Pick

"Sizzling sex, drugs, and rock-n-roll…Absolutely perfect!"

—*Fresh Fiction*

"Emotionally touching, funny, and curl your toes hot!…a non-stop thoroughly enjoyable read."

—*Book Lover's Inc.*

"I just can't seem to get these rockers out of my system. I can't wait to read each band member's book."

—*A Buckeye Girl Reads*

"Olivia Cunning has written a perfect erotic romance… amazingly hot."

—*About Happy Books*

"Hot, steamy, humorous."

—BookLoons.com

SINNERS ON TOUR

Double TIME

OLIVIA CUNNING

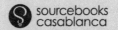
sourcebooks
casablanca

Published by Sourcebooks Casablanca, an imprint of Sourcebooks, Inc.
P.O. Box 4410, Naperville, Illinois 60567-4410
(630) 961-3900
FAX: (630) 961-2168
www.sourcebooks.com

Library of Congress Cataloging-in-Publication Data

Cunning, Olivia.
  Double time : Sinners on tour / Olivia Cunning.
    p. cm.
  (trade paper : alk. paper) 1. Rock groups—Fiction. 2. Bisexual men—Fiction.
3. Women rock musicians—Fiction. 4. Man-woman relationships—Fiction.
5. Triangles (Interpersonal relations)—Fiction. I. Title.
  PS3603.U6635D68 2012
  813'.6—dc22

2012024629

Printed and bound in Canada
WC 10 9 8 7 6 5 4 3

Dedicated to the memory of
Randy Rhodes,
the first rock star I ever mourned.
He disembarked from
the crazy train much too soon,
but his legacy will always survive
in his haunting guitar work.
Dude, you rock.

Chapter 1

"TREY." THE SOUND OF Brian's deep voice tugged at Trey's heart. His soul. His will. Brian comprised Trey's hopes. His dreams. Embodied his love. His desire. Represented his past. His present. His future. Everything Trey had ever been or ever could be, he associated with the man. Trey knew Brian would never love him. Not with the same all-encompassing, soul-wrenching possessiveness with which Trey loved him, but they maintained a close friendship. It wasn't nearly enough for Trey, but was better than nothing.

"Trey?" Brian whispered against his ear, his bare chest pressed against Trey's naked back. "I want you."

The flood of lust that coursed through Trey's body was punctuated with an inrush of breath. *Yes...* "Now?"

"Shh," Brian breathed. "Quiet. Or someone will hear us."

Trey was naked. Had he gone to bed naked? He didn't remember. It didn't matter. In the darkness, Brian pressed him facedown on the mattress of his bunk on Sinners' tour bus. Trey felt Brian's weight over his back. His warmth seeped into his skin. The scent of leather, Brian's sweet aftershave, and male surrounded him. Trey closed his eyes and relished the sensations. The texture of Brian's skin. The raspy quality of his breath.

Emotion washed over Trey. His only regret was that they weren't face to face, so he couldn't stare into Brian's intense brown eyes, bury his hands in his messy, shoulder-length hair, and kiss his firm lips as he took him. Whenever Brian visited him, it was always like this. Face down. Total surrender.

Trey felt Brian's cock against his throbbing ass. He relaxed, opening himself to possession. Brian surged forward, filling him with one deep thrust.

"Ah," Trey gasped brokenly as a mix of pain and pleasure pulsed through the core of his body. He loved that Brian's cock was huge. That it stretched him to his limits. Loved how Brian clasped his hands on either side of his head to pin him down. It made Trey feel helpless. Fucked. Used. Exactly how he needed to feel, because he knew this wasn't right. Brian loved another.

Trey lifted his hips slightly in an attempt to get his own attentive cock into a more pleasurable position.

"Don't move," Brian growled. "Take it."

Trey took it. No pain now. Just intense, pulsating pleasure. Brian fucked him harder. Harder. Until Trey wanted to scream *I love you, I love you, I love you* at the top of his lungs. He didn't dare. He knew Brian would disappear the moment he said anything that remotely stupid.

Trey bit his lip and struggled to lift his hips off the bed. He wanted Brian's hands on his cock as he fucked him. Stroking him from base to tip. Giving him pleasure. Making him come. Come by his hand. In his hands. The hands that created the guitar music that was as much a part of Trey as it was of Brian.

"Brian?" he whispered. "Please."

"No."

Trey groaned and rocked his hips, rubbing his cock against the mattress. He needed to come so bad. *Oh, please. I need it. Need you.*

"Hold still, Trey. You know how this works."

Trey stopped moving. Brian had been visiting him like this more and more frequently. Especially since Brian had gotten his wife, Myrna, pregnant. It was pretty much a nightly occurrence at this point. Trey wanted him. Not just in bed. In his life. Each moment, he felt Brian slipping further away and Trey didn't know how to hold on to him.

Brian. Stay with me. Please.

"Trey?" A hand grabbed Trey's shoulder and gave him a hard shake. "Trey! Wake up. It's time."

Trey opened his eyes. The Brian of his dreams vanished and was replaced by the real Brian. This one was *not* fucking him good, hard, and selfishly up the ass. This one was fully clothed and grinning at him from just outside the curtain of Trey's bunk. Trey's balls tightened unexpectedly and he reached down to pull off his sock. He buried his cock in the soft, warm cotton. His belly clenched. Muscles at the base of his cock gave a hard spasm. He came with a tortured gasp.

Goddammit. He ruined more socks that way.

"Sorry to interrupt your wet dreams, dude," Brian said, "but we've got to catch a plane. Like immediately. Get dressed."

Still disoriented, still trembling with the aftereffects of his unexpected orgasm (while Brian watched—he'd undoubtedly relive that in his fantasies for weeks), Trey forced himself to sit up on his bunk. Feet dangling over the edge, he bent his back at an uncomfortable angle so he didn't whack his head on the tour bus' ceiling. "What time is it?" Trey rubbed his eyes and blinked in the overly bright cabin lights.

"Three."

"In the morning? What the hell, Brian? I need sleep."

"Myrna's in labor."

Trey's heart twisted unpleasantly. "She's not due for…"

"Two weeks. I know. It's the real deal though. She's already at the hospital." Brian grabbed Trey's arm and jerked him out of his bunk to the floor. "Hurry up. I will not miss the birth of my first child."

"I don't understand why I have to go," Trey said.

Brian looked a little hurt and Trey immediately wanted to take that comment back.

"You have to go because I need you there," Brian said.

"Fine. I'll go. Whatever," Trey said as if his heart wasn't singing with delight. Brian needed him? There was a first time for everything, he supposed.

Trey rearranged his boxer shorts and located his jeans on the floor next to their new soundboard operator's empty bunk. Rebekah's bunk didn't get much use. She and the band's drummer, Eric Sticks, spent most nights in the back bedroom claiming they were still on their honeymoon. Seven months of honeymooning was a bit much by anyone's standards. Even Trey's. Trey hopped into his pants, tugged a T-shirt over his head, and began his search for a spare sock.

Brian chuckled at him when he tossed his ruined sock in the garbage. "That must've been some dream. What was it about?"

Trey raked a hand through his long bangs. "These three really hot chicks," he lied without missing a beat. "I had three cocks and each of them was sucking one."

Brian quirked an eyebrow at him and Trey's heart skipped a beat. The man was so fucking gorgeous, it was a sin. "Weird."

But not as weird as having homoerotic dreams about your best friend. Your married best friend who was about to become a father.

"Did you get plane tickets already?" Trey asked.

"Your brother's jet is meeting us at the airstrip. It's already on its way. Should be landing by the time we get there."

"So Dare's coming with?"

"Nope. Just you and me."

Alone on a private jet. Trey was pretty sure they wouldn't be initiating each other into the mile high club. Bummer.

By the time they reached the hospital four hours later, Brian was in a panic. When Trey hesitated on the threshold of Myrna's delivery and recovery room, Brian grabbed his arm and hauled him inside.

"I didn't miss it, did I?" Brian asked the doctor who was between Myrna's legs with his bloody surgical gloves trying to ease a black-haired head out of something Trey wished he had never ever seen. Oh fuck. That had to hurt.

Trey's eyelids fluttered, the floor disappeared from beneath him, and everything went black.

The squall of a baby and the declaration, "It's a boy!" flittered around Trey's semiconscious mind. That and some strange ammonia smell just beneath his nose.

"Come on, gorgeous," a soft feminine voice said nearby. "Open your eyes for me. The messy part is all over now."

Trey regained full consciousness with a sudden intake of breath. He instinctively knocked the offensive smelling salts from beneath his nose and sat up.

"There, he's back with us," someone said from the opposite side of the room. The doctor maybe? Trey couldn't get his eyes to focus.

"Did I pass out?" Trey asked.

"Out like a light, buddy," Brian said from beside Myrna's bed. He chuckled much too gleefully.

"You can*not* tell anyone about this," Trey said, struggling to climb to his feet. He leaned his back against a wall to steady himself. He hated hospitals. He'd spent far too many hours in them as a child, including one entire summer when his father had been serving his residency and his mother had decided to ride a bicycle across the country. Just the smell of a hospital made his skin crawl.

"Yeah right," Brian said. "I'm having T-shirts made. I wanted to wait to cut the cord, but you refused to wake up in time to watch."

Trey's stomach did a summersault. *Cut the cord?* Yuck. "Sorry I missed it." Not.

"That's okay. I got it on film."

"Great…" Trey ducked his head to hide his crinkled nose.

A stunning brunette dressed in pink scrubs bent down to enter Trey's field of vision. She stroked his hair out of his face. The slim brows over her striking blue eyes drew together in concern. "Feeling better now?"

He grinned at her and she flushed. "I think I'll live," he said.

Her hand slid to the back of his head. "You bumped your head." Her fingers found the scar that ran beneath his hair in a wide arch over his left ear. She traced the ridge with her index finger. "What's this?"

Trey captured her hand in his and pulled it away from his scalp. "Old war injury." If getting hit in the back of the head with a baseball bat during a bar fight could be considered war. That little incident had landed him in a hospital for days. Not one of his better memories. "You have really pretty eyes," he told the nurse, still holding her hand.

Her breath caught, pupils dilated slightly as she focused on his interested gaze. "Thank you," she whispered, lowering her lashes to hide her deep blue eyes.

Trey released her hand and she sagged against the wall. He turned his attention to the bed, glad a blue drape cloth concealed whatever the doctor was doing between Myrna's legs. Trey was pretty sure the doc was giving Myrna stitches and he did *not* want to know why that was necessary.

"So where's this baby we've been waiting to see for nine months now?" Trey asked.

Brian waved him over to the bed. Trey approached cautiously. Myrna looked exhausted, and he knew better than to tick her off. He was prepared to make a run for it, if necessary. Brian wrapped an arm around Trey's shoulders and they gazed down at the bundle in Myrna's arms. A miniature, red-faced Brian jabbed his fist in his mouth and sucked earnestly. Trey's heart skipped a beat before melting inside his chest. Brian's son was the most perfect thing Trey had ever seen in his entire life.

Brian scooped up the baby and handed him to Trey. Trey drew his little body against his chest and stared down at him in breathless awe.

"We named him Malcolm Trey," Myrna said. "After Brian's father. And, well, *you*."

Trey tore his gaze from the small wonder to gape at Myrna. "Me? Why would you name him after me?"

She smiled. "It seemed appropriate to name him after the two most important men in Brian's life."

"We want you to be his godfather," Brian said.

"I…" Trey was honored, but he wasn't an appropriate godfather. He was scarcely responsible enough to take care of himself. How could they ever expect him to be responsible enough to care for their child? "I don't think…"

The baby in his arms gurgled, and Trey looked down to find him staring up at him with unfocused brown eyes. His father's eyes. Brian's eyes. Brian had made this. This perfect, beautiful little person.

Brian was a father.

Trey glanced at Brian and the enormity of it all stole his breath. Brian didn't notice Trey. He only had eyes for his son. His pride in the little guy was tangible.

Trey turned his attention to the baby in his arms. He stroked Malcolm's cheek and then touched his tiny hand, fascinated with his tiny fingers. His tiny fingernails. Tiny knuckles. Everything so tiny. Malcolm gripped Trey's finger with surprising strength. "You're going to be a master guitarist like your daddy someday," Trey told him.

Malcolm scrunched up his face and Trey laughed, totally enamored with Brian's son. The son born from the love Brian shared with his wife, Myrna. The son Trey could have never given Brian no matter how much he loved him. Trey took a steadying breath, kissed the baby's forehead, and handed Malcolm back to his father. "Here. I'll probably break him or something."

"Good-lookin' kid, ain't he?" Brian pressed a kiss to Malcolm's temple.

"Of course," Myrna said, love shining in her hazel eyes as she stared up at her husband and son. "He looks like his father."

"He has your lips," Brian said.

"And your hair."

Trey chuckled. Father and son both had tufts of black hair sticking up in all directions.

"I hope he has your brains," Brian said.

"And your talent," Myrna added.

"He's perfect," Trey said, unable to resist the impulse to smooth Malcolm's fuzzy hair with his palm. It did no good. The baby's downy black hair immediately returned to standing on end.

"You'll be his godfather then?" Brian asked.

Trey lifted his gaze to Brian's. As if he could deny him anything. "Yeah. I guess so."

Brian smiled. "I think you need to get busy, Mills—find yourself a nice girl and make Malcolm a best friend. You're already nine months behind."

"Ha! Like that's ever going to happen," Trey said flippantly, but something inside him wanted that. Wanted something he and Brian *could* share. Pride of their respective sons. He could almost picture Malcolm and Trey Junior playing together in the backyard, learning how to play guitar together, getting into mischief, growing. Trey *Junior*? What the fuck was he thinking? There would never be a Trey Junior. He didn't even like kids. Not even cute little shits who were cursed with the name Malcolm Trey. The baby cooed and Trey melted into a puddle of mush. Okay, so there was *one* exception to his dislike of kids, but only one.

"I should probably leave you three alone so you can bond as a family or whatever."

"You can stay," Myrna said. "You're part of our family."

He appreciated the gesture, but Trey knew better. Things would never go back to the way they'd been before Myrna had crashed onto the scene. He'd been sulking over it long enough. It was time to finally let Brian go. As agonizing as that decision was for Trey, he'd lost all hope of Brian ever returning his feelings. Brian belonged to Myrna. Belonged *with* Myrna. And Malcolm. Trey had been fooling himself into thinking Brian might eventually come to think of him as more than a friend, but now he didn't even want him to. He wanted Brian to continue to be a wonderful husband and an amazing daddy. Myrna deserved that. Malcolm deserved that. Trey couldn't interfere with something that important. It wouldn't be right.

"You know I hate hospitals," Trey said. "I'm going to go see what Dare is up to. Hang out with my big bro in his McMansion until we have to head back to the tour bus. You can call me if you need me to change a diaper or something."

"You're willing to change diapers?" Brian asked.

Trey chuckled at his startled expression.

Trey glanced down at little Malcolm who was making a face that led Trey to believe he was already cooking up a ripe diaper in his honor. "Nah, but I'm sure I can talk some sweet fangirl into doing it for me." He winked at Brian.

"You will not use my son as a chick magnet, Mills," Brian said.

Trey laughed and then bent over the bed to offer Myrna a hug. She met his eyes and cupped his cheek. "You okay?" she whispered, seeming to recognize that Trey was moving beyond his infatuation with her husband. Giving up on Brian. Letting her win. She'd been infinitely patient with him. And trusting of her husband. Because she'd recognized the truth far sooner than Trey had. Brian didn't love him—not the way he wanted him to—and he never would.

Trey leaned closer and whispered, "Love him enough for both of us. Okay? Just promise me that."

Her hand pressed against the back of his head as she hugged him close. "I will. I promise."

When he stood upright, he offered Brian a vigorous, one-armed bro hug. He met Brian's intense brown-eyed gaze steadily. "Good-bye." He could scarcely get the word out through his constricted chest and throat. Brian obviously had no clue that there was significance behind that single word of farewell.

"Later," Brain said. "If I don't see you before, we have a show tomorrow night."

"Wouldn't miss it," Trey said with a smile.

Brian's gaze shifted to his son's face. "Yeah," he said breathlessly. Trey could practically see his separation anxiety and pictured Brian onstage with a baby sling strapped to his chest above his electric guitar and tiny, sound-blocking headphones on Malcolm's fuzzy head. So not Sinners' style. But totally Brian's.

Trey kissed Malcolm's forehead. "See you soon, godson. Don't break too many hearts."

Brian chuckled. "Look who's talking."

Trey left the room, forcing himself not to look back at the scene of domestic bliss he left behind. He really needed to do something fun to take his mind off things. Something or some*one*. What he needed was sex. His drug of choice.

The pretty, young nurse who had woken him with smelling salts stood just outside the delivery room door. When he walked past her, she perked up and grabbed his arm. She'd been waiting for him. Too easy.

"Hey," she said breathlessly. "Hey, um, Trey, right?"

He offered her a crooked grin, and she flushed before lowering her wide blue eyes to his chest. He watched her, noting the submission in her stance, the way she swayed toward him slightly. The way her thumb stroked his bare arm just above his elbow.

"Um…" she pressed onward. "I was just about to take a break and wondered if you'd like to go grab a cup of coffee with me."

Trey's heart rate kicked up a notch. He turned and took her firmly by both wrists, pressing her back against the wall, their bodies separated by mere inches. He bent his head so his breath would caress her ear as he spoke to her in a low voice. "You don't want coffee."

Her pulse raced out of control beneath his fingertips. "I don't?"

"No, but I know what you do want."

"What's that?" Her dark blue eyes flicked upward to meet his. She'd already surrendered, and he rarely turned down a good time.

"A hard, slow fuck against the wall."

"Here?" she whispered, her eyes wide.

He didn't dare laugh. That would have broken his spell over her. "In that supply closet." He nodded down the hall.

He held her gaze in challenge, daring her to deny him. She tore her gaze from his and peeked around his body for witnesses before grabbing a handful of his shirt, racing down the hall, unlocking the supply closet, and dragging him inside. The instant the door closed, she wrapped both arms around his neck and plastered her mouth to his. He let her kiss him. Let her touch the hoop piercing his eyebrow and the ones in his ear. He'd show her the one in his nipple, but she was still a little skittish and he knew if he took the upper hand too quickly, she'd balk and either leave or pretend he'd taken advantage of her.

"You're so sexy," she murmured against his lips. "Why are you so sexy? I shouldn't be doing this."

By *this*, he assumed she meant unfastening his belt, tugging at his T-shirt, rubbing her firm breasts into his chest, biting his lip.

"I don't want you to think I normally do this kind of thing," she said, her hand slipping into his silk boxers to toy with his hardening cock.

He did this kind of thing almost daily, but he wouldn't make the mistake of telling her that.

"Take off your pants," he whispered.

When she obeyed, he knew she was in this until the end. Which he estimated would be approximately fifteen minutes in the future.

"Are you really in a rock band?" she asked.

Trey chuckled. Couldn't help it. Did she seriously not know who he was? It had been a while since a woman had jumped him without knowing he was notorious for this kind of thing. "Yeah, I'm really in a rock band. And I play an actual instrument."

"Guitar?"

He grinned. "How did you guess?"

The excitement in her eyes led him to believe she wasn't half-naked in a supply closet at work because she wanted famous-guitarist Trey. She was pantsless and submissive because she wanted bad-boy Trey. He was all about giving her exactly what she wanted. The walls were concealed behind floor-to-ceiling shelves, so he pressed her back up against the door and trapped her arms on either side of her head. She gasped when he lowered his head to kiss her neck. He nibbled, suckled, and licked the pulse point under her jaw until she began to fight his hold with impatience.

"You're driving me insane," she said. "Do you have a condom?"

"Are you in a hurry?" he murmured.

"Kinda. My fifteen-minute break is almost over."

"You're going to be late." He nipped her earlobe and released her wrist. Trey's left hand moved down her body and gave her breast a gentle squeeze before moving between her legs. She clung to his hair and then fingered the tiny hoops in his ear, then his eyebrow again.

"Do you like piercings?" he whispered. "I have a couple more."

"Where?" she whispered.

"I didn't wear the one in my tongue. Didn't realize I'd have a sweet pussy to lick this early in the morning."

She moaned in torment. When Trey's fingers found her clit, she cried out. Damn, she was swollen. And wet. And eager. He liked eager. The chase meant nothing to him. He just liked to fuck. Kissing her neck, he stroked her clit rhythmically.

"There's another in my nipple," he whispered.

Her hand moved to his chest. She found the ridge of his jewelry under his T-shirt, and then she slid her hand up under his clothes to finger it.

"Pull it," he encouraged. "It makes my balls throb."

"Do you like that?"

"Try it and see."

She tugged and he shuddered. "Oh," she gasped when his hard cock leaped against her thigh.

"Come for me." He rubbed her clit faster in wide circles until she shuddered hard with an orgasm. Her gasping breaths in his ear made him want to join her in bliss. He lifted his head to look at her then. "Where do you want it?"

Dazed, she gazed up at him. "Where do I want what?"

"My cock."

"I have more than one choice?"

He slid a finger inside her slippery pussy and she jerked. "There's here." A second finger probed her ass and her eyes widened. "Back here." He licked her lip and then the ridge of her teeth. "In here." He slid his hand up from her wrist to intertwine their fingers. "Your capable hands." He lowered his head to whisper in her ear while he palmed her full breasts with both hands. "Or you can hold me between these. If you're really kinky…"

"What do you want?" she asked breathlessly.

"No preference." Which wasn't exactly true. Seeing the startled look on her face when he'd probed her ass made him crave some backdoor action, but that probably wasn't the best choice for her if she had to go back to work.

"Regular," she whispered.

Regular? Since when was anything he did regular? He stifled a laugh, trying to be sensitive to her feelings. "I assume by regular you mean vaginal sex."

She nodded.

"Say it."

He found a condom in the back pocket of his jeans and tore it open with his teeth. She watched him as if amazed, but she didn't say a word as he applied it.

"Tell me what you want," he pressed. He had already decided she needed the added psychological stimulation to get off. Demands and directions. Whatever she liked was fine by him. He was game. "I want you to say it."

She grabbed his hair in both fists and said, "A slow, hard fuck against the wall, just like you said."

"Where do you want me?"

She shuddered as if the very thought had her near orgasm. "Inside."

"Inside what?"

"M-my vagina."

"Your pussy?"

Her hands tightened in his hair, and the last shred of her resistance crumbled. "My cunt. Fuck it hard, Trey."

He lifted her off the floor, pressing her against the door for leverage, and then directed his cock inside her. He loved losing himself in mindless fucking. No worries. No heartache. Just pleasure. He gave her what she wanted, possessing her with hard, deep, slow strokes, but she gave him what he needed to. A temporary reprieve from his turbulent thoughts and his perpetually broken heart. Trey concentrated solely on sensation. He felt no emotional connection as he thrust into her. Never did. Hadn't since Brian had made love to him back in high school and he'd tossed his heart at the guy's feet. Twelve years of sex without love. Twelve years of love without sex. And now that Trey had given up on Brian ever loving him or *making* love to him, he just felt hollow. Empty. Desolate. He doubted anything could fill the empty chasm inside. Certainly not some pretty nurse he'd just met and was fucking in a supply closet. He didn't even know her name. Didn't care to.

When she came, he followed her over the edge, his release bringing him that state of tranquility he craved. He wished it lasted longer than thirty seconds. And didn't have to be followed by a whole lot of awkwardness. He pulled out and removed the expended condom, tossing it in a convenient garbage can on the janitor's cart, and then refastened his jeans and belt. He let her find her panties and scrub pants. Waited until she was dressed before he looked at her. Not that he didn't want to watch the hot stranger he'd just fucked slide her panties up her legs. He just knew that if he did, she'd start seeing things that weren't there. Feelings. With feelings came attachment. With attachment came complications. That was the last thing Trey ever wanted.

"I…" she said breathlessly.

"You don't have to say anything," he said. He pinned her with the look that got him almost anything he wanted. He'd perfected it as a child, modified it as a man, used it unabashedly. She flushed and leaned against the door for support.

"Sometimes a beautiful woman just needs a hard, slow fuck against a wall with a perfect stranger. I understand."

She gazed at him, looking more dazed than a pothead at a Grateful Dead concert. "Yeah… Perfect."

"I'll leave first. I wouldn't want you to get in trouble."

"Yeah…"

He waited for her to collect enough sense to move out of the way of the door. One hand on the doorknob, Trey took her chin between his thumb and forefinger and kissed her trembling lips. "That is the best sex I've ever had against a door in a hospital supply closet."

"Yeah…"

"You're an amazing woman."

"Will you call me?" she gushed.

He shook his head slightly. "I want to keep my memory of this moment untainted. Let's not complicate it. Let it be what it's meant to be. Pleasure for the sake of pleasure."

Her face twitched with disappointment, but she nodded.

He gave her a gentle kiss on the forehead and then let himself into the corridor. He strode toward the bank of elevators at the end of the hall.

Hot nurse a fuzzy memory already, Trey dug his cell phone out of his pocket and called his brother.

"What's up?" Dare answered.

"Brian and Myrna had a boy." Trey smiled at the thought of holding Brian's perfect son for the first time. "They named him Malcolm Trey."

Dare sniggered. "What the fuck are they thinking? Poor kid."

"You home?"

"Yeah, but I'm busy."

Trey grinned. "Busy, huh? What's her name? I'll help you entertain her."

"Not that kind of busy. Remember that stupid contest our publicist came up with: Guitarist for a Year with Exodus End? Today we're auditioning studio musicians to identify the winner. We do need to find someone to take over for Max on rhythm guitar, but this is fuckin' stupid." Max was the lead singer of Dare's band, Exodus End. Max had also played rhythm guitar until recently. "We hoped his carpal tunnel surgery would get us out of this mess, but the surgery fucked up his hand even more. He can't stand the pain of playing, and he's been advised not to move his wrist for several weeks."

"That should make jerking off a challenge," Trey said.

"As if Max needs to jerk off."

True. The man could have any woman he wanted.

"Hey," Dare said, "you should come try out. We can make it seem like you entered the contest."

"You know I can't do that. I'd never leave Sinners. Not even for you." Trey stepped on the elevator and made his way down to the lobby. The well-built guy in the elevator smiled at him and let his eyes drift down Trey's body with appreciation. Trey had to admit he was tempted by the open invitation, but he had a powerful need to hang out with his big brother. Dare understood him. Trey needed that at the moment. More than he needed more meaningless, but amazing, sex with yet another attractive stranger.

"You can help us decide then," Dare said, drawing Trey's attention from the way elevator-guy was gnawing on his lips and making Trey want to kiss him. "We've narrowed it down to five guitarists based on their demos, but there's no way to know how many times they redid them before sending them in. They'll all be playing live for us in about an hour. They can't fake that."

Trey stepped off the elevator, winking at Open Invitation before wandering toward the exit to find a cab.

"Okay, sure. Sounds like fun." Trey's phone beeped. "I'll be there in a few. I've got another call."

"Later."

Trey disconnected and checked his phone's screen. *Mark?* Shit. He considered ignoring him but knew Mark would just keep calling and calling until Trey finally talked to him. The guy could not take a hint. Might as well get this over with.

"Hey," Trey answered.

"Are you in town?" Mark asked.

"I'm on tour. You know that."

"The Sinners' News Blog said you flew into L.A. this morning because Brian's wife was in labor."

Trey wasn't sure how the owners of that blog knew what was going on with Sinners so quickly. Sometimes they knew more about

Sinners' goings-on than Trey knew and he was living it. He guessed he couldn't deny that he was in town. "Yeah, they had a little boy. Adorable little shit."

"Yeah, that's what the site said. 7 pounds 9 ounces. 21 inches. Named him Malcolm Trey. Are you still at the hospital? I could stop by."

Stalker alert! "Mark, we've been through this. I'm not interested in a relationship with you." Men! They could be such a pain in the ass. Especially if they didn't know what they were doing back there. Trey had slept with Mark more than once. They'd met in Portland over a year ago and after relieving him of his anal and oral virginity, Trey had taken him to get a tattoo. The guy had moved to Los Angeles a few months later. Trey suspected it was because of him, as Mark was relentless in his pursuit. Trey had no problem fucking him, but when Mark had started trying to forge a commitment, Trey was finished with him. The guy could not take a hint. Or blatant rejections. Or flashing neon signs that read: *Go the fuck away.*

"Who said anything about a relationship? I just wanted to congratulate Brian," Mark said.

"Do whatever you want. I've already left the hospital."

"Oh." Mark hesitated. "Are you hungry? I could take you out for breakf—"

"No, I've got plans."

"What kind of plans? Are you seeing someone else?" The jealousy in Mark's voice was so fucking annoying Trey considered hanging up on him. But then Mark would just call back and blame a bad connection or some stupid shit.

"Yeah," Trey lied. "I am seeing someone. I'm seriously dating a woman right now."

"Bullshit," Mark said.

"It's not bullshit. I've sworn off men for the rest of my life." When the lie had formed, Trey hadn't meant it, but now that he'd said it, he decided it was the best idea he'd ever had. Women he could deal with. Men either broke his heart or complicated his life. Exhibit A was upstairs bonding with his son. Exhibit B was on the phone. Exhibits C through triple X were scattered across the US and Canada waiting for Sinners to pass through their area again.

"Whatever, Trey. Come over to my place tonight and I'll make you dinner. Suck your cock."

Mark was a decent cook. And he did suck good cock. He was also exceedingly easy on the eyes and had a spectacularly tight ass, but the guy needed to move on. Trey had tried to hook him up with a few different men, but Mark was too hung up on Trey to consider anyone else.

"I can't."

"Can't or won't?" he challenged.

"Don't want to—how's that?"

Mark sighed loudly. "I'll call you tomorrow."

"Mark, what do I have to do to convince you that it's over between us?"

"I'll call you tomorrow."

Shit. Trey was going to have to get his number changed. Again. He honestly didn't understand why some people couldn't take a hint. He didn't want to be in a relationship. Why was that concept so difficult for his sex partners to grasp?

Chapter 2

REAGAN LEANED AGAINST THE brick wall and clung to the neck of her red, electric guitar as if it was her lifeline. *Breathe, Reagan, breathe. If you don't win this competition, it's not the end of the world. Maybe you were meant to be a barista for the rest of your life.*

"You should have taken some Dramamine like I did," an emo-punk hybrid, who was wearing more eyeliner than a three-dollar whore, said. He was also a finalist and set to go into the sound booth right after her. "You look like you're going to hurl."

She felt like she was going to hurl. Why was she here? She'd sent in that demo tape never thinking Exodus End's manager would actually call her to audition for the band. Over five thousand guitarists had sent in a demo tape, too. How had she ended up in the top five? They were fucking with her. Had to be. She was a complete unknown. Of course, Dramamine guy was an unknown too, but that confident son of a bitch in the corner looked familiar. She was sure he'd been in some popular eighties band at one time.

Dramamine turned to look at Hair Band Hasbeen and sighed remorsefully. "We made it this far, at least."

"I think I must be dreaming," Reagan said. Dramamine's hair definitely looked like something out of a bizarre dream sequence. How did he get it to stay sticking straight out to one side like that? And who thought the burgundy and green stripes through his jagged-cut bangs were a good idea? "How often does a mega-famous, amazing band like Exodus End let unknowns audition for their group?" Reagan continued.

Dramamine opened his mouth to answer, but Reagan prattled on. "Never, that's when. I can't believe I'm actually here. In Dare Mills's house. Doing an audition with Exodus *fucking* End." She checked a clock on the studio wall. "In twenty minutes." She swayed and Dramamine grabbed her shoulder to keep her on her feet. She removed her guitar and set it against the wall. It didn't usually feel heavy, but today if felt like she had an elephant hanging over her shoulder. She massaged her temples with both hands. "I think I'm going to pass out."

"You're hyperventilating. Breathe more slowly."

"I can't help it." She needed to keep talking about something to keep her mind off things. She patted Dramamine on the chest. "Hey, what's your name?"

"Pyre."

She lifted an eyebrow at him. "No shit?"

"Well, that's my stage name."

Lame.

"It's short for Vampyre," he added.

Wow. Okaaaay.

"I'm Reagan. It's short for Reagan. I'm not into vamps. What are you going to play, *Pyre*?"

"The three Exodus End songs we all have to play."

"'Bite.' 'Encore.' 'Ovation.'" She ticked the song titles off on one hand. She'd been practicing them for days. And every other Exodus End song ever released in case they threw a surprise at her. Like a pop quiz. They probably wanted to make sure whomever they hired could really take over the duties of rhythm guitarist—and what better way to do that than to request a surprise song? Reagan would rather play lead guitar than rhythm, truth be told, but Dare Mills wasn't the one being replaced. Maximilian Richardson was giving up rhythm guitar and just sticking to vocals. At least, that's what she'd been told. She hadn't actually met him or anything. In fact, they'd been ushered into this studio and hadn't had the opportunity to meet any of the band members. So much for her plan to win them over with her sweetest smile. Probably for the best. At the moment she doubted she could produce a decent grimace, much less a smile. "What about the solo of our choice? What are you going to play for that?" she asked Pyre.

"'Temptation.'" Another Exodus End song. A great solo, heavy on technique, but not speed.

"Nice choice."

"What are you going to do?" Pyre asked.

"Sinners' 'Gates of Hell.'"

"Are you foiking insane?" Pyre asked, his eyes wide in astonishment.

"What do you mean? That solo is awesome!" she said, her heart thrumming with excitement. She hearted Sinners. Their lead guitarist, Brian Sinclair, was an absolute god.

"That solo is impossible," Pyre said. "Foiking Master Sinclair has seven fingers on each hand or something. No mere mortal can do that solo justice."

Reagan grinned. "You can't play it?"

"No one can play it like Sinclair does. You should pick something easier."

"Let her play it." Hair Band Hasbeen saw his way into their conversation. "If sweet-tits blows her chance, it's one less piece of competition for us to worry about." He grinned to himself as he stared at her ass.

Reagan bristled. "What are you going to play, dildo? 'Mary Had a Little Lamb?'"

The guy rolled his eyes and shook his head in disgust. "It's not like they're going to want to hire a chick guitarist anyway. Who'd you sleep with to get an audition, baby?"

Reagan gave him a once-over and wrinkled her nose in disgust. "Not you, old man."

Pyre chuckled. "Ouch."

"You got a problem, douche bag?" Hair Band grumbled.

Pyre's stance turned threatening. Reagan supposed she could let the two of them get into a fistfight. It might make it easier for her to outplay them if they broke their fingers on each other's faces. Might. But she stepped between them to try to defuse the bomb instead. Pyre looked like he hadn't seen a protein-containing meal in months, and Hair Band had apparently subsided on a beer diet since he'd given up on wearing snakeskin-print spandex. It probably wouldn't have been an interesting fight. More likely pathetic than anything. Reagan figured she was tougher than the two of them put together. "Easy, guys," she said. "We're all a little on edge here. No need for you to get your panties in a bunch. Mine are bunchy enough for all of us." She pressed a hand to the center of Pyre's chest. Though his stance was confident, his heart hammered out of control against her palm. Pyre wrapped an arm around her waist and drew her closer. Using her as a human shield, no doubt.

"Are you the finalists?" a deep voice asked from somewhere behind her. Its low tone seemed to caress Reagan's back. A shiver of delight streaked up her spine.

Reagan turned to identify the speaker and almost fell on the floor. Trey Mills, the rhythm guitarist of Sinners, stood just beside the studio door. He checked her out a little and then a little more. Just enough to make her want him to inspect her closely. And naked.

Black-haired, green-eyed, and exuding sexual energy, the man was gorgeous onstage, but up close his sensual charm overwhelmed her. What was he doing here? Not that she wanted him to leave or anything. More than anything she wanted to challenge him to one of Sinners' dueling guitar solos. The ones he and Sinclair performed onstage together. She always wondered if she could outplay Trey. At every Sinners' concert she'd attended (eleven and counting), she'd wanted to charge up on stage and challenge both of Sinners' guitarists to a little competition. Somehow, she'd managed to keep herself in the mosh pit instead of storming the stage.

"Fuck. If Mills is in this contest, we're all screwed," Hair complained. "Nepotism much?"

Trey grinned and Reagan's heart dropped into her combat boots. "Nope, I'm not in this. I'm helping with the judging. Good luck." He opened the door and disappeared into the studio.

Reagan sighed in feminine bliss. Freakin' gorgeous man. And then his words sunk in. Trey Mills was going to be listening to her play?

She grabbed Pyre by the front of his ripped-up, electric blue T-shirt and gave him a panicked shake. "Hey, do you have any more of that Dramamine on you?"

The four members of Exodus End sat in the small recording booth facing a large window that overlooked Dare's music studio. Trey took a seat next to his brother in front of the soundboard and immediately had a set of headphones thrust in his direction. Trey held one earphone up to his ear.

"Listen to this guy," Dare said and played a demo for Trey.

Trey's heart skipped a beat. Six-stringed perfection filtered into his delighted ear. "Is this a joke?" Trey asked.

"A joke?" Dare asked. One dark eyebrow lifted over a piercing green eye.

"This is Brian," Trey said. "I'd know his playing anywhere."

"It's not Brian. Some guy named Elliot." Dare tapped on the empty CD case. It had a plain white insert with the name Elliot scrawled across it in black marker.

"El-li-ot," Logan, Exodus End's golden-haired bassist, said in a perfect impression of E.T.

"Phone hooooome," their drummer, Steve, added.

"Are you guys fuckin' bored or what?" Max, their lead singer, asked. "You need to take this shit seriously." He had a brace on his left wrist and a scowl on his devilishly handsome face. Not that Trey noticed. He wasn't interested in men anymore. Not even ones who looked as good in a black tank top as Maximilian Richardson did. Besides, Max was straight. Trey didn't bother with straight guys. What was the point?

"Frieeend," Logan said to Max and pointed at him with one finger. Trey could almost picture it glowing at the tip.

Steve snorted with laughter.

Max just rolled his eyes. "I think you need another beer, Lo."

"I need some pussy," Steve said.

"You always need pussy."

"This *is* Brian," Trey insisted and no one would convince him otherwise. The longer he listened to the guitarist's demo, the more certain he became. And the more angry. "Someone must have pirated some of his material. Fuckin' rip-off artists piss me off."

Max said, "I guess we'll find out when they audition. Can't fake that kind of talent."

"So what do they look like? A bunch of douche bags?" Dare asked.

"You haven't seen them?" Trey asked and set the headphones down. Not because he didn't love to hear Brian play, but because the longer he listened, the more ticked off he became that someone would use his friend's material that way.

"No, we're going into this blind. Our manager's brilliant idea to make a contest out of this has turned into a major pain in the ass. We don't care what the winner looks like. We just want the right sound. Chances are we know some of them and Sam didn't want us to be swayed by that either. Is Sam even here today? Fuck no. He's in New York with some all-girl goth band he's trying to sign. So now this stupid contest he came up with is all on us."

Trey's gaze shifted from one gorgeous man to the next. Did they really expect him to believe that they didn't care what the newest member of their band looked like? They all worked out and had excellent physiques. Tribal tattoos accentuated the cut of their hard-muscled bodies. Their long, well-kept hair made the girls go wild and they wore just the right amount of leather. Maybe they didn't want the newbie competing for their women and secretly hoped he was a toad. Or maybe they were so pissed at their manager they really wanted this unorthodox way of picking a new band member to back-fire. Trey doubted that. He knew how serious this band was about its career. They wouldn't have gotten this far if they lacked sense. Too bad their manager didn't share it. He was all about promotion.

"Well?" Logan prompted. "What do they look like?"

"I didn't notice," Trey said. "One of the guys brought his girl-friend along with him. *That* I noticed." Well, he had also noticed the weird-looking guy who'd been hanging on her, but mostly because he couldn't figure out what she saw in him. Must be the guitar thing. Some girls had a thing for musicians no matter how fugly they were. Still, something about that woman had been unquestionably raw and sexy. Too bad she was taken. Trey didn't chase after women who were taken. There were enough single ladies out there to meet his every need. Why fuck up some other guy's miserable relationship?

Max sighed loudly. "Might as well get this over with. If they all suck, we get to go home, right?" He flipped a switch and spoke into a mic that fed into the sound booth. "Send in victim number one."

There was a heavy window shade pulled down to block those auditioning from view. Victim number one was a phenomenal instrumentalist. As was number two. Max scribbled notes on a pad of paper while the rest of them just listened. Were all vocalists anal? Sinners' lead singer, Sed, would have probably done the same thing. When guitarist number three began to play, Trey jumped to his feet, knocking his stool over backward. He leaned forward and squinted at the glass in front of him as if it would give him X-ray vision and he could see through the shade blocking his view.

"That's Brian," Trey said.

"El-li-ot," Logan insisted.

"You guys have taken this joke far enough. He needs to be in the hospital with his wife and new son."

"Trey, it's not Brian," Dare said. "No one is fucking with you."

"I'll prove it's Brian. Don't you think I know his sound? I've played guitar with him for eighteen years." Trey turned on the microphone. "Play the solo to 'Gates of Hell.'"

There was a screech in the booth as the guitarist stopped playing in the middle of 'Bite.' A second later Brian's most insanely complicated and fast solo filled the booth.

Trey scowled at Dare. "I *told* you it was him. No one can play that solo like he does. Not even me."

"Why would we go to all this trouble to fuck with you, Trey?" Dare asked.

"How the hell should I know?"

Trey exited the studio and opened the door to the sound booth. "Ha ha, Brian, very funny." Except it wasn't Brian playing 'Gates of Hell' to perfection. It was that woman. Her dirty-blond hair was cut into a short, sassy style. She wore faded army-green cargo pants, combat boots, a plain white tank top, and not a stitch of makeup. She held her red Stratocaster with authority and played it as if it were her little bitch. The woman was a fucking goddess.

Chapter 3

REAGAN SLAPPED HER HAND on her guitar strings to stop their vibration. Trey Mills had burst into the recording booth and scared the shit out of her. He stood there in the open door gaping at her and setting her heart aflutter. The last time she'd felt like this was the day she'd met Ethan Conner, and that had turned out to be the most fucked up experience of her life. She didn't need this kind of nipple-tingling distraction right now. She needed to concentrate on her audition.

Max's voice came through the speaker overhead. "Send the wannabes home. We don't need to hear anymore. We've found our man."

"Woman," Trey called.

"What?" Max asked. "We want Elliot."

"I'm Elliot," Reagan said. "Reagan Elliot."

"Well, I'll be a son of a bitch," Max grumbled.

"Where did you learn to play like that?" Trey asked her.

Wait just a fucking minute—did Exodus End just hire her? She'd won? Really? She played a victory screech on her guitar and carried the note with way too much whammy for polite company.

Trey stepped closer to her and she caught the scents of cherry, leather, and sex on him. "You didn't answer me."

"Self-taught," she told him.

"You sound so much like Brian, I thought you were him playing a prank on me."

"Brian?" When she realized to whom he was referring, her eyes felt like they were going to pop out of her head. "You mean Master Sinclair?"

He nodded slightly.

"Seriously?" She smiled, her heart thudding like a jackhammer. "That's quite a compliment."

"Especially coming from Trey," Dare Mills said from the doorway.

There should be a law against the Mills brothers standing in the same room. Separately they were murder on a woman's ability to think straight. Together? Reagan's mind went entirely numb. Other areas of her anatomy were fully attentive, however. The pair looked somewhat alike. Both had green eyes. Trey's were sultry, as if he'd just woken up after a long night of fucking some lucky girl's brains out. Dare's were piercing and made her feel naked, exposed, and liking it. Trey's hair was short in the back, longer in the front. By flopping in his face, his bangs drew attention to those bedroom eyes of his and made him look mysterious. Naughty. Oh so naughty. Dare's hair was all the same length, settling a few inches below his collarbones, and made him look wicked. Dangerous. Oh so dangerous. Trey had a bad-boy vibe, accentuated by his various piercings. Dare had a similar vibe, but more feral. Dare's sexy shadow of beard growth made Reagan crave some whisker burn on the insides of her thighs. She wasn't sure how long she stood there staring at them and imagining them making her a very happy woman—together, separately, together again—but they allowed her inspection as if they were used to it.

"I'm Reagan," she gushed and rushed forward with her hand extended in Dare's direction.

Dare gripped her hand firmly, measuring her up as a fellow musician, not as a woman. Damn it. Well, actually that was for the best if they were going to be working together. Oh yeah, they'd be working together. Awesome!

"I'm Dare Mills."

"Yeah, you are." She broke out in nervous laughter and wished someone would tranquilize her before she made a bigger ass of herself.

Maximilian Richardson entered the room and Trey had to grab her shoulder to keep her on her feet. Electrifying sensations radiated through her flesh from where Trey touched her. She turned to look at him in amazement. He stared back, looking just as stunned.

"We'll want you to play a few songs with us before we have you sign an official contract," Max said, "but you're one hell of a guitarist. How is your band not already signed?"

She tore her gaze from Trey and forced her attention to Max. *Forced* her attention to Max? What the fuck was wrong with her? The leader of one of the most successful metal bands past, present, and undoubtedly future was addressing her, talking about contracts and making all of her wildest dreams come true and she was thinking how much she'd like to spend a few moments alone with Trey, just so she could hear the timber of his voice again. Well, maybe she wanted to do a few other things while alone with him, but he could talk to her at the same time. At least when his sexy mouth wasn't otherwise occupied.

"My band broke up several months ago," she told Max. "The lead singer's wife had a baby. Bands don't usually last long once members start having kids."

Trey's hand dropped from her arm and he shuffled past his brother, who gave him a look of empathy and a squeeze on the shoulder. Was it something she said? Her brow furrowed as she tried to figure out why Trey would care that her band had broken up. They hadn't been all that great. No real spark between them. Once Trey was out of the room, half of her brain returned. The gushing fangirl half. "Oh my God, I'm so excited. You guys are so amazing! I've been a fan of yours since high school. I really appreciate you giving me this opportunity."

Exodus End's bassist, Logan, and drummer, Steve, squeezed into the small room. Her band shuffled around so they could all fit into the small space. Her band. *Hers*. Oh my God, this had to be a dream. She pinched her arm as hard as she could. "Ouch. I guess I'm not dreaming," she muttered.

"You wail, sweetheart," Steve said. "What's your name?"

"Reagan."

She shook hands with Logan (long, golden hair, gentle blue eyes, and hot) and Steve (soft waves of shoulder-length brown hair, dreamy brown eyes, and hot). Snuck another peek at Max (dark brown, trendy short hair, deep hazel eyes, and hotter) and then Dare (silky, sleek jet-black hair, intense green eyes, and the hottest). How would she survive being in a band with this many luscious and talented men without her panties spontaneously combusting?

"Reagan, we love your sound," Max said. "We'd like to head down to Dare's practice room and jam through a few songs together to make sure you're compatible with the group as a whole. Unless you have something better to do."

In twenty minutes, Reagan was supposed to be at work serving coffee to stressed-out customers in knock-off Armani suits. Did that count as something better to do? "Fuck no, I don't."

"Great," Dare said. His wide smile was like a double-shot of espresso to the happy lobe of her brain.

Reagan followed the group through the maze that was the north wing of Dare's sprawling mansion. She'd never been in a house that had wings before. That entire section of his house was dedicated to the band. Gold and platinum records lined the hallway. Bits of Exodus End's history: Photos of the band at award ceremonies and playing live shows, guitars, posters, backstage passes, drumsticks, and other memorabilia covered every square inch of wall space. Dare's interior decorator obviously frequented chain restaurants. She wished she had time to examine it all and learn the history behind each piece.

They passed another recording studio packed wall to wall with Steve Aimes's ginormous drum kit and other percussion instruments.

"Do you take that entire thing on tour?" Reagan pointed into the open door.

Steve chuckled, his brown eyes sparkling with mischief. She had the feeling she'd need to keep a close eye on that one, which would not be a chore but a privilege. "Naw, that's my old kit, which I use mostly for special studio recordings. I just take the essentials on tour."

"His essentials take up half a semitruck," Logan said.

"Says the man with four hundred bass guitars," Steve countered.

Reagan gaped. "Four hundred?"

"Not quite that many," Logan said.

"Three hundred and ninety-nine," Steve amended.

Reagan had one good electric guitar, one cheap piece of crap, and one acoustic. She was far out of her element here. Could she handle going from zero recognition to instant infamy? She didn't know, but she was about to find out. There was no way in hell she was giving up this opportunity.

They passed another room that looked like a tastefully decorated high school gymnasium. The highly polished wooden floor gleamed beneath modern-styled chandeliers. A huge, fully stocked bar took up the majority of the far wall. Some chairs were stacked against one wall, but the rest of the room was empty.

When Reagan paused and gaped through the spectacular archways, Dare said, "The ballroom."

"We have a ball in there, all right," Logan said.

"Parties?" Reagan asked.

"A few," Dare said.

"Will I be invited to the next one?" she asked eagerly.

Dare chuckled. "I'd say so."

The other band members continued down the corridor and entered the next room, talking and laughing about various party memories. Reagan caught movement out on the expansive patio outside the floor-to-ceiling ballroom windows. Everything in this house was huge. She wondered if Dare lived here alone. Seemed a waste of space for one person. She had no doubt that he had an easier time forking out millions of dollars for this place than she had coming up with mere hundreds for rent each month.

The man outside the windows pulled his shirt off over his head and tossed it on the ground.

"Is that Trey?" she asked breathlessly.

Trey pushed something on the ground with his toe and a huge Jacuzzi set into the slate patio began to bubble.

"Helping himself to my hot tub again," Dare said. "I keep telling him he might as well move in. He says he doesn't want to impose. The dipshit imposes all the time."

Reagan looked up at Dare and was momentarily dumbfounded to find she was having a conversation with one of the most famous guitarists on the planet. One of her idols. "I think I said something back in the studio that upset him. Does he really care that Bait-n-Switch broke up? We weren't very good, to be honest."

"I'm pretty sure he's never heard of Bait-n-Switch," Dare said. His hand slid up into his long, silky hair and he scratched his head before tucking the black strands behind one ear. "No offense."

"None taken. Do you have any idea what I said to set him off?"

Dare smiled at her. "He has a lot on his mind. Brian Sinclair's wife had a baby this morning. What you said about kids causing bands to break up—"

"Oh shit! I didn't mean Sinners." She tore her gaze from Dare to watch Trey kick off his shoes. He looked entirely too depressed. "I'm going to go talk to him. Can you give me a couple minutes?"

"Sure, we need to get our instruments tuned up anyway."

Reagan had completely forgotten that she was still carrying her guitar strapped around her neck and shoulder. She looked down at it wondering if it was wise to take it out near the rolling hot tub water.

"Do you want me to take that into the practice room for you?" Dare asked.

Reagan was dumbfounded by his thoughtfulness. Weren't rich and famous rock stars all assholes? "I'd really appreciate that, Mr. Mills."

Dare laughed. "Oh please. No one calls me Mr. Mills besides my lawyer. Call me Dare."

She smiled wondering why he would need a lawyer. "Thanks, Dare." Reagan lifted the strap over her head and handed her guitar to him.

He held it in one hand and wrinkled his nose at it as if it had an infectious disease. "You know, since Max won't need his guitars anymore, he'll probably give you a few high-quality instruments to use until you find something more to your liking."

Max played custom-made Gibson Les Paul guitars. *Expensive* custom-made guitars. "Are you serious?" she blurted.

Dare chuckled. "Completely. I bet you're a little overwhelmed at the moment. Go talk to Trey. Put a smile on his face for me. Just don't take too long. My band can be sort of diva when you make them wait." He winked at her and carried her guitar down to the practice room where various clangs and twangs were being produced.

As soon as she recovered from Dare's flirty wink, Reagan rushed across the polished floor of the ballroom and slid into the bank of windows. Trey stood with one toe in the hot tub water. The rest of him was completely exposed. *Completely.* He turned his head at the sound of her graceless crash and offered her a crooked grin before slipping into the water.

In those five seconds that his naked body had been in view, she'd snapped enough mental pictures to get her through several nights of adventure with her favorite vibrator. Trey's body relaxed into the water and he sat there facing the windows, staring at her with the most unreadable expression she'd ever encountered. He obviously thought she was a total idiot, a klutz, and an embarrassment to the human species. Oh well. She'd made worse first impressions in her life.

She opened one of the French doors and heard a faint beep. She glanced around looking for its source.

"I think you just triggered the alarm," Trey said.

"Shit! What do I do?" Panicked, she slammed the door shut behind her.

"Now you've triggered the alarm *and* locked yourself out of the house." He chuckled and hauled himself out of the hot tub. Naked, gorgeous, and dripping, Trey padded to a different door that led into some sort of changing room. Reagan scarcely heard the beeps as he entered some code into a touch pad on the wall. So much blood was rushing through her ears she would have had difficulty hearing a jet engine. As he crossed the enormous patio in Reagan's direction, she couldn't take her eyes off him. She prided herself on keeping her head when it came to men, but this one... Must be all the excitement of the day catching up with her and making her giddy with duh-ness.

Trey made things worse (*better?*) by coming to stand before her instead of returning to the concealing water of the hot tub. Displaying no signs of self-consciousness, Trey stood there and waited for her eyes to drift from his bare feet to his thickening cock to his flat belly to his... thickening cock. Why was he getting excited? Surely not because she was there. She glanced around looking for the typical bikini-clad, sexpot supermodels these rock stars spent most of their time with. She found she actually was the only female in attendance. *Weird.*

"Do you want to join me?" he whispered close to her ear.

He didn't touch her, but her entire body responded with electric jolts of lust that converged between her thighs. His low voice did jittery things to her already frayed nerves and she laughed. She laughed at Trey Mills instead of shedding her clothes and jumping into the hot tub with her ankles behind her neck. She bit her lip, suppressing the urge to slap herself in the forehead repeatedly.

"I'll take that as a no." He turned and started back to the hot tub.

She caught his well-muscled arm and scarcely stifled an excited gasp. He paused and glanced over his shoulder to melt her into a puddle of Reagan pudding with those maddeningly sexy green eyes of his.

"I…" she shrieked. *Shrieked?* What in the fuck was wrong with her? *Keep it together, Reagan. Keep it together.* She cleared her throat. "I didn't come out here to join you in the hot tub. I came to challenge you to a guitar duel." *What? No, not that.* She'd come out there to console Trey about Sinners. To tell him there was no way Brian would ever leave the band. But what did she know? She didn't know Brian. She was just a hopeful fangirl.

His eyebrows lifted with interest. "A guitar duel?"

"Yeah. I have to go practice with my band." She sucked in a breath of pure terror. She was certainly running through a wide gamut of emotions this morning. "My band… Exodus End," she mumbled. "Oh my fucking God!"

Trey laughed.

Reagan took a deep steadying breath. "After we're done practicing, I want to duel you, Trey Mills."

"At high noon?" He whistled the theme to some old spaghetti Western.

"After you're done with your soak in the hot tub."

"And if I win, you'll join me in the hot tub?"

Her heart skipped several beats. "If that's what you want."

He stroked a lock of hair from her cheek. "That's only the beginning of what I want, Reagan."

She laughed again. She really was just nervous, but she knew it sounded like she was laughing at him. Rejecting his advances. Never in a million years would she purposely laugh at Trey Mills. And yet, she kept doing it. He dropped his hand, a confused scowl on his handsome face. Reagan wanted to strangle herself.

"If I win the duel, we're going to the skate park," she said. *The skate park? What am I? Thirteen?*

"You skate?"

"Sometimes," she admitted. *Oh God, he thinks I'm an immature idiot.*

"Sounds fun."

Liar, liar, lack of pants, I'm on fire. "Yeah. Good. See you later, then." Mortified by her complete lack of poise, she fled into the house through the door Trey had left open and followed the sounds of music to the practice room.

"There you are," Dare said. "I was starting to think I was going to have to come rescue you from the hot tub and my brother's libido."

Reagan's cheeks flamed. That might have been a possibility if she hadn't made a complete fool of herself.

"She's not stupid enough to fall for that player," Max said.

Oh, but she was. Stupid. For that player.

With his good hand, Max took Reagan by the wrist and led her into a large closet beside the practice room. They faced a wall that had guitars hanging from one end to the other on pegs. Some were Dare's. Some Max's. Some Logan's bass guitars. All drool-worthy. Reagan sighed in bliss. Who needed men when you had guitars? She wanted to roll around on them naked. Which would probably be a tad uncomfortable, but she didn't care. She was in lust with every instrument in the room.

"Dare pointed out that I won't need my guitars," Max said, "at least for a while, so take your pick."

"I couldn't," Reagan said, even as her fingers itched to grab the black guitar with electric blue flames directly in front of her.

"At least try one out. I'd rather give them to you than get rid of them. Think of it as a gift."

"Okay," she gushed and lifted the guitar from the hooks in the wall.

"Nice choice," he said.

She had the sudden urge to burst into tears. Maximilian Richardson had paid her a compliment. And let her *touch* his guitar. Even better, let her *play* his guitar. How was she ever going to get used to this?

Once they had her hooked up to an amplifier, Max called out songs and everyone followed his lead. Reagan was really glad she'd practiced all of their songs to prepare for the audition. She actually knew what she was doing, and they seemed impressed that she was keeping up with them. Sweet!

As she played with her new band, she had to continually remind herself that to really serve them as a musician she should mimic Max's sound as closely as she could. It wasn't much of a challenge. Max was a great guitarist, but Dare was the real six-stringed talent in the band. Reagan played with her usual heart, but damn if it wasn't hard to concentrate in the presence of this many great musicians. These men were her inspiration. They were rock gods. *Gods.* And they already accepted her into their fold as if she belonged there. They played through about half of their set list. After several songs Reagan began to relax, but she was careful to keep the sound consistent. She spread her feet apart for balance, closed her eyes, and nodded her head in time with Steve's hard and heavy beat that was made cohesive by Logan's low bass. She let Max's incredible voice carry her away. Paid extra close attention to Dare, to complement his hard, edgy sound rather than compete with it. When the song ended, Reagan opened her eyes to find the members of Exodus End staring at her.

"What?" she said, her face flaming again.

"Band meeting!" Steve called and climbed out from behind his drum kit accompanied by several loud thuds and clangs.

Did a band meeting include her? She looked to Max for direction.

He hooked his microphone into its stand, noticed her looking to him for guidance, and said, "Stay here, Reagan. We'll be back in a few."

Her stomach dropped. She was being excluded. They'd changed their minds. She knew this was too good to be true. And she'd mistakenly thought she was doing well. Fitting in. She'd been fooling herself into believing this miracle was part of her reality.

"Okay," she said with a cheerfulness she did not feel.

It had been a phenomenal dream the forty minutes it had lasted.

The band filtered out of the room, leaving her alone. She played one of Bait-n-Switch's old riffs to keep herself occupied while she waited. A pair of bare feet entered her line of vision. Her head snapped up.

"Is that the riff you want to duel me with?" Trey asked. "I'm not familiar with it."

"It's a riff I wrote, but it isn't any good."

"I kind of like it. Do you want to use it in our duel?"

Trey snagged Dare's guitar from its stand and lifted the strap over his head. The wide strip of studded leather rested at an angle across Trey's well-defined bare chest. The body of Dare's white guitar settled low in front of his pelvis. A no longer naked pelvis. Trey was still shirtless, but he'd put on his jeans. Gnawing on her tongue, Reagan stared at his nipple ring for a long moment before remembering that he'd asked her a question.

"Naw. Too easy. You pick a riff."

He lifted an eyebrow at her. "How about the intro to 'Crazy Train?'"

She loved this man. He had excellent taste. Reagan tore into the intro of "Crazy Train" without waiting for a signal. Flying through the series of building notes with no problem, she paused and Trey echoed what she'd played. When he reached the end, she upped the tempo of the intro and played it again. He echoed her perfectly. She played it faster still, concentrating so intently on the notes that she didn't notice he'd edged closer until his arm brushed hers. She stumbled over a series of notes, the strings feeling awkward under her trembling fingertips. He was left-handed and she was right-handed, so the necks of their guitars faced opposite directions. Scowling at her mistake, Reagan pressed on. Trey copied her, down to purposely making the same error she'd made. She glanced up at him and grinned. He grinned back and winked at her. The next few notes she played sounded like drowned cats choking on strangled chickens. Her heart thundered in her chest. She lowered her gaze to his mouth. A spasm gripped her pussy as she watched the tip of his tongue slide over his lip. God, she wanted him to kiss her.

As if he were a mind reader, Trey turned, lowered his head, and claimed her mouth in a deep, hungry kiss. Stunned, she pulled away and lifted a hand to slap him. She caught herself just in time. She got lost in his eyes, her hand suspended millimeters from his angular jaw. He tilted his head so that her fingertips brushed his cheek and then turned his head to caress her tingling flesh with his lips. Gentle, sucking kisses on the tips of her fingers drew a groan of longing from deep within her. She wrapped both arms around his neck and pulled him down to meet her desperate kiss.

He quickly took control, applying a gentle suction to her lips and then teasing them with hints of an expert tongue and tender nibbles. She tugged him closer, wanting to press against his hard body. Chaotic screeches wailed from their guitars as their strings rubbed against each other.

"You two do *not* make beautiful music together," Dare said as he returned to the room.

Reagan jerked away from Trey and discovered he hadn't been holding onto her at all. All the contact between them had been her

doing. Oh God, she'd thrown herself at him. She should be mortified, but she wasn't. She wanted to throw herself at him again and
keep throwing herself at him until he caught her.

"Does this mean I win?" Trey asked, his deep voice doing strange
things to her nipples.

She chanced a peek at the front of her thin white tank top.
Yep, her arousal was apparent. She crossed her arms over her chest.
Why had she decided against a bra that morning? As a card-carrying
member of the itty bitty titty committee she didn't really need to wear
a bra most days, but one would have concealed her high beam issue.

"Did I say you could borrow my guitar, bro?" Dare asked.

Trey removed the guitar and handed it to Dare. Reagan squeaked
in surprise when Trey drew her against him and claimed her mouth
in another kiss. Glad she hadn't been the one to initiate the contact
between them this time, her arms slid around him to draw him closer.
For once in her life she wished a guitar wasn't hanging around her
neck so she could relish the full length of Trey's lean body against
hers. Feel his rigid arousal against her damp mound. Why was she
melting against him instead of trying to fend him off? Why was she
stroking the cool, smooth skin of his back as if she hadn't just met
the guy? What was it about this man that was so utterly irresistible?

Trey's mouth moved to her ear. "I want you," he whispered.

A shiver of pure delight snaked down Reagan's spine, and she
shuddered with complete surrender.

God, yes, take me you sexy, sexy man. Right here. Right now. Any
way I can have you. I want you too.

"Trey, we need to talk to your latest conquest for a moment,"
Dare said. "Do you mind?" He waved at the open door in get-the-
hell-out-of-here-twerp fashion.

Latest conquest? Could a man who made her feel this special be
a player? She realized that's exactly what made Trey a good player.
She was so going to get her heart broken. And while that realization

totally sucked, she'd deal with it when the time came. There was no way she was shying away from that opportunity. Or that man.

"I'll meet you in the hot tub," Trey said to Reagan.

Probably not a good idea, but she had lost their duel. Might not have if he hadn't touched her. Kissed her. Drove her to utter distraction. Thank God he had. Otherwise they might be heading off to the skate park. Yeah, not exactly her best idea.

"I'll be there in a bit," she said, her heart thudding in anticipation.

Trey moved from her loose hold and slid past the congregated members of Exodus End. Reagan's face flamed. Again. They'd all been watching that. What must they think of her?

"We talked," Dare said.

They all looked so serious. Reagan swallowed. Here it comes. Dreams smashed against the rocks.

"We want to sign you for the upcoming concert season," Max said. "The first half of the tour is US. The second half is world. We leave in three weeks. Can you get your shit, um… *stuff*, in order before then?"

"Of course!" she gushed.

"Awesome," Max said. His welcoming smile faded. "We do have a few concerns."

"Concerns?"

"First, you're a woman."

She lifted a brow at him. "Last time I checked. Is that a problem?"

"Potentially," Max said. "Things happen on tours that might offend you."

She snorted with laughter. "I am unoffendable, Max. Trust me on that."

"We're guys," Logan said. "We're not used to having to behave ourselves."

"Why would you have to behave yourselves?" Reagan asked.

"You're a woman," Steve said.

"I think we've already agreed on that point."

"We don't want you to get freaked out and leave in the middle of the tour," Dare said.

"No chance."

"You'll undoubtedly see things…"

"I get it. You guys party. You fuck sluts. You cuss and argue. You lose your minds and break shit. Whatever. I can handle it."

They exchanged glances.

"I can handle it," she insisted.

"All right, but we're going to be pissed if you back out on us."

"I won't."

"Our second concern…"

The four of them shifted their gazes to the floor. It must be a pretty big concern to make four balls-of-steel rock stars unable to meet her eyes.

"We all noticed that you are…" Steve murmured.

"Fucking hot," Logan blurted.

"Yeah, hot," Max agreed. "But…"

"You need a makeover, sweetheart," Dare said.

She was fucking hot, but she needed a makeover? She set her jaw to control the anger rising up from her chest. "I see. And if I refuse?"

"You'll be destroyed by the tabloids."

"We know you're in this for the music, Reagan, and so are we, but… we kind of have this reputation of…"

"Looking gorgeous," Reagan said flatly.

"If you don't want to be a part of that, it's okay, just know that you're going to hear about it," Max said.

"Remember that time Dare cut his hair?" Logan said. "You would have thought it was a national emergency."

"I'll think about it," Reagan said. If she didn't get a makeover, she was going to end up the frog in a group of princes. Just freaking wonderful.

"We also think you might need a personal bodyguard," Steve said. "When our fans see you…" He produced a low growl that made Reagan feel like willing prey.

"A bodyguard?" she managed to say.

"We have security. They're just not used to keeping too close an eye out for one individual. We wouldn't want you to get hurt."

She lowered her chin and gave them all her frostiest look. "Look here, guys. I'm not some delicate flower. I've been in my share of mosh pits."

"We wouldn't want you to get hurt," Dare repeated. "It would put our minds at ease."

She scrubbed her face with both hands knowing she was going to cave. "Fine. I know someone who can guard my body."

"You know someone?"

"Yeah, my roommate is in security. As overprotective as he is, he'll totally get off on it." Having her best friend, Ethan, on tour with her would be fun. He'd help ease her nerves as well as protect her body.

"So you're signing on with us?"

"Fuck yeah, I am."

And then she was going to celebrate in a hot tub with Trey Mills.

Chapter 4

TREY LEANED BACK AGAINST the edge of the hot tub and closed his eyes. He wondered if Reagan would actually stay true to her word or if she'd back out of their bargain. He couldn't quite figure her out. It unsettled him a little. He liked it a bit too much.

An excited squeal grew in pitch and volume from the hall in the house. Trey's eyes snapped open and, through the ballroom windows, he watched Reagan sprint down the hall and into the changing rooms that led to the pool area. She stopped beside the hot tub and shook a piece of paper as if it were a winning lottery ticket. "A one-year contract with chance of renewal," she yelled.

"Awesome."

"Money. More money than I could make in ten years."

"Exodus End is loaded."

Her gleeful smile faltered. "You don't care. You don't even know me." She pulled out a cell phone and pushed a button before jabbering into it at a million miles a minute. "Ethan. Ethan. Listen. I won the contest and—Yeah, yeah, I won. I just signed a contract with Exodus End. I'm going to be their rhythm guitarist on this year's tour." She paused while whoever Ethan was responded. "Yes, you told me so. You can gloat later." Trey should have known a woman like Reagan would be taken. He started to climb out of the hot tub. Reagan's eyes widened and she darted around the tub to push him back in. "Stay," she said.

Trey laughed and stood in the roiling water with his hands on both naked hips. Oh well. So he couldn't fuck her. He could still hang out with her as a friend. He liked her already. She was interesting. Different. Hot as hell. A great kisser. Why would she kiss him like that if she had a boyfriend?

"Do you want a job?" she said into her phone. "They want me to hire a personal bodyguard. You'd have to come on tour with me." She rolled her eyes. "No, that's not why. Just think about it, okay? It pays a lot, benefits and everything, but I can't talk right now. I've got a date in a hot tub with Trey Mills."

Date?

Reagan disconnected the call. She kissed her contract and then headed back into the changing room.

Now where was she going? Trey shook his head and returned to his seat in the hot tub. Reagan came back a moment later in her hot pink panties and white tank top. Okay, that was totally unfair. He couldn't be expected to think of her as a *friend* in that outfit. He couldn't think at all when he noticed the twin bumps of her nipples straining against her top.

"I didn't wear a bra today so I'll have to wear my shirt in the hot tub," she said when she noticed him ogling her. "Maybe I should just go topless."

He couldn't find words. He was too busy trying to register hers. She stepped in the hot tub and the water concealed her shapely legs from view. Damn, he was hard as granite already. If she went topless…

"You're right. I'm being silly," she said. "It's not like you've never seen a pair of tits before. Am I right? Mine aren't even that great."

Before he had the chance to confirm or deny her assumption, Reagan grabbed the hem of her shirt and peeled it off over her head. Her beautiful breasts rose and fell as she removed the tank top and threw it on the side of the hot tub. A grunt of protest escaped Trey as she sank into the water and hid those small globes of flesh with their tempting pink tips from view. He rubbed his tongue against the ridge of his upper teeth to curtail the urge to flick it over her nipples. Despite what she claimed, her breasts were perfect and he very much wanted to show her just how great he thought they were. Reagan sat beside him, within arm's reach, but not touching him. And while he figured he could probably pounce on her now and get down to business, something stopped him. He wanted to talk to her even more than he wanted to fuck her. Very bizarre. Mostly because he really, *really* wanted to fuck her.

"Dare said that Brian had a baby this morning," she said.

"Yeah, I never thought Brian would ever be able to push it out through such a little hole. It was fuckin' brutal."

She laughed and splashed water at him. "You know what I mean. His *wife* had a baby. Boy or girl?"

Trey couldn't help but smile. He kind of wanted to hold the little guy again already. "Boy."

"Have you seen him?"

"Yeah, I was there when he was born." He purposely left out the fainting part. "He looks like his father."

"Niiiice," she said.

Trey laughed. "Got a thing for Sinclair?"

"Oh my God, the man is delicious."

Couldn't argue with that. Trey happened to agree.

"When I said my band broke up over a kid, I didn't mean that Sinners would break up."

She touched his arm and that electric sensation he'd felt earlier snaked across his skin again.

"Brian won't let us down," Trey said. "Still, things are… changing."

"Is that bad?"

"In some ways, yeah, but in others…" Trey sighed. "I guess things can't stay the same forever."

"Thank God," she said. Her grayish-blue eyes turned skyward. "I thought I was going to be serving coffee for the rest of my life."

"Is that what you do for a living?"

"Pssh, no. I'm the rhythm guitarist for fucking Exodus End. Don't you know anything?"

She tilted her head at him and shook her head. She was so genuinely beautiful it took his breath away. He grinned. "Congratulations. How long have you been playing?"

"Three years."

Trey almost swallowed his tongue. "You learned to play like that in three years?"

"I played cello before I picked up the guitar, but yeah."

"What are you—some kind of prodigy?"

She shrugged. "I've won a contest or two."

"Do you still play cello?"

"I played for my dad, not myself. He's a music teacher. He started me on violin young, but as soon as I could hold a cello properly I switched."

"Was he strict?"

She laughed. "Not exactly. I just liked to make him happy. There wasn't much joy in his life after my mom divorced him. He still has all the programs, certificates, ribbons, and trophies from my competitions hanging all over his den. I need to call him and let him know I'm going on tour with Exodus End." She laughed. "He's so going to hate it."

"I'd think it would make him proud."

She talked out of the side of her mouth as if disclosing a great secret. "He despises rock 'n' roll. It led to the great rebellion of my teen years and me moving out here to Los Angeles on my twenty-first birthday. Growing up, he wouldn't let me listen to anything but classical music."

"My mom was the same way but with folk music." Trey

attempted to suppress a shudder. He still had nightmares about being forced to play "Kumbaya" for all eternity in his personal hell.

"How long have you been playing?" she asked.

He was almost embarrassed to say. "Uh, fifteen years or so." More like eighteen, but who was counting?

"I love your sound," she said. "You complement Brian as if he was your soul mate."

"And you play just like him."

She blushed. Damn, he wanted to kiss her again. She was tough for a woman, yet there was something sweet about her. The combination stirred something within him. The fact that she played guitar like the man he'd loved for over a decade stirred him even more.

"Who's Ethan?" he asked. If she said he was her boyfriend, Trey was going to break his own rule about interfering in other people's relationships. He wanted this woman. His typical take-em-or-leave-em feelings for the opposite sex did not apply in this case.

"My best friend," she said.

"*Only* friends?" Messing up a romantic relationship where the partners were best friends would bother him even more, but he'd still give it a go because there was something unique about this woman. Something he wanted to identify, to get to know, to understand.

"Well, we used to date," she said, "but… uh, let's just say I wasn't enough for him."

Not enough for him? Was the guy a moron? "You're kidding, right?"

"Ethan's great. Really. Too bad he likes men. I caught him fucking some guy in my shower. Talk about a shock to the system. Especially since I'd stripped off all my clothes to join him."

Trey lowered his eyes. He wondered if homosexuality bothered her. He tended to be very open about his bisexual nature, but he'd sworn off men that morning, so it was no longer applicable. Right?

Somehow he didn't think that line of logic would fly with Reagan, but what she didn't know wouldn't hurt her.

"You aren't some kind of homophobe, are you?" she asked.

Trey laughed and lifted his gaze to meet her questioning eyes. "Uh, no," he said. "Not at all."

"Good. What happens in a person's bedroom is no one's business but his own. It would have been nice to have some sort of warning though. I had absolutely no clue that he was gay. We used to go at it like rabbits." She scowled and a distant look settled over her even features. That guy, Ethan, had really hurt her. Trey could tell. Yet, somehow she'd forgiven him enough to continue to be friends with him. She must be fairly open-minded about such things. He hoped.

"So you asked this guy, Ethan, to be your bodyguard?"

She smiled at him. "Yeah, he'd do a good job. He's very protective of me. Maybe a little too protective. He keeps scaring away my boyfriends."

"Do you have a boyfriend now?"

She looked up him. "Do you think I'd let you kiss me if I had a boyfriend?"

There were plenty of women out there who'd let him kiss them (and more) with their boyfriends watching. "I don't know you well enough to say."

"I wouldn't."

He believed her.

"Do you have a girlfriend?" she asked.

"Do you think I'd get into a hot tub naked with you if I did?"

"Yes."

He laughed. "I don't have a girlfriend. I'm not really the commitment type."

"What type are you?"

"The just-looking-for-a-good-time type."

"That's too bad."

His heart sank. He wasn't sure why. Usually if someone wasn't interested he just blew it off. He ducked his head and lifted his gaze to meet her eyes. "Maybe you could change my mind."

She laughed. "Does that line actually work?"

He'd never thought to use it before. Probably because it would have complicated things. He didn't like complications. He wasn't sure what had changed since this morning to make him crave a few complications. As long as they involved Reagan Elliot. "That wasn't a line," he said.

"I'm not buying it, Mills."

He leaned close to her ear and she stiffened. He waited until goose bumps rose along her neck and shoulder before he spoke in his well-practiced seductive voice. "You know what you need?" She shivered and Trey leaned an inch closer so his warm breath would caress the damp skin just below her ear. "A hard, slow fuck against a wall."

Her breath caught.

"*That* was a line," he whispered into her ear.

She slapped at his shoulder. "Well, I would have fallen for *that* one."

He leaned back and cocked an eyebrow at her. "You would have?"

"Yeah, because it's true. That's exactly what I need. A hard… slow… *fuck* against a wall."

Trey's balls throbbed incessantly. The way she said "fuck" made him feel like he was already sheathed deep inside her body.

"You're just the man to give it to me," she said in a husky, breathless voice.

His heart skipped a beat. He reached for her, and she grabbed his head between her hands just before his lips met hers. She stared deeply into his eyes and then winked.

"That was a line," she said and shoved him away.

He laughed and once he got started, he couldn't stop. He collapsed against the back of the tub and covered both eyes with his wet hands. He might have found his match in this woman.

"Is it safe to join you?" Dare asked from the edge of the hot tub.

Trey was glad his brother had found the decency to put on swim trunks.

"We're just talking," Reagan said.

"Just talking? You must be a married woman or something," Dare said.

"Nope."

"Trey's moving slow today. Did he use his hard, slow fuck against a wall line?" Dare settled into the tub across from Trey.

Reagan gasped in indignation.

"Apparently so."

"Jackass," Trey grumbled.

"You're the jackass," Reagan said.

Trey shrugged. "What can I say? I love sex."

Reagan stared at him for a moment and murmured something that sounded like, "Me too," before she turned her attention to Dare. "Did everyone go home?"

Dare reached for the glass of cola he'd set beside the hot tub and took a sip. "Yeah. This is the first break we've had from touring in a while. We need some time apart."

"Maybe I should go," Reagan said. "I wouldn't want you to get sick of me."

Dare met her eyes and held her gaze. "I don't think that's going to be a problem, Reagan."

She flushed. Trey scowled. Dare didn't need lines to attract women. He just had to sit there and give off Dare-a-mones.

"Did you want something to drink?" Dare asked Reagan.

Damn it. Trey should have asked her first.

"I am a little parched."

"I'll get it," Trey offered. When he started to stand, Reagan grabbed his thigh to keep him seated. His naked thigh.

His cock thickened in a surge of hot lust.

"You're naked," she reminded him.

And he would have been fine climbing out of the hot tub naked before she'd touched him. Now if he left the water, he'd embarrass himself in front of his brother. When she didn't move her hand, he eased toward her. Wanting her to touch him, not just there, but everywhere.

"I've seen him naked before. I wasn't overly impressed," Dare said and took another sip of his Coke. "Harold!" he yelled.

A moment later Dare's servant/butler/whoever appeared beside the tub. "Did you need something, Mr. Mills?"

"I have guests."

"Right." Harold turned to Reagan and Trey. The shine of the afternoon sun on his bald spot was almost blinding as he bowed slightly. "Would you like a beverage? A snack? Cherry sucker?"

Trey nodded.

"What do you have?" Reagan asked.

"Anything your heart desires," Harold said.

"Sex on the beach?"

"Anywhere your heart desires," Trey said.

Reagan slid her hand farther up Trey's thigh and he stiffened. In more than one location.

"I should probably abstain," she said. "I have to find the correct bus home."

Abstinence should not be a word in this woman's vocabulary. Trey's gaze lowered to the shadows of her dusty-pink nipples just beneath the surface of the water. He bit his lip so he didn't start with the come-on lines again. Her fingertips stroked sensual trails up and down the inside of his thigh. She moved within inches of his crotch and then away again. An inch closer this time.

Oh God.

"Don't worry about it," Dare said. "Have a drink if you like. If you get wasted, the driver can take you home in the limo."

Reagan's eyes brightened. "You have a limo?"

"The band has a limo," Dare said, "so technically you have a limo too."

"No. Feckin'. Way." Her hand squeezed Trey's thigh and he almost leapt out of the water. "Did you hear that, Trey? I have a limo."

Trey murmured in her ear, "We should go for a ride."

"That would be fun. We could swing by work and I can quit. Or get fired. I don't really care."

"Why would they fire you?" Dare asked.

"Because I'm supposed to be there right now and I didn't even call to let them know I wasn't coming. Not very responsible of me."

"So typically you're a responsible person?" Trey asked.

"I'm wearing nothing but my panties in a hot tub with a pair of rock star brothers—one of them naked. Does that sound responsible to you?"

"I don't have a problem with it," Dare said and laughed.

Reagan grinned. "I have a tendency to do what I want, when I want. Fuck the consequences."

Trey leaned close and pressed his nose to the outer ridge of her ear as he spoke in his most seductive voice. "Can I be the consequences?"

She turned her head and lifted an eyebrow at him. "Are you always this naughty?"

"This is well-behaved for Trey," Dare said and laughed again. His brother was having a grand time at his expense. Trey would get him back for this at his earliest opportunity.

"I figured as much." Reagan leaned closer until her lips were a hairsbreadth from his. He couldn't remember ever wanting to kiss a woman so bad. But for once in his life he wasn't sure how to make the first move. Her signals were all mixed and driving him to distraction. He couldn't figure out what he needed to do to get what he wanted from her. Probably because he wasn't sure *what* he wanted from her. Maybe he didn't want anything from her. Maybe he just wanted her. Period.

"Do you know what I do to naughty boys?" she asked.

"Tease them to their limits and then shoot them down," Dare guessed and took a nonchalant sip of his beverage.

Reagan grinned. "Exactly."

Well, fuck, if she was just going to shoot him down anyway, he might as well push the envelope.

"Do you know what I do to naughty girls?" he asked, locking her gaze with his.

"What?"

"I put in my tongue piercing." He ran a fingertip down the center of his tongue.

"And?" She actually sounded bored. What the hell?

"I flick it over their clit until they scream."

"What do they scream?"

"Oh, Trey. Fuck me. Please."

She tilted her head and stared above his head in contemplation. "Not very original."

Dare chuckled. "This is sweet," he said. "Reagan, I think I love you."

"Shut up, Dare," Trey grumbled. He shot a look of disgust over his shoulder at his brother's smug face.

Reagan's wet hand caressed Trey's cheek and he turned his head to look at her. "Do you know what I'd say?"

He knew he was walking into something, but he couldn't seem to help it. "What?"

Her face went slack, eyes closed, mouth opened in that unmistakable look of feminine bliss. "Oh, Trey, I'm so empty right now. Don't make me come without your thick cock pounding me hard. And deep. And fast. Oh yes, give it to me. Harder. Oh please, harder."

Trey's mouth went dry.

She opened her eyes and grinned devilishly. "Can you tell me where the bathroom is?"

He had no idea what a bathroom *was* at that moment. Did she really expect him to form a coherent response?

When Trey did nothing but gape at her, she glanced at Dare. "Bathroom?"

It took Dare a long moment to answer. "Uh, yeah. There's one in the changing room." He flung a wet hand in the general direction of the house.

"Thanks." Reagan climbed out of the hot tub. Water coursed from her beautiful body and left wet footprints on the pavement in her wake. Trey watched the sweet globes of her ass flex beneath the clinging satin of her panties as she trotted toward the house. When she was out of sight, he relaxed against the edge of the hot tub and emitted a tormented groan.

"She is fucking luscious, isn't she?" Dare said.

Trey sat up straight. "Are you going to pursue her?" He'd hate to have to compete against his brother for a woman, but Reagan kept tempting him to break his usual patterns.

"I would," Dare said, "but A, she's in my band and I won't jeopardize my career for a woman, and B, I think she likes you."

"I think she's just fucking with me."

Dare chuckled. "And I am totally getting off on that."

"You would."

"I've never seen a woman go head-to-head with you before. They either think you're the biggest jackass on the planet or they are seduced before you offer them a second glance. She's different. I think she'd be great for you."

"You do?" Trey glanced back at the door Reagan had disappeared through, hoping she'd return quickly. He already missed the sight of her. And the sound of her husky voice. And the slight lift at the corner of her mouth when she was teasing him. And the feel of her hand on his thigh.

"She'll keep you on your toes." Dare's teasing grin faded. "How did it go this morning?"

"How did what go?" Trey asked, head reeling from the sudden change in subject.

"Seeing Brian with his son."

Trey's heart skipped a beat. "Oh that. Well, I…" He covered the center of his chest with one hand. The emotional anguish of earlier returned—hot and raw as ever—like a branding iron burning a hole through his heart. When he'd been concentrating on Reagan, that pain had been completely absent. She was just the distraction he needed. "Brian belongs with Myrna. I've decided… It's time for me… I'm moving on."

Dare slid around the periphery of the hot tub and wrapped an arm around Trey's shoulders. "You okay?" Dare said, his voice husky with emotion.

"I think so."

Dare was the only person on the planet who knew how much Brian meant to him. The only person. In true big-brother fashion, he'd advised Trey to let Brian go for years, but when he couldn't, Dare had been the caring ear Trey had needed whenever things got too painful to bear.

"Do you need to talk about it?" Dare asked, his hand moving to the side of Trey's head to press his temple against his shoulder. Trey couldn't ask for a more understanding big brother.

"I think it needs to sink in for a few days. It's still kind of new."

"You know where to find me if you need me. I'm always here for you. You know that."

Trey smiled and patted the center of Dare's bare chest with one hand. "Thanks, Dare."

"Oh my God, you two are so fucking gorgeous," Reagan said from the patio behind them. "My vibrator is going to get one hell of a workout tonight."

Not if Trey could help it.

Chapter 5

REAGAN CONSIDERED WHETHER SHE wanted the vision in her head to become a reality. Dare sitting on the edge of the hot tub, pulling her hair while she sucked his cock. Trey fucking her from behind in the hot, roiling water at the same time. When she'd come out of the house and seen the two of them close—touching, cuddling almost—her panties had nearly burst into flames. She needed to get a grip. As much as she wanted to suck Dare off, she knew it would be a bad idea. If they got involved sexually, it would complicate their professional relationship. The music had to come first, even though she wished she was the one coming first and second, before the pair of gorgeous brothers came all over her.

She stared at the matching tattoos on their shoulders—Dare's on his right, Trey's on his left. Red flying V guitars with the saying *Flying V Forever* beneath both. She opened her mouth to ask about them about it (because she'd never seen either of them touch a flying V guitar), but when her eyes met Trey's and then Dare's, the only thing she could think of was becoming the filling in a delicious Mills brothers sandwich.

"I should probably go," she said, before her throbbing, achy pussy convinced her to do something she'd regret.

The butler-guy appeared beside her. Just in time. She grabbed the two drinks from his serving tray and downed them both in quick succession.

"Are you sure?" Dare said, releasing his hold on his little brother and staring up at her with those piercing green eyes.

She set the two empty glasses on the serving tray and nodded vigorously. "Yeah. I have a lot of things to get in order before we go on tour." Total lie. She couldn't tell him the truth though. *Dare, I have to leave before I rape you and your brother in the hot tub.* Not exactly admirable. But oh so true.

"Harold, could you call for the car?" Dare said. "Reagan needs a ride."

Oh yeah. The car. She'd get to ride in a limo. That was almost as good as a threesome with two of the sexiest guitarists on the planet.

Okay, not even close, but it was still pretty cool.

"I need to head out too," Trey said and stood from the water. Her eyes followed the happy trail of hair on his lower belly to his oh-so-gorgeous but now flaccid cock. It pulsed to life as she stared. Jeez, what was wrong with her? She loved sex as much as the next girl, but it wasn't usually the only thing on her mind. She should probably stay as far away from Trey Mills as possible. "Do you mind if we share a limo?" he asked Reagan.

Reagan bent to retrieve her discarded tank top from the edge of the hot tub and pulled it on over her head. "Not at all," she said nonchalantly. She tugged on the fabric so it wouldn't cling to her hard nipples. Not making much progress with that really.

Trey nudged her when he sauntered past her. Making sure he had her attention, no doubt. He collected at towel from the edge of the hot tub and began to rub it over his skin. Now was that really necessary? He turned and she caught a glimpse of his perfect ass. Well, perfect except for the ridiculous tattoo that decorated one cheek. A unicorn, rainbow, and calico kitten had no business on the man's ass. It was a travesty.

At her startled inrush of breath, Dare burst out laughing. "You really need to have that thing removed, bro," Dare said.

Trey followed their line of sight to his ass. He blew out his cheeks and released a slow breath. "Lost a bet," he said to Reagan.

She laughed. "I have one of those." She slid the band of her panties down to show the single word tattooed on her right hip. It said LUNCH beside an arrow that pointed toward her mound.

Trey produced a sound that made Reagan fear he needed the Heimlich.

"What is it?" Dare asked, straining his neck to try to see around Trey.

"Nothing," he said and wrapped his towel around her waist. He reached for his clothes and got dressed, while she dried off her legs with his towel.

She shook her head and laughed. "My bandmates have a sick sense of humor."

"I know the feeling," Trey said.

"My *ex*-bandmates," Reagan clarified. She peeked around Trey's body to grin at Dare. "You guys wouldn't make me get LUNCH tattooed on my hip, would you?" She winked at him and showed him her tattoo.

The shocked expression on Dare's face deserved to be captured on film and hung in a gallery. "That's pretty fucked up," he said.

"Oh, I get it now," Trey said and laughed. "The arrow is pointing to your box. Lunch box."

"A little slow on the uptake today," Dare said. "Too little blood in your brain, bro?"

"Shut up. What kind of ass would make a woman get that tattooed on her hip?"

"Same kind of ass that would make you and Brian get matching girlie tattoos on your asses," Dare said.

"I got off easy," Reagan said. "Our bassist lost the same bet. He has a tat on his ass that says Emergency Entrance with an arrow that points to his... I'm sure you can guess."

"I refuse to ever introduce you to Eric," Trey said. "If he hears that, I know what tattoo I'll be forced to get the next time I lose a bet."

Dare massaged the bridge of his nose. "I'm so glad my band-mates aren't douche bags."

"Me too," Reagan said. "Should I come back tomorrow? I should probably practice for the tour on decent equipment. My guitar is a piece."

"Yeah, you should do that. Do you need me to send the car for you?"

Hmm, let me see... Ride in the limo back to Dare Mills' fabulous mansion or take the city bus and hoof it from the nearest stop? Hard decision.

"That would be appreciated. I don't have a car."

"Just tell the driver what time he should pick you up in the morning."

"Will do. Thanks again for giving me the chance to even audition." Oh no, the gushy fangirlness was returning. "I can't believe I'm going on tour with Exodus End. This is so freaking amazing!"

"We're lucky to have you," Dare said, obviously just being a nice guy. Reagan was the lucky one.

"Thanks," she managed to say. "I'll see you tomorrow then."

"Later, Dare," Trey said.

Trey waited for her outside the dressing room. She removed her wet panties and tucked them in her pocket before slipping into her cargo pants and combat boots. Trey led her back through the maze that was his brother's house and out the front door to the portico over the driveway. A sleek, midnight-blue limousine sat waiting for them. Reagan squeaked excitedly and gave Trey a crushing hug before diving through the open door into the backseat. The white leather seats were arranged in a u-shape around a console in the middle of the floor. Fluorescent blue tube lights circled the perimeter of the ceiling giving everything a sultry blue glow. Before Trey even settled into the seat beside her, she was already fiddling with the console in front of her shins.

"Is this a wet bar?" she asked.

Trey reached for a remote control and started pushing buttons. Music blared from the speakers.

"Oh, I love this song!"

He pressed another button and the center of the console slowly rose to eye-level. "Do you want something to drink?"

"I'm drunk on life. And two inhaled sex on the beach cocktails, but you can have something, if you'd like."

"I'm hungry for lunch, actually," he said.

Her face flamed. She never should have shown him that tattoo. "I like you and all, Trey, but I'm not ready to spread my legs and offer you lunch." Okay, that was a total lie, but he didn't need to know that. She had to play a little hard to get. Very little.

"I meant food. I haven't eaten all day."

Her face fell. "Oh."

"Are you hungry?"

"Yeah, sure. Can we stop by my work first? I need to quit my job."

He lifted a phone receiver and handed it to her.

"I don't want to call them. I want to do it in person. From a limo. I might even moon them."

"Where to?" a deep voice came from the phone receiver.

"That's the driver," Trey informed her with a grin.

"Oh. Right. I've never been in a limo before." She hugged Trey again before lifting the phone to her ear. "Hi, can you fit this long thing through a coffee shop's drive-thru?"

"That shouldn't be a problem, madam."

She giggled and covered the receiver with her hand. "He called me madam," she told Trey.

He grinned at her crookedly, his head tilted just so, and she melted.

"I will need the address," the driver said in her ear, drawing her out of happy-Trey-land.

"Right." She gave the driver the address and hung the phone back in its cradle. "Lunch is on me," she said. "Where are we going?"

"How about Spago Beverly Hills?"

Her jaw dropped. She couldn't afford that place. She hadn't gotten her huge signing bonus from Exodus End yet. "Lunch is on you."

"I would very much like lunch to be on me." He lifted an eyebrow at her, his gaze flicking toward her crotch and then back to her eyes.

She swatted his shoulder. "You're so naughty."

"Usually works pretty well for me. Not so much with you."

He was so wrong. She was utterly seduced. She had no idea why she wasn't making out with him right now.

In a limo.

That belonged to Exodus End.

Her band.

She covered her mouth with one hand to hide her cheese-eating grin. She didn't resist the urge to hug Trey again. He was entirely huggable. Entirely lickable. Entirely fuckable. They'd get to that eventually. She was too distracted to give him the undivided attention he deserved.

"What do you want to do after lunch?" he asked.

Was she seriously going to lunch at Spago with Trey Mills? When had her life become a dream? Oh yeah, about three hours ago. "Don't you have important rock star stuff to do?" She tilted her head and shook it at him. He grinned. Again, she melted.

"I'll have to head back to the Midwest tomorrow for the next Sinners show, but I'm free tonight."

If she spent the entire day with him, she'd be flat on her back with his tight body above her by dusk. She felt the flush of desire creep up her throat. "I'm in," she said without hesitation.

The phone in the console rang. Trey picked it up and listened to the driver speak on the other end. "Did you want to order any coffee?" he asked Reagan.

She shook her head. "The coffee here sucks. Guys come for the scenery. Just pull through and stop at the window."

She took the remote and started pushing random buttons. A TV came out of the ceiling. The song switched to something very hard and heavy. The window that separated them from the driver slid down. At last, the moonroof in the ceiling opened. She climbed up on the console and popped up through the moonroof. The driver eased the limo forward until she was even with the drive-thru window. She waved her arms but no one noticed her. "Tell him to honk," she called down to Trey.

The horn blared the intro to the Exodus End song "Bite." Stacy, the college student Reagan usually worked with, turned at the sound of the horn. Her dark eyes widened and she yanked the drive-thru window open.

"Reagan! What in the world?" She gaped at the limo and then pointed at Reagan. "Hank is pissed that you didn't show up for work. He says he's going to fire you."

"Tell ol' Hank to come here," Reagan said.

"Why are you in a limo? Did you win the lottery?" Several of the other baristas were at the window trying to see through the tiny opening. Every last one of them was wearing a teeny weeny yellow polka dot bikini.

"Better," Reagan assured her.

"What could possibly be better than winning the lottery?" Stacy asked.

"Oh, I don't know…" Reagan said, sure her face was about to crack from the huge smile she couldn't seem to curtail.

A hand pressed against her lower back and Trey peeked out the moonroof beside her.

There was an ear-splitting scream from within the coffee shop. "That's Trey Mills!"

"Hiya," he said and stuck his arm out of the limo's roof to wave.

"Oh my God, Reagan, are you dating Trey Mills?" Leah squeaked, shoving the other bikini-clad baristas away from the window as she attempted to climb out of the tiny opening. Not going to happen. "That *is* better than winning the lottery!"

"She keeps turning me down," Trey said.

Reagan slapped at him. "He lies."

"Reagan, will you be my girlfriend?" he asked.

She looked down at him, knowing he was teasing her. Knowing he expected her to say no. His grass-green eyes were full of mischief. "Yeah, sure, Trey. Why not? Consider yourself saddled with a steady girlfriend."

Trey's eyes widened and he sort of melted down through the open moonroof and disappeared from sight. She laughed, wondering what he would say to get himself out of that arrangement.

"What are you doing? Causing another spectacle?" Hank yelled through the window. "This is the last straw, Reagan Elliot. I cut you some slack when you hosed down a customer with club soda."

"He was being a dick," Reagan said. The four women behind Hank nodded in agreement.

"I turned a blind eye when you wore combat boots with your bikini instead of the required heels."

"Hey, I said if you made it through an eight-hour day in those foot-killers I'd be willing to wear them." She shrugged.

The sound of Trey laughing rose up through the open moonroof.

"And now you're blocking the drive-thru with your obnoxious limo," Hank said.

"There's no such thing as an obnoxious limo. I just stopped by to quit. I don't need this fucked-up job anymore."

"Just like that?" Hank bellowed out the window. "No notice or anything?"

"Yeah, just like that." She snapped her fingers. "Later." She pursed her lips and crinkled her brow as if concentrating. "Actually, I won't see you later, Hank. Split my last paycheck between all my honeys. Bye, girls! I'll miss you!" She waved at her ex-coworkers. They waved back excitedly.

She dropped back down into the limo and grinned at Trey. "That was awesome," she said.

"I thought you were going to moon them."

"They do call it a moonroof for a reason, but I'm not wearing any panties, so I think I'll skip that part today."

"Did you really wear combat boots with a bikini?"

"Is that a problem?"

He shook his head. "I'd just like to see it is all."

"I don't wear a bikini to work anymore." She grinned again. Couldn't help it. "I wear a guitar now."

"And nothing else?"

"It wouldn't bother me. Would it bother you?"

"I'd definitely be bothered. Hot and bothered."

The phone in the center of the console rang. Trey answered. "One moment. Let me see if I can get reservations at Spago."

Trey dug his cell phone out of his jeans pocket. Reagan was not dressed to rub elbows with the rich and famous. It didn't sound all that fun to her, really. Trey slid his finger down the screen of his phone looking for the right number.

"You'll never get reservations on such short notice," Reagan said.

He glanced up at her and blushed. She noticed for the first time that he had a light spattering of freckles on his nose. She wanted to kiss them all.

"I... uh... have connections with someone there. They always get me in."

She took his phone to make sure she had his undivided attention. "I'm impressed. Really," she said, "but honestly, I'd rather get a burger and a beer and eat while cruising around in the back of a limo. With you. Just you." She looked up at him. "But if you'd rather I behave properly in public—"

He snatched the phone out of her hand and tossed it into the seat on the opposite side of the limo. The driver's phone hit the console, and Reagan found herself buried under one hot and eager man. Heavy on the hot.

Dear Lord, the man could kiss. Trey's lips were soft yet strong against hers. He applied just the right amount of pressure and suction—rubbing with lips, caressing with tongue—to drive her mad with desire. He nipped her lower lip and then drew it into his mouth to suck it gently and soothe it with the tip of his tongue. She knew she was clinging to his back, rubbing her heat against his thigh and panting with excitement, but the incurable tease in her had gone on vacation and for a long moment she let Trey drive her to distraction without even considering pushing him away.

"Sir," a tinny voice said from somewhere in the middle of the car. "Sir! We're blocking the drive-thru."

Reagan slapped around at the console, trying to find the phone receiver. When she finally wrapped her hand around it, she turned her head to break Trey's kiss. He stared down at her, his heavy-lidded eyes partially closed, and a pulse of hot lust surged through her pussy. He seemed to be waiting for her to give him the proper cue, but all she could do was stare up at him and imagine the feel of his cock filling that hot, achy emptiness between her thighs.

"Sir, are you there?" the driver said exasperatedly. "Damned rock stars," he muttered.

Reagan lifted the receiver to her ear. "The damned rock stars would like to drive around for a while. Head north along the coast. Just keep driving. We'll let you know when to stop."

"Yes, madam," the driver said sheepishly.

She tried to hang up the phone, but she couldn't reach. Trey took the receiver and set it in its cradle. When he shifted, his cock pressed against her mound. Had he been unexcited, or even half-hard, she might have stood a chance, but he was hard as stone. She shuddered and, heaven help her, moaned. His breath caught, and his gaze shifted to her face. The sultry look he gave her set her ablaze. Trey buried both hands in her hair, tilting her head back slightly as he stared down into her eyes.

"I want to kiss every inch of you," he murmured and ground his cock against her mound. "Then I want to lick every inch. And touch. Then suck. Then fuck." He gave her hair a hard tug. "Every inch."

She wanted to shout, *Yes, Trey, kiss me lick me touch me suck me fuck me, all of me, all of me!* but it came out as an incoherent gasp.

"I will find all your spots. Pleasure you until you beg me to possess you. When I finally do, I'll plunge into you hard. Deep."

She could practically feel him inside her. "Fast," she gasped. "Hard and fast."

"Slow," he murmured and lowered his head to kiss her jaw. His lips scorched a trail down her throat. When he reached her collarbone, he paused. "So slow." He rubbed against her again and she spread her thighs so he slipped lower. Their clothes prevented him from surging into her body, but she felt him there, gyrating against her opening in slow, sensual arcs. "I want to make you come hard, so hard, but only after I spend hours worshipping your body."

"I bet you say that to all the girls," she said.

The light stubble on his chin was rough against her nipple as he used it to push the neckline of her tank top down. His tongue slid against the erect bud and her stomach clenched with need.

"Jealous?" he whispered, his breath teasing her nipple. He sucked it into his mouth and rubbed it with circular motions of his tongue.

"A little," she admitted. "Now that I'm your steady girlfriend, I expect you to pleasure only me."

He tensed. She waited for him to deny her as his girlfriend so she could find the sense to tell him to get off her, not to get her off. It wasn't as if she'd never had a one-night stand before, but she always regretted them in the morning. She didn't want to regret anything with this man. She kind of liked him. Getting tangled up with him sexually too quickly would ruin that. There'd be the awkwardness and the niceties and then he'd never call her again. She wasn't an idiot. She knew how players operated.

"Yeah," he said, "only you, Reagan."

Well, that just pissed her off. Lying to her to get her to submit? Wrong.

She shoved him onto the floor of the limo and sat up, concealing her reddened, very excited, and suddenly lonely nipple under her top again.

"What?" Trey said, sitting on the floor at her feet, looking all tousled and aroused and completely flabbergasted. Damn him for being so irresistible. And knowing it.

"I do have feelings," she said. "And I'm not stupid, so don't think your lies are going to work on me."

"What lies?" The man was a fine actor. He honestly looked like he had no idea what she was talking about.

"*Only you, Reagan*," she said, mimicking that sultry, bedroom voice of his.

"What lies?" he repeated. "I meant that. I want that. With you. Only you."

"You want what with me, Trey? Sex?"

"A committed, steady relationship. I want to try it for the first time in my life. With you, Reagan. Don't take it lightly. If you think the idea doesn't scare the piss out of me, you're wrong. But, I think…" He shifted his gaze to the ceiling. "Never mind. Forget it."

"You've never been in love?"

"I didn't say I've never been in love. I said I've never been in a steady, committed relationship."

Reagan scowled and crossed her arms over her chest. "So you cheated on the woman you loved?" Ethan had cheated. She couldn't be with a man who cheated again. It hurt too much.

"No, it was one-sided. Bri—the person I was in love with didn't love me back. I kept hoping that would change given enough time, but… I want to move on. I didn't think I'd ever feel that way—didn't think I'd ever give up—but today has been one kick to my system after another and here you are all perfect for me. I don't think I should ignore that."

She snorted. "You think I'm perfect?"

"No, I think you're pretty fucked up, Reagan. Perfectly fucked up."

She tightened her arms, which still crossed her chest, and rubbed her upper arms. "You're fucked up too."

"Exactly."

She watched him for a moment, looking for the smooth operator who separated women from their panties with such ease, but Trey seemed completely sincere. She'd be able to tell if he was just saying what he thought she wanted to hear to get into her pants, right? She supposed there was an easy way to tell.

"Okay, we'll try this serious relationship thing on one condition."

"I have a pressing condition in my pants."

She shook her head at him, needing him to be serious. "I don't quite trust you yet. I still think you just want to fuck me and then dump me. Which, okay, fine if that's the truth then I can handle that, but don't make me love you and then break my heart."

"Why would I open my heart to you if that was the case?"

"I'm not sure if you're opening your heart or just making up some bullshit story to get laid."

"I'm not. Honestly, Reagan, I have no problem getting laid. If that's all I wanted, I can find it anywhere." He stared up at her for a long moment and, when she didn't back down, he released an exasperated sigh. "What's your condition?"

"That we spend the entire day together on a completely platonic level."

"That's a sucky condition."

"No sucking either."

He laughed. "Okay, fine. Platonic. I can do that. That's where we hold our breath, try not to come for a really long time, meditate and stuff, right?"

She laughed. "No, baby, that's tantric."

"I was hoping that was what you meant," he said, a devilish grin on his handsome face. "But if you did actually mean platonic, I think I can manage it for one day."

"And you have to pass the Ethan test." No one ever passed the Ethan test. Her heart would be perfectly safe from Trey Mills's clutches.

"That's two conditions. You get one or the other."

Only fair, she supposed. He'd never make it through a platonic day anyway. "Fine. You just have to make it through the day without a single come-on, caress, or stolen kiss. And no flirting."

"Agreed." He extended a platonic hand. "Shake on it."

She took his hand and shook it, surprised when he didn't try to prolong the clasping of their hands. "It's a deal then. One platonic day together."

He released a relieved breath. "Thank God the sun goes down in six hours. You said nothing about a platonic night."

Why did the man have to be so feckin' perceptive?

Chapter 6

TREY HAD NEVER HAD so much fun not having sex with a woman. They'd had burgers and beers while watching a ballgame in the back of the limo. Had he wanted to steal a kiss, rip off her clothes, fuck her senseless? Every second. But he'd somehow managed to behave. She'd cheered for the San Diego Chargers, and just to get her all up in arms, he'd pretended to be a fan of the opposing team. He hadn't paid enough attention to the game to remember who had won.

After the game, they'd taken a walk on the beach. Talked. About music. He'd never met a woman who knew so much about music. He'd hung on her every word. Was it because he was thinking about the way her kiss tasted, the heat he'd discovered between her legs, the cute way she squinted in the sunshine when she looked up at him? Only about half the time. She was genuinely interesting. He wasn't just pretending she was interesting to get laid. He'd talked to women this way when he had no interest in them sexually, but this? This was new for him. This being totally turned on by a woman he genuinely liked blew his mind. Why had he thought this was a bad thing? Because he'd always felt like he was being untrue to Brian, that's why. Screwing around with people he didn't care about didn't feel important. Every time Brian entered his thoughts, Trey still felt guilty for liking Reagan so much. It felt like he was cheating on Brian. It seriously messed with his head so he made an effort not to think about Brian. With Reagan beside him, it was easier than he'd thought it would be.

He and Reagan found a skate park on the beach and she talked a couple of dudes into letting her borrow their skateboards. She ollied and kickflipped like a pro. Trey tried to keep up, but he hadn't been on a skateboard in about ten years and it showed. The skater dudes were impressed with Reagan's abilities. Trey knew they were all thinking about fucking her. He could see the hunger in their eyes. Even though Trey spent most of their skate park adventure scraping his bruised body off the ground in a most unimpressive fashion, she left with him—much to her captive audience's dismay—and they'd continued down the beach.

She spotted a drink shack and lit up with excitement. "I'm thirsty. Are you thirsty?"

He needed a Tylenol and an icepack for his elbow more than a beverage, but how could he say no to that eager look on her face? "Yeah, sure. What do you want?"

"Vanilla shake."

He bit back a quip about vanilla sex.

A Frisbee landed at Reagan's feet and a big, slobbery, yellow dog barked at her excitedly. He wagged his tail and nudged the plastic disk with his nose.

"He doesn't bite! Would you mind tossing that this way?" some guy yelled from near the waves.

Reagan gave the dog a scratch behind the ears and then tossed the chewed up bit of plastic toward the waves. She chased him a couple of steps and then stopped dead in her tracks. She glanced at the line at the drink stand and then at Trey.

"Go play with the dog," Trey said. "I'll get your drink."

Her happy laugh was all the reward he needed as he found the end of the line.

While Trey waited for the cashier to make Reagan's vanilla milkshake, he watched her throw the Frisbee down the beach for the Labrador retriever again and again. The dog's owner was watching her almost as closely as Trey was. The dog was in total puppy love as she scratched him behind the ears, took the tooth-marked plastic disk from his mouth, and gave it another toss toward the lapping waves.

"Here you go," the girl behind the counter said. "One vanilla shake. One cherry slush."

Trey tore his attention off Reagan long enough to pay for their drinks. When he turned around, drink in each hand, he found Reagan laughing with the owner of the yellow lab. Trey hurried to her side. He wondered how many women the guy picked up this way.

"No he didn't. Really?" Reagan said to the attractive, tan, and athletic dog owner. She had this way of holding one eye closed when she thought you were full of shit. It made Trey wonder what she looked like when she had an orgasm.

"Yeah. I thought for sure she was going to call the cops on me."

Trey sidled closer to Reagan. She smiled at him when he handed her the vanilla shake, but she immediately turned her attention back to the dog guy. "So why didn't she?"

"Riley didn't mean to hurt her," he said and turned to his dog. "Did you, boy?"

Riley took several backward steps, his tail wagging, and produced a loud *WOOF!* in agreement.

"He was just looking for love. Weren't you, boy?"

Woof! Woof!

Trey slurped his slush as loudly as possible, hoping to regain Reagan's undivided attention. A harsh, jabbing pain radiated up the back of his throat and pounded incessantly behind his right eye.

"Ah, God. Brain freeze!" Trey yelled and covered his eye with his free hand. "Fuck. Why does that hurt so bad?"

Reagan laughed at him. "Suck it more slowly next time," she advised.

He had fifteen lines he could have used at that moment, but he had to keep things platonic between them for another hour or so.

"Are you okay?" she asked as she watched him wipe tears out of his eyes. He'd take a broken nose over brain freeze any day.

"I think I need to walk it off," he said and gave the loser and his dog a pointed look.

"This is Scott," Reagan said, misinterpreting Trey's tell-this-guy-to-get-lost look.

Trey nodded at him without taking his eyes off Reagan. He'd never felt so possessive of a woman before. He didn't even want Scott to look at her. The fact that Scott was using a dog as an excuse to flirt with her made him pretty lame in Trey's book. Of course, if Scott had a medal of valor, five Olympic gold medals, and a Nobel prize hanging around his neck, Trey would have still thought he was lame. He was hitting on Reagan and Trey couldn't touch her in such a way to make it clear that she was his. Trey had to be very careful not to give her a reason to blow him off. One more hour to behave. And then once he met her condition, all bets were off. If she tried to push him away again, he'd just have to take the upper hand and see how she reacted. He was starting to understand her signals. Maybe.

"We should probably head back to the limo," Trey said, careful not to put emphasis on that last word. That would make him as lame as Scott. Trying to impress the girl with material possessions. He didn't need stuff to impress a woman. But, hello, they had a limo at their disposal.

Reagan nodded and took a long sip of her milkshake. Her face twisted in pain and she covered one eye with her free hand. "Brain freeze," she gasped.

"You should—"

"Suck it more slowly next time?"

"You can suck it as fast as you want." He winced as soon as it was out of his mouth. He was so used to turning every phrase into innuendo it happened automatically.

Reagan laughed. "Don't worry. I'll suck it real slow. It will last longer that way."

As turned on as he was by this woman, there were no guarantees he'd last at all. No matter how slow she sucked. He stared at her mouth as he took another slurp of his slush, holding the frigid beverage in his mouth to warm it slightly before he swallowed this time.

Reagan bent and gave the dog another scratch behind the ears. "No more humping elderly women in wheelchairs, Riley. It's not nice."

Riley barked and wagged his tail. Trey laughed.

"Bye, Scott," Reagan said without looking at him.

Two points for the Trey-ster. Trey so wanted to take her hand and hold it as they walked away, but he had a little over an hour to keep his hands to himself.

"So I take it you like dogs," Trey said.

"I love dogs. Do you have a dog?"

"I had one when I was a kid. He got hit by a car. Haven't had one since."

Reagan's features softened with sympathy and she slid a *comforting* hand down his back. Damn, he was horny. Even that small contact had his cock at full attention.

"I'm sorry," she said. "You haven't had any pets since?"

"Just Eric Sticks."

Reagan laughed. "I can't wait to meet Eric. He seems like so much fun when I've watched interviews of you guys."

"You've watched interviews of Sinners?" He wondered what she thought of him. He didn't say too much during interviews. Their lead singer, Sed, liked to hear himself talk.

"I'm kind of obsessed with Sinclair."

Trey completely understood that obsession.

"I love his sound. It speaks to me," she added and took another draw off her milkshake.

"I honestly thought you were him at that audition. It's amazing how much you sound like him."

"I've been practicing. Could you introduce me to him? I promise not to turn into a gushing fangirl." She covered her chest with one hand. "Much."

"He's used to gushing fangirls."

"Are you?"

"Yeah. But I like it. Brian never did."

"Thanks for the tip. I'll try not to prostrate myself at his feet, kiss his boots, and repeat his name like a mantra to the rock gods."

Trey wanted to make her repeat his name like a mantra to the *sex* gods. "You should play for him," he said, trying to keep his train of thought from slipping. Not doing so well with that, thanks.

She paused, her bare toes scrunching in the sand. Damn, even that was sexy. When she didn't say anything, he lifted his gaze to meet hers. "I'd rather play with you."

Trey bit his lip, the urge to spill another come-on line overwhelming. He wasn't sure, because the blood rushing through his head on its way to his cock was rather loud, but he might have actually produced a verbal groan of longing.

"You're censoring yourself, aren't you?" she asked and touched his chest with her fingertips. His heart thundered in his chest.

"I'm trying so hard to be good," he admitted.

"Why?"

"I'm not sure. If you ditch me, I can easily find someone else to entertain me."

Her features hardened and he knew he'd said the wrong thing.

"The thing is, I don't want anyone else. I like you, Reagan."

"How often do you use that line?" she asked.

"Never," he said honestly.

She smiled and he was glad she believed him. "I was sort of hoping you'd stop trying to be good and just be yourself. I keep glimpsing this naughty guy and I'd like to get to know him a little better. I'm not sure why I gave you that platonic ultimatum. I've been wishing I hadn't for the past three hours."

"If I give free rein to my naughty side, I won't be able to keep my hands off you."

She cocked her head to the side, her gaze trained on his mouth. "What about your lips?"

"They'd be all over you too."

"And your tongue?"

Now he was sure he groaned with longing.

She stared into his eyes as if contemplating her options. "Do you want to come back to my place? It's not far from here."

"I'd like that."

"Just so you know, this doesn't mean you're going to get laid, Trey Mills."

She was killing him here.

"It guarantees it," she added.

Heat flooded his lower belly and spread to his groin. He wasn't going to make it all the way to her place. He didn't care how close it was.

He draped an arm around her shoulders and drew her closer, hurrying her toward the limo parked at the far end of the beach. Her warmth melted into his side as her arm moved to rest against his lower back. Her fingers brushed his side.

She nodded toward the waves. "Beautiful sunset."

Trey glanced at the horizon. The sun had just kissed the ocean. The sky was ablaze with shades of pink and orange. He'd never been so happy to see a sunset in his life. Even though she'd recanted her stupid platonic ultimatum, he'd somehow made it through without dying from blue balls. Two points for the Trey-ster.

"I had fun with you today, Trey," she said, "but I think I'm going to have a lot more fun with you tonight."

"I think that's a safe assumption."

—⁓—

Reagan climbed into the limo and slid around the white leather seat to give Trey room to join her. Had she really just invited Trey back to her apartment? And promised him sex? Jeez, just because her pussy had been wet and swollen since he'd kissed her earlier didn't mean it was a good idea to come on to him so strong. He had way more self-control than she did. When he ducked into the car, his long bangs obscuring one sultry green eye, and pinned her with a look of pure lust, she had no regrets. Other than dirty feet from walking barefoot down the beach and dog-germ hands. As much as she wanted to touch Trey, she decided she needed a shower first. That last coherent thought fluttered out the moonroof when he looked at her like she was his favorite cherry dessert.

The limo's door closed behind him and he settled beside her. He leaned close so that his nose brushed her cheek near her ear and his warm breath tickled her earlobe. "Later," he said in a low voice, "I'm going to make love to you slowly and appreciate every inch of that gorgeous body of yours, but right now…" He sucked a sharp breath between his teeth as if his own thoughts were torturous. "Right now I'm going to devour you."

Eyes wide, she turned to look at him. His mouth captured hers in a deep, sucking kiss. His tongue flicked against the inside of her upper lip and she groaned, opening her mouth to his possession. His lips tasted of cherry and some unique flavor that could only be described as Trey-licious. She leaned into his hard body, pressing her breasts against his chest.

He shifted and she found herself belly-to-belly with him and sprawled across the backseat of the limo. He moved his thigh between her legs and pressed it firmly against the throbbing ache that longed to be filled by him. She squirmed, needing rougher stimulation, and felt the evidence of his desire against her hip. He tore his mouth from hers and met her eyes. "I want you," he said. "Reagan." He buried one hand in her hair and tilted her head back so he could move those sucking kisses of his to her throat. "Reagan."

"I want you too," she said breathlessly.

"Say my name."

"Trey."

He moved his hand to brush the straps of her tank top down until her breast was exposed. He flicked his tongue over one nipple and her entire body tensed.

His hands skimmed down her sides, drawing her tank top down to her waist. She got lost in a sea of sensation, unable to keep track of where his hands were, his lips, his tongue. She'd never been this excited in her life. Cool air bathed her crotch and she wondered when he'd managed to unfasten her pants. She lost track of that thought when his tongue flicked against her swollen clit. Her hips buckled and she cried out. He rubbed the flat of his tongue against her several times and then lifted his head. He reached for his cherry slush and took a drink. Reagan almost had time to collect her scattered thoughts before he lowered his head and dribbled a trail of frigid ice over her hot and achy flesh. She groaned when he lowered his head to warm her with the friction of his tongue and lips.

Within seconds her womb tightened and the first ripples of orgasm gripped her aching center. "Trey, Trey, Trey!" she chanted as she came, wishing he was inside her as her core clenched with hard spasms of pure bliss.

"You're gushing," he said as if in awe and started lapping at her freely flowing juices. "You taste so good," he murmured, "Reagan mixed with cherry."

Still trembling with aftershocks of release, she chuckled. The guy had a thing for cherry. He continued to lick and suckle her while he removed her pants. Her panties, which she had taken off back at Dare's house, were still in her pocket. With nothing on but her tank top around her waist, she found herself mostly naked while Trey was still fully clothed. Didn't seem quite fair. She wanted to see him. Touch him. Kiss him. Taste him, too.

She sat up in the seat and reached for his shirt, tugging impatiently at the fabric along his back. He caught her hands and locked fingers with her, his tongue still dancing over the heated flesh between her thighs.

"Trey," she whispered desperately. "I want to touch you."

"I couldn't stand it," he said. "After I come, you can touch me as much as you want. I'm much too excited right now though."

His tongue plunged into her body. Twirled inside her. Withdrew. Plunged inside again. Twirled. Withdrew. She writhed against his face, unable to control the motion of her hips. Oh dear God, if he kept that up much longer she'd come again. He released one of her hands and softly, gently stroked her quivering belly. Her hand moved to his hair and tangled in the long silky strands. She tried to tug him upward, to direct him to her throbbing clit, but he resisted, still teasing her pussy with that talented tongue of his. She felt her tank top go taut against her waist. He grabbed her hand, did some fancy twist, and the next thing she knew her wrist was trapped at her side, imprisoned by her own shirt.

He lifted his head and said, "Don't interfere," before nipping her clit. Her entire body jerked. He flicked the sensitive nub with his tongue, sucked on it until she was writhing against his face again, and then switched to suckling her swollen lips.

"You're killing me, Trey," she said breathlessly. "Will you just fuck me already?"

He lifted his head and chuckled. "I thought you'd never ask."

He wanted her to ask? If she'd known that, she would have asked ten minutes ago. He shifted back to kneel on the floor between her wide open legs. The cold air that bathed her slick heat reminded her how much she needed him inside her. She struggled to free her wrist from her twisted tank top and, once free, she sat up and reached for Trey's belt. He was checking the pockets of his jeans frantically.

Reagan unfastened his belt and worked at the buttons of his fly. Trey had his wallet out and was digging around inside. When Reagan got his pants open, she reached inside and carefully pulled his cock out of his pants.

He shuddered. "W-wait," he breathed.

His cock was magnificent—long and hard, tipped with a large, thick head that she wanted to suck almost as much as she wanted it inside her.

"Hurry," she whispered. "God, I want you."

"Fuck!"

"Yeah, fuck. That's what I had in mind."

He grimaced when she rubbed her thumbs over his cock head in wide circles.

"You wouldn't happen to have a condom on you, would you?"

"Not on me, no. You're supposed to put it on you and put it *in* me." She chuckled.

"I don't have one with me."

She groaned. "Please tell me you're joking."

He bit his lip and shook his head. "I probably lost them one of the times I hit the deck at the skate park. Or when I bought our drinks. Or at Dare's house. Or at the hospi—"

She released a frustrated breath. "Maybe there's a drugstore nearby. We'll send the driver in." She peeked out the window and found they were in a familiar parking lot. "Oh, I'm home. I do have condoms upstairs."

Trey breathed a sigh of relief. "Awesome. I'm dying to bury myself inside you."

Chapter 7

WHEN ETHAN HEARD REAGAN fumbling with her key in the lock of the front door, he glanced up from the boxing match he was watching on TV. Wide smile on his face, he climbed to his feet and prepared for her excited launch into his waiting arms. He probably shouldn't love it when she was excited about something, but Lord he missed the feel of her body against his. As far as Ethan was concerned, any excuse to embrace Reagan Elliot was a good excuse.

The door swung open and she stumbled into the room, pulling some laughing guy into the apartment by his T-shirt. Barefoot, she tossed her boots on the floor near the entryway, which freed her hand to grab onto the guy with both hands. So she could pull his mouth against hers and kiss him hungrily.

Ethan's smile faded. She'd brought home another dipshit who was in no way good enough for her. Ethan straightened his spine, prepared to use all six feet two inches of his muscular frame to its full, intimidating advantage.

Said dipshit wrapped both arms around Reagan's narrow back to deepen their kiss and kicked the door closed behind him. "Where's the bedroom?" he said against her lips. His hands moved to squeeze her luscious ass. Ethan stifled an angry growl.

Reagan drew away, took the guy by the hand, and took two steps in the direction of her bedroom when she noticed Ethan standing there. At least she had the decency to flush.

"Oh, Ethan," she said. "This is... This is Trey. My, um,

new…*boyfriend*?" She glanced at this Trey fellow and he smiled at her like the dipshit he was.

Boyfriend? When in the hell had that happened? Ethan would have known if she'd so much as gone on a date with anyone. She still confided everything to him. The dipshit, *Trey*, stepped forward, his hand extended in greeting. Ethan got his first good look at the guy and his gut clenched with a powerful longing. Wow. The man was sex incarnate. This guy was straight? Ethan had a hard time buying that. Ethan's lust was never wrong. He could pick out a piece of hot tail from a mile away, and this guy was the hottest tail he'd ever laid eyes on.

"Hey," Ethan said and accepted Trey's hand. He could smell Reagan's sex all over the guy, so either Trey was very confused or in denial. Or, in a perfect world, bisexual. "Nice to meet you."

"Likewise," Trey said, his gaze raking down Ethan's body. Yeah, this hunk of hotness was not everything Reagan thought he was. She hadn't been able to accept Ethan's sexuality. She wouldn't be able to accept this new guy's either.

"How come you haven't mentioned Trey before?" Ethan asked Reagan.

Her cheeks went pink again. The woman cursed like a sailor, but talking about her love interests made her blush. "Well, I just met him today."

"Moving a little fast, aren't you?"

Reagan scowled at him and then smacked him in the arm. "Shut up. If you try to mess this up for me I'll shave your head in your sleep and superglue the hair to your balls."

Ethan knew she'd do it, too.

Trey's sexy green eyes began to roam the apartment. He draped an arm around Reagan's narrow waist and rested his hand on her hip as if getting comfortable to stand there for a while. Apparently he realized that Ethan was on a mission to keep Reagan out of her bedroom for as long as possible.

"So tell me about the audition," Ethan said to Reagan, trying not to stare at Trey's mouth. The man had a beautiful mouth. A beautiful mouth that would look phenomenal wrapped around Ethan's hard, thick…

Reagan's eyes widened and she went animated. The way she reacted when she was really excited about something. Ethan loved to get her excited. "Oh my God, can you believe it? They liked my playing so much they didn't even finish listening to all the contestants. I'm going out on tour with Exodus End in three weeks."

"And Sinners," Trey added absently. He reached into his pocket and pulled out a red lollipop. He unwrapped it and stuck it in that beautiful mouth of his. Ethan's belly clenched and his cock stirred to life.

Reagan looked up at Trey in question. "Sinners?"

"Yeah, we're co-headlining with Exodus End this tour."

"You mean we're going to be on tour together?" she said, the pitch of her voice rising with each word.

"Dare didn't mention that?"

"No," she squealed and bounced up and down on the balls of her feet.

Ethan chuckled. She was so adorable when she was excited.

"Such a fucktard," Trey commented and tugged the sucker out of his mouth.

Ethan practically felt the tug of Trey's suction on the head of his cock. Mercy, the man was sensual. And judging by the sidelong glance he offered Ethan, he knew it.

Reagan hugged Trey, her entire body trembling with excitement. "And just when I thought my day couldn't get any better."

"Your night's going to get a whole lot better," he murmured into her ear. "If we ever make it to the bedroom." He lifted his gaze just enough to catch Ethan staring at him. He grinned crookedly and then sucked that lollipop back into his mouth.

Ethan stifled a groan. "So you're in a band too?" Ethan asked.

Reagan spun around to gape at him. "This is Trey," she said, shaking her head at Ethan. "Trey *Mills*. Ethan, get your brain out of cold storage. I talk about the guitarists of Sinners constantly. How talented they are. Do you ever listen to a word I say?"

Ethan racked his brain for a name he'd heard amongst Reagan's ceaseless prattling about guitarists and could only come up with, "Brian Saint Claire?"

"Brian *Sin*clair," Reagan said and rolled her eyes at him. "Brian's the lead guitarist for Sinners. Trey is rhythm."

Rhythm? Ethan bet the man knew quite a few things about rhythm, and if not, Ethan would be more than happy to show him.

Trey winked at Ethan, a knowing grin on his face. He pulled the sucker out of his mouth and gave it a few flicks with his tongue before sliding it back into his mouth through his tightened lips. In. Out. In. Out. The fucker was tormenting Ethan on purpose. Trey moved to stand behind Reagan and wrapped both arms around her waist. She leaned back against him and Ethan gritted his teeth. Ethan didn't know why he didn't just move on. Things would be a lot more tolerable if he didn't still love Reagan or if he wasn't attracted to men, but he had both problems and wasn't sure what to do about it. Well, *besides* getting rid of these guys she brought home as quickly as possible. Funny, he didn't think his usual intimidation tactics would work with Trey. Trey was probably well aware of Ethan's instant attraction to him. Ethan wondered if Trey was attracted to him as well or if he really was just fucking with him because he found giving men blue balls amusing.

"You said something about finding me a job, too," Ethan said to keep Reagan talking and out of the bedroom. He'd been doing piece-work since he'd left the force. Some high-profile bodyguard work for celebrities and low-profile security at events, but nothing long-term. A more steady flow of income would be a welcome change. Especially since it meant he got to keep an eye on Reagan. He worried about her constantly. She was too reckless for her own good. Exhibit A was standing right in front of him giving that lollipop one hell of a blow job.

"The band thinks I'll need a personal bodyguard. I think they're—"

"Absolutely right," Trey said. "Fans don't usually intend to harm anyone, but they can get carried away. No one wants to see you hurt." Trey pulled the sucker from his mouth and placed a series of gentle sucking kisses on the sensitive spot just below Reagan's earlobe. Her eyelids fluttered, and she clung to Trey's thighs with both hands. "He'll probably spend most of his time trying to protect you from me," Trey murmured in a sexy growl.

"Then he's fired," Reagan said.

Ethan cleared his throat. Trey stared him in the eye as he drew his tongue up along the side of Reagan's neck. Ethan's balls clenched. What a fucking bastard. He had to know that would turn Ethan on. Why was he torturing him?

"So what exactly will my duties be?" Ethan asked, trying to ignore the way Reagan was rubbing her sweet ass against Trey's crotch. Ethan still remembered how well that ass fit his palms while she rode him. How hot and slick and tight her pussy felt as it slid up and down his length.

Trey paused and looked up at Ethan. "You talk too much." He lifted his hand and stuck his half-eaten sucker in Ethan's mouth. "Where's your bedroom, Reagan? Or I could just bend you over that sofa there and finish what we started in the limo."

Limo?

"This way," Reagan said and grabbed a handful of Trey's T-shirt. She tugged him into her bedroom and shut the door before Ethan could come up with another stall tactic.

Shit. Where were his sound-blocking headphones? There was no way he'd be able to survive listening to those sexy sounds Reagan made when she was getting it good. And Ethan had no doubt that Trey Mills was going to give it to her good.

Chapter 8

Trey was glad when Reagan shut her bedroom door and removed her very distracting roommate from sight. He hadn't even made it through a day and he was already thinking about being utterly seduced by a man. Well, one man. The big, gorgeous alpha male in the living room. Trey knew Ethan would hold him down and fuck him good and hard when he needed it. It would be nice to let someone take charge for a change. His last few lovers had been total bottoms, which had its perks, but sometimes Trey wanted a man who took charge and… Wait. Wrong! What was he thinking? No more men. No submissive bottoms. No alpha tops. Not even a healthy switch. No men. Period.

Reagan turned on a lamp, opened the top drawer of her dresser, and rummaged around until she produced a small box of condoms. She blushed when she moved to stand before him. "Only two left. I hope that's enough."

"We could always borrow some extras from Ethan."

Reagan's eyes widened. "I couldn't."

Trey was starting to think there was still something between the roommates. Something more substantial than friendship. "Do you still care about the guy?"

"Well, I might if he wasn't gay. Can we not talk about Ethan? I'd much rather concentrate on you."

But would she still want to concentrate on him if she knew that Trey tended to be as attracted to the same sex as much as he was attracted to the opposite sex? Except he'd given up on men. Yeah. He only wanted women. And at the moment, he only wanted Reagan. He would not allow himself to imagine how unbelievable it would feel to have Ethan's weight against his back as he filled him from behind. Trey seriously needed to get busy with Reagan so he could orient his thoughts back where they belonged. On his new *girl*friend. Who was smoking hot, a lot of fun, interesting, and with whom he had more in common than any other person he'd ever met, with the exception of Brian.

Brian.

Trey grabbed Reagan around the waist and pulled her up against his chest before lowering his head to kiss her breathless. He would not be thinking about Brian either. Just Reagan. She was everything Trey could ever possibly want in a woman, and he wasn't going to mess this up by thinking about men.

Reagan tugged at Trey's T-shirt impatiently and he released her long enough to pull it off over his head. She removed her tank top as well, freeing her small, perky breasts to his eager gaze.

"You're beautiful," he said, touching her face, her shoulder, her rosy nipple.

"Show me," she whispered.

He smiled. "I'd be happy to."

He took her hand and led her to the bed. He kissed her neck while he worked at the button of her cargo pants and released the zipper. Starting at her throat, he licked his way down the center of her body as he slowly lowered her pants to the floor. She kicked them aside and tugged him to his feet. "Let's go take a shower."

"Shower?"

"I have sand all over my feet. And I smell like dog."

"You smell like pussy," he corrected, and it had his motor revving on high.

She chuckled. "That too."

"That's a good thing. Trust me."

She stared down at her hands and pulled a face of disgust. Okay, he supposed he could survive showering with her if it would allow her to relax.

Trey glanced around the room, looking for a door to a connecting bathroom. There was a sliding closet door and the door they'd entered, but nothing that led to a bathroom. "Where's your bathroom?"

"There's only one in this apartment."

He was surprised when she opened the bedroom door and walked out into the hall completely naked. Wasn't Ethan out there? Trey kicked off his shoes and followed her. Ethan was indeed out there, and the way he looked at her told Trey what he'd expected all along. Ethan wasn't homosexual; he was bi. For years, Trey had searched for a bisexual partner. They weren't easy to find. Women, sure. He'd encountered plenty of bisexual women, but bisexual men willing to admit to it were more of a rarity. Of course Trey would discover the perfect lover the day he vowed to give up men forever. Murphy's Law.

Ethan's dark eyes flicked from completely-naked Reagan to half-naked Trey. Trey lifted an eyebrow at him in question. He couldn't believe that Reagan hadn't picked up on this guy's vibes. Was she completely clueless or just seeing what she wanted to see? Ethan grabbed a pillow, hugged it to his abdomen, and turned his attention back to the boxing match he was watching. His enormous biceps strained beneath his skin as he clutched the helpless, blue sofa pillow. Trey expected it to rend in two at any moment.

"Trey?" Reagan called from the bathroom. "Did you get lost?"

"I'm coming," he said.

"Not without me, you aren't."

He chuckled. The woman made his heart sing. It was stupid of him to even entertain thoughts of anyone but her. When he entered the bathroom, she was bent over the tub adjusting the temperature of the water. All that slick, rosy flesh between her legs instantly grabbed his complete attention. Considering his sexual ADD, that was saying something. Reagan tugged the lever, sending a steady gush of water out of the showerhead, and then stepped into the tub facing the spray. Trey followed her without hesitation.

She turned to look at him standing behind her in the shower and laughed. "You forgot to take off your jeans."

"You have stolen my ability to think coherently."

She turned and wrapped her wet arms around Trey's neck. Her smoky blue eyes were full of mischief when she said, "Is that so?"

His hands slid over the slick skin of her back to her hand-filling rump. He loved a woman with a succulent ass. It gave him something to hold on to. Trey jerked her against him and rubbed her mound against the hard length of his cock through his pants. "Do you feel what you do to me?"

"I haven't even started with you yet, Trey Mills."

He grinned. "Is that so?"

"Yeah. There's something about you that makes me want to do very naughty things." Her tongue flicked out and she bent her neck to toy with the piercing in his nipple.

"I feel the same way," he said. "That's why I'm still wearing my jeans."

"But I want you naked." She leaned back, her mound pressing more firmly against his cock, and unbuttoned the topmost button of his jeans. "Can I take these off?" She looked up at him coyly. Her short blond hair clung to her damp cheeks, framing her lovely face to perfection. He was surprised his wet jeans didn't start steaming.

"Help yourself," he murmured, pulling away just enough for her to release his fly and ease his pants down his thighs. She squatted down in front of him as she lowered his pants to his ankles and teased the head of his cock with her tongue when it came within reach.

He gasped at the slight contact. He didn't usually spend all day seducing a woman before he earned his prize, so his body was not used to this level of denial. He hoped he could hold back long enough to give her the pleasure she deserved. Her hand moved to cup his balls and he almost leapt out of his skin.

"Easy," he whispered.

She shook her head. "Let me help you with this." She removed his sopping jeans and used them to cushion her knees as she lowered herself to kneel before him.

He'd wanted to pleasure her for hours before he let himself have his release, but she was right. He needed this. He could give her those hours of pleasure after. It wasn't as if he planned on leaving right after he came. Another rarity for him.

"Just relax," she murmured and sucked his cock into her mouth.

He watched her through half-lowered eyelids. Hot water struck his chest and poured down his belly and thighs. Her hands moved to his hips as she bobbed her head faster, sucked harder. She was pretty good at this... for a woman. He watched her, forcing his mind to focus on her. Only her. She didn't deserve to be compared to anyone else. Man or woman. She was wonderful. Beautiful. Sexy. Talented. And oh God, he was going to come.

"Reagan," he gasped as he found release.

She moved her head to the side, stroking him with both hands as he came so hard his fluids struck the wall behind her. She lifted his cock and licked his scrotum until he grabbed her hair in both fists to get her to stop. His knees felt wobbly enough as it was.

"Trey. My hair," she complained.

He immediately released his handholds and smoothed the damp locks. "Sorry. I just really, really needed that. You've been driving me crazy all day."

She climbed to her feet. "Now we can start from the beginning again."

Now he could worship her body as she deserved. He retrieved a bar of soap and lathered a washcloth until it was dripping with frothy suds. He washed her skin slowly, making sure the rough, foamy cloth stroked every inch of her flesh. He especially enjoyed her reaction when he sank to the floor of the tub, lifted her foot, and washed between her toes. She held onto his head for balance and alternated between moaning and giggling. He washed her other foot and then slowly worked his way back up her body. Wishing soap was cherry flavored, he paused to lick the tattoo on her hip. It was way past lunchtime. Trey moved slowly up her body, the washcloth no longer soapy. When he stood before her, she wrapped both arms around his neck and plastered her wet body against his. He reached for the soap and then lowered his head to kiss her. He washed her back as he explored her delectable mouth with his tongue.

She tore her mouth from his. "Take me to bed," she said, her eyes focused on his lips.

"You don't want to try that slow, hard fuck against a wall?"

She chuckled. "You make me weak in the knees and it's all slippery in here. I don't think that's a good idea at the moment."

"Maybe later, then," he said and claimed her mouth again.

He moved the soap to wash his arms as they surrounded her body. He rubbed the soap over her hips, then his, making the shower about both of them now. She took the soap from him and washed his back, his ass, the tops of his thighs. Her hands moved to his shoulders and she dropped the soap.

They weren't really washing each other anymore anyway. They were getting to know each other's bodies. As the warm water rinsed the suds from their entangled bodies, Trey filled his hands with her plump ass. She moaned in his mouth when he dug his fingers into the soft, yielding flesh and massaged the cheeks together before tugging them apart and massaging them together again.

"Trey," she whispered into his mouth.

"Hmm?"

"I love the way that feels."

"That's good," he murmured.

"But you know what would feel better?"

"Hmm?"

She moved her mouth near his ear. "If you did it while I rode you."

Couldn't argue with that logic. "Mmm hmm."

"The bedroom is that way." She nodded toward the door.

"I don't want to let you go." He loved the way her curves fit him. How perfect his cock felt nestled against her lower belly. How the hardened tips of her small breasts pressed into his chest. He didn't think he could take his hands off her delicious booty if he tried.

There was a knock at the door. "The temp agency just called. I have to go fill in for a night shift," Ethan said. "Are you two going to stay in there all night? I need to take a shower."

"Roommates," she murmured in annoyance.

Trey didn't think Ethan was so bad. He kind of wished Reagan would let Ethan join them. She kissed Trey and then tugged out of his grasp so she could shut off the water. The fluffy blue towel she grabbed from the shelf above the toilet did a lot to hide her distracting curves and give Trey enough sense to step out of the tub. He didn't even bother with a towel, just followed her out of the bathroom knowing the faster they reached her bedroom, the quicker he could get her back into his arms.

Ethan grunted in annoyance as they passed. When he closed the bathroom door behind him, Trey heard him say, "What in the fuck are these doing in the tub?"

"I think he found your jeans," Reagan said with a laugh.

The smile she delivered over her shoulder pushed the last shred of control beyond Trey's reach. He grabbed her around the waist, lifted her several inches off the ground, and carried her to the bed. The towel dropped to the floor as he tumbled her onto the mattress. He stared down at her in the lamplight, giving his eyes a moment to feast on her beauty. A woman's body was a work of art. One to be explored and appreciated. Every curve, every valley, every freckle a treasure to discover. Every nerve ending a challenge to ignite with pleasure. Now, where to start? There wasn't an inch of Reagan he didn't want to get to know intimately.

She lifted both arms in his direction. "Come here."

He grinned. "I'm still enjoying the view."

"I think it's time for my close-up."

Trey climbed onto the bed with her, kneeling at her side. She scooted toward the center of the bed to give him more room. He caught her hand and drew her knuckles to his lips. That was where he'd start. The part of her that had first drawn his interest. Her talented hands. Trey massaged her palm with both hands as he nibbled and suckled her fingertips. He licked and blew. Kissed and caressed her hand as if there was nothing more desirable than her fingers, her knuckles, her palm, her wrist. He watched her reactions, taking note of the things she liked best. Sharp nips to the flesh at the base of her thumb made her suck in excited breaths. Flicks of his tongue to the center of her palm caused her to squirm. Suction at her fingertips made her back arc slightly off the mattress.

"Trey," she whispered, her face flushed with desire. "Aren't you going to make love to me?"

"I thought that's what I was doing."

"You know what I mean. I want you inside."

"You're not ready yet."

"Yes," she groaned. "Yes, I am. I've been ready all day."

"You just think you are." He lifted her hand and placed it on his belly. "Touch me. Show me what you like. Not to give me pleasure, but what part of me feels best beneath your hand."

She slid her hand down his belly and reached for his cock. He'd known that's what she'd go for first because she was impatient and hadn't really internalized his instructions.

She stroked him gently from base to tip. "Does that feel good?" she asked him. "Or do you like a firmer grip? Tell me what you like."

"Later," he promised. "This is about what you like. What does it feel like in your hand?"

"Hot and smooth. Firm. I like the way the skin moves beneath my hand when I stroke it."

"Is there any part of me that you like to touch more?"

She shook her head.

"How do you know? You haven't touched me everywhere yet."

Her brow crinkled. "I've never met a guy who liked to be touched anywhere but his cock. Wouldn't you rather just get down to business?"

"This is how I do business." He decided the back of her knee was the next location he wanted to explore. "Lost your chance. My turn again." He rolled her onto her back and moved to kneel between her ankles. He stroked the skin behind each knee. Lightly at first, which made her giggle, and then with more pressure. He lowered his head to kiss, lick, and suckle the back of one knee and then the other. When she started squirming, her succulent ass caught his attention. That was next on his agenda. He slid his hands up both thighs and grabbed an ass cheek in each hand. He massaged her ass roughly as he trailed gentle kisses up the back of one thigh.

"Oh," she gasped when he reached one cheek and sucked as much of it into his mouth as possible. He continued to massage the soft globes of tissue as he feasted—kissing, sucking, biting, licking until she was writhing on the bed below him. He flicked his tongue over her anus, once again wishing he had his stud piercing in his tongue. Next time they made love he'd show her a few tricks. "Wait!" she gasped brokenly.

"Wait for what?" he murmured. He flicked his tongue over the same spot and she shuddered. "Does it feel good?"

"W-weird."

"Do you like it?"

"I-I don't know."

He licked her there one more time and then slapped her ass. She tensed and then surprised him by hooking an arm and leg around his body and tumbling him onto the bed beside her. "I have to have you, Trey."

"You don't like to be touched?"

She shook her head. "I love it. I want to do the same to you. Explore every inch of you with every inch of me, but I need this." She grabbed his cock. "And I need it now."

"I need a condom."

Reagan scrambled from the bed and retrieved the condoms from the nightstand. She didn't seem to notice that her bedroom door was open or that Ethan was standing there in his towel scowling, but Trey did.

Trey watched Ethan while Reagan tore open the condom and unrolled it down his length. He still hadn't decided if he should alert Reagan to her roommate's presence or allow him to enjoy the show when Reagan straddled him and directed his cock into her heavenly warmth.

"God, I've never needed fucked so bad in my life," she said between clenched teeth. She rode him hard.

"Never?" Ethan grumbled.

Reagan paused and glared at Ethan over her shoulder. "Get out of here."

"I won't be home until morning. Be sure to lock all the deadbolts before you go to sleep."

"Trey's here. I'll be fine. Stop worrying so much."

Trey lifted his hands to her breasts, rubbing his thumbs over her nipples.

"You mean he's not going to leave as soon as he blows his load?" Ethan said.

"Nope. I'll still be here in the morning," Trey said. "Have fun at work."

He heard Ethan say something that sounded a lot like, "Lying bastard," under his breath before he slammed the door.

"I'm really sorry he's like that," Reagan said. "I don't know why he's so protective."

Trey knew, but he wasn't about to tell Reagan that her roommate was still in love with her. Despite the reduced flow of blood to his brain at the moment, he wasn't a total idiot.

Reagan lifted her hips until Trey fell free of her body and then flopped down on the bed beside him. "What a mood killer! God, I could strangle him right now."

Trey didn't think it would be too hard to get her back in the mood. He rolled on top of her and cradled her face between both hands. "Forget about him," Trey murmured and kissed her lips. His hands moved in perfect unison as he caressed her breasts, her sides, her hips. His mouth moved to suckle her jaw, her throat, her earlobe. When her tension faded and her body relaxed again, he took his cock in his hand and directed it inside her. He dug his toes into the mattress and possessed her with those hard, deep, slow thrusts he'd been promising her all day. Her hands explored his back and butt as he drove himself into her.

"Look at me, Trey," she whispered.

He shook his head. He never looked his lovers in the eye when he was joined with them.

"Trey," she said more firmly. "Look at me."

He lifted his head to glare at her. She smiled gently, her steady gaze locking with his. He couldn't look away. Didn't want to look away. He saw her. Not as just a body to sate his lust or a personality to amuse him, but all of her. Reagan. The pleasure in his groin intensified. He didn't understand it at first. Why his heart was pounding so hard. Why he wanted to do more than fuck her. He wanted to possess her. Why he couldn't look away from her eyes. Why he felt so alive and excited and afraid all at once. That emotional connect that he never allowed himself to feel? He felt it. He felt it in Reagan. With Reagan. And for some reason he liked it.

He buried his hands in her hair and tilted her head back, still staring into her eyes. He allowed himself to become immersed in her. Not just his body, but his heart, his soul, his thoughts and emotions. She awakened something within him. Something he'd been denying himself for far too long.

"Why do I feel this way?" he whispered. He hadn't meant to, but once he'd said it, he hoped she could give him an answer, because he was at a total loss.

"What way?"

He wasn't sure how to explain it to her. "Like... like this is important."

"That it means something?"

He nodded slightly and continued to stare down at her, waiting for her to elucidate him.

"I don't know, Trey, maybe you're in love with me."

He would have laughed at how preposterous that teasing statement was, if it hadn't hit so close to his suspicions. "Maybe," he whispered and closed his eyes so the emotions didn't overwhelm him and he could enjoy the pleasure her body offered.

Trey knew he couldn't fall in love with someone in one day. It wasn't possible. Yes, it had been that way with Brian, but he'd been young and impressionable. They'd been friends for years before his feelings had changed with one stolen kiss. Trey was older now. Wiser. He couldn't actually be in love with her already, but he did feel *something*. Something was a hell of a lot more than the nothing he usually felt.

Trey moved faster within her, seeking release so he could finish this and return to that uninvolved state he felt after having sex with someone. He was now quite sure that he wasn't ready to get involved with anyone. Especially not with a woman who made him feel this much this quickly. And definitely not so soon after giving up on Brian. He wasn't ready for another emotional attachment yet. He had to get away before she broke his heart. He'd never given anyone but Brian that power over him before.

"What's wrong?" Reagan whispered. Her lips brushed his jaw.

"Nothing," he lied.

"Something's wrong. You've lost your rhythm."

He hadn't even noticed. Not only did she make him feel too much, but she obliterated his concentration. "Sorry." He'd never apologized in the bedroom in his life. What in the hell was wrong with him?

"Maybe if you'd stop fighting it."

He paused and stared down at her. "Fighting what?"

"The connection between us."

"I'm not fighting anything."

She smiled slightly. "If you say so."

She planted both hands on his chest and pushed at him until he pulled out with a grimace. She rolled him onto his back. "Let yourself feel it, Trey. Feel me."

She stroked his chest with both palms.

"I want to be close to you," she said. "Will you let me? Even if it means I'll get my heart broken later, it's worth it."

"I won't hurt—"

"Shh," she murmured, her lips moving to his chest to suckle kisses across his skin. "No words, Trey, just feel."

Just feel. She made it sound so easy. He felt her touch, the warmth of her body, the tickle of her bangs as they trailed down his belly. He felt affection for her—a bubbly warmth in his chest. Beneath her touch, he felt desire and need. When she moved to straddle his hips and directed him back into her warmth, he felt blinding pleasure.

And more. He'd experienced the same thing as he stared into her eyes the first time their bodies had joined. He eased his eyes open a crack and found that she was staring at him as she rose and fell over his body. He closed his eyes again, his heart thudding like mad in his chest. She gently brushed her fingertips over his quivering belly as she rode him with a slow, steady rhythm. It scared the hell out of him to know she was looking for an emotional connection, not a quick and easy release. He was sure a lot of his lovers had wanted the same, but he'd never even considered it before. Before now.

He took her ass in both palms and massaged its cheeks as she rose and fell over him. Her motions became more sensual as she churned above him. His thoughts scattered as nothing but pleasure mattered.

"Trey," she gasped.

He opened his eyes, wanting to see her face the first time she came with him buried inside her, and their gazes locked. He lost himself in that instant. She held nothing back. She was completely open to him and it was the most beautiful thing he'd ever seen in his life. She smiled gently. "There you are," she said.

He sat up, shifting her hips until she was comfortably impaled by his cock. She wrapped her arms and legs around him and snuggled her face against his neck. He held her for a moment, his mind racing. What was he doing? He realized that he'd told her he wanted her to be his steady girlfriend, but he hadn't thought that meant he'd become emotionally invested. That would make it so much more difficult to let her go when the time came. Just thinking about letting her go had his arms tightening around her.

I'm fucked, he thought. And not in the good way.

"You are all kinds of freaked out about this, aren't you?" she said into his ear. She pulled away and cupped his face as she stared into his eyes. "Tell me."

He shook his head. There was no way he could describe what he was feeling. Besides, he didn't want her to know. He hadn't even come to terms with it yet. How could he be expected to share it with her?

She kissed him gently and then stared into his eyes with tenderness. "Given time, maybe as little as ten seconds, I think I could love you, Trey Mills. How does that make you feel?"

"I'm used to people falling in love with me," he said. And it usually annoyed him. A twinge of hurt crossed her eyes and he was sorry he hadn't chosen his words more carefully. "What I'm not used to is thinking that I could feel the same way."

Her eyes sparkled in the lamplight as she smiled at him. "So there is something special between us. You feel it too?"

"It scares the shit out of me."

She laughed. "Oh God, me too." She kissed him hard on the mouth. "I'm terrified you're going to crush my heart, but I don't want to slow down, do you?"

He contemplated her question. Yeah, he did want to slow down, but he was pretty sure it was too late for that. He was falling hard and fast for Reagan Elliot. His entire world had been shaken to its core in one short day, and there was no turning back now. "I think it's time I held nothing back. Do you think you can handle that?"

She laughed. "Probably not, but I'll scrape what's left of me back together tomorrow. Tonight I won't hold anything back either. And if it doesn't work out between us, it doesn't work out."

He stroked her hair away from her beautiful face and smiled as he stared into her eyes. Knowing that she had the same reservations, but also wanted to throw them aside, made it so much easier for him to bare his soul. Well, most of it. "I hope it does work out."

She smiled. "Me too. I'm going to let myself love you now. Don't freak out on me."

He laughed. "No promises."

"But I want promises," she whispered. "Even if they only extend through tonight."

Promises.

"You make me feel whole," she said. "Like that piece that's always been missing has been filled. I didn't even know it was there until you touched on it."

Trey's heart thudded as he tried to find words to describe what he was feeling. He'd felt something very similar to this before. With Brian. "Move with me, Reagan. I feel… connected." More than that, but he wasn't sure how to describe it. "Like I need you in order to recognize my true self."

She smiled gently and kissed him before raising her hips and lowering them, bringing their bodies apart and together. "This is undoubtedly the craziest thing I've ever done, and I've done some crazy things in my life, Trey Mills."

"It's just sex, Reagan."

She shook her head. "With someone else this would just be sex, but with you… I need to shut up. I'm going to end up scaring you more than I already have."

"The damage has already been done." He nibbled her neck, her jaw, suckled her earlobe. "Don't stop now."

He slid his hands over her smooth back, delighting in the texture of her satiny skin.

"With you…" She rubbed her face against his temple. "You make me feel wonderful inside and out."

He tipped her onto her back and grinned down at her. "Enough mushy stuff." He couldn't concentrate on giving her physical pleasure when he was trying to analyze feelings he wasn't ready to identify. He watched her face while he plunged into her body, looking for those telltale signs that gave him clues as to what she liked best. He found her rhythm quickly and discovered she moaned the loudest when he pounded her hard and ground his pelvis when he was buried deep, and again when he was inches from falling free from her body. He concentrated on giving her what she liked. Sweat trickled down the side of his face. His stomach muscles and hips began to tremble with fatigue, but hearing her reaction and watching her orgasm approach was well worth the effort.

"Oh, Trey. I'm coming."

He slid a finger into his mouth to wet it. When her body convulsed with release, he reached beneath her and slid his fingertip into her ass. He repeatedly flicked it against the inner rim of the tight ring of clenching muscle. Her eyes widened with astonishment and then squeezed shut as her body took its pleasure.

"Oh God," she gasped as her back arched off the bed.

She cried out as her pussy gripped him in hard spasms. He took a deep, shaky breath, fighting the urge to follow her in bliss. They had all night to get to know one another and only had two condoms.

When her body went limp, Trey shifted his arms to either side of her body to rest on his elbows. He brushed her sweat-damp hair from her face and waited for her to open her eyes. He grinned while she struggled with the effort to pry her eyelids open.

"That was amazing," she gushed. "Did you come? I wasn't paying attention."

He shook his head.

"Does that mean there's more?" She had that same my-life-is-a-dream-come-true look on her face that she'd sported when flittering her contract at him by the hot tub.

He bit his lip and nodded.

She made a fist of victory and shouted, "Yes!"

Trey laughed and lowered his body to snuggle her close against his chest. Still buried deep inside her, he rocked his hips slightly. She shifted to wrap her legs around his waist, her heels pressing into his ass to encourage deeper penetration. Her arms circled his body and drew him closer, her hands sliding over his sweaty back.

"Closer," she murmured. "I want you closer."

He buried his face in her neck and nuzzled her throat. "I don't think I can get any closer," he said, his words muffled by her flesh.

Her arms and legs tightened around him. "Try."

He drew his arms against her, until he was touching her with as much of his skin as possible. She sighed in contentment and turned her face into his hair. "Thanks for indulging me. Most guys hate to cuddle."

"I love it," he said and grinned. "Brian calls me Mr. Cuddles."

"*Brian* does?"

Her hold on him loosened and his heart sank. He'd been so at ease that he'd let his guard down and forgotten that he was playing the role of a fully heterosexual man. "Several girls complained to him." Even that little lie closed a part of him to Reagan. He wasn't sure if he felt relieved or sad that he couldn't tell her everything.

She squeezed him again. "I'm not complaining."

"I'm even better at it after I come," he said, digging his toes into the mattress and rocking forward to remind her that he was still hard and yet unfulfilled. At least sexually. He was feeling pretty good about the connection between them. Like he could tell her *almost* anything.

"What's your favorite position?" she asked.

He lifted his head to look down at her in question. "Mine?" Several of his favorite threesome encounters, where he and Brian had simultaneously pleasured a woman, filled his mind. He loved working his cock against another man's while being buried inside a woman. Trey could feel a blush of heat rise up his neck. Reagan was in no way ready for that bit of information. "No one has ever asked me that," he said truthfully.

Her brow furrowed. "Why not?"

"My lovers tend to let me please them."

"You already did that. Now it's my turn to please you."

"You please me by letting me please you."

She closed one eye and gave him her you're-full-of-shit look. "No one is that selfless."

He shrugged. "Believe what you want."

"If you won't tell me, I'll figure it out for myself."

She went limp beneath him, her arms straightening at her sides, her legs falling open. She planted her heels in the mattress and rocked her hips to encourage him to thrust. He began to move with her, pulling back and thrusting forward with a deep, steady rhythm. She watched him as the pleasure she offered washed over him and he began to take her faster. His eyes drifted closed as he lost all semblance of rational thought and focused solely on finding release. Reagan shoved him onto his back. He groaned as his cock fell free of her body, and that glorious building sensation in his groin abated. And then he was inside her again. He regained enough sense to remember he should touch her. Give her pleasure. She took his hands and held them as she began to rise and fall over him, taking him deep within her and grinding her hips before rising again. She continued to watch him as she rode him and he soon lost himself to the pleasure again. With nothing to concentrate on but Reagan's heat, her friction, Trey allowed himself to be completely immersed in sensation. After several minutes she climbed off of him and settled on her hands and knees facing the end of the bed. She didn't need to tell him what she wanted. She was trying different positions to see which he enjoyed the most. Truth was he loved them all. He shifted to kneel behind her and slid inside her. He held onto her ass and rubbed her anus with both thumbs as he plunged into her slick core.

He caught her reflection in the mirror above her dresser. She was watching him again.

"Trey, just fuck me. Don't worry about bringing me pleasure right now."

"You don't like it?"

"It feels fantastic. I like that look on your face when you lose your train of thought. I want to see it again."

And he wanted her to have what she wanted. He moved his hands to rest gently on her hips and pumped into her body. Every muscle in his body was taut, every nerve ending alight with sensation. It didn't take him long to find his peak. She tried to pull away again, but he held her firmly by the hips and increased his tempo until he found the pinnacle of pleasure. Involuntary spasms gripped the base of his cock in hard, pulsing waves. He called out in triumph, his head tilted back in abandon, as he spent himself within her. Inside Reagan.

Reagan.

When his body went limp, a sweet tranquility washed over him. He collapsed forward, arms wrapping around Reagan's waist as he pressed her back to his front. His hands moved to hold her breasts; his lips moved against the back of her shoulders as he produced repetitive sighs of contentment. No awkwardness after. Just togetherness.

Reagan's arms began to tremble with fatigue and though she didn't complain, Trey released her and pulled out of her body. He stripped the condom from his softening cock and tossed it somewhere. He didn't know where, he just wanted to wrap his body around his woman and nestle his bare cock against that scrumptious ass of hers.

"So doggie style is your favorite?" she murmured once he had her tucked securely against his chest and trapped in the tangle of his arms and legs.

"There are more than three positions," he said drowsily.

She squirmed so that her butt rubbed against his cock. "Good point. Trey?"

"Hmm?" He was almost asleep already. Not that he planned to stay that way for long. He just needed a little nap before they made good use of that second condom.

"Promise me something?"

"What's that?"

"Next time we'll come together."

He grinned and nuzzled her soft hair. "That's a promise."

Chapter 9

ETHAN POURED HIMSELF A cup of coffee and sat down at the breakfast bar. He probably should just go to bed—he'd had a long, dreadfully boring night guarding a meat-packing plant—but his thoughts were too turbulent to sleep. The guy, Trey, had spent the entire night with Reagan. Ethan had thought for sure that Trey would be gone by the time he got home. It had been that thought which had gotten him through his shift. Otherwise he would have left the job to check on her and encourage her new *boyfriend* to leave. Ethan had peeked in on them when he'd first arrived and found them entwined in her bed looking exhausted yet sated. At least he hadn't had to listen to them go at it all night. That would have been torture.

He took a sip of his coffee. He couldn't blame Reagan for wanting someone to love. He didn't like it, but he had blown his chance with her. It had been his fault, not hers. He knew it wasn't fair of him to try to keep her to himself, but he couldn't stand the thought of her with another man. Reagan's bedroom door creaked open and he smiled to himself. "Did you sleep well?" he asked her.

"Definitely," Trey's deep voice sounded behind him. "Reagan's bed is much more comfortable than the bunks on the tour bus. And she's a fantastic cuddler."

Ethan scowled into his cup of coffee. So it wasn't the light of his life emerging from her bedroom, but that dipshit she'd brought home the night before. Ethan glanced over his shoulder and found the guy dressed in a T-shirt with a towel wrapped around his hips. Trey looked even sexier in the morning with his hair all astray and a shadow of beard growth on his jaw—the bastard. At least he didn't have a lollipop in his mouth this morning.

"Your jeans are in the oven," Ethan told him and turned his attention back to his coffee.

Trey chuckled and Ethan wished he didn't have to hate him.

"There's a place they haven't been before," Trey said. "And they have been in a lot of unusual places."

"They were still wet." And the faster they dried, the faster Ethan could shove him out the door. Then Ethan could console Reagan when she became upset that her new *boyfriend* had already taken off on her. She needn't know that Ethan had bodily removed Trey from the apartment, right?

"The smell of coffee woke me." Trey glanced hopefully in the direction of the coffeepot.

"I didn't take you for a morning person."

"Went to sleep earlier than usual," he said with a devilish grin. "Reagan wore me out."

Ethan's heart skipped a beat. The man was utterly, devastatingly gorgeous when he smiled. Maybe instead of kicking him out of the apartment he could catch his attention in another way. He'd love to take a go at him. The only thing that kept Ethan perched on his stool instead of reaching for the half-naked man in his kitchen was the memory of Reagan's face when she'd caught him with Joseph. She'd been devastated. If Ethan made a move on Trey, she'd probably never forgive him. He couldn't take that chance.

"Help yourself," Ethan said, waving a hand at the coffeepot.

Trey glanced around the kitchen and peeked in a cabinet looking for a mug.

"That one," Ethan said, pointing at the cabinet next to the stove.

Trey opened the cabinet indicated and retrieved a mug. And

dropped his towel. Ethan stifled a moan. The man had a perfect ass. Well, except for the ridiculous tattoo on one cheek. "What in the…"

Trey glanced over his shoulder at Ethan and followed his line of sight to his ass. "Lost a bet." He ran a hand over his flank. "People keep telling me to get it removed, but it's a great conversation starter." He grinned as if to prove his point.

Ethan chuckled. "You dropped your towel on purpose, didn't you?"

Trey shook his head. "Why would I do that?"

"Hell if I know. Put your jeans on."

"Do you find my tattoo offensive?" he said, opening the now-cold oven and pulling out his jeans, which were so stiff they could probably stand on their own.

"No, I find your ass distracting. If you don't want me to come over there and…" Ethan pressed his lips together so he didn't continue that thought. "Put your jeans on."

"Two days ago, I would have told you to make me." He shook his jeans out and hopped from one foot to the other as he put them on. Ethan forced himself not to stare at Trey's cock as he pulled his jeans up and tucked it into his pants. "But things have changed."

"What's that supposed to mean?" Ethan asked as he watched Trey pour a cup of coffee.

"Reagan," he said, as if saying her name explained everything. And in actuality, it did. They were on exactly the same wavelength, and it only made Ethan want him more. And not because he thought it would get rid of him. On the contrary, he wanted him to stick around indefinitely.

"I hope you have better luck with it than I did," Ethan said. He took a sip of his coffee and watched Trey put the carafe back in the coffeemaker.

"Sugar?" Trey asked.

Ethan pushed the sugar bowl in his direction. Trey circled the counter and took a seat next to Ethan before shoveling spoonful after spoonful of sugar into his cup.

"So how was work?" Trey asked, stirring his coffee with the sugar spoon. When he licked it, Ethan's entire body tensed.

"It sucked."

"What do you do exactly?" Trey glanced at him and Ethan got lost in his emerald green eyes for a long moment.

"Depends on the day," Ethan said. "Last night I guarded big slabs of beef."

Trey paused. "I like my beef big. The bigger the better." He tossed the spoon on the counter and massaged his forehead with one hand. "Sorry. It's a habit. I need to watch what I say."

Ethan chuckled. "What's the longest you've ever gone without a man?"

"I have no idea what you're talking about." He averted his sexy green eyes as he took a sip of his coffee. He reached for the spoon and added more sugar.

It was only a matter of time before Trey messed things up with Reagan. Ethan just had to be patient. And not be the one who Trey strayed with. After Trey and Reagan inevitably broke up, then maybe Ethan would have his chance with Trey. Ethan watched him wrap both hands around his coffee mug. The man had phenomenal hands. Long, strong fingers. Thick wrists. Sinewy forearms. Ethan tore his gaze away and stared into his empty coffee mug with a scowl. It was hard to be good when temptation sat on the stool next to you. Close enough that with each breath, Ethan caught Trey's scent mingled with Reagan's. The combination blew his mind. Ethan decided he should head for bed. He could think about having sex with Trey and jack off. No one got hurt that way.

"So do you always guard big slabs of beef?" Trey asked. "Any experience dealing with heavy metal fans?"

Ethan turned his head to look at him. "I've done security at a lot of concerts."

"Metal concerts?"

Was he questioning Ethan's ability to guard Reagan? "A few."

"She's going to be a superstar. Are you ready for that?"

Abandoning his plan to head for bed, Ethan climbed from his stool to get more coffee. "Is *she* ready for that?"

Trey chuckled. "It definitely fucks with your mind. If you aren't careful, you start to believe the things people say, both good and bad. You're a god. A talentless hack. A sellout. The best thing that ever happened to the planet. A menace to society. It's enough to drive a person nuts."

"How do you deal with that stuff?"

"Trust only the people who are living it with you and the people who knew you before you became famous."

"She knows she can trust me," Ethan said. He took a seat again. His arm brushed Trey's as he settled on the stool, and he stifled a groan of torment. The man was utterly delectable. Even when he wasn't trying to be.

"Don't betray that trust. She's going to need you." Trey caught his eye and held his gaze. "Almost as much as she needs me."

Ethan's first instinct was to protest. Reagan didn't need anyone but him. He would protect her until the end. Keep everyone at minimum safe distance. No one would touch her or even look at her. He knew that wasn't realistic, and though he only managed to hold Trey's gaze for several seconds before he had to look into his coffee again, Trey was right. Reagan would need Trey, or someone in a similar position, to go to when things Ethan couldn't understand weighed her down.

"She's important to me. Her happiness is important to me." Ethan had no idea why he was spilling those feelings to a man he hardly knew. A man who happened to be his competition for the woman he loved. Except Ethan wasn't competing anymore. He was sitting on the bench watching from the sidelines like some loser.

"I know," Trey said. He clapped him on the back. "It's important to me too."

Trey's hand slid down Ethan's back. It took every shred of Ethan's willpower to stay on his stool and not tackle Trey to the floor and rip his clothes off.

"So have you always been in security?" Trey asked. His gaze drifted down Ethan's body and he shifted on his stool uncomfortably. "You definitely have the right build for it."

"I used to be a police officer."

"Used to be?"

Ethan nodded. "I got fired for beating the shit out of a suspected child molester. Police brutality."

"I don't blame you."

"Well, I might have gotten off easier if I hadn't already been on probation for beating the shit out of a guy who assaulted his wife."

"You probably just got carried away."

"Like I did when I beat the shit out of a guy for raping a sixteen-year-old girl?"

Trey winced. "I guess."

The thing was Ethan didn't regret getting violent with those criminals. Not at all.

Trey touched his knee. "Do you miss it?"

Ethan shrugged. "Sometimes. I have too much of a temper to be any good at it. I enjoyed protecting the innocent and hurting those who hurt them, but that's not what the job is really about."

"So now you guard... *beef*?"

Ethan scowled. "Uh. Yeah."

"Good morning," Reagan said in a sleepy voice behind them. "I need coffee."

Ethan shouldn't have looked at her. She'd put on her panties and a T-shirt, so most of her was covered, but the messy hair, blurry eyes, and the sexy smile she gifted Trey were too much for him to handle.

Trey wrapped an arm around her narrow waist and directed her to stand between his legs with her back against the counter. He drew her against his chest, embracing her with easy affection. Ethan couldn't decide what he wanted more at that moment, to be the person wrapped in Trey's strong arms or the man holding Reagan. How could he want both of them? And be jealous of both of them? This was a total mind fuck.

"You can share my coffee," Trey murmured against her cheek.

She leaned back and accepted Trey's cup. She took a sip and pulled a face of disgust. "This isn't coffee. It's syrup. How much sugar did you put in this?"

"Enough," he said and took his cup back to take a sip.

"I'll get you a cup," Ethan said and rose to make Reagan's coffee. He knew how she liked it. One sugar and a splash of milk.

"You're such a good roommate," she murmured, relaxing against Trey again. He seemed to be holding her up. "When do you have to get on the plane?" Reagan asked. Her hands tightened, clenching his shirt.

"A few hours. When's the limo supposed to be here?"

She glanced at the clock on the wall in the living room. "Fuck," she murmured. "In twenty minutes." She clung to him, pressing her face against his shoulder. "Do you think the band will mind if I show up like this?"

"I'd say they wouldn't mind at all," Trey said, "but if you want them to concentrate on their music instead of your gorgeous ass, you might want to put on some clothes."

Ethan extended her cup of coffee toward her. She gave Trey a leisurely kiss, her hands messing up his bed-hair even more, and then reluctantly drew away and took her cup of coffee. "I guess I'll shower. Maybe try wearing a little makeup today."

She moved away from Trey and sipped her coffee on her way back into her bedroom.

"Are you leaving on a trip?" Ethan asked Trey, not knowing if he wanted him to stay or go.

"Yeah, I'm still on tour. Just came back for one night. Brian's wife had a baby yesterday. We have a show tonight."

"He's going to perform in a concert the day after his wife had a baby?"

"We scheduled our tour dates so he'd have a week off when the baby was born, but Malcolm decided he wanted to come out two weeks early."

"So you'll be gone for two weeks?" Ethan wondered how mopey Reagan would be during that time. She obviously liked this guy. She wasn't going to like being away from him for two weeks so early in their relationship.

"Yep. Then we have a week off. Then we're going back out on tour with Exodus End." He grinned. "And Reagan."

"And me," Ethan added.

"I guess that's right. Should be fun." Trey's ornery grin did strange things to everything in Ethan's boxer briefs. He wasn't sure "fun" was the right word. Torture might be more appropriate.

Chapter 10

REAGAN ALMOST SWALLOWED HER tongue when Harold showed her into the kitchen and she found Dare slicing fruit on the dark, granite countertop of the kitchen island. He was shirtless. His hair wet from a recent shower. Beard stubble recently trimmed. His expression dreamy and contemplative. Dare Mills. Yum-to-the-um.

Dare glanced up from his task and smiled at her in welcome. "There you are. I never got your number yesterday so I couldn't call and let you know that today is a no go."

Reagan's heart sank. "A no go?"

"Max went to Vegas with Logan to blow off some steam. Steve took off to the wilderness somewhere, and I have sudden plans to go to Hawaii. I'm leaving tonight."

Reagan's excitement waned. How was she supposed to get ready to go on tour with them if she didn't practice with them?

"He has a girlfriend there," Trey said.

"I haven't seen her in a while."

Trey slipped onto a barstool, picked up slices of strawberries with his fingers, and popped them into his mouth. "You could have called me, Dare. I would have relayed the message."

Dare just kept right on slicing a peach as his little brother helped himself. "I tried to call you. It kept going to voice mail."

"I probably need to charge my phone."

"So I had an idea," Dare said to Reagan. "You wouldn't learn much you don't already know by hanging out here in the studio for two weeks without the band. Have you ever been on tour?"

"Not really," she admitted. "All of Bait-n-Switch's gigs were local."

"Why don't you go with Trey and hang out with Sinners for a couple of weeks? Learn what goes on behind the scenes."

"Besides the beer and pussy?" Trey said, helping himself to slices of Dare's peach now.

Reagan whipped her head around to glare at him.

He chuckled. "Kidding."

"Sure," Dare said with a grin as he rinsed an apple in the sink situated in the center of his kitchen island. He started to cut the apple into thin slices on a cutting board. "Trey gets all the beer and pussy he wants, whenever he wants it."

Reagan scowled. "I bet he does."

Trey grabbed her around the waist and pulled her to stand between his legs with her back to the counter. "Yours is the only pussy I want. I will take a beer though."

Dare snorted. "That's another reason you should go on tour with him, Reagan. To keep an eye on him. I think his record for celibacy is about twelve hours."

"I've gone a few days without," Trey said.

"A few *days*?" Reagan bellowed.

"How many more tour dates does Sinners have?" Dare asked.

"Eight shows in the next fourteen days. Then a week of rehearsal for the new show with you guys, and then back on the road again for… I don't remember. A long fucking time."

"So that means fourteen days without sex." Dare laughed. "He won't make it, Reagan."

"Don't worry. I am perfectly capable of jerking off for a couple of weeks," Trey assured her. He took a slice of strawberry and used it to trace her lips. The very idea of him with his hands on some other woman, his cock inside some other woman, another woman watching him come, had her seething.

"I think Dare has a great idea. If I go on tour with you and Sinners, I won't be so anxious when I start out with Exodus End."

Trey fed her the slice of strawberry. "Well, if you want to go, I don't see why you can't. All the other guys have brought a woman on tour with Sinners in the past. About time I took advantage of that privilege."

"And you can help me practice my music, too," she said, really warming up to the idea now. "And maybe Brian can help me work on my triplets."

"I'm sure he'd be happy to."

"Really?" she said, wrapping her arms around Trey's neck. "He's such an amazing guitarist!"

Dare cleared his throat.

"You *all* are amazing guitarists," she hurriedly rectified.

"We're all amazing guitarists," Trey amended.

Reagan smiled. "Right. *We're* all amazing guitarists."

"If you're coming along, you better go get packed. Brian's supposed to be here in an hour to fly back to Oklahoma City to meet up with the bus for tonight's show in Topeka." Trey smiled sweetly. "I wonder how his little one is doing."

"He called this morning and said Myrna was checking out of the hospital. I think she and the baby are coming out to the airstrip to see him off."

"Aw," Reagan said. "I'll get to see baby Sinclair?"

"If you hurry." Trey patted her butt. "We've got to make it in time for the show tonight. Have the limo run you home."

"What do I bring?"

He leaned back to look her over. "A box of condoms and some energy drinks."

She rolled her eyes and shook her head at him.

"Just pack as if you're going on a two-week vacation. I don't know what you need to bring. Chick stuff."

"Don't bother bringing your guitar," Dare said, slicing a pear now. "You can grab one of Max's from the practice room."

She pecked Trey on the lips. "I'll be right back," she promised and raced toward the front door to find the limo before she regained her senses and changed her mind.

—∕∿∿∕—

As soon as Reagan was out of earshot, Trey picked up a peach and threw it at Dare. It stuck to the center of his bare chest.

"What the fuck, Dare? Why did you put me on the spot like that?"

"I knew you were too stupid to think of it on your own." He peeled the piece of fruit off his chest and popped it in his mouth.

"Are you even going to Hawaii?"

"No. I broke up with Cassidy weeks ago. The rest was true though. Max and Logan went to Vegas as soon as Steve took off into the wilderness. Can't blame Steve for heading out. You know what he's like. He needs trees."

"And you're going to just stick around here by yourself?"

"I'll probably do a little entertaining." He grinned. "Or be a little entertained. So how did things go with Reagan last night?"

Trey checked over his shoulder to make sure she hadn't returned unexpectedly. "She's phenomenal."

"Yeah. I thought you'd like her. Is she okay with your bisexual side?"

"She doesn't know. And I'm not going to tell her. I'm giving up men."

Dare shook his head at him. "Right, Trey. Good plan," he said sarcastically.

"Her ex is bisexual. She caught him cheating on her with a man. She's not very open to that kind of thing."

"Hmm," Dare said, munching on a slice of apple, his green eyes reflective. "You should dump her now then. She'll just wind up hurt when you put your snake in a dark tunnel."

Trey threw another slice of peach at his idiot brother. "I won't be putting my snake in any dark tunnel. Unless it's hers. I want this to work between us. I want a normal relationship. Last night was amazing. I want to keep that going."

"Trey, you can't deny what you are. You need to find a woman who accepts that part of you as part of the package. You'll never be happy if you give up men entirely. I know you won't."

"Just butt out. Okay? Let me do this my way."

Dare sighed and reached for a pineapple. He hacked off the top with more force than necessary before grabbing some fancy gadget that trimmed it into a neat, hollow cylinder. "Just don't chase her off, Trey. We need her for the tour."

"I'm not going to chase her off. I'm going to make her mine."

The doorbell rang. Trey's heart thudded with excitement, and he stood up from the barstool. "I bet that's Brian."

"Don't wet yourself there, Trey."

"Shut up." He hadn't seen Brian in over a day. He had a lot to tell him. And he missed him. A lot. Just because Trey had given up on Brian loving him didn't mean that he'd fallen out of love with the man. Trey didn't know if he'd ever stop loving Brian. Not completely.

By the time Trey made it to the foyer, Brian and crew were already inside the house. Brian had a diaper bag slung over one shoulder, a baby carrier in his free hand, and was trying to coax Myrna into a nearby chair.

"I'm fine, sweetheart," she said, "really."

"Since when did they start letting women out of the hospital after one day of rest? It's insane," Brian insisted. "Please, baby, sit. I don't think you should be out of bed yet."

"Brian, I'm fine. Just a little tired."

"Did you call Jessica?"

"Yes, I called her. She said she'd meet me here and stay with me at the house until you get back from tour. And when she's unavailable, Aggie said she'd help out too." So Myrna had agreed to let the lady Sinners—Sed and Jace's respective fiancées—help her out. Trey was actually surprised that she would admit to needing help.

Brian breathed a sigh of relief. "I'm so glad they both agreed to stay with you. I can't imagine leaving you alone right now." Trey decided she'd done so only to give Brian some peace of mind.

Malcolm grunted in his carrier, and Brian set it on a decorative table, oblivious to the expensive vase he pushed aside. He had the baby out of his seat and cradled against his shoulder in record time. When Brian sniffed Malcolm's tiny baby butt, Trey burst out laughing.

"Hey, Trey," Myrna said. "Enjoy your day off?"

"You might say that," Trey said and came further into the room.

"Is it time for him to eat?" Brian asked Myrna.

"It's only been an hour," she said with a weary smile.

"He made a noise," Brian told her.

"They do that sometimes, sweetheart. You're spoiling him."

"Ah, God, I miss him already." Brian cradled Malcolm in the crook of his arm and hummed some lullaby version of the Sinners song "Good-bye Is Not Forever" while gently bouncing him up and down.

"He's going to puke on you if you aren't careful," Trey warned.

Brian pointed to a white spot on his shirt and grinned as if it were some treasure to behold. "He already did."

The doorbell rang again. Dare had just taken a step into the room but stopped in his tracks and went to the door.

"Is the baby here?" Trey heard Jessica squeal from the front door.

"Uh, yeah, I think he came with his parents," Dare answered.

Jessica breezed into the room, looking absolutely stunning as usual—a strawberry-blonde bombshell who looked like she belonged in a *Playboy* centerfold instead of in a courtroom. Trey was pretty sure some of her clients were repeat offenders just so they could see her again. Jessica gave Myrna a quick hug. "I'm so glad you called me," she said. Jessica noticed Trey and gave his arm a squeeze as she zeroed in on Malcolm. "Oh," she said, clutching her hands in front of her chest. "He's adorable. Let me hold him."

Brian in no way looked prepared to hand over his son until he had no choice, but the pride in Jessica's excitement at seeing his child was apparently a good motivator. He handed over the kid but stayed beside her with his hand inches from Malcolm's back as if he expected Jessica to drop him on the polished marble floor at any moment.

"Oh," Jessica said again and cuddled the baby against her chest as if he were as fragile as wet paper. "Did you send a picture to Sed? He'll die when he sees him."

"Yeah, we sent the guys pictures," Brian said, still hovering over Jessica. "They bitched about missing out on the fun."

"Well, I wouldn't call it fun," Myrna said flatly. "Amazing, unbelievable, breathtaking, and wonderful, but not *fun*."

Once Brian seemed sure that Jessica was trustworthy, he moved to stand beside his wife. He stroked her auburn hair with one hand. "Are you thirsty? Hungry? Can I get you something?"

"A glass of water would be nice," she admitted.

"I'll get it," Dare said. "Harold!"

Trey watched Brian fuss over his wife, and though he was a little sad to watch Brian slip even farther away from him, Trey was glad that Brian was so happy. Absolute joy radiated off the guy. It was almost blinding.

"Who's a handsome boy? Who's a handsome boy? Who's a handsome boy?" Jessica asked Malcolm who was gnawing on his fist and gazing at her with unfocused eyes. "That's right. Malcolm's a handsome boy. Malcolm's a handsome boy."

"He's not a dog, Jess. Why are you talking to him like that?" Trey asked.

"He likes it," she said. "Don't you like it? Yes you do. Yes you do."

"Well then, he's the only one," Trey muttered.

Myrna chuckled.

"I want to hold him again," Brian said, following Jessica around the room as she continued to repeat herself incessantly. "You can hold him as much as you want after I'm gone."

"Oh God, I want one," Jessica said, hugging the baby before handing him back to his father.

"Are you sure you mean that?" Trey said.

"Yes, I mean it," Jess said. "Look at him. He's perfect."

"I'm telling Sed you said that. He'll have you knocked up in an hour. Even though he's over twelve hundred miles away."

"That's some serious potency," Myrna said.

Jessica hesitated. "My caseload at the practice is too heavy right now. I don't have time for a baby." She leaned against Brian and stared down at the tiny bundle in his arms. "Okay, fuck the job. I want a baby."

Myrna laughed. "Shouldn't you wait until after your wedding? You've been planning it for months."

"Maybe Sed and I should do what you and Brian did. Just elope. I thought I wanted a big wedding, and Sed's family wants us to have a big wedding, but even with an event planner helping us out, it is so stressful."

"Do you want a big wedding, Jessica?" Myrna asked.

"Kinda," Jessica admitted.

"Then have your big wedding or you'll always regret it."

Brian perked up. "Do you regret not having a big wedding?"

Myrna smiled. "Not at all. I didn't want a big wedding. I just wanted you."

Oh God, not the Brian/Myrna mushy mushy love stuff. Trey wasn't sure if he could handle it today.

"Maybe I should just get pregnant now," Jessica said. "I won't be showing too much in three months. I should still be able to fit into my dress. Or I could get it altered." She looked down and rubbed both hands over her flat belly.

Oh God, shoot me now, Trey thought. *Babies, weddings, and pregnancies. What will they be talking about next? Their periods?*

Dare finally managed to make it into the room to greet his guests. "How are you doing, Myrna?" he asked, taking her hand and giving it a squeeze. "You look gorgeous as usual. Are you sure you just had a baby?"

She beamed. "Oh, I'm sure," she said.

"Harold's bringing your glass of water and some other refreshments. I told him to hurry."

"Thanks, Dare."

"No problem. I hear you named that poor kid Malcolm Trey." Dare nodded his head in the direction of Brian and Jessica who were competing for Malcolm's complete lack of attention.

"It's better than Malcolm Terrance, isn't it?" Myrna asked. Terrance was Trey's real first name, but even Myrna knew how much he hated it.

"Uh, sure," Dare said. He turned toward the two kissy faces, who were undoubtedly driving little Malcolm bonkers. "Well, let's have a look at this kid. Apparently he's the biggest star in the house."

Dare slipped the baby from Brian's hold into the crook of one arm. The guy was a natural at everything. Even holding babies.

"Will you look at that? He already has his father's rock star hairstyle."

"He's adorable," Jessica crooned. "Yes he is. Yes he is. Adorable."

Trey was beginning to feel sticky from all the sap in the room.

"When do we have to leave?" Brian asked, coaxing Malcolm out of Dare's arms and back into his.

"As soon as Reagan gets back," Trey said.

"Reagan?" Brian, Jessica, and Myrna questioned in unison.

"Trey's new girlfriend," Dare said.

"Trey has a girlfriend?" Brian said in disbelief.

"Yeah," Dare said.

"*Trey* does? *That* Trey." Brian pointed at Trey.

"Yes, I have a girlfriend. Is that so hard to believe?"

Brian nodded his head. "Yes, it's very hard to believe. You've never had a girlfriend in your adult life."

"Never?" Jessica questioned, trying to get Malcolm to grip her finger in his fist.

"Depending on how you define girlfriend, I have dozens of them. Had," he rectified.

"The series of women you string along in every town aren't girlfriends; they're conquests," Brian said.

"Well, Reagan is my girlfriend. And she's going on tour with us."

"How long have you known this chick?" Brian asked.

"We met yesterday."

"And did you decide she was going on tour with us before or after you fucked her?"

"Brian, don't be crude," Myrna said. "You asked me to marry you the day after we met."

Brian scratched his head. "You're right," he said. "As usual."

"Reagan touring with Sinners was my idea," Dare said. "She's our new rhythm guitarist, and I figured it would do her good to spend a couple of weeks out on tour before she's subjected to the insanity that surrounds Exodus End. She's talented but not very experienced."

"You hired a *female* guitarist?" Jessica asked.

"Uh, yeah," Dare said. "She fuckin' rocked our faces off."

"That is so awesome," Jessica said. "I can't wait to meet her. I bet she's cool. Is she cool?"

"She must be pretty terrific if she's got Trey thinking commitment." Brian grinned at him and punched him in the chest.

"She is," Trey said. The thought of her made him smile. "Terrific. And cool."

When the doorbell rang about twenty minutes later, Trey went to answer it himself. He found Reagan on the doorstep breathless and lugging two huge suitcases.

"I didn't know what I'd need, so I brought everything."

"I told you all you needed was a box of condoms."

She thrust a paper bag at him. "I bought six dozen. Is that enough?"

Trey laughed and kissed her tenderly. He enjoyed the sensation of her lips against his so much that instead of pulling away he deepened the kiss. Her rolling suitcase tipped over as she released its handle to draw him closer.

"I missed you," he murmured against her lips.

"You did?"

"Mmm hmm." He kissed her again to prove it.

"You'd better go grab a guitar, Reagan," Dare said from behind Trey. "The jet is waiting for you guys."

Trey reluctantly released Reagan and grabbed the handle of her suitcase.

"Is this seriously my life?" she said, shaking her head and following Dare in the direction of the practice room. "I don't recall rubbing a magic lantern and making three wishes."

Trey watched her walk down the hall next to Dare until she was out of sight and then wheeled her suitcase into the parlor where everyone was waiting.

"So where is she?" Brian asked, craning his neck to look behind Trey.

Trey couldn't resist fucking with him. "She's right here in this suitcase. She's an amazing contortionist."

"A contortionist?"

"Yeah. Why do you think I fell for her so quickly? She can wrap both ankles around her neck and lick her own clit."

Brian's eyes widened. "No shit?"

"Shit no." Trey shook his head and grinned. "She went with Dare to pick out a guitar."

"Is she really that talented?" Brian asked.

"I think she could give you a run for your money, Master Sinclair."

"We'll see," he said. He lifted sleeping Malcolm to his lips and then lowered him into his carrier. "I love you, little one. Keep an eye on your mom for me. You're the man of the house when I'm away."

Jessica hovered nearby to watch the little guy snooze. Brian drew Myrna to her feet and then led her out of the room so they could say their good-byes in private. With nothing better to do, Trey went to stand beside Jessica so he could watch his godson sleep.

"He really is amazing, isn't he?" Jessica said.

Trey glanced over his shoulder in the direction Brian had disappeared. "Yeah. He really is."

"I wonder if Sed's ready to start a family." Jessica stroked the baby's cheek with her knuckles. "I sure do want one of these all of a sudden."

"It's that biological clock. Tick. Tick. Tick. I can hear it all the way over here."

Jessica shoved him. "I'm not *that* old."

She wasn't old at all. She was just fun to tease.

"You know Sed has always wanted a bunch of kids," Trey said.

"Yeah, every time we talk about it he adds another one to the brood. He thinks we need eight now."

"Do you have any idea what that's going to do to your vagina?"

"Trey!" She smacked him repeatedly in the arm.

Yeah. Fun to tease. She got riled up so easily. One of the many things that got Sed's motor running for the woman. Not that Trey blamed him. Jessica was easily the most beautiful woman he'd ever met, and Trey had met a lot of women in his day. She was way too high-strung for Trey's taste. Trey preferred someone more laid back. Like Reagan. She entered the room as if on cue carrying a guitar case in each hand. Dare had two as well.

"Reagan, we're only going to be gone for two weeks," Trey said. "You don't need four guitars."

"She wanted to bring eight," Dare said. "This was our compromise."

"They're all so beautiful. I couldn't pick favorites."

Reagan tossed a questioning look in Jessica's direction. Trey hadn't realized they were standing so close to each other. Jessica had seen him hit rock bottom, so he was incredibly comfortable around her. Hell, he was incredibly comfortable around most people. Reagan would have to get used to it sooner rather than later.

"This is Jessica Chase."

Reagan's eyes widened. "I thought you looked familiar. I saw that video of you and Sed getting it on at the top of the Eif—"

Trey shook his head vigorously and luckily Reagan realized she should keep her knowledge of Sed and Jessica's infamous sex video to herself.

"Nice to meet you. I'm Reagan Elliot."

"So you're a guitarist?" Jessica asked.

"Yeah. Can you believe this fucking shit? Yesterday I was a barista. Today I'm rhythm guitarist for the hottest metal band on the planet, dating the sexiest man in the universe, and about to get on a private jet to go on tour with a band I've idolized for years. Are you fecking serious? How did this happen?"

"Because you're talented," Dare said.

Reagan flushed. "You're making my head swell."

"You always make my head swell," Trey quipped.

"You'll have to show me that on the jet. Where's Master Sinclair? Is he here?" Reagan glanced around the room.

"He's saying good-bye to his wife," Trey said. "It might be a while."

"This is his new baby," Jessica said, lifting Malcolm out of his carrier. The baby released a cry of protest and Brian dashed into the room.

"What's wrong?"

"I just picked him up and startled him a little," Jessica said. "He's fine, Papa Bear."

"He shouldn't be handled by too many people," Dare said. "His little immune system can't handle all the germs."

Brian paled.

"I'll take him," Myrna said, walking rather slow and grimacing with each step. She collected the baby in her arms and he immediately started rooting around for a meal.

"He knows his mother already," Brian said and stroked Malcolm's hair.

Reagan dropped her guitar case and her fingers dug into Trey's arm. He glanced at her and she looked like she was about to faint or explode or something. He followed her line of sight to Brian. Trey hoped she didn't go all fangirl in front of everyone. He'd just told Jessica that she was cool.

"Is this your girlfriend?" Myrna asked Trey.

"Yeah, this is Reagan."

"Nice to meet you." Myrna examined Reagan from head to toe. Her gaze finally settled on Reagan's guitar case. "You're a very attractive woman. I have a thing for guitarists, you know," Myrna said.

Brian choked. He turned to look at Reagan and his eyes widened. "If you want to hook up with her, Myrna, you totally have my permission," he said, "but only if I get to participate."

Myrna chuckled. "I wasn't serious, baby. But you are. Serious. You need to relax. You're going to explode. Everything will be fine. I promise."

Brian sighed and kissed her temple. "I'm going to miss you. Make sure you take a picture of Malcolm every hour and send it to me. And video. Record lots of videos. I don't want to miss anything."

Myrna cupped his face with her free hand. "I will. I promise."

"Jessica," Brian said, tearing his gaze off his little family long enough to glance at Sed's fiancée. "I know Myr won't call me if there's a problem, so you'd better."

Jessica nodded.

"She can always call me if she needs anything," Dare said. "I'll be here." Trey cleared his throat and luckily Dare was a mind reader. "I'll just cancel my trip to Hawaii," he added. "No big deal."

Trey took Reagan's hand. "Let's go get on the plane."

She was still gaping at Brian, so Trey had to give her a tug. She inhaled as if startled and looked at Trey. "Plane? Yeah, okay," she said. She picked up the guitar case she had dropped.

Trey collected her suitcases. "We'll see you in a couple of weeks," he said.

Reagan said, "Nice to meet you all."

"We'll talk when you get off tour," Myrna said. "I'd love to get the perspective of a female musician for the book I'm writing."

"Sure," Reagan agreed.

"I'll be there in a few," Brian said before continuing to say his good-byes with his wife. There was a lot of open-mouthed kissing involved in the process.

Carrying two guitar cases, Dare followed Trey and Reagan toward the back of the house where the airstrip was located.

"Sorry you didn't get a better introduction," Trey said to Reagan.

"It's okay. Everyone's excited about the new baby. I understand."

"Brian isn't going to handle this separation well," Dare commented. "He's going to need your support to get through this, Trey."

Trey was always willing to support Brian. It felt kind of strange that Trey didn't consider this an opportunity to try to get Brian to fall in love, or in bed, with him. Maybe Trey's feelings for Brian were starting to change. "All the guys will be there for him. You know that," Trey said.

"But he'll need you most."

"I never realized he was such a family man," Reagan said. "I remember how crushed I was when I found out he'd gotten himself married and was no longer available. He really loves his wife though. I can tell."

"Those two are forever," Trey said and smiled.

When they reached the sleek black jet, Reagan entered first. She started squealing excitedly as soon as she was onboard. "This is amazing! Oh my God! I've never been on a private jet before."

Trey and Dare followed her aboard. They watched her dart about the cabin as she inspected the wet bar and the entertainment center. The comfortable leather captain chairs, the sofa, and the bathroom. "Room in here for sex," she announced.

A surge of lust pulsed through Trey's groin. Their make-out session in the limo that morning already had his motor running in second gear, and that little comment shifted it into third.

"Yeah there is," Dare murmured to Trey out of the corner of his mouth.

Trey was certain Dare knew that from experience.

"Reagan, sweetheart, you really need to work on your cool rock star veneer while you're on tour with Sinners," Dare said. "No matter how excited you are about something, you have to pretend it's the most fucking boring thing you've ever encountered. It's pretty much expected that you act that way. Like it or not, honey, you're a rock star now."

"I am?"

Dare nodded.

"Okay," Reagan said. "I'll try." She pretended to stifle a yawn. "I can't believe this jet doesn't have an Olympic-sized swimming pool and full spa facilities. How can I be expected to exist under these horrible conditions? Where's my fuckin' beer? It better be cold." She glanced at Dare, who laughed. "How's that?"

"Much better."

"I should probably warn you that Sinners don't live like this," Trey said. "Not even close."

"I can't wait to see the inside of your tour bus," Reagan said. "I usually have to suck off at *least* two roadies to get in to see a band."

Trey gaped at her and she laughed.

"I'm kidding," she said.

When he relaxed, she added, "It usually only takes one."

Dare tossed his head back and laughed until Trey thought he might pass out from lack of air. "She is so perfect for you, little brother."

Trey couldn't argue. He happened to agree.

———

Reagan kept one eye on the open door of the jet waiting for Brian Sinclair to make an appearance. She would do her damnedest not to go ape shit ballistic when she saw him, but as much as she'd been starstruck the first time she'd met Trey and the members of Exodus End, when she'd seen Brian she'd almost had a coronary. The man had entirely changed her life. If he hadn't influenced her style of guitar-playing, she wouldn't be in the incredible position at all. Still, she didn't want to annoy him by prostrating herself at his feet or damaging his eardrums with rapturous squeals.

She heard voices outside the open door of the jet and her body stiffened.

"Are you nervous?" Trey asked. He reached across the aisle and took her hand to give it an encouraging squeeze.

"A little. I'll try not to embarrass myself."

"Why would you embarrass yourself?"

"Because I'm about to be trapped on a jet for more than two hours with *the* Brian Sinclair."

"Last night you got laid by *the* Trey Mills."

"And it was amazing," she said, rolling her eyes toward the ceiling to express her bliss.

"If you play your cards right, you might get laid by *the* Trey Mills in the bathroom back there in about half an hour." Trey nodded over his shoulder to the back of the plane.

"Do I get a hint?"

"A hint?"

"On how to play my cards right?"

"You've been playing them right since the moment I laid ears on you. Don't change a thing."

"The moment you laid *ears* on me?"

"Yep, nothing sexier than the way Brian Sinclair plays a guitar, except finding a woman who plays just like him."

There he went again referring to Brian in a way that most men never would. She supposed they would be closer than most friends, seeing as they spent most of their lives crammed in a tour bus together. Still, something felt a little off about their relationship. Maybe it would make more sense to her when she spent more time watching how they interacted.

"Do you think Brian will show me some of his techniques?" Reagan asked. "Or are they secrets?"

"I'm sure he'd be happy to work with you. Hopefully it will take his mind off having to leave his family."

Trey stared down at his thumbs. There had been a time when Sinners had been Brian's family. And then he'd married Myrna. And now that he had Malcolm... Trey wasn't sure where he fit in the man's life anymore.

Brian climbed onto the airplane and took a seat across from Trey. "Look at the picture I just took," he said, holding up his cell phone so Trey could see the screen. In the picture Brian had his arm around Myrna who was cradling Malcolm against her chest. All three of them were smiling like idiots. Even the baby, who probably just had some gas. The picture was a little blurry because Brian had taken it by holding the camera phone in front of them with an extended arm, but the love displayed in that candid moment stole Trey's breath.

"It's great," he said.

Brian looked at the picture and smiled. "Yeah. She's supposed to send me lots of pictures until I come home in a couple days."

"A couple days? We have two more weeks of shows."

"And any day I have off I'm flying back. Dare already said I could use the jet anytime I want."

"You're going to wear yourself out."

"I don't care. Knowing I'll see them again in a few days is the only thing that got me on the plane."

"I can only imagine how hard it was to say good-bye to them," Reagan said.

Brian glanced at her and smiled warmly. "So you're Trey's new girl."

Trey loved the man's smile. It always showed in his eyes. He was so genuine. It was one of the many reasons why Trey had stayed in love with the guy for so long. Hell, he still loved Brian even if he was letting him go. Or trying to. It had been a lot easier to pretend he could move on when Brian had been out of sight.

"I guess you could say that." Reagan beamed and Trey found himself just as smitten with her smile as he was with Brian's.

"So you play guitar. Metal?" Brian asked.

The engines started and Reagan had to talk extra loud to be heard. "You're my greatest influence."

"*I* am?" Brian's brow knitted with confusion. "How long have you been playing?"

"Three years," Trey said. "Can you believe it?"

"That's amazing. Can't wait to hear your work," Brian said. His phone beeped and he grinned when he looked at the screen. He held up the display for Trey to see. "Look! He's feeding."

Breast feeding. Trey averted his gaze. He'd licked those breasts about a year ago. And now… It was going to be a long two weeks.

"Please remember to turn off all electronic devices through the duration of the flight. Make sure your seatbelts are fastened during takeoff. I will let you know when it's safe to move about the cabin." The pilot's voice came over the intercom. She had a sexy, British accent. Trey could have listened to her talk for hours. "Enjoy your flight."

Brian switched off his phone but continued to hold it in his hand on his lap. He offered Trey a depressed smile before settling his gaze on Reagan. "So tell me how you came to be the rhythm guitarist for Exodus End," he said.

She shifted into full-out gush mode, and Trey sat there grinning as she articulated every word with a hand gesture or facial expression. He'd never met anyone as animated as she was. Well, besides the few actors he knew. "So I'm at this club with my girlfriends. We all had a few too many and were trying to figure out how we were going to get home, when the bassist of my old band happens into the club. Chad's a real sweetheart. I didn't get along with our lead singer, but I'd work with Chad again. So I went to bum a ride from him and he says, 'Just the guitarist I was looking for.' I figured he wanted me to play for some new band he formed, but he shows me this ad in *Guitar Planet* for the contest with Exodus End. Go on Tour with Exodus End for a Year, or something like that. It said to enter you had to send a demo to the record company and sign a release and some other bullshit. Sounded like a big hassle to me. I didn't want to enter. Didn't think I had any business entering since there was no chance I'd ever win. As a metal guitarist, I take a lot of shit for being a chick, you know. Chad bribed me into agreeing by offering to give all my girls a ride home. Plus my friends were really enthusiastic about the idea and I was drunk as shit, so I somehow agreed to enter. I cut the demo in Chad's basement the next day and sent it in unedited. I didn't think there was a snow cone's chance in a bonfire that they'd ever pick my demo for the live audition. I just did it to get people off my back."

"How many of the entrants got a live audition?" Brian asked.

"Five out of something like five thousand."

Brian's dark brows lifted in surprise. "Impressive."

"When the contest coordinator called, I thought they were making stuff up. That Chad had put one of his buddies up to calling me and giving me a hard time. My old band members are notorious for fucking with me." She paused and lifted a hand of caution in Trey's direction. "Not fucking me. I never slept with any of them. So after about ten minutes of trying to get this exasperated dude on the phone to admit he was a friend of Chad's, it finally sunk in that I won the live audition. I was so nervous that I didn't want to go. My roommate, Ethan, talked me into it. Reminding me how I'd always regret not giving my all. I knew he was right. I'd always wonder if I didn't go through with it. I was so nervous in the studio yesterday, I thought I was going to hurl. And then Trey shows up right before the five finalists were scheduled to go into the booth for our live auditions. I think that's when reality hit me. I put everything I had into that audition. Something about knowing Trey was listening really upped my game. I'm not sure how I would have done if he hadn't showed up. I probably would have thrown up on my guitar and started crying."

"I don't deserve any credit," Trey said. "She's amazing. I actually thought she was you when I heard her play. She has the same balls-out style you play with."

Brian laughed. "Now *that* I have to see."

"I don't let my balls out for just anyone," Reagan said. She grabbed her crotch and pretended to shift her balls into a more comfortable position. "But I'll make an exception in your case."

Brian gaped at her and then burst out laughing. "So you two hooked up at the audition?"

"Afterward," Trey said.

"He beat me in a guitar duel and then I took him for a ride in Exodus End's limo." She shifted in her seat and looked over her shoulder to the bathroom at the rear of the plane. "Speaking of taking Trey for a ride."

Brian's gaze followed Reagan's to the bathroom door. His face twisted as if he were in pain and he groaned. "The doctor said I can't fuck Myrna for six weeks. I'm going to die."

Trey wasn't sure how Brian could even think about Myrna in a sexual capacity after watching her give birth. If Trey ever decided to have kids, he would insist his woman have a C-section. Just the memory of natural childbirth had Trey a bit woozy.

"When do we get to lose the seat belts?" Reagan asked.

"They'll announce it," Brian said. He lifted his phone to give it a look of longing before tucking it back in his pocket.

"So how did you meet your wife?" Reagan asked. She sure knew how to earn brownie points with Brian.

Brian grinned. "She saw me fall off a table in a hotel bar and still thought I was hot enough to take up to her room."

"And then she pushed him away for months," Trey added. At the time Trey had been torn between wanting Brian to be happy by winning Myrna's affection and wanting him to give up on her so he might have a fighting chance. The thing was, besides the two times that he and Brian had gone all the way in high school, they'd never been intimate again. Not for Trey's lack of trying. It was as if Brian had checked homosexual experience off his life's to-do list and never really thought about it again. Trey, on the other hand, had been hung up on the experience for over ten years. He was lucky that Brian had patience. He had to know that Trey still wanted him, and Brian never intentionally hurt him. Instead Brian seemed content for Trey to outgrow his infatuation. Maybe it would have been easier if Brian had just shredded Trey's heart and left him to wallow in despair for a few months instead of that constant ignore-the-situation-and-it-will-go-away stance he'd taken. Trey didn't blame Brian though. He knew how important their friendship was to him. It was as equally important to Trey. If Brian had treated him any differently, their friendship might have dissolved as well, and that might have hurt their music. Trey supposed that waiting it out had worked eventually. Maybe. His heart still fluttered every time he looked at Brian. He still thought about how connected he'd felt to the man the first time they'd made love, and how that connection had somehow lasted for twelve years.

He glanced at Reagan and found her watching him closely. Had he been staring at Brian with open longing? Shit. If he wasn't careful, she'd figure out that he was interested in men. He smiled at her and she offered him an answering smile. The connection he'd forged with her the night before returned to the forefront of his mind. He wondered if he'd carry a torch for her forever the same way he carried a torch for the first man he'd ever felt that connection with. The idea scared him, yet if she embraced it, instead of ignoring it, maybe they could build something substantial. Trey didn't know if he could handle another one-sided love affair. There was one significance difference in this relationship. Reagan was interested in him. He had to trust her intentions.

"We're now at cruising altitude," the pilot said over the intercom. "Feel free to move about the cabin. Help yourself to anything in the galley."

Reagan removed her seat belt and slid onto Trey's lap. "Do you count as something in the galley?" she asked. "I'd like to help myself to you."

"Technically I'm not in the galley, but you can still help yourself."

Reagan stole a kiss, her arms wrapping around his neck. "I'm so lucky," she whispered in his ear.

His hand slid up her shirt to slide over the bare skin of her side.

Brian sighed. "Don't mind me."

"In the good old days I would have asked you to join us. Now you're all married and boring," Trey said, peering around Reagan to see if his taunt had wiped the scowl from Brian's handsome face.

"What I wouldn't give for a time machine," Reagan said.

Brian smirked and shook his head. "Go on. Have fun. I'll sit here and mope a while longer."

Reagan unfastened Trey's seat belt and climbed to her feet. She leaned over him and spoke into his ear, not quietly enough to exclude Brian, so Trey could only conclude that she was trying to tease Brian out of his funk. "I'll go into the bathroom. You come join me in a couple of minutes so no one will suspect anything."

"Yeah, okay. Good plan," he said with a chuckle.

He watched her walk down the wide aisle and close herself in the bathroom.

"She's cute," Brian said. "Kind of a tomboy, but I can see why you like her."

"Does it bother you?" Trey asked.

"Does what bother me?"

"That I have a steady girlfriend."

"It's a little sudden, but of course it doesn't bother me. I'm happy for you. I hope it works out. You deserve the love of a good woman."

Trey wasn't sure why that made him a little sad. He wanted Brian to like Reagan. He also wanted Brian to be insanely jealous and tell him he wasn't allowed to love anyone but him. He knew it was fucked up to still feel that way, but at least he no longer *wanted* to feel that way. That was progress, wasn't it?

"I'll try not to make her scream too loud."

Brian chuckled. "Fuck her brains out. You know I wouldn't consider your misery if our positions were reversed."

Positions reversed? Trey pictured himself dragging Brian into the bathroom. Shoving him against the wall. Taking everything he wanted from him. Trey bit his lip and rose from his seat, hoping Brian didn't notice how hard he was all of a sudden. Of course, Brian would probably think he was hard for Reagan, not him. Trey's desire was as fucked up as his feelings were. He had a lot of work to do.

He retrieved a strip of condoms from a box in the paper sack he'd brought onboard and headed for the bathroom. He knocked and then opened the door. Entirely naked, Reagan reached into the corridor and jerked him into the small bathroom before securing the door behind him. The lavatory was a bit larger than a standard airplane bathroom, but not by much. Trey pressed her against the wall behind the door and claimed her mouth with a deep, seeking kiss. He needed that senseless, disconnected release he was accustomed to. He didn't give her time to draw him out of his shell this time. He squeezed her breasts and then released his belt and the fly of his jeans. He tore his mouth away from hers long enough tear a condom open with his teeth.

"Trey?" she gasped in question.

He silenced her with another kiss. He just wanted to come. He didn't want to talk. And he didn't want to think about Brian. Or even Reagan. He just needed a body to lose himself in for twenty minutes. Was that so wrong?

He pushed her up the wall and struggled to hold her there with one hand while he used his other to guide his cock into her receptive body. Once inside her, he shuddered with delight and shifted both arms to hold her securely while he thrust up into her. Things were going exactly as he'd envisioned until she began to touch him with a tenderness he didn't deserve. He tore his mouth from hers. "We need to hurry," he lied to explain his need for impersonal urgency.

"Look at me, Trey," she said.

He buried his face in her neck. "I need to concentrate."

She grabbed two handfuls of hair and jerked his head back. "Look at me," she demanded.

He opened his eyes and then his mouth to tell her she didn't have a right to treat him so harshly, but before the words even formed he got lost in her loving gaze.

"There you are, lover," she murmured. "That's what I want."

They stared at each other as their bodies moved together with an increasing tempo. Reagan's cries of ecstasy started as a soft coo and soon escalated to screams of enthusiasm. Trey got caught up her vocalizations and started answering them with shouts of his own.

"Come with me," she chanted. "Come with me. Come with me."

"Yes, yes, yes," he answered.

Her hips buckled and her fingers dug into his scalp as she cried out in ecstasy. He pumped into her vigorously and let go. He forced himself not to close his eyes as his body claimed release and was rewarded with the look of pure bliss that settled over her lovely face. "Oh God, Trey, I'm coming so hard." He almost dropped her when her entire body went taut.

"That's it, baby. Get off."

If he hadn't already come, the sounds she made as she found release would have sent him over the edge. After a long intense moment, she sagged back against the wall, wrapping her arms around his body to draw him against her. "Fuck," she gasped in his ear. "That was amazing."

He murmured something against her throat in agreement, so glad she'd made him look at her and hadn't allowed him to treat her like a meaningless sex partner.

Trey released her begrudgingly, and she did her best to clean up in the tiny sink while he looked for the best place to dispose of his condom.

"Trey?"

He glanced up to look at her.

"Is there something more between you and Brian than friendship?"

Trey hoped she took his shock for denial instead of acceptance. "No. Why would you think that?"

"Just a few things you've said. And the way you look at him."

"What way is that?"

"Like you love him."

"I do," he said. "I love all the members of my band. They're like my family."

While she pulled her T-shirt over her head, he turned to face the wall and mouthed, *Shit, shit, shit* repeatedly. How had she picked up on that so easily? And if he was that transparent, how come Brian never recognized it?

"Do you think he heard us?" She bumped into him as she struggled to put on her panties.

"I don't know if he heard me, but I'm sure he heard you. You were screaming like a horror picture bimbo."

She slapped him on the arm. "Was not."

"How about I ask him?"

"Don't," she pleaded. She grabbed his arm and spun him to face her. "I didn't mean to get that loud. You got me carried away. I forgot where I was."

Three points for the Trey-ster.

He waited for her to squirm into her pants before he opened the door. He took the seat across from Brian, stretched his legs out in front of himself, and crossed them at the ankles. He folded his arms behind his head and sighed in contentment. Brian, who had been staring out the window, turned his head to look at him.

"Done already?" Brian asked.

"Had to hurry. We'll be landing soon."

Brian shook his head. "I couldn't tell if you were killing her or screwing her. There isn't a dead body in the bathroom, is there?"

Before Trey could assure Brian that he hadn't murdered Reagan, she exited the bathroom and sat on the far end of the sofa. Her face was beet red.

"I didn't hear anything," Brian told her. "But if you scream like that on the tour bus, Eric will tease you and Sed will cuss you out for making him horny. You might want to borrow a gag from Jace."

"I thought you didn't hear anything," Reagan said.

"I didn't. Just sayin'."

Reagan grinned at Brian. "Can I get my guitar out now? I brought one acoustic with me."

Trey wasn't sure how the woman could think about working. He wanted to take a nap.

Brian perked up, his gloomy expression replaced with one of interest. "Yeah. Let's hear what you've got."

Reagan found the thickest of her guitar cases and opened it to reveal a black lacquered acoustic guitar. "This baby sings," Reagan said, strumming the strings lightly. "Max did a great job breaking her in."

She carried the guitar over to the sofa and sat with the instrument on one thigh.

"Good. You're right-handed," Brian said, leaving his seat to sit beside her. "Not a lefty like Trey. He does everything ass-backwards."

"I think that's part of the reason why you two complement each other so well," Reagan said, smiling first at Trey then Brian.

"Takes him twice as long to learn a riff."

"You're just a freak of nature," Trey told Brian.

"So I've watched all sorts of videos of you playing solos, but they never really catch your finger movements in the upper register. I sort of made up my own technique, but the notes never sound as crisp as yours. They all run together at that speed."

"Show me," Brian said.

Reagan played the triplet repeats of the solo to their newest single, "Betrayed." She had to strum incredibly fast, because an acoustic sounded nothing like an electric guitar and wasn't ideal for soloing. Brian watched the fingers of her left hand as they moved over the fret board.

"Don't squeeze," he said. "Tap." He tapped the tops of her fingernails. "Short taps."

She followed his instruction but still didn't get the same quality of note that Brian got. He extended a hand. "Here, I'll show you."

She handed him the guitar and watched his fingers in rapt attention as he played the solo several times in a row. He didn't bother strumming more than he would his electric guitar, so it didn't sound much like a solo as most of the notes were almost silent with no pickups to amplify them. "I'll show you on an electric tonight," he said.

"I see what you're doing." She took his hand in hers and flipped it over to inspect his fingertips and then her own. "I need to work on some new calluses. Yours are more off-center than mine. I'm not hitting the strings in the same spot."

"Instead of trying to copy me, maybe you should work on your own sound."

She grinned at him. "But I like yours. Wish I would have come up with it first."

"Why don't you play some of the stuff you wrote?" Trey suggested. He still remembered the mesmeric riff she'd been playing in Dare's studio when he'd taken her up on her challenge to duel. He'd watched her for several minutes before he found the sense to interrupt.

She flushed. "I'll just embarrass myself."

Most guitarists started out copying the guitarists they admired, and that would serve her fine as she took over for Max, but when she pushed to the next level in her career, she'd need to find her own sound. And be confident that she owned it.

Brian patted her knee. "You've got the talent. You'll get there." He climbed to his feet and found his seat. He reclined it. "I'm going to catch a little nap. Didn't get much sleep at the hospital last night. I'd appreciate it if you two would keep the orgasmic screaming to a minimum."

Trey stood and reached into an overhead bin. He pulled out a pillow and blanket and tossed them at Brian, hitting him dead in the face. If Reagan hadn't already expressed her suspicions about Trey's feelings for Brian, Trey would have chosen a less violent delivery, but he had to be careful not to show her how much he cared about him.

"Thanks," Brian said sarcastically and stuffed the pillow under his head. He spread the blanket over his body and clutched it to his chest.

Trey turned the lights in the cabin down and winked at Reagan, who was sitting with her guitar still on her lap and watching him a bit too closely. Trey sat beside her on the sofa and took the guitar from her. He set it carefully on the floor and drew her into his arms. "We never got to cuddle after our initiation into the mile high club," he murmured near her ear.

She shifted onto his lap and wrapped both arms around his neck. He mostly just held her for the next hour and stroked her skin tenderly. They exchanged a few sweet kisses, but Trey was far too preoccupied with Brian's situation to intensify the passion between himself and Reagan. Brian wasn't happy and if Brian wasn't happy, none of the band was happy. Even though Sed led the band and they all looked to him to fix any logistical problems, Brian was their keystone, and without his talent, they had nothing to center themselves around. They all depended on him to be their creative focus. Trey was pretty sure Brian could stick it out for the next two weeks, but what of the next year? They'd just put out a new album they needed to promote. They were co-headlining with Exodus End all across North America, then Europe and Australia. Asia. South America. Brian might be able to fly back to see Myrna and Malcolm when he was within a few hours flight time, but from the other side of the globe? There was no way.

"What are you thinking about?" Reagan asked, her hand moving to stroke the tension from his forehead.

"The end of Sinners."

She glanced at Brian who was out cold and drooling all over his pillow. "Maybe the band just needs to take a year off."

"Maybe." But then Sed and Jess would probably have a kid or twelve and they'd be in the same place. "I'm never having kids," he muttered under his breath.

"Me neither," she said.

Trey glanced down at her. He hadn't meant to say that aloud and was surprised that Reagan wouldn't want kids. Didn't all women want them?

"You don't want kids?"

She shook her head. "Do you have any idea what they do to your vagina?" she said. "No thank you."

Trey laughed and squeezed her against him. "My perfect woman."

Chapter 11

REAGAN CARRIED TWO OF her guitars onto Sinners' tour bus. Behind her, Brian and Trey had divvied up her remaining luggage and followed her onboard. Her stomach fluttered when she noticed *the* Eric Sticks sitting at the dining table, poring over musical scores. His untamed black hair, with a streak of canary yellow that started at his left temple and continued down a finger-thick strand that fell to his collarbone, caught her attention first. Then his ruggedly handsome features. Then his long, sinewy body and masculine hands. He glanced up, barely gave Reagan a second glance with a pair of piercing blue eyes, before his gaze settled on Brian. "Pictures," he demanded and flicked a beckoning hand at him.

Brian dropped Reagan's luggage and brushed past her to sit next to Eric in the booth. He began flipping through pictures on his cell phone. He'd been so excited when he had been allowed to turn on his cell phone after landing and found he had six new pictures and a video of Malcolm sleeping in his bassinet for the first time. While Eric ooo-ed and aww-ed over baby pictures, Trey struggled with Reagan's abundance of luggage.

"I brought too much, didn't I?" she asked.

"You think?" Trey laughed and stacked her four guitar cases on the only sofa on the bus.

"Maybe we should store them underneath the bus," she said.

"Good idea."

"You're not going to introduce her?" Eric asked. He lifted his gaze from Brian's three-minute-long, baby-sleeping video to look at Reagan.

Brian elbowed him in the ribs. "This is Malcolm's first meal."

Eric looked at the picture and grinned. "Niiiice."

Trey stared at her as if he had no idea how to introduce her to Eric. Eventually he said, "This is Reagan. She'll be on tour with us for the next two weeks. Dare's idea."

Eric scratched behind his ear. "Dare's idea?"

"I'm Exodus End's new rhythm guitarist. Taking over for Max," Reagan explained.

"Oh. Max's carpal tunnel syndrome. Pussiest reason for giving up guitar that I've ever heard. So why are you touring with us instead of rehearsing with them?"

"I think they're afraid that I'm not man enough to go on tour with a rock band."

Eric's gaze traveled down Reagan's entire length. "I'd hazard to guess you aren't man at all."

"She's also Trey's girlfriend," Brian said.

Eric's head snapped around in Brian's direction, his bright blue eyes wide with astonishment.

"I know, right?" Brian said.

Trey cringed. Reagan wondered why it made him uncomfortable.

"Let's go put some of your stuff under the bus," he said.

A loud mechanical sound came from near the front of the bus. Before Reagan could figure out its source, Trey took Reagan's arm and directed her to stand with him between the captain's chairs along one wall while a good-looking young man maneuvered his wheelchair down the aisle.

"You ready to head out, Brian?" the man asked. "We'll be on the road for hours. The other bus and equipment trucks are already in Topeka. They've started setting up."

"Yeah, let's go," Brian said. "Where are the rest of the guys?"

"Jace and Sed went to get some necessities," Eric said. "Jon left with the other bus. Jake's napping."

"Rebekah?"

Eric smiled and glanced at the back bedroom's closed door. "She's getting dressed."

"We need to store some stuff under the bus," Trey said to the man in the wheelchair.

The man started when he noticed Reagan crammed between Trey and the wall. "Sorry, I didn't see you there." He extended a hand in Reagan's direction. "I'm Dave. I run the soundboard when Rebekah lets me."

Reagan reached around Trey to shake Dave's hand. She had heard about Sinners' bus accident and that their soundboard operator had been paralyzed in the crash. She hadn't known that he was still part of the crew.

"You better be glad Reb didn't hear that," Eric said.

Dave grinned and ran a hand through his sandy blond hair. "Rebekah is my younger sister. Also one of Sinners' soundboard operators."

"And my wife," Eric said. "She's a little kinky. Just to warn you."

Trey laughed. He'd never heard Eric apologize for his wife's kinkiness before. Of course, she'd been the only woman on the bus for the past seven months and the guys were used to her emerging from the bedroom dressed as a vampire or an umpire. She would then corral her husband into the back bedroom and a whole lot of happy emanated from that area of the bus for the next couple of hours.

"So Dave is your brother-in-law?" Reagan asked Eric as she worked out the dynamics of the bus occupants.

"Yep."

"What are you working on?" Brian asked Eric, finally taking his attention off his collection of photos to look over the scores of music. "New Sinners' songs? We just released the last album. Don't you ever take a break?"

Eric collected his music and stuffed it into a folder. "It's not Sinners. It's for Hot Dog Junkie."

Brian laughed. "I still can't believe you named your new band that. Why not call it Wiener Eater? Maybe Trey—"

"Let's go put this stuff under the bus," Trey interrupted loudly. He reached for two guitar cases and handed them to Reagan. He grabbed the larger of her two suitcases and another guitar case and encouraged her to head toward the exit.

"Eric has a new band?" Reagan asked as she made her way back toward the exit.

"Some punk/emo/goth hybrid thing he's working on with Jon Mallory. They're still in the planning stages mostly."

"What about Sinners? Is he leaving?" Reagan asked. She couldn't imagine Sinners without Eric Sticks in the band.

Trey shook his head. "Side project," he said. "Sinners is still his main focus."

Reagan descended the steps and waited at the bottom for Trey to join her. She followed him to the side of the bus where he opened a compartment underneath.

"I should have asked you which guitar you wanted to keep out," he said as he rearranged some luggage so he could fit three of her guitars and one of her suitcases in the cramped space.

"They're all awesome. I'm glad you chose so I didn't have to."

Once Reagan's things were stored safely underneath the bus, Trey shut the hatch and then reached for her. He drew her against the length of his body and kissed her.

"Don't pay attention to what the guys say," he said, still thinking about how Brian had almost revealed Trey's homosexual tendencies to Reagan on the bus with that wiener eater remark. He wasn't ready for Reagan to know that about him. Wasn't sure if he ever wanted her to know. Trey did feel uncomfortable about hiding it from her, but since men were no longer on his menu, there was no sense in complicating his new relationship with Reagan with all those skeletons in his closet. There was an entire army of skeletons in his closet. And a few sailors. "They joke around like that a lot."

"I should hope so. They're guys. I'm sure Exodus End does that a lot too."

Trey laughed. "They're a bit rowdier than we are."

"Rowdier?"

"Yeah. Dare figured if you couldn't handle the five of us, there's no way you could handle the four of them."

"Well, don't take it easy on me."

"Sinners BC was an entirely different animal," Trey said. "We've mellowed over the past year."

"Sinners BC?"

"Before chicks."

"Well, don't mellow for my sake," Reagan said. Her hands slid down his back to squeeze his ass. "I happen to like you naughty. The naughtier, the better."

Trey grinned and lowered his head to kiss her. He knew he liked this woman. Even though she claimed to like him naughty, if she had any idea how truly deviant he could be, he was sure she'd go running for the hills. He'd start her on naughty lite and see how she handled that first.

"Good, you guys are back," Sed called from several yards behind the bus. He was carrying several brown paper sacks. Jace, who was walking beside him, smiled a greeting before noticing Reagan's hands on Trey's ass. He blushed and averted his gaze. Sed glanced at Reagan long enough to ascertain that she wasn't Brian. "Brian's here too, right? You didn't leave him in Los Angeles, did you?"

"He's on the bus torturing Eric with baby pictures," Trey said.

Sed smiled. "I can't wait to hold the little guy."

"Jess said she wanted one," Trey said and winked.

Sed's blue eyes widened. "Jess wants a baby?" he asked breathlessly.

"She's totally in love with Malcolm. Her biological clock is ticking at warp speed."

"You're fucking with me," Sed said and scowled.

"She seemed to genuinely want a baby to me," Reagan said.

Sed spared her a second glance. "We're getting ready to leave. You need to get lost now."

Her face fell.

"Fuckin' Sed," Trey grumbled. "She's with me."

"That's obvious," Sed said.

"And she's staying with me," Trey added.

"I'm Jace," Jace said to Reagan and smiled warmly.

"Oh God. Cute!" Reagan exclaimed and released Trey to grab Jace in a face-to-bosom, double-armed embrace.

Jace's various chains rattled as he tried to extricate himself from Reagan's bear hug. She finally released him, took a second look at him, and hugged him again.

"Jace doesn't like to be touched," Trey tried to explain as he tugged on Reagan's arm. "But I like it."

"Oh, sorry," Reagan said as she released Jace for good this time. "I didn't mean to attack you like that. I've never seen you smile before."

Jace blushed again and stared at his boots.

"So she's staying on the bus?" Sed asked, sounding none-too-happy about the fact.

"Yeah, for the next two weeks," Trey said.

"I'm Reagan. Exodus End just hired me to be their rhythm guitarist."

Sed and Jace both stared at her as if she had sprouted wings and took flight to Crazyland.

"No shit?" Sed shoved his grocery sacks in Trey's direction. "You can tell me all about it later. I need to call Jess."

Trey managed to grab the sacks before Sed released them. Sed dug his phone out of his pocket as he stomped up the bus steps.

"He's kind of a jerk," Reagan said.

"*Kind* of?" Trey said.

"He's different once you get to know him," Jace said. "He's like that with strangers. Doesn't know who to trust."

"True," Trey agreed. "It's been a while since I've seen him act like that. He must've thought you were a groupie."

"That excuses him being a jerk?" Reagan asked, her eyebrows raised high above her grayish-blue eyes.

"You'll have some groupies of your own soon. Then you'll understand why it's easier to be an asshole when they're around."

"So you're an asshole to your groupies too?" Reagan asked.

Trey started backpedaling. "Well, no, I—"

"Trey just uses them for sex," Jace said and headed up the stairs after Sed.

Trey was going to invest in four sturdy ball gags. One for each of the members of his big-mouthed band.

Reagan managed to stifle a laugh as she watched Trey try to come up with something to say after Jace dropped that bomb. She didn't care that Trey had a long list of sexual conquests. One didn't get as good in bed as he was without a lot a practice. It wasn't as if she was clueless about what went on backstage. She had a few acquaintances in the business. No one as famous as Trey—well, until yesterday—but even small-time bands had plenty of women to keep them entertained.

"If you're going to get upset every time one of your band members reveals one of your dirty little secrets, you're going to go nuts."

Trey raked a hand through his long bangs and held them out of his eye. "I'm not upset."

"You don't think I know these things already?"

His face fell. "What things?"

"That you've slept with a lot of women."

He released his hair and it dropped to conceal one eye again. His typical devil-may-care expression replaced the worried one of just a moment before. "You're not the jealous type?"

"If I was, I wouldn't last as your girlfriend for three seconds. I see the way women look at you."

"You do?"

"I can't blame them."

He grinned that sexy smile and even though it made her heart race, she couldn't resist teasing him. "I want to take a pair of scissors to those bangs as much as they do."

His sexy smile faded and he looked up at his bangs. "You don't like my haircut?"

She bit her lip and shook her head. "It's much too sexy. It makes me want to grab you and do naughty things with you."

He laughed. "One of these days I'm going to get used to you fucking with me and quit falling for your taunts."

She produced an exaggerated pout. "And ruin all my fun?"

The bus engine started and Trey took her hand. "Time to sequester ourselves in a small space with six or seven other people who like to fuck with me."

"This should be fun."

Reagan paused at the top of the stairs. There was a lean man with a foot-tall, blond mohawk behind the wheel. How many people were crammed onto this bus?

"Hey," the guy said, rubbing one eye and blinking rapidly as if he'd just been pulled from a deep sleep. "Are we finally ready to roll?"

"Let's move," Dave said. He'd given up his wheelchair, which was folded and tucked behind the drivers' seat. He had a pair of metal crutches resting against the side of the sofa beside him.

Reagan offered a hand to the driver. "I'm Reagan."

"Jake."

"You'll want to get to know him. He's our guitar technician," Trey said.

Jake squeezed her hand before honking the bus's horn. "And occasional driver."

"Nice to meet you. I'll harass you later."

"Booyah!" Jake said.

Reagan walked down the bus aisle and looked for an empty seat. Sed was sitting in one of the two captain's chairs talking into his cell phone and flipping through the pictures on Brian's phone with a huge smile on his face. "I'll be home in two weeks. Get off the pill now." He paused. "I'm sure." Another pause. "I'll still marry you even if you're as fat as a hippo. I'll just put you on a diet after the baby is born." His face fell and Reagan couldn't make out Jess's words, but she was definitely yelling. "What?" he said. "What did I say?"

Brian was in the other captain's chair watching his cell phone anxiously. Sed waved it around as he tried to talk himself out of the hole he'd dug himself into with his fiancée.

Jace had settled onto the sofa across from the captain's chairs. He was on his cell phone too, texting at a hundred miles an hour and blushing again. He looked tough and so cute at the same time. Reagan wouldn't mind sitting next to him for the entire journey to Topeka. There was a narrow space between himself and Dave, but not enough space for Reagan to sit. She didn't think it was appropriate to sit between them and wiggle until they gave her some space. That left the booths around the dining table. The bus moved and Trey placed a steadying hand on her lower back as she stumbled.

Reagan shuffled to the dining area and sat across the table from Eric Sticks. He offered her a smile when she'd settled against the wall. Trey slid into the booth beside her.

Eric's gaze searched Reagan's face. "Should I know you?" he asked after several minutes.

"What do you mean?"

"New guitarist for Exodus End. Trey claims that you're his girlfriend. Either you're a close personal friend of Dare's or famous."

"Neither."

"She entered that Guitarist for a Year with Exodus End contest," Trey explained.

"She won?" Eric asked.

Reagan nodded.

"Are they hoping to use a hot woman to get some new fans?" Eric asked.

Trey's arm wrapped around her waist and he drew her closer to his body. "I can see why you might think that, but they hired her before they saw her. Completely based on the merit of her guitar work."

"Don't think a woman can hold her own?" Reagan asked. She knew she was part of a male-dominated profession, but she didn't tolerate double standards. At all.

Eric shook his head. "Never crossed my mind. I was much more confused by Trey claiming to have a girlfriend than by you going from unknown to a soon-to-be world famous guitarist. I figured Trey must be doing a favor for his brother."

Reagan took Trey's hand and looked into his eyes. "Why does everyone find it so hard to believe that you actually like me? Do I have spinach in my teeth?" She bared her teeth at him.

Trey pretended to scrape something out her teeth. "There you go. Now they'll believe that we're involved for sure."

Reagan smiled at him.

The bedroom door opened and a petite blonde emerged wearing a sexy waitress uniform. The fabric was pink gingham with a lacy ruffle around the bottom of a short skirt. Petticoats made the skirt stand out and revealed her white thigh-high stockings and the pink ribbons circling the tops of her legs. The bodice of the uniform was low cut and showed off her cleavage—something Reagan had never had—to perfection. The young woman's platinum hair was swept up into a sloppy knot. Canary yellow strands, the same shade as Eric's long strand of hair, surrounded her face. She sashayed her way to the table and handed a drooling Eric what appeared to be a menu.

Reagan looked from Eric, who was perusing the menu with interest, to the woman who was snapping her gum and scratching behind her ear with the end of her pencil.

"What can I get you, sugar?" she asked Eric in an exaggerated Southern accent.

Reagan turned her head and found Trey grinning at the pair.

"Uh…" Reagan wasn't sure what was going on. Eric had said his wife was kinky, not a waitress.

"What's today's special?" Eric asked.

"The sixty-nine is on special, sugar. Is that what you want?" The woman paused with her pencil hovering over her pad of paper.

"I have a big appetite today. I think I'd like an appetizer to start things off."

"I have a real nice hand job available to whet your appetite for the main course," she said.

"Does that come with special sauce?"

"It's available with either cooling or warming lube."

"Mmm. That sounds good. I'll take the hand job with cooling lube, followed with the sixty-nine special, hold the orgasm. I'll follow that with a thick sausage in a pair of buns with some extra cooling lube sauce."

Rebekah grinned. "Excellent choice, sugar. Will you need any dessert?"

"I'll decide on dessert later," Eric said. "But you might want to grab the chocolate syrup and whipped cream from the fridge. I'm feeling artistic."

Rebekah wrote down Eric's order and then turned her attention to Reagan. "Can I get you anything, sugar?"

Reagan's eyes widened. Trey burst out laughing. "This is Eric's wife, Rebekah," he said. "She's just messing with you."

"Tonight I'm Eric's waitress," Rebekah said.

"I'm Reagan."

Rebekah winked and tucked her pencil behind her ear. "Nice to meet you."

"Miss," Eric said in a highly annoyed tone. "Is my appetizer ready yet? I've been waiting for almost a minute."

"It's right through that door, sugar," Rebekah said to her husband. To Reagan, she said, "We'll chat later. Nice to have a bit of estrogen on this testosterone cruise."

Eric slid from the booth and slapped Rebekah on the ass. "You can expect a very large tip tonight, babe."

Rebekah smiled seductively. "You know I aim to please."

Eric wrapped an arm around her waist and palmed her breast. "I love you."

They paused at the small black refrigerator long enough to collect a bottle of chocolate syrup and a can of whipped cream before shutting themselves in the bedroom.

Reagan scowled. "Does she serve him like that all the time?" Not that it was any of her business, but she was all about empowering women.

"It's a two-way street. Tomorrow Eric will probably dress up for her and satisfy one of her kinky little fantasies."

"Do you like that kind of thing?" Reagan asked. She picked up the menu Eric had left behind and found a list of sexual acts. She'd only tried about half of them.

"Rebekah is really creative," Trey said. "And Eric is well aware of exactly how lucky he is. I wouldn't mind engaging in a few of their games. Looks like fun."

Reagan pointed to a selection on the menu. "I don't even know what this is."

"I could tell you," Trey said. He leaned closer to whisper in her ear. "But I'd rather show you."

"Give me my phone, Sed," Brian said in the living area. "I need to call Myrna."

"She's sleeping," Sed told him. "Jessica said she looked wiped."

"Is she okay?"

"She's fine. Just tired. Relax, Sinclair."

Brian slapped the cell phone out of Sed's hand. "You relax."

Trey offered Reagan a weary smile and then slid from the bench. He picked Brian's phone off the floor and yanked Sed's phone out of his hand.

"Hey, I was talking—" Sed protested.

Trey handed Brian his cell phone. "Don't call her if she's sleeping. She needs rest," he said to Brian. "Go show Jace and Dave your pictures. They haven't seen them yet."

Brian's angry glare softened when his phone's screen saver caught his eye. He squeezed himself in between Jace and Dave, who immediately stopped what they were doing to distract Brian before he throat-chopped Sed.

Trey lifted Sed's phone to his ear and winced when Jessica's healthy tirade greeted his eardrum, "… if you expect me to have eight kids, then you'd better be prepared—"

"Jess, it's Trey."

"Oh what, is he *hiding* now? Coward. Knock him upside the head for me, will you?"

Trey smacked Sed in the forehead and received a punch in the thigh for his efforts. "Done. Listen, can you have Myrna call Brian as soon as she wakes up? Doesn't matter what time it is or if he's onstage, tell her to call him."

"How's he doing?" Jessica asked.

"Worse than you can imagine. You know that greenish hue he gets before he goes on stage?"

"Yeah."

"Multiply that by a thousand. I'm going to give him the

phone. You be sure to tell him how great Myrna and Malcolm are doing."

"She's been crying on and off all day. She's having a hard time with this separation too. Aggie finally got her to lay down for a while." If Brian heard that, Trey knew Brian would commandeer the bus and head back to L.A. Not that Trey blamed him. Trey didn't like to hear that Myrna was upset either. The woman was Brian's rock.

"Didn't you go to law school to learn how to say exactly the right thing?" Trey said to Jessica. "Work your magic."

Trey turned and thrust the phone in Brian's direction. Brian was having a bit too much fun making Jace look uncomfortable by describing the entire birthing process. "Jess wants to talk to you," Trey said.

"Is something wrong?" Brian asked.

"Nope. Everything's great."

Jace offered Trey an accusatory glare. Aggie had probably been texting him about the entire situation. The band needed to sit down and come up with a game plan to get Brian through this. He'd already scheduled a red-eye flight back to L.A. for the next morning. When would the man sleep?

"Thanks for getting me off the hook with Jess," Sed said. He rose from his seat and stretched his arms over his head.

"I don't think you're off the hook," Trey said. "Are you ever going to learn to think before you start saying stupid shit to her?"

Sed lowered his arms and shrugged. "Probably not." He went to the fridge and found himself a beer. He turned to Reagan sitting in the booth at the dining table and said, "Do you drink beer, Trey's Girlfriend?"

Reagan's frosty expression made Trey grin. Most girls went limp when Sed so much as entered a room.

"Sorry, I forgot your name," Sed said and scratched the back of his neck as he inspected the ceiling.

"It's Reagan, and yes, I like beer."

Sed grabbed two beers and slid into the booth across from Reagan. He twisted off a bottle cap and extended his peace offering to her. She hesitantly accepted it and took a swig. Deciding Brian had been temporarily placated, Trey slid into the booth beside her. "I could put in my tongue piercing now, if you'd like," he whispered in her ear.

"Why wouldn't I like that?" she said with a grin.

"Depends on if you want to talk or make out. It makes me talk funny."

"And he clicks it against his teeth and drives us all nuts," Sed added.

"I can't sing with it in either, so I only wear it for special occasions."

"And he has enough special occasions to keep the hole from growing shut." Sed laughed and flipped his bottle cap at Trey. It pinged off his shoulder.

Trey glanced sidelong at Reagan. In all of his "conquests," he'd never once considered what it would be like to have to answer to them once he settled on a more permanent relationship. It had never even entered his thoughts. He kept waiting for Reagan to get upset and tell his man-whore self to get lost, but she brushed it off with no problem.

"He keeps hinting that he has some talent with the thing but hasn't proven it yet." Reagan stifled a yawn. "I'm currently unimpressed."

Sed laughed. "Sounds like a challenge. Are you up for it, Mills?" He took another swig of his beer, his eyes fixed on Trey as he tilted his head back and swallowed.

Reagan slid her hand up Trey's thigh and brushed her knuckles over his fly. "Nope. He's not up at all."

The sudden stirring in his groin was about to brand her a liar.

"Eric and Rebekah already claimed the bedroom," Trey reminded her. "Not enough room in my bunk to do a good job."

"You better put your name on the bedroom sign-up sheet for tonight. And put your tongue where your mouth is."

He tilted his head to one side as if perplexed. "Isn't my tongue *always* where my mouth is?"

She grinned and took a drink of her beer. "You know what I meant. Back your claims with some evidence."

"Sed," Brian called from the adjacent living area. "Jess says you owe her five orgasms for that comment about her getting fat. She also claims to love you for some reason and says she will talk to you later."

Sed grinned. "She still hasn't figured out that I sometimes say shit to piss her off so she'll 'punish' me." He finger quoted punish. "Making that woman come is a privilege, not a punishment."

"When's the wedding?" Reagan asked.

Sed lifted his brows and stared at the ceiling as he made a mental calculation. "Eighty-seven days."

"Are you doing anything special?"

"Hell if I know. Our mothers are hashing that stuff out. My job is to show up in a tux and repeat some vows. My mom wants to make sure the ceremony is traditional and momentous. Jess's mother wants it to be Hollywood's social event of the year. So Mom's taking care of most of the wedding stuff, and her mother's taken over plans for the reception. I don't have a clue what's really going on. I'm glad I'm on tour right now and can avoid most of the bullshit."

"I think Jessica is ready to elope," Trey said. "She seems pretty stressed out about it all."

Sed paused with his beer bottle halfway to his mouth. "I should probably jump on that opportunity, but then she'd get pissed that I didn't let her have her huge wedding."

Sed knew how to handle his fiancée without her even knowing she was being handled. Which was good, because if Jessica knew Sed made a concerted effort to keep her either placated or riled, that would have really pissed her off. The guy was smarter than he looked.

"I'm never getting married," Reagan said. "I mean, what's the point? I guess if you want to raise kids together…" She glanced at Trey. "What do you think?"

Trey shifted uncomfortably in his seat. "Well, I guess it depends. My parents have been happily married for over thirty years."

"Mine too," Sed said.

"Then you have Eric's parents. He doesn't even know who his father is. His mother dumped him off when he was a little kid. I don't think a marriage would have made a bit of difference in that situation. I still don't know a thing about Jace's family situation other than his parents are both dead. And then there's Brian, whose parents get along okay, but their parenting skills could use a complete overhaul." He glanced over his shoulder at Brian, who was sitting in one of the captain's chairs now, staring off into space. "Some people should be married. Brian should be married. Other couples? I'm not so sure."

"I think it's important," Sed said. "With the right woman, of course."

"Eric and Rebekah rushed into it, but they work. I think it was inevitable between the two of them. And then Jace…" Trey's gaze shifted to their quiet bassist. "He asked Aggie to marry him and she said yes, but they don't seem to be in any hurry to make it official. So yeah, it depends. I don't think all couples have to get married or even should get married. Though it would be nice if all kids had a nice stable home to grow up in."

"Single parents can do a good job too," Reagan said.

Inwardly cringing, Trey wrapped an arm around her stiff body. He'd forgotten that she'd been raised solely by her father. "I didn't mean to suggest that they couldn't. Why are you thinking about marriage?"

"Everyone keeps talking about it." She turned her face into his shoulder. "It's not my favorite subject, trust me."

"So if I asked you to marry me, you'd say no?"

She looked up him, her eyes wide. "You wouldn't!"

"You're right. I'd never ask a woman to marry me before she got to experience the power of my tongue piercing."

She laughed and relaxed into his side. Yeah, the marriage talk made him uncomfortable too. He was glad they were on the same page again. Trey's phone rang. He discreetly slid it out of his pocket and was careful to hide the screen from Reagan as he checked who it was. If it was one of his exploits, he wouldn't answer. He was surprised to see Dare on caller ID. Not that his brother didn't call him on a regular basis, but he'd just seen him that morning, so he wasn't likely calling to shoot the breeze.

"What's up?" Trey answered.

"Is Reagan there?" Dare asked.

"Nope, left her passed out in the jet's bathroom."

"Let me talk to her. Sam is pissed and I figured I'd better warn her." Sam was Exodus End's manager. Trey was pretty sure that Reagan hadn't even met him yet.

"Why is he pissed?"

"She is his publicity stunt. Hard to publicize her when she's there with you."

"Does she have to go back?"

"Just let me talk to her."

Trey passed the phone to Reagan. "Dare wants to talk to you."

She gave him a puzzled look and accepted his phone. Trey wasn't sure why the thought of her returning to L.A. so soon gave him a sinking sensation in his stomach.

"Give him my number. I'll talk to him," Reagan said. She recited her number for Dare several times to make sure he had it. "Thanks for the heads up." She laughed at something Dare said. "I think I can handle him. Do you need to talk to Trey again?" She smiled at Trey and shook her head at him before telling Dare good-bye and trying to figure out how to end a call on Trey's phone. Trey took his phone and buried it in his pocket.

"Are you going back to L.A?" he asked.

"Not if I can help it. The dude wants to dress me up, take pictures, and do some sort of publicity campaign with Exodus End's hot, new, chick guitarist." She rolled her wide blue eyes at him. "No thank you."

"You're probably going to have to do it anyway."

Her nose curled. "What part of tomboy don't these people understand? I don't like to be fussed over."

"I bet you clean up real nice," Sed said. It was impossible to have a conversation on the bus without everyone knowing about it.

The icy glare she sent in Sed's direction made it perfectly clear that she did not consider his statement a compliment.

"My wife makes hand-embroidered corsets," Jace said. "If you'd like, I'm sure she'd be happy to make you some for your stage attire."

"Wife?" several bus occupants chorused.

"Girlfriend. Fiancée. My woman. Whatever you want to call her," Jace said.

"I'm not sure I have the right figure to pull off a corset," Reagan said.

There was a general mumbling of disagreement, though everyone seemed to have their eyes focused conspicuously elsewhere to avoid her ice-glare.

"What part of hot chick don't you understand?" Trey said. "I think I need to fuss over you more."

Her phone rang and her stomach fluttered with nerves. She pushed against Trey to get him to stand up out of the booth. "I'll take this in the bathroom." She hurried into the small room near the back of the bus and slid the door shut.

Reagan's hands were shaking as she answered the call. She'd pretended to be cool about Exodus End's manager calling, but it was far from the truth. If he was thinking of exploiting her looks, he was going to be sorely disappointed. She didn't have any aspirations to look like the ideal beauty. She just wanted to play her guitar. Sometimes she wished she'd been born with balls.

"Hello?" She hoped her voice wasn't shaking too badly.

"Is this Reagan Elliot?"

"Yes."

He laughed. "I wasn't sure if Dare gave me the right number. He likes to fuck with me. Thinks it's a good time. I'm Sam Baily, your manager. Well, manager by way of Exodus End."

She had a manager. Feeling a tad overwhelmed by all the changes in her life, she closed the toilet lid and sat down. "Dare said you had an issue with me touring with Sinners."

"It's not that I have an issue with Sinners. I just found out you're a woman and I swear I could not have devised a better outcome to that contest. The fans will love it."

"Do you really believe that? It's really hard to get metal heads to take a female guitarist seriously. It might be best to hide me behind the drum kit so they don't know I'm there." She hated that people saw her as female first and musician second. She'd loved that Exodus End had conducted the contest blind. She doubted they'd have chosen her if they'd known she was a woman. And if they had chosen her knowing that, she'd have always wondered if they'd really liked her music or were more interested in her ass.

"Are you kidding, doll? We're going to work this from every angle. The band thinks you have star potential, both as a musician and a performer."

Reagan rubbed her eyebrow with one finger. "They've never seen me perform."

"Something about band practice. Anyway, doll, you need to get back as soon as you can. I'll set up some appointments. Fashion consultant. Hair designer. Makeup artist."

"I'm not really the kind of woman who likes that kind of thing," she said.

"Don't worry. You won't have to pay for any of it."

"I won't be back to L.A. for thirteen days," she said, "and then I'll be rehearsing with the band for the shows. I don't think this will fit into my schedule."

"You'll make it fit, Reagan." His carefree tone suddenly turned hard. "It's in the contract you signed."

She probably should have consulted a lawyer before she'd signed that contract. For all she knew it might say she had to have her brain transplanted into a cyborg body. "Well, you'll have to wait until I get back to L.A. Technically, my contract doesn't start until then anyway."

He paused for a long moment. "Suit yourself. I'll have your itinerary prepared for when you're back. You'd better clear your schedule."

"I should thank you for coming up with that contest. I'm not sure how you got the band to agree to something like that."

"I can be very persuasive."

Reagan wasn't sure what he meant by that. "Well, in any case, thanks."

"No thanks necessary. Just don't disappoint us."

"I'll do my best."

"Your best plus ten percent," he said. "Call if you need anything to prepare for the tour or if you decide to come back to L.A. early."

After they disconnected, she sat there for a long moment, her heart hammering. How could anyone give ten percent more than their best? Unless they were holding back to begin with. She never held back. She'd be okay. This was her dream. It would all work out. Her best would be good enough. And if it wasn't, she could always find a new job. She made a mean cup of coffee.

She sat there for a long time, wondering if she'd made the best decision in signing with Exodus End and in joining Sinners on tour. This was all a huge change for her. Maybe she'd jumped in a bit too fast. She wasn't sure if she was mentally prepared for this.

A knock at the door startled her out of her musings.

She stood up immediately and slid the door open. "Sorry," she said. "I didn't mean to hog the bathroom." Trey stood on the threshold with a devilish grin on his handsome face.

Instead of letting her exit, Trey urged her back inside the small bathroom and slid the door shut.

"What did he say?" Trey asked. His voice sounded a little off, though she couldn't figure out why. Maybe the acoustics in the bathroom?

She leaned back against the sink vanity and looked up at him. "That when I get back to L.A. they're going to try to turn me into a sex object."

"Does that bother you?"

She lowered her gaze. "I don't know."

"If Sam pressures you into doing something you don't want to do, talk to Dare about it. He knows how to handle Sam. And if Dare won't listen to you, I know he'll listen to me."

He stripped her T-shirt off over her head. She wasn't really in the mood for sex. At least she wasn't until Trey lowered his head and sucked her nipple into his mouth. Something hard flicked over the sensitive tip until she moaned and clung to his hair in surrender. That explained why his voice sounded a little off. He'd put a stud in his tongue for her.

"Are you sure this is a good idea?" she whispered.

He lifted his head, releasing her breast with a loud sucking sound. "I thought you might need a distraction."

Reagan was convinced that Distraction was Trey's middle name. He lowered his head to her other breast and she watched him rub the delightful metal ball near the tip of his tongue over her rapidly hardening nipples. "Trey. Trey," she murmured. "What's your middle name?" She suddenly wanted to know everything about him. His favorite color. His shoe size. Who he took to prom.

Trey lifted his head and grinned at her. "I'm not telling you that. You'll laugh."

"I won't. I promise. I want to know more about you." But not so much that he should stop what he was doing. She clung to his head with both hands and directed his mouth to her breast. He sucked and stroked her tender nipple as his hands moved to the waistband of her pants. Oh God, what would that stud feel like against her clit? She pushed his hands aside impatiently and unfastened her pants, shoving them down over her hips to her ankles and kicking them and her boots aside in one hurried motion.

He lifted her to sit on the edge of the cold vanity. A hard tremor shook her entire body. He began his descent, his mouth moving down the center of her chest. His lips, tongue, and that hard metal ball blazed a trail of pleasure across her skin. Her belly clenched as he suckled and licked his way down her stomach.

"It's Sol," he whispered.

"Soul?" She felt a spiritual connection with Trey. There was no questioning that, but she didn't have any idea what he meant.

"My middle name is Sol. Like the sun."

Reagan giggled.

"I told you that you'd laugh. My dad is incredibly clean-cut and my mom was a flower child. Dad picked out my and Darren's horrible first names, and Mom picked out our ridiculous middle names."

"Darren?"

"Dare," he clarified.

"Oh. But Trey isn't a horrible name."

"Terrance is."

"Nah, it's not bad. At least you weren't named after two presidents."

"If you tell me your middle name is Bush, I'm not sure I'll be able to continue."

"Nope, it's worse than Bush."

"Most things are worse than bush." He drew his fingers through the small triangle of pubic hair on her mound.

She slapped him while stifling a grin. "Naughty."

"So tell me what it is or I won't be able to concentrate. I'll be too busy trying to think of presidents' names. Is it Kennedy? Reagan Kennedy is kind of cute."

"I wish."

"Johnson? That's almost as good as bush." He glanced up at her and actually flushed. "I mean if you like cock. Which I don't. But you probably do."

She covered his mouth with one hand. "It's Eisenhower."

Trey sniggered. "You don't expect me to actually believe that," he said, his words muffled by her hand.

"I'll show you my birth certificate sometime. My father is the quintessential Republican, and my mother couldn't care less what he named me. Can we not talk about our parents? It's a major mood killer."

She moved her hand and pushed his head down gently, wanting to know what magic that tongue jewelry of his was capable of inflicting. This was *not* the sexiest conversation they'd ever had.

"I will never complain about my name again, Reagan Eisenhower Elliot."

"You have no reason to, Terrance Sol Mills."

Trey shuddered. "Now that you know all my secrets you have to stay with me forever."

Reagan laughed and threaded her fingers through his silky hair. "I don't think I could learn all of your secrets in a lifetime, Trey Mills."

"Another reason to stick around." His lips brushed her belly and goose bumps rose to the surface of her skin. "I have some good ones."

He suckled a trail down her lower belly, occasionally drawing the metallic ball in a circle as he made his way to the rapidly swelling flesh between her thighs. When the tip of his tongue flicked her clit, she sucked a ragged breath through her teeth. The anticipation was killing her. He seemed intent on increasing her need rather than alleviating it. His lips moved up to her belly again, sucking a spot just beneath her navel that drove her absolutely insane.

"Trey. Trey," she chanted.

"Hmm?" he murmured against her belly. He traced the rim of her belly button with his tongue, catching the stud on her skin and tugging it in a way that made her head swim. Now if only he'd take that circular tracing a little lower.

Fingers tangled in his hair, she pressed his head downward. He allowed her to direct him where she wanted him, his delightful tongue working against her swollen lips and then between them to her throbbing clit. He latched on with a hard suction and flicked his stud against the sensitive bit of flesh. Orgasm rapidly approached. She fought it, wanting more. It felt so good that she wasn't ready for it to end. She wondered what his tongue would feel like a few inches lower. She pressed his head down again and he released her clit. He changed the way he moved his tongue, tracing the rim of her opening repeatedly and then pressed a bit deeper. Deeper still. The contrast between his softer tongue and that hard little ball had Reagan writhing against his face. He moved a few inches down without her prompting, catching the ball in his tongue on the rim of her anus and tugging repeatedly. No penetration. Just teasing the surface. She shuddered.

Reagan wasn't much into anal play, but even that felt amazing. He nibbled on one swollen labium and sucked it into his mouth, rubbing that wondrous stud along the slick surface slowly at first and then faster, increasing her building excitement with each stroke. He repeated this on the other side and then latched onto her clit again. The flick of tongue sent her over the edge. He slammed two fingers into her pussy as she came, rotating them in wide arcs, working against her clenching muscles.

As her tremors stilled she became aware of her hands gripping his hair and the steady stream of swear words she was shouting into the small room. Her body relaxed against the counter and the mirror at her back. She released his hair and smoothed it with both hands.

"Sorry," she murmured. "I got carried away."

He licked a trail up her belly, his face tilted so he could look at her as he made his way upward. "That's the whole point," he said. He latched onto her nipple, sucking and flicking her favorite bit of metal in the world against the sensitive peak. His fingers began to glide in and out of her body in the same rhythm.

"Can I tell you something?" he asked.

"Yeah. Of course."

"I've never had sex without a condom."

She smiled. "That's good. Very responsible."

"Have you?"

She could feel the heat of embarrassment rise up her face. "Well, yeah, but only with steady boyfriends. After we both got checked out at the clinic, of course. Does that thought bother you?"

He shook his head. "Do you consider me your steady boyfriend?"

Oh, that's what this was about. "Yeah. I suppose I do."

"Do you want to make an appointment at the clinic with me?"

She nodded.

He grinned. "Good, because I forgot to bring a condom again. If this keeps happening, I'm going to end up with a permanent stiffy."

She laughed and hugged him. "I don't think that would be so bad."

Chapter 12

REAGAN COULDN'T KEEP HER hands off Trey. She had watched him from the crowd at numerous Sinners concerts so she knew what to expect, but watching him get ready for the show gave a whole new meaning to the man's stage persona. He inserted hoops and studs into all of his piercings, but removed that glorious one from his tongue that he'd shared with her earlier. He gelled his hair so his bangs covered his eye as usual, but a shorter strip down the center of his head stood on end. She watched him button up a worn plaid shirt and slide into his baggy jeans. She helped him fasten leather cuffs around his wrists and several chains around his neck. He added another pair of silver chains to hang in loops along one hip. Hell, even his white socks in tacky contrast with his black canvas shoes were trademark and reminded her who her boyfriend really was—*the* Trey Mills. A hole in his jeans just inches from his crotch continually drew Reagan's attention. If she stuck her finger in that hole—and she had several times—she could slide her fingers over the black silk of his boxers. Standing backstage, sucking on a cherry sucker, and rocking up on his toes with nervous energy, Trey Mills was a walking aphrodisiac.

"I want you again," she murmured in his ear, grabbing his black leather belt in both hands. It had silver eyelets down its entire length, which gave her ideas. "I want to use this belt to tie you to the bed and tease you for hours."

He popped his sucker out of his mouth and asked, "Which part are you going to tease?"

"Every inch."

"Even my toes?"

"Especially your toes."

"If you're into bondage, we can hit Jace up for some restraints. I think he still has some on the bus."

"Jace?"

"Yeah, he's a badass in the bedroom. He and Aggie even give couples lessons in BDSM when he's off tour. If you really want to get kinky, let me know. I'll schedule an appointment. They have a dungeon in their basement."

Reagan's eyebrows drew together. "I thought Aggie made corsets."

Trey grinned. "She's a woman of many talents. She also dances."

"She's not dancing anymore," Jace said. "Not professionally."

He was so quiet Reagan hadn't even realized he was standing right beside her. Jace's platinum blond hair was spiked. His dark beard stubble stood in stark contrast to his light hair and had been recently trimmed. He wore his usual black leather jacket, white T-shirt, and snug blue jeans. His outfit was made even more biker by his heavy black boots, black leather belt, and the wide studded, leather cuff on his left wrist. She'd never seen Jace wear anything else. She suspected he wore his jacket and boots to bed. In the Sinners concerts she'd been to, Jace always hung to the back of the stage. Now that she knew him a little better, she assumed it was because he was shy. There was an edge to him that she'd never quite understood, but if he was a dom in the bedroom, it made a little more sense. "I suppose you're her one-man audience," Reagan teased.

Jace shuddered and his eyes glazed over. Hot damn, Reagan could only imagine how sexy the man looked when he fucked. As if she wasn't turned on enough by Trey already, she didn't need Jace pushing additional buttons.

"She insisted on having a stripper pole installed in our bedroom," Jace said. "It had nothing to do with me."

"I'm sure it had everything to do with you," Trey said and shoved him in the arm.

So Brian's woman was a sex professor, Sed's looked like a centerfold, Eric's dressed up for him, and Jace's had a pole in his bedroom and a dungeon in his basement. Reagan was dating the most sensual member of the band and he had to find her sexual expertise sadly lacking. He'd be bored with her in a week. She better up her game.

"Hey, Jace," she said, "Trey and I want to schedule a session in your dungeon."

"Trey hates pain," Jace said.

Trey licked his sucker and Reagan was momentarily transported back to the tour bus bathroom and the things he'd done to her with that tongue. "He's right. I'm not a fan of pain."

"Is that all there is to your sessions? Pain?" Reagan asked.

"My sessions?" Jace said. It was too dark to know for sure, but Reagan imagined he was blushing. He did that a lot and it softened that edge of danger in him just enough to make him adorable. "Yeah, I'm pretty much on the receiving end of lots of pain, but there are other things we can show you. Do you want me to text Aggie and see if she has any openings that week we're in L.A.?"

Reagan hoped she sounded confident when she said, "Yeah. I'd like to try it."

Trey wrapped both arms around her and moved her body to face his. He hugged her against him and whispered into her ear. "You're not worried that you aren't adventurous enough for me, are you?"

Was she that transparent? "A little," she admitted.

"I have tried pretty much every sexual thing you can imagine."

Her heart sank. "Oh."

"If you want to try new things, I'm more than willing to participate, but don't do it for my benefit."

"I don't want you to get bored with me."

He smiled and tapped her nose with his sticky sucker. "No chance."

She didn't believe him.

"Well, there is one thing you can do to keep me interested," he said.

She looked up at him, wishing she could see his expression more clearly in the limited illumination behind the darkened stage. "What?"

"Fuck me with the lights on so I can stare into your eyes."

She laughed. "That was almost romantic, Trey."

He tilted his head and she could almost make out his impish look in the darkness. She was familiar enough with it to know how irresistible he looked when he did it. "Would it be more romantic with candles? I don't usually look people in the eye when I have sex with them."

"Why not?"

"Apparently it makes me fall in love with them."

She laughed and patted the center of his chest. "Yeah right, Trey."

"Thirty seconds," someone said from near the stage.

Trey kissed Reagan and pulled away abruptly, reaching for the red and white guitar someone was holding in his direction. He slid the strap over his head, and one of the road crew checked the wireless transmitter that was attached to the back of his guitar strap. A pat on the shoulder and he moved to stand beside Brian next to the stage's steps. Trey said something to him that Reagan couldn't hear and Brian nodded.

Trey slipped a pair of earbuds into each ear and then after a few seconds climbed the steps and trotted across the stage in the darkness. Jace followed him and then Brian ascended the stairs. Reagan moved to stand near the bottom of the steps beside Sed, who was waiting for his cue to enter the stage. Someone handed Reagan a set of earphones. Dave grinned up at her from his wheelchair when she accepted them. She put them on and could hear Rebekah giving out instructions to the band, and then she could hear Eric and Jace start the low-toned intro to Sinners' latest single, "Betrayed." She'd never seen them play this song live. Didn't know what to expect. She was as excited as the cheering crowd in the stadium. Probably more so. She was close enough to touch them. She had touched them. Some of them more so than others.

The curtain dropped and the blinding stage lights flashed on as Brian and Trey entered the song with a pair of solos that complemented one another perfectly. Every band had something that set them apart, and that was Sinners' thing. They had two amazing guitarists—Brian who played like he was soloing constantly, and Trey who either complemented him by enriching Brian's soloing style with intricate pieces of his own or underlying it with more subdued rhythmic sounds that focused even more attention on Brian's wailing melodies. Reagan had always been a fan of Master Sinclair. It was a shame she'd never noticed how empty his guitar work would sound without Trey backing him. A strange feeling of pride suffused her as she watched Trey play on the opposite side of the stage from where she stood. She needed to get closer. Sed patted her shoulder and she started. She looked up at him and found him grinning at her. Since when did Sed Lionheart have dimples? She had no idea what he was grinning at her for. Maybe he thought it was funny that she was drooling over her own boyfriend, but whatever it was, the opportunity to ask him vanished when Rebekah said, "Sed, in three seconds," in Reagan's headphones and Sed took the steps to the stage.

When Sed jogged across the stage, singing the first lyrics of the song, the entire crowd roared their approval. Had Reagan been in the crowd, she'd have been screaming right along with them, but as it was, she couldn't take her eyes off Trey. When he fingered his fret board, she envisioned those talented fingers on her. In her. When he bounced on his toes rhythmically, she imagined him driving his cock deep into her body. When he started to sing backup vocals, she remembered what his cries of pleasure sounded like in her ear when he came. She was halfway to orgasm before they reached the end of the first stanza. She never would have guessed that watching the man perform would get her so worked up.

The guitar solo in this song was one of Sinners' amazing dueling pieces. Brian climbed up on the ego riser at the center of the stage and Trey joined him. The pair leaned against each other as they played, and Reagan's thoughts raced in all sorts of inappropriate directions. The pair of them played together perfectly. It was almost as if they were making love to each other with music. Erotic thoughts swarmed Reagan's mind. If they just turned their heads toward each other, they could kiss. Holy hell that would be hot. At the end of the solo they stepped away and returned to opposite ends of the stage. Their spell over her broken, Reagan wondered where those thoughts had come from. She'd never thought watching her boyfriend make out with another man would be sexually stimulating. What was it about Trey and Brian that had her heart pounding?

Sed entered the song again and an unexpected twang alerted the guitar technician, and anyone else paying attention, to a snapped guitar string. Jake grabbed a replacement instrument and switched it out with Brian before Reagan had even comprehended what happened. With only a few notes missed, Brian got right back into the song on a different guitar, while Jake hurried to remove the pieces of the broken string and replace them with a new one so Brian could get his preferred instrument back as soon as possible.

Before the show, Reagan had followed Jake around learning all she could about how the equipment was managed for well-known bands. She'd been particularly excited to find out she wouldn't have to tune her own guitars or replace the strings. Technicians would do that for her. She was liking this gig more and more.

The song ended and the crowd erupted in cheers. While Sed did his usual thing and talked to the crowd about how great they were, Trey headed to his microphone for a little crowd interaction of his own.

"This crowd is hot tonight," Trey said.

Someone in the audience yelled something that Reagan couldn't hear. Trey apparently heard it though, because he chuckled and said, "I won't argue with that, sweetheart." His deep voice sounded even sexier echoing through the enormous, jam-packed stadium. Reagan was so going to jump his bones the second the performance ended. If he didn't stop looking so freaking irresistible, she might not make it that long.

Sinners segued into their crowd favorite, "Twisted." They usually ended a show with that song. Sinners' show had evolved since she'd last attended one. Reagan was stunned when Jace took the ego riser and played a bass solo in the middle of the song. The crowd ate up every minute of it. Reagan couldn't take her eyes off Trey even then. Maybe he looked so good to her while up onstage because they'd spent the last couple of hours apart. Or maybe it was the way he played a guitar like he wanted to have sex with it. That guitar didn't know how lucky it was, but Reagan did.

Reagan didn't think her heart rate returned to normal for the first thirty minutes of the band's set. Near the end of the sixth song, someone moved to stand beside her. She turned and instantly recognized Sinners' ex-bass-player Jon Mallory.

He tugged her headphone back and said in her ear, "Hey, cutie. You look lonely."

"That will be remedied as soon as Trey's finished."

Jon grinned. "So you're Trey's hook-up for tonight."

Reagan wasn't sure why that little statement made her spitting mad. "I'm Trey's hook-up every night."

Jon chuckled. "Sure, sweetheart. Whatever you need to believe to remove you from your panties."

"Fuck off," she said and shoved his hand from her headphone.

He shrugged and someone handed him a bass guitar. Reagan watched him in confusion until she saw a white baby grand piano rise from the center of the stage with Jace at the keyboard. Jon played bass in this song while Jace played piano. How could she have forgotten that? Eric's voice singing the chorus was another unique part of this amazing song. During Jon's entire short time onstage, he tried to upstage the rest of the band. Reagan wasn't sure why they didn't push him off the stage and into the pit, but Jon's three minutes of fame (or idiocy) ended quickly and Jace was back on bass by the guitar solo.

Jon paused next to Reagan on his way offstage. He pulled back her headphone again and said, "I'm finished now if you don't want to wait for Trey. Or we can get in a quickie and he'll never even have to know about it."

"Are you fucking serious?" she asked.

"Jon, leave Reagan alone," Jake said, his blond mohawk looking somehow threatening in the alternating colors of the stage lights. "If she doesn't kick your ass, I will."

"No respect," Jon said. Some girl in the audience standing on the floor near the end of the barrier gate waved at Jon. She flashed her tits at him and he lifted his guitar strap over his head. "Never mind. I've found my own good time."

He handed his bass guitar to Reagan, who had no idea what to do with it, and sauntered over to the giggling fangirl who'd caught his attention. Jake took the guitar from Reagan and she returned her attention to the stage wondering how much she'd missed while Jon had distracted her.

The next song was Sinners' new ballad, "Fallen." It was common knowledge that Trey wrote the song about his addiction to painkillers and his recovery. It had never occurred to Reagan that Sinners' two ballads had both been written by her boyfriend until that moment. He truly was a sensitive soul. Intermixed with that unmistakable naughty streak. Near the middle of the song, Trey took the mic and recited a soliloquy in a somber tone.

"Sometimes when your world crashes down from above and you think there's no way to claw yourself out of the rubble of your life, a hand reaches for you. Finds you. Drags you from the depths of despair and refuses to let you go." Trey looked across the stage at Sed. Reagan felt the emotion behind Trey's words in her chest. Tears sprang to her eyes and the lights blurred. When Trey and Sed sang the chorus in a perfectly harmonious duet, the tears started to fall. She didn't even try to stem the flow. She couldn't remember the last time a song had touched her so deeply. With a few words spoken before a crowd of thousands, Trey held her heart. Completely.

Four songs and two encores later, the lights went down for the last time. The second Trey stepped off the stage, Reagan pounced on him. He was always sexy, but watching him onstage had saturated her panties and reinforced her love for him. "I don't think I've ever wanted you this badly."

"Oh yeah?" he murmured close to her throbbing ear. Even with the headphones the music had been loud.

She grabbed two fistfuls of his T-shirt and started walking backward, too fixated on Trey to even care if things were in her way. "I don't even need foreplay."

He chuckled and gave her a kiss on the temple. "I'm going to go take a shower in the dressing room before we head out."

"Can I join you?"

"Next time. We have an appearance at a mall tomorrow, so we need to leave as soon as possible. Even before the equipment is packed up. I need to hurry."

"So take a shower on the bus. Preferably after we spend a couple hours in the back bedroom. Unless Eric and Rebekah…"

"Rebekah is riding on the other bus tonight. She has to help tear down the sound equipment. That bedroom is all ours. Why don't you go change the sheets on the bed?"

Reagan scowled. "Are you rejecting me?"

He laughed. "Not in a million years, baby. I just need to cool down a little."

"I like you hot."

"Do you like me having heat stroke? I need too cool off. I'm so overheated I'm nauseous."

She wanted him desperately and it was as if he'd totally lost interest. "Fine, go take your shower."

He kissed her gently and left her standing in the corridor outside the dressing room. She crossed her arms over her chest and stared at the closed door. If she didn't know better, she'd think he was avoiding her or hiding something from her. He probably just needed a moment to himself. And that's all he was getting. A moment. If he wasn't on the bus by the time she changed the sheets, she would drag his wet, naked body to the bus no matter how much he protested.

"Real classy, Reagan," she said to herself as she shuffled toward the bus, not sure why she was off to change the sheets without his assistance. The guy already had her wrapped around his finger.

Chapter 13

TREY CLOSED THE DRESSING room door and leaned against it. He'd like to say he was surprised to see the gorgeous, naked man waiting for him, but he wasn't. It's the reason why he'd had to talk Reagan into going to the bus without him. Jake had alerted him to this situation right after the show when Trey had handed his guitar to him. If it had been a woman waiting for him in the dressing room, he would have brought Reagan in to make sure his past lover knew that he was serious, but since it was a guy... Well, Reagan didn't need to know this man rocked Trey's world every time he came to Topeka.

Trey had spent the hours Reagan had been learning about guitar technicians contacting his usual Topeka entourage and telling them not to come backstage. He'd even taken their names off the guest list. He wasn't sure how Xavier had managed to get past security.

"Can't do this tonight, Xavier," Trey said.

Xavier pouted. "What are you talking about? We do this every time you come to town."

"I'm in a relationship right now. Put your clothes on." Trey stared at the floor, not wanting to look at Xavier's lean body or admit that it turned him on.

"A relationship? What kind of a relationship?" Xavier asked.

Trey forced himself to look into Xavier's dark eyes. "A serious one."

Xavier chuckled. "You don't do serious relationships, Trey. If you did, I wouldn't be satisfied having you only a few nights a year."

"Don't make this harder than it has to be. Get dressed and leave so I don't have to call security."

"Now you're threatening to call security? You don't have to make up stories to get me to leave. If you're no longer attracted to me, just say so."

The problem was Trey was still attracted to him and knowing that he couldn't have him made Trey want him even more. The man had the most luscious and sensual lips on the planet. Trey could almost feel them against the back of his shoulder and at his nape. And Xavier's hands. His firm grip always stroked Trey to orgasm within minutes. Trey tried looking anywhere but at Xavier's proud, rigid cock, but his eyes seemed to have a mind of their own. Trey wanted to be possessed by this man, not in the spiritual way that Reagan possessed him, but the physical way that she couldn't.

Xavier approached slowly. He moved like a cat, his graceful limbs drawing him across the room in long, fluid strides. A long-distance runner, Xavier had a lean, athletic build that made Trey's belly quiver. "Why do you lie to me, Trey Mills? I see the way you look at me. I know you want me."

Trey shook his head. "I am in a relationship," he said. "Reagan is... Reagan is... Reagan..." Xavier was standing so close that Trey could feel his body heat, smell the mix of aftershave, cocoa butter, and arousal on him. His dark skin looked so warm and smooth and inviting, especially the hard cock situated inches from prodding Trey in the belly.

"A woman?" Xavier laughed. "And you are monogamous with her? This woman?"

Trey nodded.

"How long have you been together with her?"

Trey almost didn't want to admit the truth. He'd only been with Reagan a short while and he was already craving some man-on-man action. It didn't help that Xavier was one of his favorite lovers, and he usually looked forward to their times together. "Three days."

Xavier cupped Trey's face and ran his thumb over his cheek. "So new. How sweet. I will wait for you to return to me next time. I am a patient man, but also logical. A man who likes cock as much as you do will never survive a monogamous relationship with a woman."

"I really care about her," Trey said. He did. Xavier was wrong. Trey would make it work with Reagan. He just needed someone to keep the naked men out of his dressing room and things would go much better. Out of sight, out of dirty mind.

"She's a lucky woman. You should tell her I said that."

Not in ten million years.

Trey slid around Xavier's tall body and headed for the connecting bathroom. "I expect you to be gone by the time I'm done showering."

Xavier groaned. "You test a man to his limits, Trey. That might be why I'm so in love with you."

Trey picked up Xavier's discarded shirt and tossed it at him. "Now who's making up bullshit stories?"

"Believe what you must."

Trey entered the bathroom and locked the door. He wasn't sure if he'd locked it to keep Xavier out or to keep himself from inviting him in. Trey had to take a shower though or Reagan would know he was keeping things from her. He wanted to be completely honest with her about everything. Well, except for his past attraction to men. She didn't need to know about that, but everything else... completely honest. He was still trying to convince himself that he was being honest with Reagan when he finished his shower and found, with a strange mix of relief and disappointment, that Xavier had done what he'd asked and left.

He wasn't prepared to find Reagan waiting for him outside the dressing room door. Had she seen Xavier leave? That was bound to bring up all sorts of questions he wasn't prepared to answer.

"Feel better?" she asked in a clipped tone.

Shit. She knew about Xavier. Why else would she be pissed off at him?

"Not really. I'm clean now, but I need some alone time with my woman to alleviate the rest of the heat in my body."

He drew her against him and kissed her, hoping that he could distract her enough to make her forget all those questions that must be swarming around in her mind.

She pulled away. "Is there a woman in there?" she asked. "Is that why you tried to get me out of the way?"

"A woman?" Trey said, feigning astonishment. "Of course not. Don't you trust me?"

"You're not acting very trustworthy," she said, wrapping her arms around her body to shut him out. "I can't think of any other reason why you'd want to get rid of me so quickly after the show."

"I didn't want to get rid of you." He went to the dressing room and pulled open the door. "Go ahead and have a look. There are no women there."

She didn't look inside. She turned and started walking down the corridor as fast as her legs could carry her.

Trey jogged to catch up with her. "Why are you mad?"

"If you're going to cheat on me, break up with me now, Trey," she said, her eyes trained on the door that led outside. It was as if she couldn't get away from him fast enough.

"I'm not going to cheat on you, Reagan."

"Because trusting someone and having them cheat on you? It fucking rips your heart out." She slammed the door open with both hands, startling several of the crew who were loading things into the semitrailer outside.

Trey finally caught up with her at the bottom of the tour bus steps. He grabbed her by both arms and turned her to face him. His heart gave an unpleasant lurch when he saw the tears swimming in her eyes.

"Reagan," he said, "don't be upset. I wasn't cheating on you. I wouldn't do that. If it came to that, I would break up with you first. Okay? I promise."

She covered her face with both hands. "Don't look at me. I can't stand for people to see me cry."

He tugged her against his chest and she buried her face in his shirt. "I can't see," he said, rubbing her back with both hands. "I don't understand why you're so upset about this though. I swear nothing happened."

"You're hiding something from me. I know you are."

"I'm not." He hated to lie, but damned if the truth wouldn't hurt her more. He was serious about not cheating on her. He would never do that to anyone, especially not someone he cared about as much as he did Reagan.

"You are, Trey. I know you're not telling me something. I'm not stupid." Her arms went around his back and she drew him closer. "Just tell me. Even if it hurts. I want to know."

"The truth?" *Half-truth.* "You're right." She made a pained sound in the back of her throat, but he pushed on with his explanation. "There was someone waiting for me in my dressing room. I didn't go in there to fool around with them. I went in there to get rid of them. Okay? Every city I go to, I have several people who are used to hooking up with me after a show. It's going to take a while for them all to realize I'm not available anymore. That I have a girlfriend now and I'm not interested in them."

"So you *were* trying to get rid of me earlier."

"I was trying to avoid hurting you, Reagan. I had no intention of cheating on you and I didn't. I just didn't want you to have to deal with a jealous ex-lover."

She looked up at him and smiled in relief. "Thanks for telling me the truth."

Half-truth.

"You can tell me these things, Trey. I'd rather know than have you hide them from me."

"Okay. Next time something like that happens, I'll tell you." But there were things he couldn't tell her. If she was this upset over finding out that he hadn't cheated on her, how would she react if she knew the person who'd been waiting for him in his dressing room hadn't been a woman as he'd led her to believe, but rather a man?

Chapter 14

REAGAN WASN'T EXACTLY AN early riser, but the members of Sinners slept most of the day away. She supposed she'd have to get her sleep cycle more in sync with the up-all-night, sleep-all-day lifestyle of the average rock star, but for now she was wide awake at seven a.m. and the bus was still and silent. Trey was snoring softly beside her. He'd earned his sleep after the hours of pleasure he'd gifted her the night before. It was almost as if he was trying to prove something or make up to her for some wrong that he continued to deny. Not that she was complaining. The man was a phenomenal lover. She believed that he hadn't cheated on her, but she wondered how long it would be before he did. The opportunity was always there. It would be so easy for him to give in to temptation. She'd just have to trust him. No matter how scary that thought was. Ethan's cheating had ripped her apart inside, and she didn't care for an encore. But if she wanted to be with Trey, and she did, she knew she couldn't spend every moment they were apart seething with suspicion.

Reagan inched toward the edge of the mattress, trying not to disturb Trey as she got up. She had to pee and a shower sounded like a little piece of heaven, but Mr. Cuddles apparently had some extrasensory perception of when his bedmate was about to vacate the premises. Trey's arm wrapped around her waist and he tugged her against him, spooning up against her back and tangling her in his arms and legs until she was trapped. He murmured something unintelligible against her hair. She relaxed into his warm body and told her protesting bladder to shut up. This was nice. There was no place she'd rather be. She gently stroked the skin on his forearm, concentrating on the rhythm of his breathing. She could have lain like that for hours. If she hadn't had to pee so bad.

She carefully untangled her body from his and hurried out of bed. He lifted his head off the pillow and blinked at her. "Where you going?" he asked, his voice slurred with sleep.

"To the bathroom."

"You coming back?"

"How long are you going to stay in bed?"

"Depends on if you come back." He grinned at her and dropped his head on her pillow, burrowing into it and inhaling deeply. "I already miss you."

No wonder he got anything he wanted. He was so sweet and unashamed of it. He wasn't manipulative, exactly. Persuasive. That's what he was. "I'll be back," she promised as she slipped into her discarded panties. She'd thought about getting some guitar practice in and working on the technique Brian had shown her on the plane, but spending the day in bed with Trey sounded a lot more entertaining. She was a little disappointed that Brian had left immediately after the show and would be gone until they played in Saint Louis the next night, but she understood that his family obligations came before indulging a fangirl guitarist with lessons on his grandeur.

Reagan put on her clothes from the day before but rummaged around in her suitcase until she found everything she needed for a shower.

"Looks like you plan on doing more than going pee," Trey said.

"I'm going to take a shower." She was sticky with cum. Trey had used condoms the night before, but he'd peeled them off at the last moment and spurted on her belly. Her back. Her ass. Her breasts. Probably other places too. She'd lost track. At the time, it had been incredibly sexy, but now she needed to feel clean.

After her quick shower—there was a limited supply of water on the bus—she found her purse in the dining area and checked her phone for messages. Her father had called and left a message. "I spent all day Sunday wondering if you're alive or dead." She had meant to call him. She made it a habit to call him every Sunday, but so many things were happening that it had slipped her mind. He would probably be at work, but she'd leave him a message so he knew that she was safe. He'd never wanted her to leave Arkansas. He'd been convinced that she couldn't take care of herself. Or maybe he'd been more worried that there'd be no one to take care of him anymore. She'd taken over the role of domestic goddess when Mom had left. Cooked, cleaned, did the laundry. She sometimes worried that Daddy ate canned tuna every night and wore dirty socks, but she also knew that she had to make her own life. Catering to her father for twenty-one years had been long enough.

She was surprised that he answered when she called.

"Is everything okay, Reagan?" he asked gruffly.

Her heart started to pound. She already knew that Daddy wouldn't approve of her going on tour with a rock band. Of making her dream to become a professional guitarist a reality. If he had his way, she'd have become a concert cellist in some orchestra. Yawn.

"Everything is wonderful, Daddy," she said, her voice giving away none of the anxiety in her chest. She wanted him to be proud of her. She didn't want to listen to him berate her for having dreams that did not match his. "I have some exciting news."

"I thought you were dead. Or worse. Strung out on drugs."

"I don't do drugs," she said flatly. He was big on stereotypes. "I did win a contest."

"A music contest?" He actually sounded excited.

"Yeah."

"So you're going back to cello?"

"No, it wasn't an orchestral contest. It was a rock guitarist contest."

Silence. She could picture the look of displeasure on his face. She'd seen it enough times.

She pressed on. "I've been selected to be the rhythm guitarist for Exodus End while they tour the US and world this year. This is an amazing opportunity for me."

More silence.

"So if I forget to call you, I'm probably doing drugs or sleeping around with tattooed freaks or showing off my ass on stage."

More silence.

Something, Dad. Say something.

"I've got to go," she said after a long moment of listening to silence.

"Be careful, Reagan."

The phone clicked in her ear as he hung up. "I love you, Daddy."

She sank into the booth at the dining table and stared down at her phone. She figured she'd never make the man proud. She might as well let that dream go. Her cell phone sounded, alerting her to the receipt of a text message. She viewed it without much thought.

You took what's mine, bitch. Don't think you'll get away with it.

She sucked a deep breath into her lungs and erased the message before thinking better of it. She'd probably received the message by mistake. She'd never taken anything from anyone. Why would someone threaten her? She suddenly wanted to talk to Ethan. She dialed his number. He picked up on the first ring.

"Reagan?" His deep voice was groggy with sleep.

"Another late night?" she asked. Her heart was still pounding, but she felt safer just hearing his voice.

"Yeah, lucky me."

"Sorry I woke you."

"I'm glad you called. I've been wondering how you've been. I didn't want to come across as a paranoid, overprotective asshole, so I somehow managed to keep myself from calling you."

"You are paranoid and overprotective."

"But not an asshole?"

"Usually not."

He laughed. "So why did you call? Everything okay?"

"Mostly."

"New boyfriend getting on your nerves already?"

"No. Trey's wonderful. I called my dad this morning. Told him about the tour."

Ethan groaned. "I can imagine how that went."

"And then... I got a strange text message."

"Strange? Strange how?"

"Threatening."

"Someone threatened you?" Ethan no longer sounded groggy. "Who sent it?"

"I don't know. I deleted it. I didn't think to check."

"I can probably get the information from the phone company, but it will take some digging and persuasion."

Ethan's means of persuasion were far different from Trey's methods.

"What time did you get it?" he asked.

"Right before I called you."

"Seven thirty-ish your time."

She nodded.

"Reagan?"

"I'm here. Yeah, around seven thirty."

"I'll see if I can find out who sent it. If you get another one, make sure you don't delete it."

"It scared me," she admitted.

"What did it say?"

"'You took what's mine, bitch. Don't think you'll get away with it.'"

"Probably some jealous ex of your new boyfriend's. It was most likely an empty threat, but I'll still check up on it. Are you still scared?"

"I feel better now." Ethan always made her feel safe. She was thinking she overreacted. She'd never been threatened like that before.

"If you need your bodyguard a couple weeks early, I can fly out. Where are you now? On your way to Saint Louis, right?"

"How did you know?"

He was quiet for a long moment. "I sort of mapped out your entire trip based on the tour dates posted on Sinners' website."

Reagan laughed. "See. You are paranoid and overprotective."

"You can count on it."

"I'll be okay, Ethan. Thanks for being there when I needed you."

"You can count on that too."

Chapter 15

SEVERAL DAYS LATER, STANDING in the dressing room of the venue in Indianapolis, Trey held his cell phone in an iron grip. "What do you mean, you're stuck in traffic?" Trey asked Brian. "We have to be onstage in twenty minutes."

"It can't be helped, Trey. I didn't order a car fire on the interstate in an attempt to annoy everyone."

"If you'd quit fucking running off to L.A. every frickin' night—"

"I have other obligations now, Trey. I know the word 'responsibility' isn't in your vocabulary, but maybe you should think about someone other than yourself for five goddamned minutes."

Trey hated arguing with Brian. The man had a skill for laying on a guilt trip. "I'm not thinking of myself. I'm thinking about those twenty thousand fans who paid to see us perform and who expect us to be onstage at ten o'clock. Not ten thirty. Not eleven. Ten."

"So stall them for half an hour. I'll be there. I'm just going to be late."

"Stall them? What are we going to do? Put Jace onstage to do his knock-knock joke routine?"

"You'll think of something."

Out of the corner of his eye, Trey caught sight of Reagan laughing with (or at) Eric. "You know what? We'll just start without you."

Trey hung up before Brian could say anything else. Trey found Sed drinking a beer with several fans who'd scored VIP passes from a local radio station.

"Brian's going to be late," Trey told him.

"Late?" Sed glanced at the clock. "Like how late?"

"At least thirty minutes."

"Fuck. The crowd will go berserk by then." Sed set his beer down and headed toward the dressing room exit. The last of the opening bands was finishing up their set. Trey knew what Sed's plan was. Try to keep the Kickstart onstage longer. Trey had a better idea. At least he thought it was great. He started after Sed.

One of the fans grabbed Trey's arm. "Is Master Sinclair okay?" she asked, her eyes full of concern.

"Yeah, he's just stuck in traffic. No worries."

By the time Trey caught up with him, Sed was talking to Kickstart's soundboard operator. The guy shook his head and pointed at his watch. Sed wiped a hand over his face and stared up at the rigging over the stage.

Onstage, Kip Forrester, the lead singer of Kickstart, yelled, "Are you ready for Sinners to rock your faces off?"

The crowd roared and then followed Kip in chanting, "Sinners, Sinners, Sinners." He was doing his job as a great opening act by getting the crowd pumped up for the headlining band.

Trey took Sed by the arm and led him to a quieter hallway behind the stage. "If we make them wait an hour before we start the show, they'll probably riot."

"That's what I was thinking. William says there's no way Kickstart can do another encore. Any ideas?"

"Reagan can fill in for Brian."

Sed looked at him as if he'd said, "Reagan can walk on water."

"Just to get us started," Trey clarified. "As soon as Brian gets here, he can take over."

"I don't think our fans will like that much. Most of them come just to see Brian." He paused. "And me."

Sed was never short in self-confidence.

"Do you have a better idea?" Trey asked.

"Yeah, I do. We'll tell Brian he can't go back to L.A. after every show. Put our foot down with him. This is bullshit. I thought he was going to pass out onstage in Saint Louis."

Trey scoffed. "Good luck with that, Sed. He's not going to give up seeing his family for anything."

"I understand where he's coming from, but we only have one more week on the road. He fucking looks like the walking dead. He's stretched too thin and not doing a good job at anything. Not performing. Not taking care of himself or his family."

Even though Trey was pissed at Brian, he didn't like anyone saying bad things about him. Not even Sed. "He's doing his best."

Sed snorted derisively. "You don't really believe that."

"He's just trying to do too much right now."

"And failing at everything. Go see if Reagan is up for this idea. We'll try it. We might have to do the entire show twice, but at least we won't have an out-of-control crowd." Sed rubbed his jaw. "I hope."

Trey grinned, his heart drumming with excitement. "She'll do great. Everyone will love her."

Sed chuckled. "I think you're a tad partial, Trey."

Trey hurried back to the dressing room and found Reagan chattering at Jace, who listened intently to her entire one-sided conversation and nodded occasionally but said nothing.

Trey moved in behind her and wrapped his arms around her waist. He probably should have okayed this plan with her before bringing it up with Sed, but how could she refuse? And if she did, Trey was sure he could get his way with very little effort. He knew she kind of liked him.

Reagan covered his hands with hers and pressed them against her belly, encouraging him to hold her more tightly. "Are you ready to go onstage?" she asked.

"Are you?"

She laughed. "Yeah, I can't wait to do my first show in two weeks. I'm getting anxious."

"I meant are you ready to go onstage tonight?"

She turned around in his arms and gave him a questioning look.

"Brian's going to be late, so I thought you could stand in for him for a couple of songs until he gets here."

"No way! I haven't rehearsed. I'd make a total fool of myself."

"You know all of Sinners' songs. You'll do great."

"Trey, I can't do this."

"I already told Sed you'd do it. Don't make me look like an ass."

Her eyebrows drew together and she pinned him with a heated stare. "You're being one, why not look like one?"

Trey tilted his head just so and held her gaze with his. "Please."

"Don't 'please' me, Trey Mills. That look will not get you everything you want."

"Even if I want to please you?"

Her lips twisted as she tried to suppress a smile, and he knew she was going to cave. "You always please me," she said.

"So you'll do it?" he pressed.

"Sure. Why not?"

He kissed her neck and murmured in her ear, "You're getting the extra-large tongue stud tonight, Reagan Elliot."

"You're supposed to sweeten the deal before I agree to your terms, not after."

"Are you objecting?"

She wrapped both arms around him and stared up into his eyes. "Absolutely not."

"I guess we'd better let the stage crew know there's been a slight change in the show tonight."

Eric tapped Trey on the shoulder. "Uh, Trey, I think Reagan is great and all, but I don't think this is the best idea."

Trey lifted an eyebrow at him. "What would be your best idea?"

"To wait for Brian."

"They're going to hate me, aren't they?" Reagan said. "I'd hate me if I was waiting to see Master Sinclair perform and some tomboy stepped out on stage in his place."

"They'll love you, Reagan. I guarantee it."

Reagan didn't feel right borrowing Brian's guitar without his permission, but his equipment was already tuned up and synced to the amplifiers, so switching out guitars now would have put undue stress on the sound crew. She was excited to get her first real taste of the limelight, but she could hear the restlessness of the crowd. Uneasiness settled in the pit of her stomach. What was she doing here? And why did she always do exactly what Trey wanted her to do? She couldn't even get mad at him about it. Not when she so eagerly did his bidding and then benefited from his happiness. Because a happy Trey was a generous Trey.

Trey rubbed her back and smiled at her. "You ready?"

"Are you sure about this? I don't know 'Betrayed' very well. It hasn't been out very long."

"You played it perfectly five minutes ago."

Yeah, but there hadn't been forty-thousand eyeballs on her five minutes ago. Rebekah gave them their cue to enter the stage, and Trey gave Reagan an encouraging squeeze before he climbed the steps and crossed the stage to its far side. Jace gave her a set of knuckles in the shoulder and followed Trey. Sed, who stood behind her, nudged her toward the stage. She found the taped X on the stage where she was supposed to stand in front of Brian's stomp pad. She knew the notes but had no idea which amplifier she was supposed to switch to and when. This was going to be a disaster. Trey owed her a lot more than a session with his talented tongue to make up for this.

Eric thudded the bass drum and Reagan jumped as if it was a

shotgun blast. Jace's bass line entered and she found proper fingering on the strings of Brian's guitar. Her head started swimming and she realized she had forgotten to breathe. She gasped for air and played the first chord. Bright lights hit her in the face and she winced, but she somehow kept playing. She'd been fooling herself into thinking she was half as good as Master Sinclair. Every slight variation in tone made her cringe. No one else seemed to notice. The crowd, what little of it she could see with the blinding lights in her face, was enthusiastic for the music. They didn't seem to notice that someone else was playing the role of their favorite guitarist. Sed entered the stage and the audience roared their approval. He paced the stage as he sang, lifting his hands to the roof and getting the crowd to mimic his motions.

Reagan glanced across the stage at Trey, who nodded at her in encouragement with a huge smile on his face. Okay, this wasn't so bad. She could do this. Her eyes began to adjust to the bright lights, but the heat coming off them was brutal. Sweat slickened her lower back and the nape of her neck. When the solo approached, she wasn't sure if she should mimic Brian and head for the ego riser at the front of the stage or just stay put and hope the crowd didn't notice Brian had sprung a set of boobs since his last performance.

Trey headed for the front of the stage and nodded his head in that direction to get Reagan's feet moving from where they'd rooted themselves into the stage. She stubbed her toe on a foot pedal but somehow managed not to fall flat on her face as she joined Trey on the ego riser. He leaned against her, just as he did when he played with Brian, and an undeniable connection flowed between them. She'd never experienced anything like it. The feeling of oneness was even more pronounced than the one she felt when they made love. She closed her eyes and let the music carry her away with Trey. She might have been lost in that sweet nirvana forever if a shoe hadn't whacked her dead in the forehead. She faltered and stepped back off the riser instinctually. If Sed hadn't been there to steady her, she would have fallen on her ass. She finished the solo near the back of the stage. Getting hit with a shoe had hurt, but more than that, she felt utterly humiliated. Someone nudged her arm and she opened her eyes to Trey's concerned expression.

"Are you okay?" he mouthed.

She didn't know. She'd suffered far worse injuries falling off skateboards, but this had stung more than her pain receptors. It had stung her pride. The fans didn't want to listen to her play. She didn't blame them. And she was certain Exodus End's fans would react the same way when they saw her trying to replace Max.

The song ended and, without waiting for instructions or looking at anyone, Reagan removed Brian's guitar. She handed it to Jake on her way backstage. She could hear Sed talking to the crowd, but she wasn't really interested in his words. He said something about kicking the ass of whoever threw that shoe. And a bright new talent in the guitar world. Someone to watch out for. Someone to throw shoes at, he meant.

She'd almost made it to the door that led to the dressing rooms backstage when Brian burst through the door and she staggered backwards. He steadied her with both hands.

"They actually started without me? I can't fucking believe this," he said.

"You have nothing to worry about, Master Sinclair. Your adoring audience awaits," she said and jerked out of his grip before racing to Sinners' empty dressing room.

She went straight for her cell phone and dialed Ethan. He was there. He was always there. He listened to her tirade about the entire incident from before the show until the instant she'd called him. And then he listened to the confession of her fears. And then her discourse of self-pity. And finally her indignation at being treated that way for doing someone a favor. After she'd unloaded all of her feelings, Ethan said, "Are you ready to give up and come home then?"

"No, I'm not ready to come home. You don't think one little catastrophe is going to make me give up this dream, do you?"

"Nope, but with all that bitching, I thought maybe you'd changed your mind about what you wanted."

She wished he was there so she could glare at him. "I just needed someone to talk to."

"And where is that wonderful boyfriend of yours?"

"He's onstage right now."

"Does he know you call me every time you have a problem?"

"If you don't want me to call you anymore, I won't."

"I do want you to call me, Reagan. I just wondered if he knew."

"When he's around, the last thing on my mind is my stupid little problems."

"And the first thing on your mind?"

She grinned to herself. "His tongue."

Ethan chuckled. "I bet. So other than getting hit with a shoe, how is everything going? Are you learning how to be a rock star?"

"Not a very good one," she admitted.

Chapter 16

SED HAD ASKED THE entire band to be there when he confronted Brian. They were there, but not a one of them looked the least bit happy about it. Trey felt sick to his stomach. He already knew what Brian would choose. It wasn't them.

Brian yawned as he came out of the bedroom with his carry-on bag slung over one shoulder. He paused when he noticed his bandmates blocking his route off the bus.

"I called and cancelled your flight," Sed said.

Trey wasn't sure if Sed was bluffing, but it seemed a pretty extreme measure even for Sed—king of extreme measures.

"You did what?" Brian asked, his weariness instantly replaced with rage.

"You're not going back to L.A. tonight."

"Get out of my way," Brian demanded.

"You look like shit, dude," Eric said. "We all think you should stay on the bus tonight and get some rest. You can go back to L.A. the day after tomorrow when we have three days between shows instead of just one. And then we have two more back-to-back shows before our week off. You can see them as much as you want then."

"When we're not rehearsing for the new tour," Sed added.

"Don't pull this shit with me right now," Brian said. "It's the last thing I need."

"Could Myrna come see you instead?" Jace asked. "Bring the baby with her?"

"Malcolm is too young to travel." The hopeless look on his face was like a knife to Trey's heart. Trey had been so caught up with Reagan, he'd failed his best friend. Brian shouldered a lot of burden right now and Trey hadn't even bothered to talk to him about it. When had they gone from a friendship where they shared everything to a couple of guys who just hung out with each other very occasionally?

Trey took Brian by one arm and pushed him into the bedroom. He caught Sed's puzzled expression just before he closed the door in his face.

"You're not going to talk me out of leaving," Brian said. "I have to go back tonight. I promised Myrna."

"Does she realize how exhausted you are?" Trey asked. He knew Myrna. She wouldn't want Brian to wear himself down like this.

"I'm fine."

"You're not fine, Brian. You can't keep going like this. Do you want to cancel the rest of the tour dates? I'll side with you no matter what. Just tell me what you want to do."

"I want to hold my son." His hand was trembling when he pressed his fingertips to his forehead.

Then that's what he was going to do. "I'll contact Jerry," Trey said. "Tell him to call off the last three shows."

Brian shook his head. "No. We need to finish out the tour. I can do this for another week."

"And then what are you going to do? We go back on the road just one week after this tour ends."

"You don't think I know that?" Trey felt the crack in Brian's voice in his chest.

Trey sighed. "You can't keep this up, Brian. What does Myrna say about this crazy schedule you're keeping?"

Brian lowered his gaze. "She tries to be strong when I leave. Says she and Malcolm will miss me, but they'll be fine while I'm gone."

"Jessica and Aggie are still helping her out, aren't they?"

"Yeah."

"Dare?"

"Yeah, everyone's great. Maybe they are fine when I'm gone. Maybe what I really want is for them to need me more."

Trey squeezed his shoulder. "Hey. Don't say that. They need you. I know for a fact that Myrna cries when you're gone. She misses you so much more than she's letting on."

Brian's breath caught and he shoved Trey aside as he reached for the doorknob. Trey probably shouldn't have told him that Myrna cried. He grabbed Brian's arm again and hauled him away from the door.

"Trey, I have to go. I'm not going to be like my father. I promised myself that I'd always be there for them both. I'm not going to let them wonder if they're important to me. Or if I love them. I'm going to tell them to their faces every goddamn day."

Now they were making progress. Brian's father had been a famous guitarist while Brian had been growing up. Malcolm O'Neil had used touring as an excuse to ignore his family, and he'd never been there for Brian when he'd needed him. "You're not like your father, Brian."

"But I could be. It would be a lot fucking easier if I was." Brian pressed his fists against his temples and took a deep breath.

"I know you, Brian. You'd give up the band before you'd do that to your family."

"It's crossed my mind."

Trey's stomach dropped. "What?"

"Leaving Sinners."

"You don't want to make music anymore?"

"Yeah, I do. I haven't figured out how to do both. If something has to give…"

Trey didn't want to even think about the possibility. "Have you talked to Myrna about any of this?"

Brian hesitated and then shook his head. Trey took his cell phone out of his pocket and dialed Myrna's number. She answered on the first ring. "Trey? Is something wrong with Brian?"

"No. The band is trying to talk Brian into staying here for the night instead of going back to L.A. He's so burnt out, but he wants to go home."

"I already told him to stay there tonight. Malcolm and I will be fine without him for a couple of days. He shouldn't worry about us so much."

"I know you're being strong for him, Myr, but he needs to hear how hard you're struggling without him so he can be all angsty and depressed, but at least he'll stop trying so hard to prove that he's not going to be like his father."

"Is that what he thinks?" Myrna asked. "That he's going to be a bad father? He's a wonderful father. A wonderful husband. How could he think otherwise? Did I do something to make him feel that way?"

"I don't think so, Myrna." Trey glanced over at Brian who had his arms crossed over his chest and was staring daggers at him. Yeah, it probably wasn't his place to force Brian to talk to his wife, but Trey couldn't stand to see him like this. Brian needed to tell her these things. She could handle it. And Trey needed to keep this band together. It meant everything to him.

"Is he there?" Myrna asked. "Can I talk to him?"

"Yeah, he's here. He's pretty pissed off at me right now, so make sure you remind him that I got in his business because he's being a douche." *And because I love him*, he added silently.

"Thanks, Trey. I'm glad you're there for him. I figured he was having a harder time than he was letting on, but he's always so happy when he's home. I didn't know he was struggling."

Trey handed the phone to Brian. "She wants to talk to you."

He snatched the phone out of Trey's hand. Trey gave Brian's

shoulder a squeeze before he left the bedroom and gave him some privacy.

The guys were still standing in the corridor, watching the bedroom door as if they expected it to explode at any moment.

"Is he staying?" Sed asked.

"Don't know," Trey said. "He's talking to Myrna."

"Are you sure that's a good idea?" Sed asked.

"I'm sure. No matter what he decides to do tonight, we have to support him," Trey said. "Even if that means we have to cancel the rest of the tour."

Sed opened his mouth to speak and Jace elbowed him in the ribs. "You're right," Jace said.

"And we might have to cancel the tour with Exodus End, too," Trey added.

They all looked at him as if he was insane. "You don't mean that, Trey," Sed said. "You know what touring with Exodus End will mean for our careers."

"Yeah, I do. If we push Brian too hard, he'll leave the band. And Sinners isn't Sinners without Master Sinclair."

Chapter 17

BRIAN STAYED ON THE tour bus for the first night since his son had been born. That didn't mean he came out of the bedroom at all or that he talked to anyone about their "baby intervention." He was probably still talking to Myrna on the phone. Or sleeping. Reagan was still pissy about what had happened onstage. Trey couldn't blame her. He was still pissy about it himself, mostly because she couldn't see how wonderful she'd been and could only think about some asswipe hitting her with a shoe. She was sitting on the sofa talking to Jace about nothing again. Trey wasn't sure why she prattled off at him on a regular basis. Probably because he was such a good listener. Or maybe because he seemed a little lonely now that Eric spent all of his time with Rebekah. Trey was sure Jace missed Aggie, but he never complained or let it show. Jace never complained about anything.

When Trey got sick of watching Eric and Rebekah play kissy-face across from him in the dining booth, he stripped down to his silk boxers and went to collect his woman. He was fine with her being pissy. He was not fine with her ignoring him.

"I'm going to bed. Are you coming?" he asked her.

"Brian's in there," she reminded him.

And truthfully, he'd rather join Brian than cuddle up to an angry woman all night, but if they didn't get this all out in the open, it was going to bite them in the ass later.

"I meant in my bunk."

"You expect me to squeeze in there with you?" She looked down the hall anxiously.

Trey rested his hands on his hips and stared at the ceiling. He wasn't having the best night of his life either. He'd thought one reason for having a steady girlfriend was so you could share this kind of thing with her.

"Forget it," he said.

Reagan grabbed the sofa arm when Jace tried to shove her off the couch. "Go to bed," Jace insisted, as if she'd annoyed him beyond his last shred of tolerance.

"Don't push me off the couch," she said, punching him in the shoulder.

"Then sit there quietly. You're giving me a headache."

"Jace," Reagan admonished.

"Me too," Sed agreed. He was sitting across from them in one of the captain's chairs, periodically glancing toward the bedroom door for signs of Brian, but otherwise sitting in gloomy silence holding a half-finished beer on his knee. Trey knew a Sed guilt-trip when he saw one.

"You guys are jerks," Reagan said.

"I'm going to bed," Trey said. "Do what you want."

He walked down the corridor and climbed into the top bunk on the right side before he tugged the curtain shut. As if he could actually sleep with his mind so full. He stared into the darkness for at least thirty seconds before a hand smacked him in the face as Reagan looked for a handhold to boost herself into the bunk with him.

He grabbed the back of her shirt and hauled her up. Much squirming ensued until they settled on their sides facing each other. He switched on the small dome light in the corner so he could see her more clearly. She looked close to tears.

He stroked her hair from her face. "What's wrong, Reagan?"

"I'm not sure if I'm ready for this."

His heart sank. "Our relationship?"

Her eyes widened and she shifted closer. "No, not that. Is that what you thought was bothering me?"

Now she stroked his hair from his face.

"I wasn't sure," he said. "You haven't talked to me since you stormed offstage."

"I haven't?" She hugged him. "I'm sorry. I guess after I unloaded on Ethan, I didn't have much else to say."

"Ethan? You talked to him about it?"

"Yeah. I called him earlier."

"So you go to Ethan with your problems instead of me?"

"I've known Ethan a lot longer than I've known you, Trey. Depending on him is a habit, I guess. I can unload on you for the next forty-five minutes if you really want me to."

He cringed. "How about you give me a summary?"

She stared at him for a long moment. "I'm not sure if I can take too many more shoes to the face," she said. "I know I'll have to win the fans over, but when I was up there I felt... I don't know. Not good enough."

"I never feel good enough. You sort of get used to it after a while. Why do you think Brian gets so worked up before a show?"

"Brian does?"

"I guess it's not as obvious with his comings and goings recently. He turns this odd shade of green and starts twitching uncontrollably. He gets a horrible case of stage fright every time we perform."

"Why would he be nervous? He's phenomenal."

Trey kissed the tip of her nose. "So are you."

She laughed. "You have to say that. You're my boyfriend."

"The crowd was stunned by your appearance, but you missed all the cheering they did for you after you ran off."

"They cheered for me?"

"Yeah, of course they did. You were awesome."

"Then why did they throw shoes at me?"

He kissed her forehead where a light bruise had formed. "*They* was a she. One person. Not everyone. And she was escorted from the stadium." And Trey actually knew that she. He'd texted her three hours before the show to tell her that he would not be available for her entertainment that night. He wondered if Reagan needed to hear that. Maybe it would make things easier for her. Or maybe it would make her angry with him. Only one way to find out. "I think she was more jealous that you were with me than anything."

"You knew her?"

Trey cringed. "She's a regular hook-up. Or was. I told her otherwise earlier today."

"So she didn't bean me with a shoe because I sucked. She beaned me with a shoe because you dumped her?"

"I think so."

Reagan released a long sigh. "Thank God. Wait. Did you tell her I was your girlfriend?"

"No, but she saw us play together. The way I was feeling when we played that solo had to be expressed all over my face."

She smiled. "That was amazing, wasn't it?"

He nodded. "Nothing like it." Except playing with Brian. He sighed inwardly. Would he ever stop comparing her to Brian? She was so wonderful and he cared about her so much. Maybe it was a compliment to continually measure her against the only other person he'd ever loved, but it wasn't fair to her. Even if she did keep measuring up to his idea of perfect. Well, perfect except for that lack of a penis thing, but there wasn't anything to be done about that. "Feel better now?" he asked. Her body language had shifted from guarded to relaxed, but he wanted to hear her say it.

She nodded. "Yeah, but I do recall someone owing me a session with a talented tongue."

He drew her against him and kissed her. "That I do, baby. That I do."

Chapter 18

USUALLY THE BAND HAD a huge party after their last show of a tour, but Brian was in a hurry to get home to his wife and baby, Sed was ready to start making babies of his own, and Jace looked like he was going to bust out of his skin at any moment. Besides, they were going back out on a new tour in eight days. It wasn't as if they were going off tour for long. Reagan sat on the sofa with her electric guitar, practicing fingerings for Exodus End songs. She knew them all by heart, but as the day that she would debut as their rhythm guitarist drew near, her anxiety grew exponentially. If she hadn't had Trey's constant reassurance, she'd have been lost.

Trey was banging around in the cabinets in the kitchenette, growing more frantic by the moment. After checking each one at least twice, he made his way to the front of the bus. "We have to stop," he told Sed, who was currently driving the bus. "I'm all out of suckers."

"Trey, it's two a.m. and we're in the middle of nowhere. Even if I was willing to stop, and I'm not, there isn't a cherry sucker for a hundred miles."

"I need one. Now."

"You haven't smoked for almost two years now. I'd think you'd be over it by now," Sed said.

"Sweetie, I think I have one in my purse," Reagan said.

He turned to look at her as if she was an angel descended from the heavens. He retrieved her purse from the counter and dropped it beside her.

"You used to smoke?" Reagan asked.

"Yeah, I had to give it up because of my mother."

Reagan lifted her eyebrows at him. "Your mother?"

"She saw me smoking in some music video of ours and called me every hour of every day harping on me until I quit," he said.

Reagan rummaged around in her purse for the sucker she knew was in there somewhere.

"And if he refused to answer, she'd call Brian," Sed said. "And if Brian refused to answer, she'd call me. And if I refused to answer, she'd call Eric. One time she called our manager."

"She's a bit persistent," Trey said.

Reagan laughed and tugged a sucker from the bottom of her purse. "So you traded one vice for another?" A folded up piece of paper fell into her lap when she lifted the sucker to Trey.

"Pretty much. Mom doesn't much care if I suck on suckers all day."

"Did the talent with your tongue come before or after you started with the suckers?" Reagan asked him.

He wriggled his tongue at her, unwrapped his sucker, and stuck it in his mouth. "I've always had an oral fixation."

Reagan started to put the folded piece of paper back in her purse, but she noticed her name written on the outside and it didn't look familiar. She opened it and found a handwritten message inside.

You took what is mine, bitch. Don't think you'll get away with it.

She felt the blood drain from her face and the piece of paper tumbled from her slack grip.

"Reagan?" Trey asked.

She blinked hard and looked up at him.

"You look like you've seen a ghost."

Trey retrieved the piece of paper from her lap and read it. His brow furrowed with confusion. "What's this?"

She snatched the note out of his hand and stuffed it into her purse. "Nothing," she said. "I'll be right back."

She headed to the bathroom with her cell phone in one hand. As soon as she was inside, she called Ethan. As usual, he answered on the first ring.

"Please don't tell me you're not going to be home tomorrow. I miss you like crazy."

"I'll be home. We're already in New Mexico."

"Okay, good. So what's up?"

"I got another message. Well, the same message again."

"Did you get the number this time? I never did get anything out of the phone company. Times like these I wish I was still on the force."

"It wasn't a text message," she said. "It was a note in my purse."

"In your purse? Reagan, that means this is someone close to you."

"Don't you think I realize that?" she yelled and realized how thin the walls were in this place.

"Who could it be? One of the band members? The crew?"

"I don't know. I don't even know what it means. You took what's mine. I haven't taken anything from anyone."

"It still sounds like a jealous ex-lover to me, Reagan. Maybe you should ask Trey if he's dated any psychopaths."

"Ha ha, Ethan. Will you be serious?"

"I am serious. Did you tell him about the last message?"

"No."

"This one?"

"He saw it, but I played it down."

"Maybe it's a practical joke. One of the guys messing with you the way guys mess with each other. Maybe the joker didn't realize how inappropriate it is."

"Maybe," Reagan said. Eric did have a strange sense of humor. Maybe he was behind it. It didn't seem like something he'd do though. Put saran wrap over the toilet bowl, yes. Send threatening messages to his bandmate's girlfriend, no.

"Well, stay close to Trey. Let him know you're worried about it. Bring the note to me tomorrow and I'll see if I can find any telling clues."

"Thanks, Ethan." Just talking to him made her feel safer.

"See you tomorrow."

She hung up the phone and left the bathroom to find Trey standing just outside. "So what did Ethan say?" he asked.

Caught. Reagan swallowed and decided to take Ethan's advice. "He said to tell you that I'm worried about this and that this isn't the first time I've gotten this message since I started dating you."

"What?"

"I got a text message a little over a week ago. Said the same thing."

"Why didn't you tell me someone was threatening you?"

"Because I wasn't sure it was real. I can't deny that it is now. That note had my name on it. It was in my purse. The message was exactly the same. Eric wouldn't pull a prank like that, would he?"

Trey shook his head. "Not his style. It's not funny."

"I was afraid you were going to say that."

"When did you get the last message?" Trey asked.

"The morning I called my father." She hadn't told him about that either. "Um, after your first concert in Topeka."

Trey nodded. "I'll make some calls in the morning. See if I can find out anything. We have no way of knowing for sure how long that note's been in your purse."

She took a deep breath and nodded. He stepped closer and hugged her. "I can protect you, you know. You don't have to keep going to Ethan."

"I know. I'm sorry. I don't usually frighten this easily. Something about this sends chills down my spine."

Chapter 19

THE NEXT AFTERNOON, REAGAN slipped into the backseat of Exodus End's limo. The man inside resembled someone's grandfather more than someone who had made a metal band like Exodus End superstars. Sam Baily was talking into his cell phone but looked up and smiled at Reagan warmly when she settled into the seat closest to the door.

"I'll call you back. I have my work cut out for me here," he said and disconnected.

What exactly did he mean by "work cut out for me"?

"So I take it you're Reagan Elliot," he said and reached across the console to shake her hand.

She was half-tempted to say, "who? I just wanted a limo ride," in an attempt to break the ice, but she didn't think this guy fucked around.

"Yes, sir."

"My assistant is dying to get her hands on you. She likes that girly sort of stuff. She'll take you shopping for some decent clothes, get your hair fixed, help you with your makeup." He tilted his head and assessed her more closely. She was five seconds from popping him in the mouth and telling him to go fuck himself. Who did he think he was?

Exodus End's exalted manager, that's who.

"How would you feel about getting breast implants?" he asked.

She was too stunned to answer at first, and when she finally could speak, the most she could muster was, "No."

"The band would pay for it."

She met his pale blue eyes steadily. "I'm not interested."

"That's too bad." He opened a tan leather folio on his lap and wrote something down. He clicked his pen with finality and closed the folio again. What was he writing? Something about her? Had she totally blown it?

She looked down at her small breasts. Would it be the end of the world if she got a little augmentation? No. But if she ever did get cosmetic surgery it would be because she wanted it, not because someone pressured her into it. "I just want to play guitar."

"That's fine. I thought you'd rather be an asset to the band instead of a liability, but we can't make you do anything you don't want to do."

Having small boobs made her a liability? She didn't know if she should be offended or hurt, so she settled on pissed. "I know I'm a nobody, but that doesn't mean you can talk to me that way."

"Forget I offered." He opened his folio and she half-expected him to pull out a sign that read "reject" and hang it around her neck. Instead he pulled out a thick piece of off-white paper and handed it to her. "That is your itinerary for the next week. Today is reserved for finding you the right look both onstage and in public. The rest of the week you'll be rehearsing for the show. Questions?"

She scanned the sheet but didn't really internalize anything it said. She was still upset about becoming a sex object, or whatever it was this guy was trying to convert her into. "Why are you so fixated on my look?"

"You're an entertainer, Reagan. It comes with the territory."

"I'm a musician."

"In the studio, you're a musician. Onstage, you're an entertainer. Get used to it. It's not up for negotiation."

She stared down at her itinerary for the day. In ten minutes, she had an appointment with a hairstylist. She rubbed a hand over the short hair at the back of her head. Was her twenty-dollar haircut that bad? And why did she need a pedicure? She wore combat boots on a daily basis.

"Reagan?"

She glanced up at Sam.

"Instead of fighting it, try having fun with it."

Easy for him to say. He didn't have to worry about the size of his boobs being a liability.

Chapter 20

TREY STARTED AWAKE WHEN the front door of Reagan's apartment closed. He hadn't meant to fall asleep. He'd been on the phone most of the morning, calling every contact in every city they'd visited in the past two weeks. He wasn't a detective, but no one seemed to know anything about Reagan's threatening messages. Not that he'd been stupid enough to ask them point-blank. He'd been more discrete than that. Trey sat up and rubbed his eyes, wishing he had better news for her. "So how did it go?" he asked her.

"How did what go?" Ethan asked.

Trey pried his eyes open and glanced at the man removing his boots by the door. Great. Just what he needed. To be alone with Reagan's sexy alpha male of a roommate. Trey decided he should head for home. He could catch up with Reagan later. No telling how long her makeover would take, and this guy made him think all sorts of things that had nothing to do with Reagan and everything to do with being fucked. The last time Trey had seen Ethan, it had been days since he'd last had a male lover. Now he'd gone weeks without being penetrated and he wasn't sure how strong his resolve was.

"I thought you were Reagan," Trey said and climbed to his feet. "She's not here?"

"Nope. Exodus End's manager took her shopping or something." Trey glanced at the clock and his eyes widened. "Shit, I've been asleep for hours. I figured she'd be home by now."

"Are you going somewhere?" Ethan asked and plopped down

on the sofa. He extended his long, muscular legs and propped his feet on the coffee table, blocking Trey's quickest escape route to the front door.

"I figured I'd better get out of your hair."

"Reagan will think I chased you off. I don't really need her to start harping on me the second she sees me."

"You could tell her I was gone when you got here."

"Sit," Ethan said.

Trey sat.

"How'd she do? Be honest. She always sounded so enthusiastic on the phone, but sometimes she acts that way to cover up her problems."

Trey tilted his head at Ethan. "She has problems?"

"Doesn't everyone?"

"I don't think she was covering up anything. We had a great time. She's amazing. Going to take the world by storm." Trey was just glad he got to be a part of it.

"Does she know about you?"

Trey's smile faltered. "Know what?"

Ethan moved so fast Trey didn't see him coming. He found himself trapped in the corner of the couch with Ethan's hard body against his side and his arm in front of his chest. "You know what I'm talking about. Don't play dumb." Ethan's breath stirred the fine hairs just behind Trey's left ear. He shuddered with longing. "Do you have any idea how often I think about you? What I want to do to you?"

Trey was pretty sure he could guess exactly what Ethan wanted to do to him. And Trey was positive that he'd like it. He pressed a hand against Ethan's rock hard chest and pretended his heart was thudding because Ethan had startled him, not because Ethan offered him exactly what he wanted. He didn't need a man to be fulfilled. Reagan gave him everything he needed.

At least that's what he wanted to believe.

"Back off, Ethan," Trey said.

"Why, Trey? Does it make you uncomfortable when I get in your personal space?"

Trey met Ethan's dark eyes. "Yes," he said. It wasn't a lie. His suddenly constrictive fly was very uncomfortable.

"Are you as hard for me as I am for you?"

"I said back off."

Ethan shifted away, but his hand went straight for the evidence. Trey gritted his teeth and squeezed his eyes shut, trying to think of something to subdue his desire, but all he could think of was being drilled by the hard, hot male beside him.

"It's okay to want me," Ethan said. "I want you too."

Trey grabbed Ethan's hand and shifted it from his crotch to his thigh. "I won't deny wanting you. That doesn't mean I have to act on it."

Trey extricated himself from the couch and hurried to the bathroom, closing the door behind him and leaning back against its solid surface. That fucking jerk. What was his game? Trey rearranged his hard and throbbing cock. He hadn't been this turned on in days. This was not a good sign. He hoped Reagan hurried home. She'd help him get his mind back where it belonged. On her.

Trey washed his face and cupped his hand to take a sip of water from the faucet. He caught his reflection in the mirror and gave himself a stern look.

"You're not going to fuck up this thing with Reagan," he said to his reflection. "So he's hot. So what? You don't need a man in your life." He almost believed that. He absolutely believed that he didn't want to hurt Reagan. He didn't know if what they had together was permanent, but it was the most real relationship he'd ever had. Even his one-sided love of Brian had never been tangible. Not something he could hold on to. He wasn't ready to let her go. Sex with Ethan wasn't worth it. And he knew how she felt about her boyfriend having sex with men. She was very clear that she wasn't accepting of that kind of behavior.

Feeling marginally recovered, Trey exited the bathroom and ran directly into a hard body. Trey backed into the doorsill to give himself an inch of breathing room, but Ethan closed the gap between them.

"What are you playing at?" Ethan asked, his obsidian gaze sending a thrill of excitement down Trey's spine.

"I'm not playing at anything."

"Why are you hiding what you are from her?"

"I'm not hiding anything."

"Denial gets you nowhere with me. I know how much you want me. I see it in your eyes. I held it in my hand."

"Maybe."

The heat coming off Ethan's hard body was feral in nature. Raw energy pulsated from every pore. There was an animal just beneath Ethan's skin and Trey very much wanted to push him to see it unleashed. He couldn't, though. He knew if he did there would be no turning back. This thing with Reagan was beautiful, tender, and loving. This thing with Ethan was hot, wild, and pure lust, but there was nothing of substance there. Fooling around with Ethan would be like all of Trey's other sexual encounters. Wham, bam, thank you, um, sir.

"No maybe," Ethan said.

Strong fingers slid into the hair at Trey's nape and tugged his head back. Ethan shifted and pressed the hard length of his cock against Trey's, which responded by leaping with excitement. "No maybe," he repeated, staring into Trey's eyes with undisguised hunger. He leaned closer, his mouth a hair's breadth from Trey's. "You want to be fucked as much as I want to fuck you."

"Maybe," Trey said. He couldn't deny it. Not with his cock straining against Ethan's. Not with his stance submissive. Not with his breaths coming in excited gasps and his heart thundering in his chest. Two weeks ago he would have shoved Ethan into the bathroom and fought him for sexual dominance, but things had changed. There were things more important to him than mindless fucking. "Unlike you, I put Reagan's feelings first."

Ethan's eyes narrowed. "What does that mean?"

"She told me why you two split. She caught you cheating on her. I won't do that to her."

"Yes you will, because you and I are alike. The soft, loving nature of a woman steals our hearts, but there is something about a hard body that gets our blood pumping. Fuck the consequences."

Trey's breath caught. "So you *are* bisexual. Reagan is convinced that you're…"

"Gay? That's Reagan's way of protecting her feelings. She doesn't want to think I still love her. She wants to think I've discovered my true nature as a gay man. She can live with that. Her realizing she's not enough for me sexually was too hard on her ego. And it will be the same when she finds out about you."

"You still love her?"

"Of course I still love her. You know how wonderful she is. I've never met another woman like her before or since."

"So you're trying to seduce me to come between us."

Ethan chuckled and he touched the tip of his tongue to Trey's upper lip. Trey wasn't quick enough to stop his excited inrush of breath. He was so turned on by this little game of domination that he was already seeping precum. He could feel the slick moisture against his thigh.

"I'm trying to seduce you because looking at you makes my dick hard. I don't have any trouble getting rid of Reagan's boyfriends and I don't do it by trying to fuck them. Honestly," Ethan murmured, the timber of his voice going low, "not many men turn me on, but the moment I laid eyes on you, I knew I had to have you."

Ethan tugged Trey's head back and kissed him. Ethan's lips were strong. They demanded surrender. For a brief instant Trey was so caught up in the moment that he didn't fight, he just felt. It felt good to let go. To let someone take control. But he didn't want this. Sure, *now* he wanted this, but in ten minutes he'd be overcome with guilt and regret. Not worth it.

Trey placed both hands on Ethan's chest and shoved. Ethan stumbled back a step and their lips separated, but Ethan still had a solid grip on Trey's hair, so Trey wasn't exactly free. His attempts at resistance seemed to turn the guy on even more. An instant later, Trey found himself pinned between the wall and two hundred pounds of pure muscle.

"You're still trying to deny the attraction between us?"

Trey shook his head. "I want you," he admitted. "But I'm saying no."

"No?" Ethan said the word as if it was part of some obscure language.

"No."

Ethan took a step back and Trey clung to the doorsill to keep from sliding to the floor.

"Fine," he said. "No means no."

Trey almost wished Ethan hadn't given up so easy. Wished he'd forced him so he didn't have to feel guilty about wanting it. When Ethan released his iron grip on Trey's hair, Trey didn't feel relief. He felt remorse. Even though he knew he'd done the right thing, some part of him wanted Ethan to make him do the wrong thing.

"Let me know if you change your mind."

Ethan entered the bathroom. Trey couldn't take his eyes off him. Not when Ethan unfastened his pants. Not when he shoved them down his thighs. Not when Ethan's massive cock emerged from his underwear. Trey's ass ached with longing as he leaned against the doorframe and watched Ethan coat his cock with lotion. The man had a beautiful organ. Slick. Wet. Darker than the rest of his bronze skin and so hard veins were visible from a distance. The head was huge and Trey could only imagine how good it would feel sliding in and out of his body. The rim tugging on his ass as Ethan pulled free and then plunged inside again. Ethan stroked his thick length with both hands. Faster. Faster. The sounds of his hands pumping his slick flesh made Trey's balls tighten. When Ethan grunted and started spurting his load, Trey's knees buckled. Ethan placed one hand on the wall behind the toilet and stared at Trey while he came—his mouth open, eyes reduced to slits, muscles tense with release. Ethan bit his lip when the last spurt of cum landed somewhere around the toilet.

Trey pushed off the doorsill, pretending he wasn't about to come down his leg, and dashed into Reagan's bedroom. He closed the door and started searching for something, anything to fill that empty ache inside. Oh God. He couldn't stand it.

He found a red dildo in her side table drawer and several tubes of lube. He coated the toy with a thick slathering of lube, fumbled with his fly, and jerked his pants down to his knees. He needed it. Needed it now. He bent over the bed and shoved the toy inside, thrusting it hard, as deep as it would go. It was a sad substitute for cock, but better than nothing. Trey crawled up on the bed, supporting his weight with his face so he could work the dildo with one hand and stroke his throbbing cock with the other. The entire time he tried to find relief, he was imagining being possessed, not by Brian, but by Ethan. The only man he'd ever fantasized about in the past had been Brian, but he would puzzle that out later. Trey was within seconds of coming when the door opened. He was ready for Ethan to fuck him now. Didn't give a shit about anyone's feelings. Just needed to be possessed and used. He turned his head, completely unprepared to see Reagan standing on the threshold with a stunned expression on her face.

Chapter 21

REAGAN'S ENTIRE WORLD TILTED on its axis. *Oh my God, I've done it again. I've turned the man I love gay.* Trey's body convulsed and he wrapped his hand around the head of his cock as if to hide the evidence of his release. His extended, vigorous, and—if the look on his face was any indication—intensely pleasurable orgasm.

"Wha-what are you doing?" she sputtered.

He squeezed his eyes shut and turned his flushed face into the mattress. "Sorry. I couldn't stand it any longer." His voice was muffled by the comforter. "I... we need to talk."

She didn't want to talk. She wanted to flee. So she did. She backed out of the room and closed the door. She turned and collided with Ethan's broad chest.

"What's wrong?" he asked.

Why did those two words always make her cry? Light-headed and dizzy, she lifted a trembling hand to her lips. "Trey is gay."

"How do you know that?"

"I saw him... saw him in there." She waved a hand toward the door behind her. "He was... getting off with..."

"Anal?"

She nodded.

"That doesn't necessarily mean he's gay, Reagan."

She looked up at Ethan for direction. He would know. "It doesn't?"

"No, *that* doesn't make him gay, but..." He lowered his eyes guiltily.

"Did he come on to you, Ethan?"

"No. I came on to him."

"You bastard. How could you?" she bellowed at him. "I really like him."

"I really like him too."

Reagan shoved her fingers in both ears. "I don't want to hear it."

Strong hands landed on her shoulders from behind and she whirled around to face Trey. Even though she was thoroughly confused, her heart thudded with anticipation and that bubbly happy feeling she got every time he was near welled up in her throat. Trey took her hands and eased them away from her ears.

"I have some things I need to tell you. I thought I could ignore them, but…" He shook his head.

Her heart thudded faster and faster. She didn't want to lose him. She'd rather not know if it meant she could keep him.

"Do you like my hair?" she said, touching the golden blond, face-framing strands. "They lightened it. I got a whole new wardrobe today. And wait until you see my new guitar," she said. "I wasn't sure if I'd like a floating bridge, I hear they're really hard to keep in tune, but it sounds phenomenal. The third pickup—"

Trey covered her mouth with one hand and lifted his gaze to Ethan, who was standing directly behind her. "Can you give us a few minutes alone?"

"Yeah, of course," Ethan said and stepped away.

"Trey," she said against his hand.

"Hear me out, Reagan."

She nodded and lowered her gaze. A dark cloud seemed to settle over her, making her skin cold and clammy.

He led her to the sofa and eased her down onto the soft cushions. When he sat on the coffee table in front of her and took her hands in his, she just wanted to wrap him in her arms and tell him it didn't matter. She could pretend like she'd never seen that. Pretend that Ethan hadn't verified her suspicions.

"I've been attracted to both men and women for as long as I can remember," he said.

Well, that wasn't what she'd expected him to say. She lifted her gaze to his. The sincerity in his eyes made her heart thud with a mixture of empathy and despair.

"Recently I decided that I didn't want the complications that come with being attracted to men. I thought I could control those urges. Deny that they exist. I wanted to be faithful to you, Reagan. I *have* been faithful to you, but…"

"You didn't do anything wrong, Trey. I'm sorry I freaked out. If that's what you need, maybe I can help, or maybe you can—"

"Keep denying what I am?" He shook his head. "I can't. I've always been very open about my sexuality. This trying to be something I'm not… I can't do it anymore, Reagan. I love you, but…"

All the air whooshed out of her lungs. Did he just say that he loved her?

"I'm saying good-bye. I can't make you happy. I'm just not cut out for a committed relationship. We'll just end up making each other miserable. Either I'll be sexually frustrated or you'll be hurt when I eventually stray. It's better to end this now before we become too attached to each other."

His face blurred behind the welling of tears in her eyes. She was *already* too attached to him. Hot trails of moisture streaked down both cheeks. Dripped from her jaw.

"Don't cry," he whispered and brushed his lips against her temple. "You'll be okay."

She took a deep strangled breath and reached for him, but he climbed to his feet and held her down on the sofa by her shoulder.

"Ethan," he called. When Trey released her shoulder, she leapt to her feet, but the arms that went around her, the shirt that absorbed her tears, didn't belong to Trey. They belonged to Ethan.

"Take good care of her," Trey said. When the front door closed behind him, she broke into wracking sobs.

Chapter 22

ETHAN'S ARMS TIGHTENED AROUND Reagan's trembling body. He drew her closer to his chest, rubbed her back with both hands, and stared at the door that Trey had just exited. Ethan had never respected a man more than he respected Trey at that moment. Ethan wished he would have had the balls to have that conversation with Reagan. Wished he'd have been man enough to let her go and spare her feelings before he strayed with a man and crushed her heart. Wished he could have put her happiness first instead of doing everything in his power to keep himself in her life. He knew he was a selfish bastard, but even knowing that, he still couldn't let her go. He loved her too much. Even if he did have to pretend he thought of her as a friend and nothing more substantial.

Ethan lowered his lips to her hair. He didn't know what to say to her. Didn't know if anything he said would make one bit of difference. He felt responsible for this entire thing. If he hadn't been so attracted to Trey and tried to make a move on his best friend's boyfriend—*God, I'm such an ass*—Reagan wouldn't be sobbing right now. She'd be laughing. Smiling. Staring at Trey with the sickening look of love that ate Ethan alive.

"Reagan," he whispered. "Shh. Calm down, baby."

"I have to go after him," she said. "I can't let him leave. He said he loves me and I think… I *know* I love him too."

She tried to pull away, but Ethan held her tight. "Reagan, he's right. You can't be happy with him. He basically told you that he'd cheat on you. I know firsthand that you don't take that well."

She punched him in the ribs. Okay, he deserved that.

"If I give him permission, it won't be cheating."

All the air seemed to vacate the room. "Permission? You never gave me permission."

"You didn't ask, Ethan. You didn't even talk to me about it. You just screwed someone in our apartment when you thought I wouldn't be home."

"How many times have I apologized for that, Reagan? I knew you wouldn't understand my attraction to men. I scarcely understand it."

"It isn't your attraction to men that I wouldn't be able to understand. It's how you could bring yourself to hurt me like that when you claimed to love me."

"I do love you, Reagan."

"Did," she corrected.

He cupped her lovely face and tilted her head back. Brushing the tears from her cheeks with both thumbs, he looked into her eyes and said, "Do."

He didn't know what he expected her to say to his confession, but it wasn't, "Argh!" She shoved him away. "Don't confuse things even more. You drive me crazy, Ethan."

"I know. I don't mean to." He just couldn't manage to regain her trust enough to direct their relationship in the way he wanted it to go. Which wasn't just friends. It had never been that kind of relationship to him. He'd let her dictate his feelings because he needed her in his life in some capacity. Any capacity. He knew he'd fucked up. He owned that mistake. He didn't know how to make it up to her though. Didn't know if he could make it up to her. Maybe if he helped her keep Trey. Would that make her happy? "I could fuck Trey for you," he blurted.

"What?" she sputtered.

"He's attracted to me. I can fulfill his sexual desires and you could trust me not to take him away from you. I want you to be happy."

"Did you seriously just volunteer to fuck my boyfriend?"

"Actually, Reagan, he's not your boyfriend. He just dumped you." Ethan jabbed a thumb toward the front door of the apartment.

"Shut up! He just needs a little time." She crossed her arms over her chest. "But not too much time." She groaned and scrubbed her face with both hands. "I don't want to lose him, Ethan. Not because of this."

"He told you what he needed to be happy."

"Do you really think we could make him happy? Me and you. Together."

"I'm more concerned about your feelings. Do you think you can handle sharing him? Even on a purely sexual level."

"With you?" She took a deep breath. "Yeah, I'd rather know he was with you than some other guy, but…" She looked up at him. "Do you think he'll go for this?"

"There's only one way to find out."

Chapter 23

TREY HESITATED WITH HIS hand on the knob of his apartment door. He wasn't sure if he wanted to be alone. Maybe he should go visit one of the guys. They were probably busy getting reacquainted with their loved ones. He wouldn't want to intrude. Maybe Dare would like some company. He stayed up late.

Trey knew he would have to get used to living alone at some point. He'd never been alone a day in his life. He'd gone from living with his parents, to living with his band in a tiny studio apartment over a drycleaners, to living with Brian as roommates, and all of those years had been interspersed with being on tour with dozens of people to keep him company. Brian had moved out to live with Myrna several months ago, but Trey had always made sure he had someone to stay the night with him or that he stayed the night at someone else's house when faced with the possibility of an empty apartment. He could call a hundred different people and he knew they'd come over to stay with him. He had plenty of friends. Unfortunately they were all friends with benefits and they'd expect sex. He wasn't ready to go back to mindless fucking. Not so soon after breaking up with Reagan. Even though he'd broken it off with her, he didn't feel free of her. He didn't really *want* to be free of her, but for once in his life he cared about someone's feelings more than he cared about his own. And it sucked.

Trey opened the door and flipped on the lights. He stepped over the threshold and froze in the entryway. It looked like home, but didn't feel like home. Certain familiar things were missing—Brian's leather jacket that usually lay discarded across the back of the sofa, the picture of Brian with his little sister that once rested on the entry table, Brian's boots by the door, Brian. Trey took a step back. Maybe he should move in with Dare. At least he'd have someone to talk to. And that's all he really wanted. Companionship. He didn't do well on his own. Never had.

His phone rang and he was so glad to have someone to talk to that he didn't even check caller ID before answering. "Hello?" He hoped he didn't sound too desperate.

"Can we talk?"

Mark. The usual dread that filled Trey when he spoke to Mark was completely lacking. He was glad to hear from him. From anyone. He hadn't answered the last twenty or so times Mark had called or texted. But now... he really needed someone to talk to.

"About what?" Trey asked.

"The tour is over now. Where are you?"

"I'm at home. Just got in."

"You're not staying with your girlfriend, *Reagan*, tonight?"

"How do you know about Reagan? I never told you her name."

"It's been the most discussed topic on Sinners' News Blog for the past two weeks."

Did they post on that fucking blog every time someone in the band sneezed or scratched his balls? "No. I'm not with her tonight. I needed a little time to myself." Though he wanted to confide in someone about his breakup with Reagan and how miserable he was to be alone, he knew Mark was not the right person. Trey didn't want to give him false hope.

"Liar. You suck at being alone."

True. "So why did you call?"

"I just want to talk."

"There's nothing to say, Mark."

"You're the one who introduced me to this lifestyle."

And Trey definitely regretted that now. He also felt like a hypocrite. He'd pushed Mark into accepting his sexuality, yet he'd hidden his own from Reagan. He should have known that it was the wrong way to handle it. If he'd have been on the other side, offering advice to a friend trying to hide who they were, he'd have told himself that he was being an idiot. That it wouldn't work. Why had he thought he could make it work? Because he'd wanted her. He still wanted her. And he'd thought she would be enough. That it would work out.

"I just need some advice," Mark said.

"On what?"

"How to win you back."

Back? Mark had never had him in the first place.

Trey rubbed a hand over his face, closed the front door, and crossed the room to sit on the comfortable, overstuffed sofa. He knew he had to be careful with Mark's feelings. Trey wasn't sure how to get his point across without being cruel. "Mark…"

"Something's bothering you," Mark said. "You sound different. Sad."

"A lot is bothering me." He reached for the remote and turned on the TV. Background noise. He needed background noise.

"Tell me. You can tell me anything."

"You shouldn't call me anymore. You're grasping at strings."

"You don't think I know that? I can't help who I love."

"And I can't help who I don't love."

There was a long pause. "How did the tour go?" Mark asked, his voice falsely cheerful. "I saw a few of the shows. When I could get off work. I tried to get backstage to see you, but…"

"It's nothing personal, Mark. No one was getting backstage. Can I ask you something?" Trey had to get his point across somehow.

"Of course."

"How do you know when you're in love?" Trey asked.

Mark hesitated so long that Trey checked his phone to make sure the call hadn't dropped.

"Why?" he asked finally. "Are you in love with someone?"

"I think so. It's just that I've loved Brian for so long that I'm not sure I can recognize it with someone else."

"How does this person make you feel?"

Trey hesitated, not sure how to describe how he felt when he was with Reagan. "Like I'm truly alive for the first time in my life."

"I feel that way too."

Trey winced. As usual, Mark was hearing what he wanted to hear. That was why it was so hard to get rid of him. "I didn't mean that I'm in love with you, Mark. I think I love Reagan." And he'd told her, hadn't he? Probably not the best thing to say to someone you were breaking up with. The sudden memory of her tear-streaked face squeezed his heart. He knew it was best that they parted ways. She could never accept the part of him that liked the feel of a hard body against his. The touch of a man. To be penetrated. Dominated. Fucked. He didn't want to hurt her more than he had to. He couldn't give up his attraction to men. He'd tried it. Maybe that made him a selfish bastard. Maybe he'd never find true love. Maybe he'd never be as happy as he'd been with her, but at least he'd be true to himself.

"She can't give you everything you need," Mark said. "Can I come over? I'll give you what you need. Just hearing your voice makes me hard. Or if you want to top, you know I'll let you." Emotionally, Trey wasn't ready for this, but physically he wanted it. His brain was telling him to hang up before he asked Mark to come over and keep him company, but his body craved the touch of a man. If he wasn't careful, any man would do. To hell with feelings and consequences.

"Trey?" Mark questioned.

Trey flopped onto his back and stared at the ceiling fan

overhead. No matter how much he wanted someone to warm his bed, he couldn't give in to that temptation. He knew he'd regret it. And Mark was the worst possible choice to appease his needs. Well, second worst. At least he hadn't given in to Ethan. He was the one Trey really wanted, but that would have devastated Reagan. "Not a good idea."

Mark cursed under his breath. "I hate that I'm so fucking addicted to you. Do you think I enjoy this?"

Trey produced a lopsided grinned. "You must. You keep coming back for more."

"You can't deny that you want me."

"I enjoy sex with you, sure, but you open up an entire set of complications I'm not ready to deal with. I know what it feels like to be in love with someone who isn't in love with you. I've lived that way for years."

"Who said I was in love with you?" Mark said.

"I think it was you."

"Are you telling me that if you had the chance to have sex with Brian, even though you knew he didn't love you in return, you wouldn't have taken it?"

"God, yes," Trey gasped. "I would have taken anything that man wanted to give."

"I feel the same way about you. You don't have to love me. Let me come over and I'll love you."

"But then you'll have hope that things will work out between us and they won't."

"Even though Brian never had sex with you all those years, didn't you still have hope?"

Trey sighed in frustration and rolled onto his side and stared at the TV screen. "Yes, but—"

"But? No but, Trey."

Trey chuckled. "Exactly. No, butt."

"Own me," he whispered. "Just in the bedroom. I promise I won't be a bother to you, if you just own me in the bedroom."

"I can't right now, Mark. I need some time to get my head on straight. Why don't you call Jacob? He'd love to keep you."

"I don't want Jacob. I want you. Don't you want me? Am I undesirable? I don't understand."

"You know I'm attracted to you."

"Then fuck me."

What would it hurt to lose himself in mindless sex? He'd been doing it his entire life without a second thought. What had changed?

Reagan. Reagan had changed everything, and though something inside him would love to go back to the way he'd been before he met her, he knew that would never be enough for him now.

"I can't, Mark. Okay? I just can't. It really isn't you. Find someone who deserves your love and attention. It isn't me."

The intercom near the front door buzzed. Trey scowled. "Who could that be at this hour?" He climbed from the sofa, pressed the button, and spoke into the speaker. "Who is it?"

"Ethan."

Trey's heart skipped a beat. "I have company," he said to Mark. "I have to go."

"Who's Ethan?"

Again with the jealous tone.

"He's Reagan's roommate. Don't call me back. I won't answer."

"Thanks for talking to me. I miss you."

"Bye." Trey hung up.

His intercom buzzed again. He rubbed a hand over his face and then pressed the button to speak to Ethan again. "Don't you think you've caused enough problems for me for one day?"

"Reagan and I talked. She thinks she can handle—" The repetitive yapping of a small dog emitted from the intercom speaker.

"You're standing in my way, big fella," the wizened voice of Mrs.

O'Neal, who lived down the hall from Trey, came through the speaker. "Quiet, Shortie." The yapping changed to a series of low growls.

"Excuse me," Ethan said to the woman. Into the intercom, he said, "Look, Trey, I don't think we want to discuss this over the intercom. Can I come up?"

"Is Reagan with you?" Trey said.

"No. It's just me."

Trey wasn't sure why he felt such disappointment. Actually, that wasn't true. He still had feelings for the woman. He couldn't turn that off by walking out the door. He did want to hear what Ethan had to say. Maybe things could work out with Reagan. Ethan knew her better than anyone. Maybe he could help Trey figure out how to proceed from here, because even though he'd said he wanted to break up with her, he didn't. Not at all. He wanted her back. Maybe he could get by with artificial stimulation. Would she wear a strap-on for him? Or maybe... He didn't know. He had to do something, though. His conversation with Mark had made him realize he needed that woman in his life. He loved her. "Fine."

Trey pushed the button to let Ethan into the building. He shoved his cell phone into his pocket and glanced around the apartment. He wasn't sure what Ethan could possibly want to talk to him about. He was probably pretty mad that Trey had made Reagan cry. Maybe he was coming upstairs to rearrange his face. He had that temper issue when he thought he was protecting the innocent. And Reagan was definitely the innocent one in this situation.

Maybe Trey shouldn't have let him into the building after all.

Maybe he could pretend he wasn't home.

A set of knuckles rapped on the door.

"Trey?" Ethan called from the hallway.

Trey's dad was a plastic surgeon. He'd do a good job of fixing Trey's face if Ethan was pissed enough to hit him. Trey took a deep steadying breath and then went to open the door.

Ethan gazed at Trey with that feral hunger that made Trey's balls throb. Damn him. Is that why he'd come? For sex? Ethan didn't look mad. Or even annoyed. He looked horny.

Ethan let himself into the apartment, rubbing up against Trey as he passed. Trey closed his eyes and tried not to be too obvious about inhaling Ethan's heady, masculine scent. Turning down Mark over the phone had been easy. Ethan in the flesh was a different story. *Focus on keeping Reagan. You haven't strayed yet. You can fix things with her. Be strong.*

Trey closed the door. Ethan reached over and turned the deadbolt. He was so close, and he smelled so good, and he felt so hard. Fuck, it had been too long since Trey had been with a man. He couldn't deny his needs. Wasn't sure why he'd ever thought he could.

Ethan's hands moved to Trey's ass. "You're mine now," he said in a low growl.

"Ethan, why did you come here?" Trey asked even though he could probably guess.

Ethan moved one hand to grip Trey's chin between his thumb and forefinger and forced his head back.

"I'm here to fuck you," Ethan said.

Trey pulled away from him. "This is what you planned all along, isn't it? To get me to break up with Reagan so you could seduce me?"

Ethan shook his head. "Don't flatter yourself. She sent me over here to seduce you. She thinks she can allow you to have a male lover as long as it's me."

Trey laughed. "That's the biggest bullshit story I've ever heard. Reagan would never say that. Just look how freaked out she was when you cheated on her with a man."

"But you didn't cheat on her. Where I snuck around behind her back to find sexual gratification, you were frank and honest with her. She's willing to try this to keep you in her life. I'd say that makes you one lucky son of a bitch."

"So I'm allowed to have sex with a man, but only if it's you," Trey said. "Do I get a say in this?"

Ethan gaped at him. Apparently, that was not what he had been expecting Trey to say. He'd probably thought he'd be naked and lubed up by now. "You don't want to?"

Trey grinned crookedly. "I don't think Reagan knows what she's getting herself into. Actually, I'm half-convinced that you're making this story up and are here because you want to be here. I don't think it has anything to do with Reagan. I think you're using her as an excuse to get laid. Or making sure you finish the deal so there is no way she'll ever let me close to her again."

"Reagan did send me, but if I didn't want to be here, I wouldn't be. You know I want you, Trey. I don't know what you're objecting to. Won't this arrangement make everything work out for everyone?"

"I don't like to be told who I'm supposed to sleep with." Though honestly, he'd wanted to sleep with Ethan the first time he'd laid eyes on him and ever since.

Ethan's cell phone rang and he started. He shifted his attention from Trey to his phone. "Yeah," he answered. "It's Reagan," he mouthed at Trey. "Yeah, I told him." He paused. "I'm not sure. He doesn't seem to believe me."

Trey was tense as Ethan spoke to Reagan. If this was happening, she was offering him the best of both worlds. A wonderful woman to love. A hot buck to fuck. But Trey still felt manipulated. He wasn't sure why. Maybe because he was the only one who hadn't had a say in the matter. Reagan and Ethan had decided this without him.

"Reagan wants to talk to you," Ethan said and handed the phone to Trey. He almost dropped it.

"Reagan," he said breathlessly.

"Hi, baby. I figured you wouldn't believe Ethan if I didn't back up his story. Are you okay with this arrangement?"

Trey's heart thudded in his chest. "I think you're going to wind up getting hurt. I've been thinking. I don't know. Maybe I could make these needs more tolerable with a dildo or…" He forced himself not to look at the temptation that was Ethan standing next to his front door. He knew a dildo was no substitute for that hot piece of flesh, but if it helped Trey keep Reagan, he could try to get by with less. Much, much, *much* less.

"That won't be enough and you know it," Reagan said. "Don't feel like I'm testing you, Trey. This was my idea."

"But thinking it. Saying it. Living it. All different things."

"If it's what makes you happy, I want you to have it. No fooling around with other women though. I don't have any male parts, but I have all the female goods. I'm the only woman on your menu. Got it?"

She was willing to do this for him? Did she love him, then? She couldn't possibly love him one millionth as much as he loved her at that moment. Some of the tension melted from his body and he smiled. "Got it." She made him happy. Just talking to her made his heart flutter. "I love you, Reagan. I want you to know that having sex with another man won't change how I feel about you. I will still love you. Always love you. Do you believe me?" Trey asked.

When she didn't say anything, his heart stumbled over several beats.

"Reagan?"

"S-sorry," she said brokenly. "I didn't expect those three little words to take my breath away. I want to look into your eyes when I say them back. Okay?"

"Okay."

"I'm going to give you and Ethan some time alone together. I just wanted to make sure you knew it was okay and that I want us to give this relationship another chance. When you need cock, go to Ethan. He can help." She said it like Ethan was a mechanic who was going to change Trey's oil.

"Don't you want to join us?" Trey asked.

She laughed, more a sound of discomfort than humor. "I'm not sure I'm ready for that."

"I'd get a lot more enjoyment out of it if we all participated."

"I do think it would be sexy to watch you two kiss," she said haltingly.

Trey grinned. "I'll send you a picture." He hoped Ethan wasn't camera shy.

Reagan groaned.

"Is that okay?" Trey asked her.

"God, yes. I think I might want to participate next time. I'm not sure if seeing you with someone other than me would make me insane with jealousy or not. Let me think about it."

"No pressure," Trey murmured. "It's just, you know how much I worship your body. Imagine if I had assistance." He hung up.

Trey backed Ethan up against the door. He stared deeply into his eyes. "Last chance to back out, Ethan. You have no idea how much I want you right now."

"I'm sure it doesn't come close to how much I want you."

Trey closed the gap between their mouths and kissed him. The kiss started hot, deep, passionate, but soon progressed into demanding, hungry, intense. Trey was so caught up in being devoured that he almost forgot he'd promised Reagan a picture. He lifted his cell phone out to the side and did his best to hold the camera still as he feasted on Ethan's strong lips and plastered his body along his hard length. He snapped a picture and then slid his phone back in his pocket so he could cling to Ethan's hard body with both hands. Ethan tugged his mouth away and grabbed Trey's hair in his fists. "I've wanted to fuck you since the moment I laid eyes on you."

"I know."

"Touch me," Ethan said in a low growl.

"Make me."

The smoldering look Ethan gave him was enough to have Trey reaching for Ethan's fly. Ethan made a sound that was part growl, part purr, and used his hold on Trey's hair to crush his mouth against his. God, Trey needed it rough like this. He wasn't sure if Ethan had picked up on that need or if he was just really worked up. Trey released the top button of Ethan's jeans. The backs of his fingers brushed against Ethan's hard stomach and they jerked their mouths apart to stare at each other. Trey slowly lowered Ethan's zipper. Ethan's breaths came in harsh, ragged gasps as Trey released his hot, stiff cock from his pants.

"I want your mouth on me," Ethan said.

"I want to show Reagan how hard you are," Trey said with a crooked grin. He retrieved his phone from his pocket and sent her the slightly blurry picture of her boyfriend and best friend kissing. He didn't wait to find out how she would respond to that image. He wanted to push her to the edge of her comfort zone and beyond.

Trey wrapped his hand around Ethan's cock and stroked it gently from base to tip. Ethan had a magnificent cock. Thick and hard. Trey couldn't wait until he filled him. Trey snapped a picture of his hand stroking Ethan's cock and sent that to Reagan before dropping to his knees at Ethan's feet. He looked up at Ethan and held his gaze as he licked the head of his cock. He held his phone up to Ethan. "Take a picture for Reagan and send it to her."

"Are you sure?"

"Yeah. She needs to get used to this, because tomorrow she's going to be personally involved in it."

"I'm not sure she's the threesome type."

Trey grinned up at him. "She's definitely the threesome type. She just needs to get used to the idea."

Ethan gave Trey a questioning look but did as he asked. Trey concentrated on licking, kissing, and suckling the sensitive head of Ethan's cock. Ethan took several pictures and sent them to Reagan.

"I knew you'd be good at this," he said to Trey. He stroked his hair gently and caressed his face. "You have the most sensual mouth."

"Call Reagan," Trey said. "Ask her what's she's doing."

Ethan dialed her number. "Trey wanted me to call you and ask you what you're doing," he said into his cell phone. He paused. "Mmm, let me hear it."

"What is she doing?" Trey asked, though he had his suspicions.

"She's masturbating."

Trey grinned. "Good. I figured this would turn her on. Give me the phone."

Ethan handed over the phone and Trey held it up to his ear. He heard the unmistakable hum of a vibrator, the sounds of her slick flesh being pounded rhythmically, and in the distance her moans of pleasure. "Reagan," he said, hoping she could hear him. "Reagan?"

"Trey," she said breathlessly.

"Does it make you jealous to see me with Ethan?" he asked.

"Jealous? No. Horny? Oh God, yes."

"Come for me, baby. Let me hear you get off."

While Trey listened to Reagan's cries of pleasure, he worked at removing Ethan's jeans. Within seconds, Reagan cried out as she came. "Was it good, Reagan?"

"It would have been a lot better with you."

He smiled. "Tomorrow I'm going to show you my favorite position," Trey said.

"Finally."

"Ethan will have to participate."

"Okay," she said breathlessly.

"We'll see you in the morning. In the meantime, think about what you want from us."

"I can't think at all right now."

Trey chuckled. "Then we'll surprise you." He hung up and put the phone back in his pocket.

"She likes this?" Ethan asked.

"Lucky for us. Are you going to help me reward her tomorrow?"

"If she'll let me."

Trey winked at him. "She'll let you."

"Can I concentrate on you now?"

"Yes, please."

Ethan eased Trey to his feet. He pulled Trey's shirt off over his head and bent his head to draw the hoop in Trey's nipple into this mouth. He sucked. Hard. The tug seemed to extend to Trey's balls. Ethan suckled a trail down Trey's belly as he lowered himself to his knees. He unbuttoned Trey's fly while he looked up at him. Ethan slowly tugged Trey's jeans and boxers down until his cock sprang free. Ethan emitted an excited gasp. He eased Trey's pants down his legs and removed the garment, pulling off Trey's shoes and socks in the process.

Trey stared down at Ethan's enraptured face. His lips were inches from Trey's cock, but he wasn't sucking it. More like worshiping it from afar. Ethan's hot, moist breath caressed Trey's most sensitive skin. Trey fought the urge to inch forward until his cock brushed Ethan's lips. After several moments, Ethan climbed to his feet without touching Trey at all.

Ethan pulled off his white T-shirt giving Trey an eyeful of glorious, muscular bulges in all the right places. He pinned Trey with a hard stare—his brown eyes intense, his expression unreadable. Trey wasn't sure why that look had him ready to drop to his knees at Ethan's feet and beg for his touch. The longer Ethan stared at him, the faster and harder Trey's heart thudded in his chest.

Trey lowered his gaze to Ethan's cock—hard, huge, and twitching with excitement. Trey couldn't wait to be filled. Stretched to his limits. He hoped Ethan hurried up about it. Didn't he realize how bad Trey needed this? Maybe he needed to be more forthright. "I have condoms and lube in my bedroom," Trey said.

"Do you want me to go get it and bring it out here?"

"The choice is yours. I'm at your mercy."

A slow smile spread across Ethan's handsome face. "You won't regret putting me in charge." He leaned closer and nipped Trey's lower lip. "Show me the way."

Hurrying toward his bedroom, Trey turned on the light and entered the large room. He went to the dresser and opened the top drawer. He had dozens of condoms inside. Lubricants. Toys designed to pleasure men. The second drawer was all for the ladies. Lady, he corrected himself. "Everything you'll need is in here," he told Ethan.

"What do you like?" Ethan asked.

"Everything," he said with hesitation, "but tonight I need to be topped."

Ethan smiled at him. "And I need to top."

While Ethan examined Trey's collection of condoms, lubes, and toys, Trey went to make the lighting in the room less glaring. He turned on several lamps and turned off the overhead lights.

"Go stand and face the end of the bed." Ethan's deep, commanding voice sent tingles of pleasure down Trey's spine. Why had Trey thought he could ever give up men? He loved being with a man just as much as he loved being with a woman. The only thing that could possibly be better was being with both at the same time. They'd get to that tomorrow. Trey moved to stand at the end of the bed and waited for Ethan. And waited. And waited. When he turned to offer Ethan a questioning look, Ethan said, "I said face the end of the bed."

Trey faced the bed again and waited some more. His anticipation built to the point that he actually shuddered when Ethan finally touched the small of his back.

Ethan planted a tender kiss at the nape of Trey's neck and

his hand slid across Trey's belly as he pulled him back against the length of his hard body. Trey felt Ethan's cock, hard and thick against his ass. He expected him to surge into his body. Just take him. Trey was okay with that. He didn't need the tender caresses and loving kisses in this sort of situation. He was no stranger to having sex for the sake of sex, so he was a taken a little off guard when Ethan started to nibble on the edge of his ear and stroke his belly, his chest, his arms.

"You have a perfect body," Ethan murmured. "And you smell so good." Ethan's hands slid down Trey's hips, his fingers tracing the ridges of Trey's hip bones.

Ethan circled Trey's cock with both hands and stroked it slowly with a firm grip. Trey leaned back against Ethan's hard chest and closed his eyes. He gasped with pleasure, quivering with unfulfilled desire.

"I want to hear you, Trey. Make some noise for me."

Ethan's hands moved faster. Trey's instincts were to grit his teeth and hold it all in, but he liked to give his lovers what they wanted so he worked on voicing his excitement. Ethan's tongue traced the outer edge of Trey's ear and then plunged inside. Trey emitted a sputtering cry.

"Damn, I want to fuck you," Ethan growled in his ear. He bit the edge of Trey's ear and held on as he stroked Trey's cock faster. Faster. Trey's heart rate accelerated out of control.

"Don't make me come yet. I want you inside me when I come. Ethan. *Ethan?*"

Ethan dropped his hands and stepped away. Disoriented, Trey tried to catch his breath.

"Is it okay if I just look at you?" Ethan asked.

No. What are you waiting for? "Um…" he said between ragged breaths. "Um… I need…"

Ethan's hands began to wander Trey's body again. He caressed the insides of Trey's thighs, cupped his balls gently, and then rubbed his hips rhythmically.

Trey whispered, "I want to feel your body against mine." His hard, hard body.

Ethan turned Trey to face him and jerked Trey against his chest. He kissed him deeply, tongue thrusting into Trey's mouth, and Trey clung to his muscular back. Ethan's rough manner totally turned him on. He wanted to be taken. Devoured. Trey's hands rubbed over hard bumps and muscular bulges. The man's ass was spectacularly firm beneath Trey's seeking palms. Ethan's hard cock prodded Trey in the belly. He wanted it to prod him somewhere else entirely.

Ethan's hands traveled down Trey's ass. When he began to massage Trey's throbbing opening, the strength went out of Trey's legs and he swayed against Ethan. *Yeah, that's the spot.*

"Do you want me to use the numbing lubricant?"

Trey shook his head.

"I'm pretty big. I don't want to hurt you."

"I want to feel you. I don't like to be numb."

An instant later, slippery fingers began to rub against Trey's opening. He widened his stance. *Yes. Now. Take me, Ethan.*

Ethan's finger slid inside Trey's body and he gasped in excitement. Much too long since he'd been with a man. Much too long.

Ethan had two fingers inside of him now. He moved his fingers in a wide arc, stretching Trey's body to accept him more easily.

"I'm ready for you," Trey insisted. "Don't make me wait. I can't stand it anymore."

Ethan applied a condom and coated his cock with excess lubricant.

Trey bit his lip as Ethan's fingers plunged particularly deep. Damn, he was excited. He was going to come so hard when he let go.

Ethan pulled his fingers free and turned Trey's body to face the opposite direction. He nudged the head of his cock against Trey's ass. Heat raced up Trey's spine. Ethan's hand moved to stroke the tip of Trey's cock, distracting him with pleasure as he sought possession. Trey leaned forward to make it easier for Ethan to enter him. He buried his fingers in the comforter at the end of the bed and relaxed.

Ethan pressed forward, claiming Trey's body one agonizingly slow inch at a time. Stretched to his limits, Trey shuddered in delight. He didn't even realize he was gasping in rapture until Ethan said, "You okay? Can I go deeper?"

There was more? Fuck yeah! "Y—yes… deeper. Oh God. You're so… thick."

"Does it hurt?"

"No. Feels phenomenal."

Ethan, completely buried now, gripped Trey's hips in both hands and ground his cock deeper.

"Ah, yes," Trey gasped and rocked back to meet him. He had all of him now. Inside.

Ethan drew back slowly and then thrust forward, hard and deep. Trey cried out as Ethan repeated the motion again. Again. He knew he wouldn't last long. This is exactly what he'd been craving—deep, hard penetration. A dominant male who knew how to give as much pleasure as he took. Trey leaned farther forward and rested his face on the end of the mattress. It felt so good. He just wanted to feel Ethan moving inside him. He didn't need anything else. Just this. Ethan slid his hands around Trey's hips and took his cock in both hands. He didn't stroke Trey's length, just held him until Trey couldn't stand it anymore and he began to rock his hips, thrusting into Ethan's hands. The only thing that could have possibly felt better was if he was thrusting into Reagan's body instead. Tomorrow he would make that thought a reality.

Trey fought orgasm. Breathing hard. Wanting the pleasure to build. To last.

Ethan slowly pulled back and then surged forward again, so deep his balls bounced against Trey.

Trey tumbled over the edge. Spasms gripped the base of his cock and his ass tightened around Ethan's thrusting cock. Ethan paused in mid-thrust and groaned. When Trey's body went limp, Ethan wrapped both arms around him and tugged him upright so that his back was pressed firmly against Ethan's belly.

Ethan's hands moved over Trey's chest. His belly. His hips. Ethan suckled and licked the side of Trey's neck until another wave of pleasure coursed through him and he shuddered.

"I'm not finished yet." Ethan turned Trey to face the post at the end of the bed. He took Trey's hands and wrapped them around the smooth wood. "Hold on tight. I'm going to fuck you until you're hard again. I won't let myself come for a long, long time."

Trey made a sound of torment but gripped the bedpost with both hands and spread his legs to give Ethan easier access.

Ethan's hands worked Trey's cock as he thrust into him gently, almost lovingly. He continued to kiss the nape of his neck as well. Trey wasn't sure why he was being so tender with him. Or why he insisted on getting him hard again. He was satiated.

"Ethan, you don't have to get me off again," Trey told him. "I'll let you finish."

"I've been thinking of all the things I've wanted to do to you for weeks," he said, his deep voice making Trey's cock twitch to life in his hand. Something about its timber excited Trey. "I lie in bed and think about you. I tell myself I can't have you. Can't touch you. You're Reagan's. I get so hard thinking about you. Wondering if you're as wonderful as I imagine." He nipped his ear. "You're even better. I deny myself any contact for as long as I can stand it and then when I finally let myself jerk off I come so hard. Like I did in the bathroom tonight while you watched. This might be my only opportunity to make those fantasies a reality. I haven't even started with you, Trey."

Would this really end up being their only time together? Trey supposed it was possible that Reagan would change her mind and things wouldn't work out, but Trey sincerely hoped that wasn't the case. He'd really like Ethan to become a permanent fixture in his sex life.

Trey was nearly in tears by the time Ethan got him hard again. The pleasure was almost too much to bear. Ethan continued to slowly possess Trey from behind. He encouraged Trey to turn until they were facing the mirror over the dresser at the end of the bed. Trey loved the way Ethan looked standing behind him. So big and powerful. The bronze skin of his hands contrasted with Trey's lighter-toned cock as he stroked him.

"Dear God, what a view," Ethan growled and sank his teeth into Trey's shoulder to quiet his cries of ecstasy as his excitement finally reached its pinnacle. Ethan's thrusts became more vigorous and shallow as he sought a quick release. His body went rigid behind Trey and he swore under his breath. Ethan's growls of pleasure as he got off made Trey's balls tighten, but he didn't come. He was a long way from coming a second time. After a moment, Ethan pulled out and massaged Trey's opening with two fingers. "Are you okay? Was that too much?"

Trey glanced at him over his shoulder and met his eyes. "Are you kidding? I never get enough. Now it's my turn."

Ethan's handsome face crinkled in confusion. "Your turn?"

"To take you."

Ethan chuckled. "Not happening. I don't bottom. Ever."

"Never?"

"Nope."

"So you're a virgin?" Trey asked, his predatory side making his heart thud with thoughts of the hunt. Trey wanted Ethan in every capacity and if he could be the first to take him, it increased his interest even further. He loved cherries.

"And I'm going to stay that way."

For now, Trey thought.

"Well, you aren't going to leave me like this," Trey said, nodding at his hard cock.

"Of course I'm not. It's not going in my ass, but I haven't tasted you yet." He licked his upper lip and Trey's knees buckled.

The man was a great kisser. Trey couldn't wait to feel those strong lips tugging on his cock. He grabbed a spare sucker from the nightstand, unwrapped it, and stuck it in his mouth. He then climbed up onto the bed and lay down on his back. Resting on the pillows, Trey linked his hands behind his head and looked down at the gorgeous man at the foot of his bed. "Get busy." he said with a crooked grin and nodded toward his erection. Trey tugged his sucker in and out of his mouth a few times and couldn't help but chuckle at Ethan's expression. He looked like he regretted allowing himself to come.

Ethan crawled up the bed and licked Trey's cock. His tongue slid up Trey's length and then flicked down to the base. Up. Down. Up. When he reached Trey's throbbing head again, Ethan suckled it with his lips, taking it in a deep kiss. Trey clung to the bedclothes beneath him. His back arched involuntarily.

Ethan gazed up at Trey. "You are so fucking sexy." He growled and placed a sucking kiss just beneath Trey's belly button. He worked his way up Trey's body, leaving sharp bite marks all the way up to his neck. "I've never met a man more suited for sex." Ethan took his sucker and tossed it aside before he grabbed his hair in both fists and kissed him. Hard. Trey didn't know how the man knew he liked to be treated roughly by his male lovers. It drove him insane with desire.

Trey moaned into Ethan's mouth.

Ethan inhaled Trey's vocalizations of excitement as he continued to kiss him. Trey knew he was chanting, "Oh fuck," but he couldn't stop. Nor could he seem to stop his hand from moving to his cock. He wanted Ethan to watch him come. Show him how much he desired him.

Ethan grabbed Trey's wrists and pinned them to the bed. "Let me do it, Trey."

"Hurry, Ethan."

The only thing that turned him on more than being treated roughly by a man was being pinned down and forced to take pleasure. The first man he'd ever been with—Brian—had done that for him and Trey had carried a torch for him for a dozen years. Trey stared up at Ethan, amazed that he had that same burning desire he felt for Brian when he looked at Ethan. He wouldn't call it love. Pure sexual fulfillment. That's what he'd call it.

"Fuck, I'm getting hard again," Ethan said, his voice gruff. "I already want you again."

Ethan tugged Trey down the bed and rolled him onto his stomach. When Ethan lay on top of him, Trey sighed in contentment. Ethan's heat and masculine scent surrounded him. Ethan rubbed his cock up and down the crack of Trey's ass, driving them both insane with need.

"Are you ready for me again?" Ethan asked.

"I never stopped being ready."

Chapter 24

ETHAN RUBBED HIS LIPS over Trey's shoulder, his tongue collecting the salt of his skin. The man had Ethan in knots. He couldn't remember ever being this crazy for anyone. The idea that Reagan was willing to share Trey totally blew Ethan's mind. When he'd suggested it, he didn't think there was a chance she'd agree, but now that he'd made love to Trey, Ethan realized he'd be willing to do just about anything to keep the man too. Perhaps together he and Reagan could keep Trey going—or coming—for years. Maybe forever. Ethan had never put forever in his equation before.

Ethan linked his hands with Trey's and pinned him facedown to the mattress. Trey was completely submissive beneath him. Dominating a strong man fulfilled Ethan like nothing else. He fleetingly wondered what it would be like to be in Trey's place. Letting himself be taken. Ethan had never considered being topped by a man before, but maybe he'd let Trey... He wasn't sure why he was thinking that way. Wasn't like him.

Ethan lifted his hips and grabbed his cock, rubbing it over Trey's slickened hole, teasing him until he began to moan and rock back against him.

"Do you want it?" Ethan asked.

"Yes."

"Too bad. I'm not ready to give it to you."

Trey squirmed. "I need to come."

"You'll come when I let you."

"Ethan," he said breathlessly.

Ethan's balls tightened at the sound of his name on Trey's delectable lips. His little game of dominance fell to the wayside and he kissed the side of Trey's neck with soft, sucking kisses. He could totally fall for this guy. Probably already had. He flicked Trey's earring with his tongue and pressed the head of his cock into Trey's ass. They shuddered in unison. Ethan hurriedly pulled out. No matter how much he wanted to fuck Trey raw, he knew he needed a condom.

"Don't move," he growled into Trey's ear.

"What will you do if I disobey?"

Ethan grabbed Trey's ass cheeks in both hands, squeezed, and separated them to tug his ass open. "I won't fuck you where you like it."

Trey whimpered and stayed perfectly still as Ethan left the bed to find a condom and more lube. When he returned to the bed, Trey was lying there completely relaxed. "Are you tired?"

"No, I can go at it all night. I just feel so much better now. Thanks."

Ethan grinned to himself. "No thanks necessary." He joined him on the bed and settled over his back. "Don't come unless I tell you to."

"Ethan."

"Don't speak either. Just take it."

Trey relaxed beneath him. "Yes," he whispered. "Give me what I need."

While Ethan struggled with the idea that he didn't just want to fuck Trey, he wanted to make love to him, he trailed kisses down the center of his back. Why did he feel this way? So tender? He'd been in love with women in the past, but men had always been just fuck-buddies to him. Entertainment purposes only. Trey's sweet surrender played with his heartstrings. He should probably forego the foreplay if he wanted to get out of this encounter still in possession of his heart.

Ethan applied a condom and coated his straining cock with

lube. Fuck, this guy made him hard. He settled over Trey's back, knowing Trey wanted it rough, but he slid into him slowly. Taking his time. Possessing him one inch at a time.

"Why so gentle?" Trey murmured.

"I'm not sure," Ethan admitted. "Raise up on your elbows."

Trey repositioned his body so that his shoulders lifted off the bed. He supported his weight on his forearms.

"Bend your back more," Ethan instructed. This would put more weight on Trey's cock so when Ethan thrust into him, he'd feel some friction between the satin comforter and his belly. Plus, Ethan could tug at Trey's nipple ring with his fingertip as he held onto his sculpted chest.

Ethan trailed kisses over Trey's shoulder blades and the nape of his neck as he found a slow steady rhythm inside him. He kept his balance with one hand on the bed, but the other he used to stroke Trey's belly, his rib cage, his nipple. He'd never made love to a man before. He'd fucked several of them, but this was different. More than the pleasure, Ethan wanted a connection with Trey. An emotional connection that went deeper than mutual sexual satisfaction.

I am so screwed. He was supposed to be serving Trey's sexual needs. Nothing more. That had been his reason for coming over here. He wasn't supposed to be getting involved. Reagan trusted him to keep his distance so she could continue her relationship with Trey. What would she do if she knew Ethan had fallen for the man she loved?

Ethan increased his tempo, deciding that if he stopped being so tender with Trey, he could find that disconnect between the emotional and the sexual again. Trey gasped brokenly and rocked back against him, meeting his thrusts no matter how hard Ethan insisted on possessing him.

"Yes. Like that. I'm gonna come," Trey gasped brokenly.

"Not until I say you can," Ethan said and pulled out.

"Oh God. Don't stop, Ethan. You feel so good. Perfect."

Ethan decided Trey was getting too much stimulation by having his cock squashed beneath him.

"Turn over," Ethan demanded gently.

Trey glanced over his shoulder at him. "What?"

"On your back."

Trey hesitated. Ethan wondered what the problem was.

"I said on your back, Trey. Or would you like me to leave?" As if he could.

Trey slowly turned onto his back. His cock was so hard and swollen that Ethan couldn't resist sliding it in and out of his mouth a few times.

"Ethan," Trey panted. "I'm seriously about to come."

"Fight it," Ethan demanded and drew Trey's cock into his mouth, sucking until Trey started to whimper. Ethan crawled up his body. Placing a kiss under his navel, the center of his chest, his neck, his ear. Trey opened his legs wide for Ethan and sighed in bliss when Ethan pressed his cockhead into his tight ass again.

Ethan lifted his head and their eyes met. Time seemed to stand still for a moment. Neither of them moved. Ethan wasn't sure if he was still capable of breathing. Trey's hand moved to the back of Ethan's neck and coaxed him closer so he could kiss him. Ethan took a deep shuddering breath against Trey's mouth and then began to move again—his strokes rhythmic and deep.

Trey's cock prodded Ethan in the belly and Ethan went down on one elbow so he could stroke his receptive lover gently with his free hand in time with his thrusts. Trey gasped brokenly into Ethan's mouth. Trey's kiss became frantic. The fingers of one hand dug into Ethan's chest, and his other hand clung to the back of Ethan's neck. Ethan broke their kiss and stared down at Trey. His sweaty face was flushed with pleasure and his sensual lips parted as he gasped in pleasure, but his eyes were tightly closed.

"You can come now, Trey, but only if you look at me," Ethan said.

It was as if Trey couldn't hear him.

Ethan thrust into him harder and stroked his cock with a firmer grip.

"Trey. Look at me." Ethan wasn't sure why it was so important to him that Trey stared into his eyes as he came.

Trey continued to ignore his demands. Ethan fucked him harder, his lip curled in anger. Why wouldn't he look at him? Harder. Harder. *Don't ignore me.*

Trey gasped in pain. "N-not so hard," he protested breathlessly.

"Look at me."

Trey squeezed his eyes shut even more tightly and shook his head.

Ethan released Trey's cock and moved his hand to grab his hair. "Open your fucking eyes, Trey."

"Ethan, you're hurting me. Don't ram into me so hard."

Ethan covered Trey's mouth with a punishing kiss.

"Bastard," Trey grumbled into his mouth.

Ethan tugged his mouth free and stared down at the flushed and sweaty face of the sexiest man he'd ever laid eyes on. "If you want me to be more gentle, all you have to do is look at me."

"Fuck you, Ethan. Pull out."

Ethan stopped thrusting and Trey went limp. He still refused to look at him. "Are you mad?" Ethan asked.

"Get off me."

"Did I really hurt you?" Ethan didn't understand why he'd gotten so angry over Trey's refusal to look at him.

"Yes, it hurt."

Ethan's heart twisted with remorse. "I'm sorry, baby. I'll make you feel better," he promised. Ethan kissed his way down Trey's body, pulling out as he trailed his tongue down Trey's sweat-slick belly. He drew Trey's cock into his mouth, but Trey grabbed his head to stop him.

"Go wash your dick," Trey said.

"What?"

"You heard me." Apparently he'd had enough of being submissive. Ethan didn't quite know how to respond.

"I'm sor—"

"Don't apologize, just do what I say."

Ethan hesitated a moment longer and then climbed from the bed to go into the connecting bathroom. He disposed of the condom. Washing his still-hard cock in the sink turned out to be more of an exercise in masturbation. The man of his fantasies had let him make love to him and Ethan had blown it by letting his temper get the best of him. *Fuck!*

"Don't clean it out," Trey called. "Just clean it off."

Ethan dried himself with a hand towel and returned to the bedroom to find Trey rubbing his balls and wincing.

"Are you okay?"

"I told you I needed to come, not that I wanted you to try to fuck me to death."

That feeling of love and connect that had extended between them was gone now. More than anything, Ethan wanted that back. He hadn't meant to hurt him. He'd just wanted Trey to look at him. He wasn't even sure why it had been so important to him at the time. Now it just seemed stupid.

"Get over here," Trey said and patted the bed beside him.

"Aren't you finished with me?" Ethan asked, feeling strangely uncertain of himself.

"Did you come in the bathroom?"

He shook his head.

"Then I guess I'm not finished with you. We're going to suck each other off and go to sleep. We'll need our strength to satisfy Reagan tomorrow. I have the feeling she's going to be really horny."

Trey was all business now, but at least he was willing to finish what they started. Ethan would be more careful with him in the future. He didn't want to ruin this. He wasn't sure he'd survive making love with Trey and Reagan simultaneously, but he was more than willing to die for their cause. Ethan crawled up on the bed, the thought of Trey's mouth around his cock made his balls throb. The first time he had seen Trey suck a red lollipop Ethan thought he would come down his leg, and now… this was no lollipop.

Trey grabbed Ethan around the waist and pulled him down onto the mattress beside him. He grabbed two fistfuls of Ethan's hair and pinned him with a glare. "I don't like pain, got it?" he said. "You can pin me down, coerce me, get rough with me, tease me to intolerable limits, but if you intentionally hurt me, I'm through with you."

"I didn't mean to hurt you, Trey. I got carried away." *I just wanted you to see me. To know who was making love to you.* "It won't happen again."

Trey nodded. "Warn me when you're about to come," Trey said and turned upside down beside Ethan, facing him.

Ethan gently circled the base of Trey's long, gorgeous cock and shifted forward to run his tongue over the enlarged head. He slowly, carefully began to move his hand up and down Trey's shaft before sucking the tip into his mouth. Trey's warm tongue flicked over the head of Ethan's cock and he tensed. The combined sensation of sucking and being sucked encouraged Ethan to pleasure Trey a bit more aggressively. He wanted it. Trey's cum. In his mouth. He stroked Trey faster—his hand gliding gently over his smooth skin— sucked Trey harder, but not too hard. No pain, just pleasure. *Let go, Trey. Let go.*

Ethan's concentration shattered when Trey's suction and tempo suddenly increased. Ethan pulled away, his head tilted back. "Oh yes," he gasped, eyelids fluttering involuntarily. The man's mouth should win awards.

Trey slapped his ass to help him collect his bliss-scattered thoughts. Ethan took a deep breath and then drew Trey back into his mouth. Stroking faster with his hand. Sucking harder. Stroking faster. Writhing his tongue. Trey's body tensed and he tried to pull out of Ethan's mouth, but Ethan kept him trapped inside as that first pulse of cum bathed his tongue. Ethan had never tasted such sweet fluids from a man. He swallowed and sucked gently as a second spurt filled his mouth. *More, Trey. Give me more.*

Trey gasped brokenly around Ethan's cock as a third hard spasm racked his body and delivered exactly what Ethan wanted.

The building pleasure in Ethan's groin broke unexpectedly and Ethan patted Trey's hip to warn him. Trey pulled back, still lost in a daze of pleasure, still stroking Ethan's cock with one hand. Ethan watched his fluids splatter across Trey's partially open lips.

Oh fuck, that was hotter than having him swallow it. To see the evidence of his release on his lover's face and lips. Ethan went limp, his body completely satiated.

"You didn't have to swallow that," Trey said breathlessly.

"I wanted it."

Ethan forced his muscles to work so he could turn around on the bed to face Trey. He cupped his jaw and traced his upper lip with his thumb, collecting his cum, fascinated by the look of it on Trey's skin.

"I never swallow," Trey explained.

"That was sexy as hell," Ethan said.

Trey's tongue darted out and sampled the fluids on the pad of Ethan's thumb. "I do lick it a little though." He grinned crookedly and Ethan's heart soared. He wasn't supposed to fall in love with him. That wasn't part of the deal, but Ethan was too far gone to care. He wrapped Trey in a solid embrace and kissed him, not sure if it was a good idea to let all the emotion come through as he devoured

Trey's salty, sticky lips. When he drew away, Trey pressed his face into Ethan's neck and snuggled closer.

"Sleepy," he murmured, nuzzling closer still.

"Let's get in the covers," Ethan suggested. Once he passed out, he wouldn't be moving for hours.

Trey released his hold on him reluctantly, but moved to the head of the bed and climbed between the covers. Ethan joined him and immediately spooned up against Trey's back. He tugged him securely against his entire length with an arm around Trey's waist, and their legs tangled together. Ethan had never been a cuddler, but he wanted to be close to this man. Not just when he fucked him. All the time. Ethan kissed Trey's shoulder lovingly and relaxed into his pillow—his nostrils filled with Trey's scent, his heart filled with Trey's love. With his passion. His light.

"I thought I was going to have to sleep alone tonight," Trey murmured. "I'm glad you came over." He linked his fingers with Ethan's and sighed with contentment.

"Me too," Ethan said gruffly. He loved a man who was free with his affection. At least now he did.

Chapter 25

REAGAN WAS IN THE shower when she heard voices in the apartment. Ethan was home and he had someone with him. Trey? Her heart gave an unexpected lurch and started to race. The erotic images she'd seen the night before played through her mind. Trey and Ethan kissing. Ethan's cock in Trey's hand. In his mouth. She didn't know whether to be aroused or jealous. Admittedly, she was a little of both. And a bit put off by the fact that she'd never be enough to keep Trey happy in the bedroom. As long as he loved only her, she'd be able to deal with it. Maybe.

The bathroom door opened. She peeked out of the shower curtain and was blessed with Trey's orneriest smile. "Can I come in?"

"We need to talk," she said. Ground rules. They needed ground rules. Her heart thudded even harder when Trey tilted his head and he did that thing he did when he wanted something. That irresistible, ornery-assed, tell-me-no-if-you-dare look.

"Talk?"

"Yes, talk."

"Okay," he agreed and entered the bathroom.

Ethan leaned in through the doorway, looking tall, dangerous, and well-fucked. The bastard. "Room in there for three?"

"We're going to talk first."

Ethan's nose crinkled and he moved back in the hallway. Reagan didn't miss the familiar way Ethan stroked Trey's hip before he shut the door behind him. Trey closed the toilet seat lid and sat on its surface.

"Okay, talk," he said. "But make it quick. You're naked and wet. I can't be expected to concentrate on words."

Reagan's belly quivered with nerves. What if they couldn't make this work? What if she had to let him go? What if he ended up feeling something for Ethan and she had to pretend like she was okay with that?

"How often do you think you'll need to be with Ethan?" she forced herself to ask and noticed she'd been rubbing soap over one arm for several minutes.

"Is this about the rules?" Trey asked.

"I think we need to lay some ground rules at the beginning."

"Can we try no rules, Reagan?"

She peeked out of the curtain to look at him. "No rules? There have to be some rules. I know you need a man in your life to fulfill you sexually, but I'm not prepared to let you sleep with anyone you choose. What's the point of being in a relationship if you're not willing to offer me some sort of commitment?" There. She'd said it. Now the ball was in his court.

He sighed and scrubbed his face with both hands. "I love you. You know that, right?"

"I think so."

He looked up at her, his gaze intense. Not at all like Trey's usual devil-may-care expression. Reagan's knees went weak.

"I love you," he said. "I have never said that to a woman in my life. Not in a romantic capacity."

"I love you too."

He smiled. "I want this thing between us to work. I think it's special."

"I think so, too."

"The sexual side of our relationship has to be completely open for it to work."

"*Completely* open?"

"What happens when I get tired of Ethan?"

"What happens when you get tired of *me*?" She didn't mean to sound like a needy banshee, but it was her biggest concern. Not that Trey would find sexual release with a man, but that he'd stop loving her. Or start loving someone else more than he loved her. She couldn't stand the thought.

"Won't happen. I already said I love you." He clutched the fabric of his jeans at his thighs. "You have to be one hundred percent okay with this part of me or you are going to get hurt. That's why I left the first time. Not because I wanted to, but because I can't change for you and I don't want to hurt you, Reagan. I won't be the cause of your tears."

"This is hard," she said.

He linked his hands together and rested his forearms on his thighs. He stared at his thumbs and asked, "Do you need time to think about it? I can go. Give you more time."

She shook her head. "I'm ready to try this. If it doesn't work out, I'll be devastated, but at least I'll know we tried to stay together."

He offered her a crooked grin. "I don't think you'll regret this decision, Reagan. Ethan and I are both here for your pleasure. And mine. And his."

She knew her body wouldn't regret it, but she wasn't so sure about her heart.

"How do you feel about Ethan committing to us?" Trey asked.

Reagan's eyes widened. The water was starting to grow cold, so she hurried to rinse off and shut off the shower. "He shouldn't have to. I mean, if he's just our sex buddy…"

Trey handed her a towel. "He means more to you than a sex buddy, Reagan. He's your best friend. Be realistic."

"I can keep sex and friendship separate," she said and wrapped the towel around her body. "He's for you. Not me."

"He has feelings too," Trey said. He rubbed a hand over his face.

"If he wants to be used as a sex toy, that's his business, but I don't think that's the case. Not after last night."

Reagan's heart gave an unpleasant lurch in her chest. "Are you falling for Ethan?"

He chuckled. "Not exactly. I like him. If I thought last night was a onetime thing, I wouldn't be sitting here discussing this with you, but if you're putting the stipulation on me that if I want a man, it has to be Ethan—nice choice, by the way—then he needs a say in this too."

Never in a million years had Reagan expected Trey to be worried about Ethan's part in this. She had been thinking of Ethan as someone she trusted to serve Trey's sexual needs and leave when she told him to, not as the man she'd been friends with for years. Not as someone who had feelings and wasn't just a nice body with a big cock to keep her boyfriend satisfied. "God, I'm such a bitch! I never once thought about Ethan's feelings in this. He just seemed so eager to take you to bed."

She grabbed the doorknob, but Trey caught her around the waist. "Ethan and I talked about this already."

"Without me?"

"We weren't trying to exclude you. More like protect you."

"I don't need to be protected, Trey. I'm a big girl."

"We both care about you and we like each other enough to commit three ways."

"Three ways?" She could feel the heat rise up her throat.

"At least in the bedroom."

Trey tumbled her onto his lap. "You can say no, Reagan. You can put up any limits you want. I want you to be comfortable with everything we do. If you don't want Ethan to be a fixture in our lives, that's fine. We'll tell him that now. I won't sleep with him again, but I honestly don't know how much deprivation I can tolerate. I lasted about two weeks last time."

She stared up at him. Last night when she'd received those

pictures of Trey with Ethan, she hadn't been jealous or hurt or confused. She'd been aroused. On fire. The jealousy hadn't spawned until that morning when she'd awoken alone and knew the two of them were cuddled up together in bed without her. "Ethan wants this?" Reagan asked.

Trey nodded. "He's emotionally invested in you, sweetheart. He wants a commitment too."

"I thought… I thought." She didn't know what she thought. She knew she loved Trey. She wanted him happy. She trusted Ethan. Then why was she so mixed up? She wrapped her arms around Trey's neck to draw him closer. God, she'd missed him lying beside her last night. She'd become entirely accustomed to him being a part of her life.

"What?" Trey asked, his hand lightly stroking her bare thigh.

"I thought we could decide this stuff afterwards. I want to make sure I like being part of your attraction to men. If it's half as sexy live as it is in pictures, I'm sold." She giggled.

"Mmmm," Trey said, his lips skimming her collarbone. "I do love you, woman."

"Did Ethan satisfy you last night?" she asked.

"Do you really have to ask?"

"He's good in bed, isn't he?"

"You would know." Trey's lips moved up her throat to her jaw. "Are we finished talking now?"

She chuckled. "Did you have something you'd rather do?"

"Ethan and I talked about all the things we wanted to do to you on the drive over. It got me all worked up."

Reagan's towel dropped to her waist as Trey's hands started to wander.

"What kinds of things?"

"We'll show you. Are you sure you're okay with this now? We can take it slower if you need to."

She smiled. "I'm ready." She smoothed his silky hair with her fingertips. "Now."

Trey tipped her onto her feet and stood. He took her towel and dropped it on the floor. "You won't need it." Trey opened the bathroom door, scooped Reagan into his arms, and practically sprinted to the bedroom.

She laughed and held onto his neck. "Eager?"

"Oh yeah."

"Me too."

"Have you ever been with two men before?" he asked her.

She shook her head and turned it abruptly when she noticed Ethan standing beside her bed, removing things from a sack and lining them up in a neat row on her nightstand.

"If you don't like it, we don't have to do it again," Trey told her. "I can keep the two halves of my sexuality separate, if necessary, but I'd much rather share everything I am with you. And so would Ethan."

She tore her eyes away from the set of red silk scarves Ethan had laid out on the bed. In that moment she realized how blessed she was to have Trey in her life. She wanted to be a part of everything he was, because she loved him. "I want that too." And how could he think she wouldn't like it? She supposed it was possible, but not very probable. "Thank you for being so patient with me, Trey. For talking with me about this. It helps with the nervousness I'm feeling."

"You don't have to be nervous. It just me. And Ethan. You trust both of us, don't you?"

"Yes."

"And if you're uncomfortable with anything we do, just let us know." He grinned. "We'll adjust our tactics."

Trey carried her over to the bed and set her down on the edge of the mattress. Ethan glanced at Trey and offered him a wink. Reagan swallowed. She wondered what the two of them had in store for her.

Trey moved to stand behind Ethan. He ran his hands over

Ethan's flat belly. "I think Ethan looks better naked," he said. "What do you think, Reagan?"

"I think you should take his clothes off," she said.

Trey pulled the hem of Ethan's tight T-shirt out of the waist-band of his jeans. Reagan's mouth went dry as she watched Trey's hands slowly slide up Ethan's abdomen, bumping over each ripped muscle as he drew the fabric upward one agonizing inch at a time. Damn, the man was lickable.

"What do you want to do to him, Reagan?" Trey asked.

"Trace all of those stomach muscles with my tongue." Her eyes widened and she looked up at Trey who was watching her over Ethan's shoulder. Had she really just admitted that aloud in front of her boyfriend?

Trey grinned at her. "So what's stopping you?"

"It's okay?" she asked, genuinely flabbergasted that Trey was okay with her licking another man's belly.

"I thought you explained things to her," Ethan said. He reached forward and gently cupped Reagan's face. He gazed down at her with those dark brown eyes of his and her breath caught.

"I tried," Trey said, pulling Ethan's shirt up over his hard pecs. With her mouth hanging open, Reagan watched Trey rub Ethan's nipples. "I don't think she fully understands that there are no limits on anything that goes on between the three of us while we're in this bedroom."

"Looks like we'll have to show her." Ethan grinned wickedly, his gaze skimming over Reagan's flesh until she had a full-body blush going on. "Unfasten my pants, Reagan."

She glanced up at Trey for his approval. She was still struggling with the "no limits" idea. And the three-way commitment thing. Trey nodded slightly and then pulled Ethan's shirt off. Trey kissed Ethan's shoulder and continued his exploration of Ethan's hard body with both hands. Reagan reached for Ethan's belt. Hesitantly, she leaned forward to trace the contours of his ripped abdomen with her tongue while she busied her trembling hands with his fly. As soon as she had Ethan's pants unfastened, Trey dipped both hands into the opening and tugged Ethan's rigid cock free.

A spasm gripped Reagan's entire body as she watched Trey's hand stroke Ethan from base to tip. Her mouth went dry, her pussy wet.

"I love this man's cock," Trey murmured.

Reagan's nervousness lessened. She was very familiar with Ethan's cock. She leaned forward and kissed the swollen head. Ethan's gasp of delight encouraged her to stroke him with the tip of her tongue. Trey grasped Ethan's shaft and rubbed his cockhead over Reagan's lips.

"Suck him, baby," Trey murmured. "Make him really hard for me."

Ethan's fingers tangled in her hair as she sucked him into her mouth. She looked up at him as she bobbed her head and found him staring down at her with tenderness. What was that look for? It wasn't as if he loved her. Actually, she was surprised he was able to accept pleasure from her. Wouldn't he prefer Trey's mouth on him seeing as he was gay?

"She's beautiful, isn't she?" Trey murmured.

"Absolutely," Ethan said.

Trey moved around Ethan and climbed on the bed behind Reagan. He pressed his chest against her back and cupped her breasts in both hands. "Can we share?" he whispered. Reagan didn't know what he meant until she turned her head slightly and found Trey gazing hungrily at Ethan's cock. She never thought she'd think her boyfriend's lust for a man would turn her on, but it did. She crossed her legs and wriggled her hips to calm the pulsating flesh between her thighs. When she released Ethan's cock, Trey guided it into his mouth. He swirled his tongue around Ethan's cockhead and then rubbed his lips over the sensitive flesh.

"Oh God," Ethan gasped. He stroked Trey's hair gently with one hand and Reagan's with his other. "The two of you are amazing."

Trey pulled away from Ethan's cock and kissed the corner of Reagan's mouth. "Now it's your turn, sweetheart." He coaxed her into the center of the bed and pressed her down on her back. "Do you think we need to tie you down?" he asked, his lips brushing lightly over her jaw and along her throat.

"Tie me down?" Her belly and thighs started to tremble uncontrollably.

"Let's see how she reacts first," Ethan said. He climbed up on the bed with her and Trey. Stretching out on his side, he propped his head up on his bent arm and used his free hand to stroke her belly.

"I like that idea," Trey said as he kissed his way down her neck and collarbone. When he caught her nipple in his mouth, she cried out. She was so turned on, she was certain he could make her come just by suckling her breast.

Ethan touched her jaw, encouraging her to look at him. "Can I kiss you?" he asked.

Reagan met his eyes and time froze. Those feelings for him she'd squashed the moment she'd caught him in the shower with that other man began to rise inside her again. She didn't answer him, just closed the distance between their lips and kissed him.

Ethan moaned in her mouth and his hand slid around her waist to draw her body closer to his. Reagan clung to Trey at her breast with one hand, Ethan with the other, and let herself feel all the pleasure, all the love that these two men brought to her life. Ethan tugged away from her sucking kiss to look into her eyes. She saw the raw emotion in his expression and she tried desperately to comprehend its meaning. Did he still have feelings for her? After all this time? But he was gay. She'd given him up because of it. He'd only dated men since they'd broken up. Not a single woman had been in his bed since then. She knew that for a fact. But maybe he did like women, too. He just hadn't found one to replace her yet.

Maybe Ethan was bisexual. Like Trey. He'd even tried to tell her that—multiple times—but she hadn't believed it. Maybe she hadn't wanted to believe it, because how could she love a man who was bisexual? And now, she realized with sudden and shocking clarity, that she didn't love a bisexual man. She loved two of them. What in the hell was she going to do about this? This wasn't how it worked. One man. One woman. That's how this was supposed to work. This love thing. She couldn't love two men. It wasn't possible.

It was inevitable.

She wasn't sure how to deal with this situation. Didn't want to think about it. Not when she had the two of them in bed with her. She'd sort out the complications later. For now, she'd just let herself feel it all and not worry about the fallout. And she knew there would be a fallout. Nothing this amazing could last for long.

"Suck my other breast," she said to Ethan, who had gone catatonic on her as he stared into her eyes. "It's lonely."

He grinned and slid down her body to claim her nipple with his mouth. She looked down at them. Trey flicking that maddening stud in his tongue over her nipple. Ethan attacking her breast as if it were a delectable feast he needed to devour.

She did. She loved them both, but she could never tell them. This was supposed to be a sexual relationship, not an emotional one. She closed her eyes and concentrated on sensation. The tug on her breasts pulled at her womb, her pussy. Trey's hand slid down her belly. Ethan's followed an instant later. Each hand reached one of her thighs and tugged her legs open. She tensed. The feel of being with two men was still foreign. The pleasure in her breasts as they waited for her to relax eventually squelched her trepidation. Her body relaxed, legs falling open in surrender.

Both men caressed the slickened flesh between her thighs. She lost track of whose fingers were rubbing her clit, stroking her labia, tracing the entrance of her vagina. She couldn't comprehend who was sucking one of her nipples hard, who was nibbling the other, who was garbling her name against her flesh. Every sense was in tune pleasure. Two fingers massaged her clit from opposite directions.

"Oh," she gasped, unable to stop her hips from writhing against their hands.

Reagan cried out as all that pleasure culminated at her center and burst in vigorous waves of release. Two fingers slid inside her as she came, working against each other as her pair of lovers prolonged her orgasm together.

Trey and Ethan released her breasts and kissed trails down her belly, their fingers still sliding in and out of her clenching pussy. When they reached her hipbones they paused. Reagan looked down at them and almost came again when they started to kiss each other. When they separated, they pulled their fingers from her body. Ethan moved his hand to Trey's mouth. Staring deeply into Ethan's eyes, Trey sucked Reagan's juices from Ethan's thick fingers. When Trey's slick fingers slipped into Ethan's mouth, Reagan shuddered. The two of them were so in tune with each other and with sharing her. Ethan gazed at Trey the same way he had looked at Reagan a moment ago. Did he have feelings for Trey? Trey just looked hungry. The love she saw in Trey's eyes when he looked at her was missing as he stared at Ethan. A little pang of sadness gripped her heart. She was sad for Ethan, because while Ethan now knew how wonderful Trey's sensuality was, he hadn't gotten to experience his love.

Trey released Ethan's fingers from his mouth and shifted to lie between Reagan's thighs. She jerked when he brushed her clit with the stud piercing in his tongue. She fucking loved that thing. He flicked her clit with the bit of metal and then rubbed her with the softer tip of his tongue before flicking it again. He plunged two fingers into her cunt and then lifted his head. She gazed down at him and watched him draw Ethan's cock into his mouth.

Ethan groaned in pleasure. That piercing must've felt great against the underside of his cock as well. After he took Ethan deep into his throat several times, he pulled his fingers free of Reagan's pussy and lowered his head to stimulate her clit again. He repeated this several times. His fingers inside her while he sucked Ethan. Her pussy empty while he pleased her clit. She was so wet, she could feel her juices dripping down the crack of her ass, hear them slurp each time Trey plunged his fingers into her body.

The fourth time Trey's tongue shifted from Ethan's seeping cock to Reagan's clit, she cried out as a hard orgasm gripped her unexpectedly. He buried his fingers inside her and suckled her clit until her hips stopped bucking.

"Oh God," she gasped, still trembling long after the waves of release subsided.

Trey rolled out from between her legs and Ethan took his place. "Fuck, she's wet," Ethan said as he lowered his head to feast on her pussy. While Trey's every motion was carefully articulated, Ethan ate her out so vigorously that she couldn't keep track of his motions or anticipate what came next. He nibbled her lips and then sucked them into his mouth. Plunged his tongue inside her. Sucked her clit. French-kissed her quivering hole until she thought she'd go mad.

Trey moved to sit on her abdomen. He slid his cock up her chest and pressed her breasts together to surround his rigid flesh. He rubbed her nipples with his thumbs in time with his strokes as he fucked her tits. She bent her neck so she could suck on the head of his cock whenever he thrust forward and it came within reach.

Ethan's thick fingers were now pounding her pussy hard and fast. His mouth had latched on to her clit and she knew he wouldn't relent until she came. Within seconds she was meeting his conditions.

Her back arched as she let go for a third time. The pleasure was so intense that tears streamed from her eyes.

"I think she's ready now," Trey murmured.

Ready? For what? She tried to open her eyes to look at him, but her body wasn't cooperating with her will.

Both men left her lying there, trembling in the aftermath of her last orgasm. She heard the crinkle of condom wrappers. Oh God, they were going to fuck her now. She didn't know if she could take anymore pleasure, but she wanted them. She wanted them both. Inside her.

Ethan moved to cover her body first. His thick cock sought entrance to her body and she opened wide for him, wrapping her arms around his neck and holding on for dear life. When he plunged into her, she cried out in bliss. God, she needed cock. She needed it deep and she needed it hard. Ethan gave her exactly what she needed.

After only a few minutes, Ethan untangled her arms from his neck and pulled out.

She gasped in protest.

"Shh, sweetheart," Trey murmured to her as he stuffed pillows under her hips to lift them off the bed. "We're not finished. I want your cum inside me."

She was too delirious to comprehend what he meant. Trey settled between her thighs and entered her slowly. Filling her with hard cock one delicious inch at a time. When he was buried balls-deep, he rotated his hips, separated his knees, and held still.

Reagan opened her eyes when Ethan moved into position behind Trey. She watched Trey's face while Ethan entered him. And now Reagan understood what Trey had meant about having her cum inside him. Ethan was using her juices to ease his penetration of Trey.

"Oh God," Trey groaned.

"You okay?" Ethan asked him.

Judging by the look of undisguised bliss on Trey's gorgeous face, Reagan guessed that he was better than okay.

"Oh God," Trey groaned again.

Ethan wrapped an arm around Trey's waist, his big hand splayed over Trey's quivering belly. Trey's cock ground inside Reagan as Ethan rotated his hips.

"Can you move?" Ethan asked Trey.

Trey bit his lip and nodded slightly. They moved slowly at first, becoming accustomed to a new rhythm. Ethan pulled out of Trey slowly, Trey pulled out of Reagan. They thrust forward together.

"Ah fuck, this is amazing," Trey gasped.

As the two men became more in tune with each other, their strokes became faster and harder.

Sweat poured from Trey's body. Reagan watched him. He seemed locked in a plane of perpetual bliss as he made love to her and got drilled hard by Ethan at the same time. She'd never experienced anything this intensely sexual in her entire life. Couldn't think of anything she wanted to share with this man more than the pleasure he was so obviously experiencing. Each time he entered her, Ethan pounded him deeper. She fought to keep her eyes open. She wanted to watch Trey's face as he rode his bliss higher and higher.

Trey's entire body went rigid when he came. He thrust deep inside Reagan and held onto her hips, rubbing his face against her shoulder and yelling his triumph against her heated flesh. Ethan pumped hard and fast into him while Trey let go.

"Ah God, Ethan. Fuck me," Trey cried, his eyes squeezing tightly closed. "Don't stop. I'm still coming."

Reagan placed a hand on the back of Trey's head, loving that he was getting off so hard, even though Ethan was mostly responsible for the added pleasure in his release. The bitterness she thought she might experience, knowing Trey needed more than her to be fully satisfied, was completely absent. She wanted him to have complete fulfillment no matter how he attained it. If he needed Ethan to find bliss, then he could have him with her blessing.

Soon Ethan followed Trey over the edge. His fingers dug into Trey's belly as his body shuddered with release and he cried out. They collapsed together, burying Reagan beneath a heap of hot, sated male. She wrapped her arms around both of them, her heart so full of love for the pair that she thought it might burst.

After a moment, Trey said, "Ethan." When he didn't answer, Trey lifted his head. "Ethan?"

"Yeah?"

"We got so carried away that we forgot to make Reagan come again."

Ethan lifted his head and smiled down at Reagan. "Well, we can't leave that business unfinished."

Was this seriously her life? Seriously? Holy hell, she was unquestionably the luckiest woman in the world.

"And I still haven't showed her my favorite position," Trey said.

Chapter 26

PULLING HIS SHIRT ON over his head, Trey entered the kitchen. He was greeted by Reagan's drowsy smile and Ethan's appreciative grin. Trey wrapped an arm around Reagan and kissed her. "How are you feeling?"

"Hungry."

"Lunch will be ready soon," Ethan said.

Ethan stirred the heavenly smelling concoction in the skillet on the stove. Trey moved to stand beside him. He rose up and offered him a deep kiss, while watching Reagan out of the corner of his eye for any signs of displeasure. She grinned. She really seemed okay with this. Actually, she seemed to relish the affection between himself and Ethan. Trey hadn't been expecting that blessing. He'd thought it would bother her to witness him openly sharing affection with Ethan. He'd never expected her to enjoy it.

"What are you making?" Trey asked, looking down into the skillet of steak slices, onions, and various colored peppers. "Fajitas?"

"Ethan's specialty. He got all of his recipes from his mother. She is a phenomenal cook."

"She has her own restaurant," Ethan said. "A mix of authentic Mexican and Tex-Mex. She was born in Mexico, but raised in Texas, so she makes the best of both."

"Is her restaurant here in town?" Trey asked. "I love Mexican food."

Ethan shook his head. "San Antonio. Maybe we can stop in when we pass through there on tour."

"Yeah," said Reagan, "that would be awesome. I haven't seen your parents in ages."

Trey offered Ethan a lopsided grin. "If you're Mexican, how did you end up with a name like Ethan Conner?"

Ethan laughed. "My dad is as white as the Pillsbury dough boy. I got my height from his side of the family too. I tower over my mom's side of the family and all of my half-brothers."

"His mom is tiny," Reagan said. "I doubt she's even five feet tall."

"Four foot eleven."

Trey realized for the first time that Reagan and Ethan had quite a history together. He felt a little left out. "So you've met each other's families?"

"Ethan's never met my dad. You can't take the Arkansas out of the man or take the man out of Arkansas, but Ethan always insists I go with him when he goes to Texas for a visit."

"It makes Mama happy. She adores Reagan. Is expecting her to give her grandchildren any day."

"She's going to continue to be disappointed," Reagan said.

"You didn't tell her when you two broke up?"

"It would have broken her heart," Ethan said and winked at Reagan.

"How many brothers do you have?" Trey asked.

Ethan turned off the burner. "Six half-brothers. My biological father knocked up my mom and they got married because of it. He was in the army and stationed in El Paso at the time. They split up a few months after I was born. They never really loved each other, you know. He had no interest in being a father. He just thought marrying her was the right thing to do. We didn't stay in touch, though I met him once when I was fifteen. I wasn't missing much. My real dad, the one who raised me, is great. My mom married him a couple years after I was born and they had a bunch of kids together. Never a moment of peace in our house. Dad is Latino, like my mom, so my little brothers don't really look like me."

Reagan laughed. "They act like his brothers though."

"Yep. They all drive me crazy. Do you have siblings?" Ethan asked Trey.

"One brother."

"Is he as delicious as you are?" Ethan asked.

"He's in my new band," Reagan said. "You'll get to meet him tomorrow. And yes. He's delicious. Dare is straight though, isn't he, Trey?"

"Yeah. One hundred percent straight."

"Maybe I went after the wrong brother," Reagan said, staring at the ceiling reflectively.

Trey and Ethan exchanged nervous glances.

Reagan laughed. "Never mind. I like this arrangement much better. The two of you are amazing separately and even more incredible together."

"It's ready." Ethan rummaged around in the refrigerator to hand Trey a tub of sour cream and a container of homemade guacamole. Trey grabbed a bottle of hot sauce off the refrigerator door and carried the fixings to the breakfast bar.

"Good," Reagan said. "I'm starving. We need to hurry and get ready for our appointment, Trey."

"Oh yeah, our STD testing/birth control appointment," Trey said. He glanced at Ethan. "You should join us."

Ethan lifted an eyebrow at him. "Why?"

"Trey wants to stop using condoms," Reagan said.

"I'm there," Ethan blurted.

"And then we have our other appointment after that."

"We do?" Trey asked.

"Don't tell me you forgot." She closed one eye and shook her head at him.

"I guess I forgot."

"Bondage training with Aggie and Jace."

How could he have forgotten that? "That's tonight?"

"Yeah."

"Bondage training?" Ethan said, deftly filling warm tortillas with meat and veggies at the stove. He set two on each plate and handed them off to Trey who set them on the breakfast bar.

"Do you want to come with us to that as well?" Trey asked Ethan. While learning how to tie Reagan properly for a night of pleasure was stimulating enough, the thought of restraining a big, tough guy like Ethan had Trey's nerve endings humming like a beehive.

"Are you sure it's okay?" Ethan asked.

"Do you really want Jace to know about your side-relationship with Ethan?" Reagan asked.

"Side-relationship?" Ethan murmured, his dark brows drawn together over his warm brown eyes.

"My band knows all about my sexual preferences. Even Jace. And we're supposed to be in this relationship as equals, Reagan."

"I didn't mean that Ethan was a lesser partner. I meant..." She climbed from her perch on a breakfast bar stool and circled the counter to wrap her arms around Ethan. "Sorry. That didn't come out right. I wasn't sure if Trey wanted his bandmates to know he dated men."

"I'm pretty sure you're the only one who didn't know, Reagan," Trey said. He grabbed a plate of fajitas and smothered them in sour cream and guacamole. He sprinkled a bit of hot sauce on them and climbed on a stool with his plate. "Can we all make up after we eat?"

Ethan secured Reagan in a tight embrace and lowered his head to kiss her. Trey paused with his fajita halfway to his mouth. He'd known from the start that Ethan still had strong feelings for Reagan and as he watched them kiss, his suspicions about Reagan still being in love with Ethan were solidified. The two didn't kiss like fuck buddies. They kissed like lovers. With all the swirling emotions and giddiness that came with being in love. Trey wondered if Reagan's feelings for him were starting to lessen now that Ethan was back in the picture. That would suck. And not in the good way.

Reagan released Ethan and smiled up at him. "Do you want to go to our appointment with us?"

He whispered something into her ear and she grinned deviously, before shifting her gaze to Trey and worrying her lower lip with her teeth. "That sounds like a plan."

"Plan?" Trey questioned. "What plan?"

"That's for us to know and you to find out," Reagan said.

Chapter 27

FROM THE OUTSIDE, JACE'S house looked like any ordinary million-dollar Georgian-styled six-bedroom, eight-bathroom home—huge, paned windows, brick walls, black shutters, and a portico—but once a person stepped into the basement, all signs of normalcy vanished. The dungeon was separated into several rooms. Trey, Reagan, and Ethan were currently in the receiving room. The walls were painted black. Silver-foil vines circled the perimeter of the room near the ceiling. The lighting was kept dim in fixtures that resembled flames, without the fire hazards. There were several red loveseats—all very formal-looking—and three shiny black doors that led off to other rooms.

Jace's fiancée, Aggie, had been the one to greet them. She'd gone all out for the occasion and was dressed in full dominatrix regale from her five-inch, spike-heeled, thigh-high boots to the sexy little leather hat on her head. Her corset, which had red roses embroidered along both sides, fit her like a glove, pressing her large breasts upward into male brain-vacating cleavage. Her long, silky black hair hung to her waist and flowed like satin around her shoulders and waist as she stalked. The woman didn't walk the way most people did. She moved like a predator. She smiled in welcome and gave Trey a big hug, her tough bitch veneer melting away as she squeezed him joyously. "It's been ages, sugar. How have you been?"

When Aggie kissed Trey's cheek, no doubt leaving traces of her cherry red lipstick on his skin, Reagan grabbed his arm and yanked.

"I've been great. How about you?"

"My custom-made corset business is really picking up. I don't have time to work the dungeon much these days. When Jace told me you were coming, I was so excited." She flicked the end of her riding crop against Trey's thigh and he tensed. It hadn't hurt. Just made a loud noise. Reagan rubbed his thigh and glared at Aggie. "Who's this?" Aggie asked, her attention settling on Reagan.

"This is my girlfriend Reagan," he said.

Aggie took her hand and shook it. "Girlfriend, huh? Never thought I'd see this one settled down." She nodded her head toward Trey. "I'm Aggie."

"Jace is such a cutie," Reagan said. "And a great listener."

Trey snorted in amusement.

"Yeah, I kind of like him," Aggie said and winked at her.

"And this is my boyfriend Ethan," Trey said.

Aggie grinned. "Now that makes more sense. Very naughty. Like our Trey was meant to be." She shook Ethan's hand. "What's our pecking order here?" She looked from one person to the next.

Reagan and Ethan exchanged a confused glance.

"Who's the top dog?" Aggie clarified.

"We reciprocate all around," Trey said. "Ethan's mostly a top, but I switch."

"What about Reagan?"

Trey contemplated Reagan for a moment. She wasn't truly submissive or dominant. She was just the goddess whose body they worshipped. "That's a good question."

"I'll work with her," Aggie said. "As for you." She flicked her riding crop in Ethan's direction. "Don't even think about disobeying. I know your type."

"Me?" Ethan said.

Aggie chuckled, a deep throaty laugh that made Trey want to crawl around on his knees at her feet. "Don't worry, sugar. Reagan will break you in properly."

Ethan gave Reagan a worried look. She smiled nervously.

"It's okay, doll," Aggie said to Reagan and took her hand. "We'll have these two studs begging for you in no time. Come with me. I need to explain a few things and find you something more empowering to wear."

Reagan swallowed and nodded. Trey had to admire Reagan's bravado. Aggie tended to be a tad intimidating until you saw what a generous heart she hid behind that tough exterior. And she did a good job of hiding it except where Jace was concerned. Jace turned the woman to mush.

"Jace is in the next room," Aggie said. "You two head in there. He wasn't expecting two of you, so make sure you explain the dynamics to him for this first scenario, Trey."

"Will do." Trey took a step toward the next room and then drew to a sudden halt. "What exactly are the dynamics for this first scenario?"

"You know I'm going to try to make a domme out of your little sweetheart." Aggie laughed with obvious delight. "We can switch things around later if necessary, but she's got the right backbone for it and I can't wait to watch that one squirm." She pointed at Ethan with her riding crop. "We'll try it this way first. I think you're all going to enjoy it."

"Trey?" Reagan said quietly, her voice wavering with anxiety.

He gave her a gentle hug and kissed her. "Trust Aggie. She knows what she's doing."

Reagan nodded.

Ethan stroked her hair. "This should be interesting." He kissed her too.

Aggie took Reagan's hand and tugged her toward one of the shiny black doors. "Both of your men are gorgeous. You are one lucky bitch, do you know that?"

Reagan laughed. "Yeah. I know."

"You're going to have to tell me how you ended up with two hotties."

When they disappeared through the door and securely closed it behind them, Ethan turned to Trey.

"You know I'm never a sub, Trey. Why didn't you tell her that?"

"I think you might be surprised by what you can be."

Trey opened the door that led to the main dungeon. He expected Jace to be all decked out in leather with a spiked collar and a black hood over his face, but nope, he looked like regular old Jace—blue jeans, white T-shirt, black motorcycle boots, and a single black leather cuff on his left wrist. He smiled a welcome at Trey, but it vanished when Ethan stepped into the room behind him.

"I thought you were bringing Reagan," Jace said.

"I did. I also brought Ethan."

Jace nodded at Ethan. "So how does this work?"

"Aggie's preparing Reagan to dominate," Trey said.

"Both of you?" Jace asked.

"And you too," Trey teased.

Jace grinned. "Not likely."

Jace moved to a series of buttons in a panel on the wall and pressed one. A mechanical grinding sound drew Trey's attention to the ceiling. A long, heavy, wooden beam suspended by chains lowered until it was at shoulder level.

"Take your shirts off," Jace said. "Once you're bound, you aren't going anywhere for a while." Jace opened a cabinet built into the wall. Trey caught a glimpse of ropes, chains, harnesses, collars, and cuffs. He wished he had more time to play with Ethan before Reagan joined them. He was in the mood to take a dominant role.

Trey reached for the hem of Ethan's shirt and pulled the garment off over his lover's head. He caught his nipple between his teeth and flicked the flesh with his tongue.

"Who should I start with?" Jace asked.

"I'll help you with Ethan," Trey offered, not even bothering to conceal his ornery grin.

"How much do you plan on struggling, Ethan?" Jace asked as if he were asking him what size shoe he wore.

"I've never been bound. I don't know."

Jace glanced at Trey. "How's his self-control?"

"What self-control?"

Jace nodded and handed Trey a set of wide wrist cuffs. "I don't think Aggie will push this too far in your first session, but we'll go with these."

Trey secured a cuff to each of Ethan's wrists. They extended halfway up his forearms and reminded Trey of gauntlets. Made Ethan look almost barbaric and infinitely sexy. Jace showed Trey how to attach the cuffs to the wooden beam which had large holes drilled through it.

"Lift your arm out to the side," Jace instructed.

When Ethan complied, he hooked the chain to Ethan's wrist cuff and threaded the chain through the hole nearest his wrist. Jace showed Trey how to secure the chain on the back side of the wooden beam. He put a carabiner clip through a chain link to prevent it from being drawn back through the hole and then took the length of chain to wrap around Ethan's hard-muscled arm several times.

"That's mostly for looks," Jace explained as he secured the end of chain through a hole under Ethan's armpit. "The cuff will hold him. The chain just makes it look more impressive."

"I'm impressed. You look sexy, Ethan," Trey said, making a mental list of all the things he wanted to do to the man's hard body.

"Is anything pinching?" Jace asked Ethan.

Ethan looked down the length of his right arm. He gave his restraint a hard tug, but it scarcely had a centimeter of give in it. "Surprisingly, no. The chain is a little cold, but it doesn't hurt."

"Trey, you restrain his other arm while I find something for you."

The second Jace's back was turned, Ethan grabbed Trey by the back of the neck with his free arm and pulled him against him.

"Do you like me like this?" he asked, his voice low and soothing. "At your mercy?"

Trey laughed. "I think I'm the one at your mercy right now."

Ethan tilted his head and captured Trey's mouth in a plundering kiss. Trey opened his mouth to Ethan's possession, kissing him back as hard as he was receiving. Ethan tugged his mouth away, his hand sliding from the nape of Trey's neck down his back so he could draw him against him.

"Trey," Jace said somewhere behind him. "You're supposed to be securing his arm, not making out with him."

"Right," he agreed breathlessly.

Ethan allowed Trey to fasten a chain to his free arm, stood still while he threaded it through a hole in the beam, and made no protest as he clipped on a carabiner to secure the chain. Trey couldn't help but run appreciative hands over Ethan's bulging biceps as he wrapped the chain around his arm. He secured the free end of the chain and took a step back to admire masculine perfection. He wanted to suck and lick and nibble every inch of the man's body. Wanted to give him so much pleasure that he begged for pain. It wasn't to be. Jace fastened a narrow cuff around Trey's wrist and tugged him to stand against the wooden beam next to Ethan.

"Take off your shirt, Trey."

He complied and tossed it across the room.

"You're restraining us side-by-side?" Trey asked.

"I could put you back-to-back, but I figured you'd rather watch what's happening to each other in the mirror this first time. See each other's reactions."

Trey focused on the mirror they faced. His gaze roamed Ethan's muscled torso and eventually met his eyes.

"Jace, you're a flipping genius."

"I just see the way you look at him. You're still very visual in your attraction to him. You haven't been together long, have you?"

Trey did like to look at Ethan, but he was attracted to much more than his handsome face and perfect body. Looks worked for this though, since they couldn't touch each other.

"Not long, no," Ethan said.

"Watch the mirror throughout the session," Jace advised. "You'll learn a lot about each other."

Trey chuckled. "Like I have to be told to watch Ethan."

"Next time you should consider hoods. Then you'll be able to tune into each other on a different level. Especially since sound is so important to Trey."

Amazing how much Jace talked when he was advising on his favorite hobby. Bondage.

"Are you ready for us?" Aggie asked through a crack in the door.

"Just a minute," Jace said.

He fastened Trey's other cuff, hooked a chain to it, and threaded it through a hole on the wooden beam. He drew it out through another hole and fastened it to Trey's other cuff. Unlike Ethan, Trey had several inches of play in his chains.

"That's not fair," Ethan complained. "I can't move at all."

"He can move less than you think," Jace said. "Okay, Aggie, bring her in."

When Reagan strutted into the room, Trey's jaw dropped. An angel in white and pink leather. White, high-heeled boots that laced up the front hugged her calves but stopped just below her knee. The short, pink skirt she wore didn't cover the cheeks of her ass, and the white corset pressed her tits up and together. She was wearing hot pink lipstick and her eyelashes were thick and heavy. Trey didn't think he'd ever seen her wear lipstick before. She looked fucking hot, but it was the confidence in her stride that made his heart pump out of control.

"Damn, baby," Ethan murmured.

"You will address her as Mistress," Aggie said.

"Damn, Mistress," Ethan said, "you look hot."

Reagan cocked an eyebrow at him. "Did I say you could speak?"

Trey watched Ethan in the mirror and had to concentrate hard on not laughing. It was obvious from his stunned expression that he'd never played this sort of game before. Aggie had been right. It would be fun watching him squirm.

"Well, no, but—"

Reagan smacked her riding crop against her boot with a loud crack. "Then don't speak."

"Mistress?" Trey asked, ducking his head respectively.

"Yes, Trey."

"May I say that you look fucking hot, Mistress?"

She smiled and then glanced at Aggie before wiping the smile off her face. "You may," Reagan said.

"You look fucking hot, Mistress."

"I agree," Ethan said. "Are you going to hit me now? You're making me all hard and horny."

Reagan's eyes widened and she looked to Aggie for direction.

"He's misbehaving. Do you give him what he wants?" Aggie asked.

"No?" Reagan asked hesitantly.

"Fuck no," Aggie said. "Trey is being well-behaved. You should reward him."

Aggie winked at Trey and moved to stand next to Jace in case Reagan needed more assistance.

Reagan strode to stand before Trey. She drew the end of her riding crop down the center of his chest and used it to flick his nipple piercing. Trey's belly tightened and his eyes drifted closed.

"Aggie said I didn't have to hit you if I didn't want to," she whispered.

Good, because Trey wasn't too fond of being hit.

"Do you want to, Mistress?" Trey asked.

She shook her head and leaned close to whisper in his ear. "I want to rub my hands all over your body while you can't get away."

"That's not playing by the rules, Mistress," he whispered.

"I want to make up my own rules."

There was a loud slap from the corner of the room and the three of them turned their attention to Aggie who was rubbing the ass she'd just smacked. Jace's. He had his head tilted back in obvious delight.

"Why don't you two take that elsewhere?" Trey suggested. "We're okay here."

"Are you sure? I haven't taught her much yet," Aggie said. Jace whispered something in her ear. She slapped his ass again and his entire body went taut.

"I'm sure," Trey said. "What do you think, Mistress?"

"I can handle these two," Reagan said.

"What? My opinion doesn't matter?" Ethan said.

"No one told you to speak," Reagan said.

"Jace does have some tension to work through," Aggie said. "I've been too busy to give him what he needs since he got off tour."

"This is unbearable to watch right now," Jace said. "I need it, Aggie."

"Need it or want it?" she asked.

"Both."

She smiled and went to a panel on the wall. "Mistress Rea, if you get into trouble, press this red button. It will make all the lights in the dungeon flash and I'll know to come check on you."

"Understood," Reagan said with a nod.

Aggie strode out of the room with an eager Jace on her heels. As soon as the door closed, Reagan tossed her riding crop aside. "You look so hot, Ethan," she purred. She approached him and rubbed her palms over every inch of his hard chest and stomach. She peppered his chest with kisses and reached for his belt. Once his fly was unfastened, she jerked his pants down to his knees and grasped his hard cock in both hands. Trey couldn't decide what was sexier, Reagan's enthusiasm or Ethan's persistent struggle against his restraints as he moaned in pleasure.

"Stand behind him, Reagan," Trey suggested, "so he can watch himself in the mirror."

Reagan glanced at Trey and her hands fell free of Ethan's body. "Damn, you look hot too, Trey," she said. She moved to wrap her arms around him, pressing her breasts against his chest as she rubbed her hands up and down his back and buttocks. She kissed his throat until he began to tremble. He wanted to touch her. Knowing he couldn't made him want to even more.

"Release me," he whispered in her ear, "and we'll both make Ethan squirm."

"Maybe I planned to release Ethan so we could both make you scream."

"What are you two talking about over there?" Ethan asked gruffly.

Reagan offered Ethan an ornery grin and moved to stand behind Trey. She slowly released the buttons of Trey's fly. "Watch the mirror, Ethan," Reagan said.

He turned his attention to the mirror. Trey made sure the pleasure registered on his face as Reagan slid her hands down into his pants and tugged his cock free of his boxers. He watched the mirror with his eyes half-closed, mostly to see Ethan's reaction as Reagan's hands slid up and down his length, but also because seeing her touch him at the same time he felt it was an incredible turn-on.

"What should I do to him, Ethan?" Reagan murmured.

"Take his pants off. I want to see all of him."

Reagan obeyed without question. Even bound to a wooden beam, Ethan's dominance was unquestionable. At least until Reagan agreed to release Trey. Reagan lowered Trey's jeans to the floor and removed his shoes and socks before stripping him entirely naked.

"I can't decide which of you is more desirable," Ethan said.

"I guess that means you'll have to want us both," Trey said.

"I do," he whispered. "Reagan, suck his sac. I want to watch him squirm."

Reagan knelt before Trey and started her pleasurable assault by flicking her tongue over Trey's scrotum. He tugged against his chains as the gentle licking became vigorous sucking. She had an entire sensitive nut in her mouth when he started begging.

"Reagan, please." His abdominal muscles began to twitch uncontrollably and he knew if the chains weren't there to keep him upright, he'd have sank to the floor.

"My turn," Ethan said. "Reagan."

She ignored both of them, intent on her task to drive Trey insane with pleasure and Ethan insane with lack thereof. When she stopped unexpectedly, Trey looked down at her. She grinned up at him and flicked her eyes to the mirror. At first he thought she was encouraging him to check out the pained expression on Ethan's face, but as he watched, she removed her lacy thong and spread her legs, leaning forward as she took Trey's aching balls in her mouth again. He couldn't take his eyes off the slick flesh between her legs. Flushed and swollen with excitement, her feminine folds begged for penetration and there wasn't a damn thing Trey could do about it.

"Reagan," Ethan murmured. "Reagan, let me go. I need to fill you."

Trey didn't know if he could actually come when his cock had been completely neglected, but the urgency in his groin had built to the point that he was involuntarily thrusting his hips. Reagan nipped the sensitive skin covering his balls and his entire body jerked. She licked the head of his cock with the flat of her tongue and then climbed to her feet. She moved to stand behind Ethan. He jerked the beam so hard that Trey stumbled as it tugged him forward then back.

"Easy," Trey complained.

"Let me go, Reagan," Ethan growled.

"You don't like to be defenseless?" Reagan asked.

"No."

"Your cock is calling you a liar. Look how hard you are."

Standing behind him, but not pressing against his back, Reagan wrapped her arms around Ethan's body and took his cock in both hands. He was already seeping pre-cum. Trey doubted he'd last more than ten seconds with Reagan stroking him that way.

"Don't come, Ethan," she said, stroking him faster. Faster. "If you come, I'm going to let Trey help me torture you with pleasure."

Ethan grunted and squeezed his eyes shut. She stroked him faster, both hands skimming over his length in gentle strokes. Trey was about to come just watching it. Ethan's gasps of excitement made Trey's ball tighten.

"Stop," Ethan gasped. "I can't hold back. Reagan? Reagan!"

Trey groaned when the first spurt of cum erupted from Ethan's rigid body. Reagan caught the second spurt in her hand and rubbed it into his flesh as she continued to stroke him.

"I told you not to come," she said, her voice hard, but behind his back she winked at Trey and grinned.

"Y-your fault," he gasped. "Okay, I'm done. Stop. Please. I can't... Oh." Ethan's entire body continued to jerk in hard spasms as Reagan continued to stroke him.

"Are you sure you want me to stop? I'm going to have Trey top you as soon as I'm done."

Oh how Trey loved this woman. His cock began to jump in excitement.

"Not happening," Ethan growled.

"Why not?" Reagan asked.

"Because I'm a top."

"Tonight you're a switch."

Reagan released Ethan's cock and moved back to Trey. She leaned close to his ear. "Do you want him?"

"God, yes. I love cherries."

Reagan laughed. "That's kind of evident in the number of cherry suckers you eat in a day."

"I mean the other kind of cherry."

Reagan's brow furrowed.

"Ethan's never been penetrated," Trey clarified. "He's a virgin."

Reagan's eyes widened. "But I thought…"

"He has always topped."

She glanced at Ethan. "We can't force him. That would be wrong."

Trey grinned at her crookedly and said quietly, "Release me and we won't have to. I'll have him begging for it in no time."

"Not a chance," Ethan, who apparently had superhuman hearing, said.

Reagan kissed Trey and then moved behind him to unfasten his restraints. As soon as he was free, he pulled Reagan against him and kissed her deeply for several long minutes.

"This is completely unfair," Ethan grumbled.

Trey pulled away from Reagan. "I agree. You're about to get all the pleasure and you're the only one in the room who's already come."

"Release me," he demanded.

Trey chuckled. "Not until we're finished with you."

Trey reached for his discarded jeans and removed the cherry-flavored lube from his pocket. Reagan watched him as he moved to stand in front Ethan. Trey coated Ethan's now flaccid cock with lube and then sank to his knees to suck him. It took Ethan a while to relax. Trey had been with enough virgins to know how to make the entire experience pleasurable, but his partner had to both trust him and be relaxed. Being restrained would make it difficult for Ethan to trust him, and he was far from relaxed. It did excite him though. Within minutes, his cock grew thick and hard within Trey's persistently tugging mouth. When Ethan began to moan and thrust gently into Trey's throat, Trey moved away. He needed to lower the beam a little. Ethan was a few inches taller than he was. Trey turned his head and found Reagan watching him with her hand up her skirt.

Trey grinned slyly. "Do you like watching that?"

She bit her lip and nodded.

"Are you rubbing yourself?"

She lifted her skirt and showed him that her fingers were buried deep inside her swollen pussy.

"Do you want me to take care of you first?" Trey asked her.

She shook her head. "I want you both. Later. Can I help you? I need something to occupy myself."

Trey climbed to his feet. "Keep him hard for me."

Trey went to the control panel on the wall and carefully depressed the switch he'd watched Jace push earlier. After the beam had lowered a couple of inches, he stopped it and locked it in place again. He turned and found Reagan bent forward at the waist sucking Ethan's cock while she plunged the fingers of her free hand in and out of her body. Ethan was watching her in the mirror with an almost pained expression on his face. That should help him be more receptive to all the things Trey planned to do to him. Trey moved to stand behind Ethan and leaned against his back. He settled his hard cock between the taut cheeks of Ethan's ass, took one cheek in each hand, and massaged them around his cock. When the tension went out of Ethan's spine, Trey slid down his body. He kissed and sucked and bit Ethan's firm backside until he started to whimper. Trey drew his tongue over the entrance to Ethan's body and Ethan shuddered, sucking harsh, excited breaths into his chest.

Trey squirted some cherry-flavored lube on two fingers and rubbed them over Ethan's tight hole, massaging in small circles until a fingertip slipped inside.

"Oh," Ethan gasped.

Trey was surprised Ethan wasn't putting up more resistance.

Trey added the motions of his tongue to that of his fingers. Lapping at the sweetly flavored lube, he caught his piercing on the rim of Ethan's entrance with each hard flick.

"Trey, Trey," he gasped, fighting his chains now.

Trey leaned away. "Do you want me to stop?"

"No, no," he groaned, "but just your finger. Put it inside. Deeper."

Trey slowly pressed one finger inside him. He peeked around Ethan's body to see how Reagan was doing. He could hear her slurping and sucking, but he hadn't been prepared for the enthusiasm she was showing Ethan's cock. And what he saw of her in the mirror was even more mind-blowing. Her thighs were slick with her cum and she was still working herself with her hand. He and Ethan were going to reward her for hours for being so wonderful.

"Deeper," Ethan urged. "Trey."

Trey forced his attention off Reagan and to what he was doing with Ethan. Trey's balls protested their lack of relief. He was tempted to skip this step and plunge into Ethan's body, but Ethan was still a little tense. Trey added more lube to his fingers and slipped two of them inside, thrusting gently in and out of Ethan's increasingly receptive body.

"Deeper," Ethan whispered.

Trey's fingers were already as deep as they would go. He began to move them in an increasingly wide circle.

Ethan was chanting to deities now.

"Tell me what you want, Ethan," Trey urged.

"Deeper," he gasped. "Harder, Reagan. Suck harder."

"Ethan, what do you need?" Trey asked, reaching for a condom from his pants pocket, while he continued to prepare Ethan for full penetration with three fingers now.

"I need fucked, Trey. Do it."

Trey pulled his fingers free and Ethan sputtered in denial.

"No, no, don't stop."

Trey rolled the condom over his straining cock and moved into place behind Ethan. He slathered lube down his length and then pressed the head of his cock into Ethan's opening. Ethan rocked back against him, wanting to be rammed, but Trey didn't want to hurt him. Not their first time. He hoped this would become a regular part of their lovemaking. They could get a little rougher next time if that's what Ethan wanted.

Trey held Ethan's hips and guided himself into him slowly, adjusting his angle if he encountered any resistance. Ethan's entire body trembled as he accepted Trey. Completely accepted him.

"Are you okay, baby?" Trey whispered, wrapping his arms around Ethan's waist and pressing open-mouthed kisses to his back.

"No wonder you like this," he gasped. "What does it feel like to have someone inside of you when you come?"

"We'll show you."

Trey began to move inside him then. Slowly at first, careful to cause as little pain as possible, and then more rapidly at Ethan's insistence. Trey hoped Ethan found release soon, because as excited as he was, he knew he wouldn't last long, especially when Reagan's hand appeared between his thighs and massaged his balls against Ethan's.

Reagan pulled away, and Trey watched Ethan's fluids jet from his body as his ass clenched around Trey's cock.

"Fuck," Ethan growled, his head thrown back in pure bliss.

Trey continued to thrust until Ethan stopped spurting and then Trey let go, shuddering hard as pleasure consumed him. He collapsed against Ethan's back, attempting to regain his breath. Trey reached over and released Ethan's restraints. The chains gave way with a loud clank and they sank to the floor on their knees, both too weary to stand.

A pair of sexy white boots entered Trey's line of sight. He glanced up at Reagan who was standing over them with her hands on her hips.

"Watching you two get off on each other really turns me on, but I think it's my turn now."

Trey figured she had more than one turn owed to her.

Reagan emitted a squeak of surprise when Ethan wrapped an arm around her waist and pulled her to the dungeon floor. "I think our Mistress needs to be taught a lesson," he said gruffly.

Now what did he mean by that? "*Ethan?*"

His chains rattled as he captured her head between his hands and stared down at her with the most intense expression she'd ever encountered. Her heart rate thundered out of control.

"What should we do to her first, Trey?"

Trey peered at her over Ethan's shoulder. "I don't know about first, but at some point tonight I want her legs wrapped around my waist and those sexy boots digging into my ass."

She tore her gaze from Ethan's to smile up at Trey. "You like the boots?"

Trey nodded vigorously.

"No one said you could speak," Ethan said and covered her mouth with a deep kiss.

Ah, so he wanted to be in charge now. She could handle that. Ethan suddenly tore his mouth away from hers and winced as Trey pulled away from him. "Where are you going?" he asked. "I like you in there. I thought I might get to be in the middle this time."

"It's Reagan's turn to be in the middle," Trey said.

Reagan contemplated what that meant for a moment. "No, thank you. I'm perfectly content to be on the very bottom."

"I thought you wanted to experience my favorite position," Trey said, a teasing grin on his gorgeous face.

"Not if it involves a huge cock in my ass."

"I'm not that huge," Trey said.

Words she'd never thought she'd ever hear a man say.

"It feels great, sweetheart. He knows what he's doing," Ethan said. His gruffness had already vanished and he peppered her face and neck with gentle kisses.

"Should we head for home?" Trey asked. "There isn't anything remotely resembling a bed in this place."

"There are loveseats in the entry," Reagan said and then flushed when she considered that they might actually take her out there and have their way with her. Aggie and Jace or some random customer might witness her shameless acceptance of two lovers.

"That there are," Ethan said and rose from the floor. "Help me with these chains," he said to Trey.

Reagan lay on the floor and watched the two of them interact. There was something different between them now. A new awareness or connection or something. While Trey unfastened the cuffs on Ethan's forearms, Ethan stared at him with unmistakable adulation. And love. Trey treated Ethan more carefully than usual, as if six feet two inches of broad-chested, muscle-bound hunk was something to cherish. When Ethan was free of his restraints, he embraced Trey and buried his face in his neck. Trey held him but didn't say anything. Reagan felt almost guilty watching their moment of sweet togetherness. Something about it made her heart ache.

And lying on the floor made her back ache.

Ethan pulled away and patted Trey's bare butt. "You can top me anytime, baby."

Reagan chuckled. Perhaps she'd been seeing a little more in that embrace than was really there.

Ethan headed for the door that led to the entryway. "Help me?" he asked Trey.

The pair left the room and Reagan wondered if they'd forgotten about her until they pushed one of the red loveseats into the room and closed the door.

"I've never moved furniture in the nude before," Trey commented.

"I've seen a few mattresses move when you're in the nude," Ethan said.

"And the earth," Reagan added.

Trey turned to look at her. "What are you doing on the floor?"

"Waiting for Ethan to teach me a lesson."

Ethan grinned. Reagan hadn't seen him smile like that for over a year. He returned to her side and scooped her up into his arms. "Your lesson will take place over here," he said and carried her to the sofa. He set her down gently and removed her corset, but left the skintight piece of leather posing as a skirt in place.

It turned out to be a lesson in pleasure. Not that it surprised her. Her men treated her well, but seeing as they were in a dungeon, she was expecting something a little more painful than having her breasts and ass worshiped by eager hands and mouths. Ethan went snooping around in the dungeon implements and found a blindfold. Reagan scowled when he slipped it over Trey's eyes.

"Find the cherry," Ethan said. He applied small spots of Trey's cherry-flavored, edible lube to Reagan's skin. Trey used his lips and tongue to find the hidden locations with Ethan's convoluted instructions of warmer and colder. It took him twenty minutes to find the spot on her shoulder, because Ethan kept redirecting him to her nipple. Another ten minutes to find the spot on her knee, because he kept Trey near the top of her thigh until she couldn't bear it any longer.

Trey was very thorough in his search and even more so when he finally found his treat. Reagan hoped Ethan put some of that lube on her clit soon. She was on fire and that's where she wanted Trey's mouth the most.

Reagan pouted when Ethan coated the head of his cock with lube and rubbed it over Trey's lips. Trey's tongue darted out and he licked Ethan's swollen head for a solid minute before he hesitated. "I don't think this is part of Reagan," Trey said.

"Ethan's cheating," Reagan said.

"You're getting warmer, Trey," Ethan said.

Trey's tongue darted out to lick at the flavoring on Ethan's cock. He was just as thorough on Ethan as he had been on Reagan. Licking and sucking. Rubbing his lips over him first and following that with his tongue. His lips again.

"Warmer." Ethan sucked in an excited breath as Trey's lips suckled off what remained of the cherry flavoring by taking the entire head of Ethan's cock in his mouth. "Hotter. Hotter. Oh God, you're hot."

Trey pulled away. "Reagan gets to pick where she wants it next."

Catching Ethan's eye above Trey's head, Reagan pointed at the heated flesh between her legs. Ethan shook his head.

"That's where I want it," she complained.

"You're being taught a lesson," Ethan said.

"What kind of lesson?"

"How to take more pleasure than you can possibly stand."

Well, that didn't sound so bad.

"Without coming," he added.

"He's big into the delayed gratification thing," Trey commented. "I wonder if he's ever experienced it."

Reagan knew he had. She used to ride him for hours and he'd just keep holding back on her until she got completely exasperated with him. "I can't ever make him come if he doesn't want to," Reagan said.

"How could he not want to? That's the best part," Trey said.

"Exactly. Must be the alpha male in him."

"You can make *me* come, Reagan. I won't hold back on you," Trey said.

"Will you make me come too?" Reagan said. "I'm not much into the delay of gratification thing either. I'd rather try for multiple orgasms."

"Hey," Ethan protested. "I thought I was running the show here."

"We just let you think that," Trey said.

Reagan laughed at the expression on Ethan's face. He apparently thought this meant he wasn't going to be involved.

"I think I've had enough cherry flavor. Now I want to taste Reagan," Trey said. Kneeling on the floor beside the loveseat, he searched blindly for Reagan's thigh and leaned over her body. She opened wide for him—one leg on the back of the sofa, the other on the floor. He kissed and sucked his way up the inside of her thigh. When he reached the wetness between her legs, he sampled it with his tongue, licking her not to bring her pleasure—though it did— but to collect every drop she produced for him. Her eyes drifted closed as she lost herself to sensation. They popped open again when Ethan joined her on the loveseat. He slid his large hands under her ass and lifted her hips off the sofa, kneeling between her legs. She noticed he'd applied a condom. She couldn't wait to find out what they had in store for her next. Trey was still swirling his tongue in her opening. He followed the raise of her hips without a problem.

"You're getting colder, Trey," Ethan said.

Trey suckled his way toward her clit. When he latched on to the sensitive nub, a spasm gripped Reagan's entire body.

"Now you're hot," Ethan said and inched forward until his cock pressed against Reagan's quivering pussy. He slid inside her, his thrusts shallow as Trey was still working her clit with that sensual mouth of his. Ethan ran a hand across Trey's shoulders and Trey lifted his head so Ethan could plunge deep—once, twice, three times—before he backed off several inches to give Trey room to lick her clit with hard, rapid strokes of his delightful tongue. When the first waves of orgasm washed over her, she cried out in bliss. Ethan rotated his hips, stretching her clenching pussy in wide circles while she came. The pleasure became too much for her and she grabbed Trey's hair to pull him away. Ethan plunged deep and then pulled out entirely. He lowered her hips to the sofa again and she lay there shuddering and gasping for air, while he moved to sit at the end of the sofa. She watched Trey sit on Ethan's lap, his back to Ethan's belly. Trey took Ethan inside his body, rising and falling over him in obvious bliss. Ethan used both hands to rub Trey's balls and cock until Trey's legs began to tremble. He pulled away unexpectedly and removed Ethan's condom. Trey sucked Ethan's cock for several minutes, while Ethan clung to the sofa cushions with both hands, obviously fighting one hell of an orgasm for all he was worth. Trey applied a new condom and held a hand out to Reagan.

"Your turn, baby. See if you can make him come."

So that's what Trey was doing. She was game. Ethan moved over a few inches so she could straddle him more easily. Facing him, she took Ethan inside, ready for another orgasm already. Watching Trey with Ethan had gotten her excited all over again.

Trey stood behind her and massaged her breasts while she rode Ethan. His hands moved down her ribs and belly. He stroked her clit with two fingers and then returned to massaging her breasts.

"Do you think she's ready?" Trey asked Ethan.

She's ready? Weren't they trying to make Ethan come?

Ethan shifted his hips to the very edge of the sofa and held her down, completely impaled on his thick cock. Trey moved between Ethan's legs and settled against Reagan's back. Slippery fingers rubbed against her ass and then slipped inside.

"Trey?" she gasped. "What are you…"

She lost her train of thought and ability to protest when his fingers began to move inside her.

"Oh," she gasped.

"I can feel that," Ethan murmured.

Trey pulled his fingers free.

"Wait," Reagan protested. "I liked it."

"Relax for me, Reagan," Trey murmured.

She wasn't sure what he meant, but she went limp against Ethan and the next thing she knew Trey's cock was buried in her ass.

She jerked upright, her body so full, she wasn't sure how to respond.

"Easy," Trey murmured. "Trust me. I won't hurt you."

It didn't hurt, exactly. There was an unaccustomed pressure within, but not pain.

Trey withdrew slightly and thrust forward.

Ethan groaned and dropped his head back against the sofa. "I can feel you move against me, Trey. Inside of her."

"That's why this is my favorite position," Trey said.

Reagan chuckled. Well, she never would have figured that out on her own.

"Lean forward a little," Trey instructed.

Reagan complied. Now that she was filled with both of them, she'd lost her inhibitions about trying this. She wanted to experience all it had to offer.

"Ride him, Reagan. I'll do the rest," Trey said in her ear.

It took her several attempts to find her rhythm. Trey held still as she rose and fell over Ethan, drawing both cocks in and out of her body with maximum effort. She wouldn't last long at this rate. Trey smacked Ethan on the shoulder. "Help her."

He'd been sitting there shuddering with his eyes closed, but at Trey's insistence, Ethan gripped Reagan's ass in both hands and helped her rise and fall. Once they found a steady rhythm, Trey began to move in shallow fast strokes, which rubbed his cock repeatedly against Ethan's on each up and down stroke of Reagan's body.

Ethan's head fell back against the sofa, his mouth dropped open, and his eyes rolled into the back of his head.

"I'll make him come," Trey said. "He'll never be able to hold out on us like this, Reagan."

She meant to agree with him, but her mind was not functioning well enough to form coherent thoughts, much less words. She could feel their cocks working against each other inside of her. It was the most wonderful, weirdest sensation she'd ever experienced.

Ethan cursed under his breath. "Fuck, I'm gonna come. I can't fight it."

Trey's fingers sought Reagan's clit to help her join Ethan in bliss. Her hips buckled unexpectedly the instant he touched her there and she cried out at the same instant that Ethan shouted in triumph, and Trey shuddered behind her with his own release.

Fan-fucking-tastic. Oh yeah. She could totally get used to this threesome thing. Even if it meant she wouldn't be able to walk for a couple days afterward. Fucking-A, Trey rocked her world. And Ethan made it spin.

Chapter 28

Trey watched Reagan's frustration build at rehearsal the next day. All the guys of Exodus End were behind her one hundred percent and she was doing great for her first attempt at rehearsing an entire, major live show, but she had no tolerance for her little mistakes. And the more she made, the more stressed she became, which made her make more mistakes until she couldn't seem to do anything right.

"Let's take a break," Max said and hooked his microphone in its stand.

Reagan rubbed her forehead while Max talked to her about letting her notes trail longer. Dare set his guitar in a stand and came over to sit next to Trey on an equipment case on the edge of the stage.

"She might do better without you watching," Dare said.

"She's doing great."

"I've seen her do great, Trey. She's stiff right now. Unnatural."

Trey had picked up on that too. "I think she's just nervous."

"That's to be expected, but she has to be able to fake it enough that the audience doesn't pick up on it."

"Maybe if your manager would stop trying to turn her into a sex symbol, she could find her music again. She's not comfortable with that image."

"He thinks that's the way to go. The band's split on that idea." They both watched Max try to get Reagan to hold her guitar lower—at heavy metal level. She typically held it a bit higher—at country western level.

"As long as you're on her side, I won't have to kick your ass," Trey said.

Dare flicked Trey's ear. "I'll do any required ass-kicking in this family."

"You're going to kick your own ass?"

"If necessary."

They watched Steve tap his drumsticks on the body of Reagan's guitar as he tried to get her to rock out to the beat. "You did it back in the studio that first day," Steve said to her. "I know you can do it."

"I think I should get her out of here for a few hours," Trey said. "She looks pretty stressed out."

"She has to get used to that too," Dare said.

"So I'm supposed to sit back and watch her struggle?"

"Nope, you're supposed to leave her to struggle on her own and let her vent to you about what assholes we all are when she sees you tonight."

Trey sighed. "All right. I'll leave my one true love at the mercy of four badass metal heads, but I won't like it."

"She's a tough chick. She'll be fine. Don't be her crutch. Be her champion."

Trey internalized his brother's words. The man could do no wrong. In Trey's eyes, he knew everything. "Dare?"

"Yeah, bro?"

"Watch out for her for me, okay?"

Dare smiled. "Will do."

"Thanks." Trey slid off the equipment case and approached Reagan who was having advice thrown at her from Max, Steve, and Logan all at once. She looked from one man to the next as if they were speaking some obscure foreign language.

"Guys," Trey interrupted. "Give her a moment to breathe."

She looked so relieved to see him that he thought she might burst into tears. He strengthened his resolve. Champion, not crutch. "I've got some stuff to do. I'll see you tonight, okay?"

Her look of desperation turned his resolve into a wet noodle. "You're leaving?"

"You'll do great, Reagan. I have faith in you." He gave her arm a rough bro-tap with his knuckles and turned to go. Maybe he should have kissed her good-bye instead.

Chapter 29

IN HER DRESSING ROOM on opening night, Reagan concentrated on walking in her new high-heeled ankle boots without breaking her neck. She'd promised Sam that she'd try this his way before reverting back to her combat boots, but Sinners' set wasn't even over yet and her toes were already complaining.

Maybe if she could stop pacing.

"Are you nervous?" Ethan asked, watching her walk past him for the fiftieth time.

"You have no idea," she said. And if he hadn't been there, she'd probably be climbing the walls with her newly polished fingernails. At least they'd listened to her when she'd insisted she couldn't play properly with the three-inch monstrosities they'd tried to affix to her fingertips.

"You look fantastic tonight. I can't keep my eyes off you."

"It only took two hours to get me to look like this."

"Is that non-smudging lipstick?"

"Yeah," she said, pressing her lips together. "Why? Is it smudged?"

Ethan wrapped an arm around her waist and tugged her against him. "Because I think you can use a distraction."

She could use a thousand distractions, but as far as distractions went, the deep plundering kiss Ethan gave her would do just fine.

Ethan's hands slid down the stiff leather of her corset and over the back of her short, tulle skirt.

"Ethan?" she whispered against his lips.

"I'll hurry," he promised.

He fumbled under her skirt and tugged her bike shorts and panties down. "Ethan?"

His kiss deepened. His fingers sought her clit. She thought she should probably protest—she had to be onstage in less than half an hour—but she surrendered instead. He continued to kiss her and touch her until she sagged against the wall behind her. Her fingers tangled in his hair and she tugged her mouth from his. "I need you, Ethan. Put it in."

She slid her hands under his tight T-shirt and sucked on his neck while he found protection in his wallet, unfastened his pants, and applied the condom. He met her eyes. The intense feral hunger in his gaze turned her knees to jelly. He grabbed her roughly and forced her to face the wall.

"Don't move," he said. The deep timber of his commanding voice alit her nerve endings with excitement.

She held still while he sought her opening with his stiff cock. He filled her slowly. She whimpered, wanting it hard and fast. Buried deep, he arranged her body to ease his possession—nudged her thighs apart, encouraged her to bend her back more. Her entire body quivered with anticipation. It had been a while since Ethan had fucked her like this. She didn't realize how much she needed it. Thankfully, he did. He grabbed her wrists and drew both arms above her head, holding her firmly. His hips began to move. He plunged into her hard and deep, possessing her with a certain fury that drove every thought from her mind. She surrendered to him completely, trusting him to fulfill her by taking her power and using her body. He pounded into her harder and faster, answering her moans of excitement with deep growls. He maintained the same rigorous motion until her pussy ached from lack of fulfillment, and even though his possession felt fantastic, she couldn't take anymore.

"Now, Ethan. Make me come."

He released her wrist and moved his hand around her body to find her swollen, throbbing clit. Two strokes of his fingertips against the overexcited nub of flesh sent her flying over the edge. Her core convulsed with blinding pleasure and she bucked her hips against him involuntarily.

Behind her, Ethan grunted. He plunged deep and tightened his arm around her waist to hold her still as he spent himself within her.

His body leaned heavily against her back as he regained his bearings. His breath came in hot and heavy bursts against her shoulder.

There was a knock on the door. "Ten minutes," someone called on the other side.

Ethan pulled out slowly and then released the wrist he was still holding. "You okay?" he asked.

"I needed that," she said and turned to face him.

Ethan chuckled. "Trey would punch me in the balls if he saw me treat you like that."

"He likes to be treated like that too."

"At least I know I'm good for something." Ethan removed the condom and worked at rearranging his clothes.

Reagan didn't have time to assuage his fears. She had to be onstage and she was quite certain her two hours in hair and makeup had been destroyed by ten minutes of hard fucking with her face smashed against wall. "We'll talk later," she promised Ethan and hurried into the bathroom to clean up, return her clothes to their proper locations, and fix her lipstick. At least her hair hadn't moved. Not that it could with the amount of product they'd gooped on it. Reagan hurried out of the dressing room with Ethan on her heels. Backstage, someone handed her a guitar, and she tossed the strap over her shoulder. The new stage setup allowed for no transition time between their set and Sinners', so when the last note of Sinners' encore went silent and the crowd roared its approval, Reagan felt her stomach drop into her boots.

"Knock 'em dead, baby," Ethan said and wrapped an arm around her shoulders to give her an encouraging squeeze. "I'm so proud of you."

When she passed Trey, who was just coming offstage, she couldn't meet his eyes for some reason. She didn't have time to puzzle out her sudden feeling of guilt.

Trey caught her arm and tugged her against his body and out of the flow of traffic from the stage. "You'll do great."

"Promise you won't watch. I'm nervous enough."

"You don't want me to watch?"

She shook her head. Accompanied by a mechanical whir, Eric's drum kit was moved offstage in one piece on a platform so Steve's could rise from the floor at the initiation of the first song. The sound of the stage realigning kicked Reagan's heart rate up another notch. This was really happening.

Trey brushed his fingers over her jaw. "If that's what you want."

"Thanks for understanding," she whispered. "I love you."

"I love you too. Now break a leg." He hesitated. "Not literally."

"No guarantees in these damned boots."

"Reagan, take your place," Exodus End's soundboard engineer, Mad Dog, said in her ear.

She pecked Trey on the cheek and entered the little door beneath the stage. It was dark under the stage, but someone in the stage crew was standing next to her platform with a flashlight. She was careful not to hit the strings of her guitar as she carefully stepped onto the flat piece of metal. She could just make out the forms of Dare at the opposite end of the stage and Logan who was between them, but farther back. She heard a mechanical whir and then the hard heavy thump of a bass drum as Steve and his entire drum kit were lifted up from behind the stage. The crowd was going insane. This was an entirely new and innovative stage design. If it worked properly it was sure to wow everyone. If not, well, Reagan would be trapped under a dark stage for the rest of her short life.

Logan entered with the deep repetitive bass line of the first song, "Ovation." His platform started to rise first, lifting him out of the floor of the stage into the spotlight. Reagan played the rhythm riff on cue and almost took a tumble when the platform beneath her lurched into motion before rising at a snail's pace. When a bright blue light hit her in the face, she forced herself not to wince. *I'm a rock star. Be Maximilian Richardson. You can do this. Don't mess it up.*

Dare entered the song and his platform didn't lift slowly like Logan's and Reagan's; it propelled him upward at a faster velocity and he used the momentum to jump out of the floor onto the main stage, wailing out his intro in true rock star fashion. The crowd went insane. Dare Mills was a star. Reagan was an imposter. She did her part though. Playing the rhythm guitar sections so close to Max's style that his own mother probably wouldn't be able to tell the difference. Assuming her mother listened to metal.

There was a sudden explosion of fire and smoke—part of the show, but it still made Reagan start—and Max appeared center stage, singing the first long note of the song like a metal angel who had descended from the heavens.

The entire crowd was one huge mosh pit. No one seemed to care that Reagan was playing guitar instead of Max. They were all too enthralled with music to pay her any mind. She watched Dare work the crowd. Logan work the crowd. Max make the people in the crowd ricochet off each other like bowling pins. Even Steve stood up behind the drum kit at one point and tossed a cracked drumstick into the audience. Reagan stuck to the song. When it ended, Max spoke to the crowd. "How are we feeling tonight, Los Angeles?"

The crowd roared its enthusiasm. Steve played a drum line to get them to settle down. "Did Sinners rock your world?" Max said/screamed/sang.

The crowd cheered again. Sinners rocked Reagan's world, too.

Especially the naughty one. She peeked over to the side of the stage, hoping that Trey had gone against her wishes and was standing in her corner. She didn't see him.

"Carpal-fucking-tunnel is a very serious malady for a guitarist," Max said, sounding incredibly grave.

"Who's a pussy?" Logan said in a deep, announcer's voice. "Max is a pussy."

Max used his good hand to give Logan the finger. "You might have noticed we have a new band member up on stage with us tonight. Reagan, come up here and say hi."

Heart racing, Reagan forced her feet to move forward, concentrating hard on not tripping over anything in her spike-heeled ankle boots. "Hi," she said into the microphone on her end of the stage.

She saw her own face on the giant screens all over the stadium and she froze.

"She's covering rhythm guitar for us," Max said. "Doing an excellent job."

Reagan felt her cheeks flame. She nodded and then took a step away from the mic.

"I love you, Reagan," some guy screamed in the audience and pulled up his shirt to flash his thin chest at her.

"That only works when chicks flash their tits at stage hands," Dare said to the guy, pointing at him with his guitar pick. "No backstage pass for you."

"'Bite,'" Reagan heard Mad Dog announce the next song in her ear. "One. Two. Three." The band followed his cue to start the abrupt beginning of the song. Logan apparently thought Reagan needed to get closer to the front of the stage. He leaned his back against hers and hopped backward, pushing her forward several steps. He repeated the motion and she almost missed a note.

"Stop it," she growled at him.

"Relax, Reagan," he said. "Have some fun."

When she scowled at him, he shrugged and went to play his bass on the opposite end of the stage.

By the end of third song, Reagan was really feeling the pressure. And her feet were freaking killing her. She glanced over at the side of the stage and caught sight of Trey standing in the shadows. Feeling stronger and somehow relieved, she took a deep breath and trotted up to the front of the stage. The guys in the front row of the audience all surged against the barrier fence as if they wanted to grab her. She glanced at Dare who grinned at her. She lifted the neck of her guitar and gyrated against her instrument slightly. Nothing too extreme. Just a little sexy. One guy launched himself clean over the barrier fence and was promptly escorted to the end of the barrier and forced back into the crowd. Reagan went down on one knee to play the next stanza and her little cluster of fanboys cheered her on. This was kind of fun. She had to be careful not to lose Max's sound though. She couldn't get too carried away.

The song ended and Max made a low growling sound in his microphone. "I see Reagan has broken out of her shell for you. Do you like it?"

The crowd cheered and Reagan found herself displayed on all the screens in the stadium again.

Reagan walked over to the nearest microphone and asked, "Would anyone be horribly offended if I took off these fucking boots? They're killing my feet."

The crowd started chanting. "Take it off. Take it off."

She popped her feet out of both boots, tossed them to a stage runner, and stood barefoot on the stage wriggling her toes in delight. "Now I can get my rock on."

She played a random string of notes that sent the crowd into a frenzy. Okay, so this was *a lot* of fun. She dug her fingers into her hair, messing it all up and feeling damned good about it. She threw up her devil horns on both fists, shaking her extended pinkies and index fingers at the crowd.

"I'm ready to get dirty," Reagan said.

Dare chuckled into his microphone. "Oh hell yeah," he said in a sexy growl.

"I'll get dirty with you, Reagan," Logan said.

"Let's all get dirty," Max yelled, and the band segued into their gritty ballad, "Stained."

Reagan made an effort to get involved in the rest of the show. Not too involved. She didn't want to overstep her bounds and upstage anyone else in the band. She felt she did an excellent job mimicking Max's guitar work and was rather proud of that, even though she felt a little disconnected from the music the entire time.

When the final lights went down and she stepped off the stage, she looked for Trey, but he'd vanished. He probably didn't want her to know that he'd been watching when she'd specifically told him not to. Ethan was there though and he gave her an encouraging pat on the back.

"You were awesome!"

"Thanks," she said.

"Good show," multiple people said to her as she was ushered through the crowd back to her dressing room. She was expected at the after-party, which was being held at the hotel across the parking lot. She wanted to find some shoes that didn't cripple her toes before she headed over.

"Nice work," Dare said to her just outside her dressing room door. "We'll rehearse again before tomorrow night's show in San Francisco. See if we can't figure out what's causing your disconnect."

So he'd noticed that, huh? She bit her lip and nodded.

"I'll see you at the after-party," he said and left her standing there feeling unsure of herself.

"What disconnect?" Ethan asked her.

"I'm not really feeling the music."

"I couldn't tell. You were fabulous up there. Everyone loved you."

She smiled. "I thought it went well. After I got rid of those fucking boots."

She entered her dressing room and reached for a bottle of water. She chugged half of it before she noticed the bouquet of flowers sitting on her dressing table. How thoughtful. Who had sent her flowers? Trey? Obviously not Ethan, because he looked as surprised to see them as Reagan did. Maybe one of her friends. Someone from the record company. Or dare she hope they were from her daddy?

She practically skipped across the room and pulled the card from the bright assortment of gerbera daisies.

Her name was printed neatly on the outer envelope. She tugged the card free and read it. Her smile faded.

You took what was mine, bitch. Don't think you'll keep it for much longer.

Ethan snatched the card out of her hand. "Fucking son of a bitch," he growled. He lifted the vase and looked at the bottom, examined the card more closely, and then the envelope. Looking for clues. A habit left over from his past police work.

"You go to the party and have fun. Just don't allow yourself to be caught alone," Ethan said, giving her an encouraging squeeze and rubbing her arm briskly. "I'll find out who sent this to you and fuck him up."

Chapter 30

THE BALLROOM OF THE hotel was packed wall-to-wall with people. Reagan searched the crowd until she caught sight of Trey surrounded by his usual posse of admirers. She hurried to his side, ignoring curious stares and the few people who called out to her as she passed. She needed to decompress and she wanted to spend some time alone with Trey. To thank him for being there when she hadn't known she'd needed him to be. And to pretend she wasn't afraid of whoever kept sending her threatening messages.

She caught the tail end of Trey's conversation when she stopped beside him. "… he never did find his pants."

No fewer than ten people laughed at whatever Trey happened to be talking about. She touched his arm and he glanced at her. A huge smile spread across his face. "Hey, Reagan. I was wondering when you'd make it. Somebody get the newest member of Exodus End a beer."

Three beers were thrust in her direction. "No thanks," she said.

"Would you like something else? Open bar tonight." He lifted his beer and his enamored audience cheered.

She shook her head and leaned close to whisper in his ear. "I want to go up to my room for a little while. Will you come with me?"

"Are rhinos always horny?"

She hesitated, her brain even more exhausted than her body was. "Um. *Yes?*"

He chuckled. "Right answer." He took a swig of his half-finished beer, handed the remainder to the nearest person, and took Reagan's hand. "Have a great night," he said to his entourage.

"Are you leaving?" asked a gorgeous redhead in a figure-hugging, purple evening dress.

Reagan's hand tightened on his. While she never got jealous of Ethan, Reagan couldn't claim she was unaffected when sophisticated, beautiful women tried to get their claws in Trey.

"Yes, he's leaving with me," Reagan said hotly.

"Easy, tiger," Trey whispered in her ear. "She writes freelance for a couple of major music magazines."

That didn't mean the woman didn't want in Trey's pants. "Then she can write about the serious relationship between Trey Mills and Reagan Elliot."

Reagan hurried through the crowd, tugging Trey behind her. She was so focused on getting to the door that she didn't realize Dare was in pursuit until Trey came to a sudden halt behind her.

"Jeez, where's the fire?" Dare said, his hand fisted in the back of Trey's T-shirt. "I have some people I want to introduce you to," he said to Reagan.

"She needs to crash," Trey said.

Both brothers offered her a look of concern.

"Of course," Dare said. "I'll cover for her."

"Thanks, Dare." She gave him a hug. "I might come back down later. I just need a few moments of peace." And to get away from the flowers in her dressing room. And that note.

"Good luck with that," Dare said.

She wasn't sure what he meant by that, but she grabbed Trey by the wrist and tugged him out in the corridor. A bunch of camera flashes went off and reporters yelled questions, but Reagan couldn't make any sense out of the chaos.

A pair of Exodus End's security guards escorted Reagan and Trey to the elevators. "Is it always this crazy?" she asked Trey.

"Exodus End only throws a party this big on their opening tour date. It will settle down. A little." Trey wrapped an arm around her shoulder and gave her a squeeze. "Overwhelmed?"

"You have no idea."

The security guards stepped onto the elevator with them and pressed the button to the eighth floor.

"Are you going to follow us all the way to our room?" Reagan asked one of the guards.

"The band has rented out the entire eighth floor. There's already security on that floor. We're just here to make sure no one tries to get on the elevator with you."

Reagan stared at the carpet inside the elevator as the car lifted to their floor without incident. Trey rubbed her back but didn't say anything. He seemed to realize she craved quiet and calm. She knew she had signed up for this, and she didn't regret it, but it was going to take some getting used to. She'd never imagined she'd need security to ride a freakin' hotel elevator. And she'd never thought she'd crave their protection.

When they exited the elevator, they found several additional security guards. They didn't escort her to her room, but they watched her closely until she and Trey were safely inside.

—⁓—

The instant Trey had Reagan alone in the hotel room, he tumbled her onto the king-sized bed. "Everyone said you were phenomenal tonight. How did it feel to be up on stage in front of all of those fans?"

"I was nervous until I saw you standing in the shadows at the side of the stage."

"You saw me?"

She nodded.

"Shit. Sorry. I know you said you didn't want me there, but I couldn't resist. Do you know how sexy you are when you play?" He rolled on top of her and captured her hands in his.

"It's the corset, isn't it? It makes me look like I actually have boobs."

Her tits did look fantastic in her corset, but that wasn't what had drawn him to watch even though she'd forbidden it. "It's that face you make when you let the music take you. It's even hotter than the face you make when you come."

"I don't make a face."

He grinned. "Yeah, you do. I hope I didn't make you self-conscious about it. It would ruin my life if you stopped making it."

She laughed. "I highly doubt that." She scowled. "I'm not sure the fans like me taking over for Max."

"They loved you. Trust me. They were a little upset by the change at first, but you won them over. Once you kicked off your shoes and got a little dirty for them."

"It's easier to be yourself when you're not pretending to be something you're not."

"Where's Ethan?" Trey asked.

"He had some errands to run." She changed the subject. "I'm just glad we could sneak away from the after-party. I'm too tired to pretend I'm social."

"Are you too tired to make love? Because I haven't been able to think of anything but you all night."

"Me and the past lovers who've been following you around all day."

"I told them to get lost. I really am committed to you. I'm sorry I spread so much love around before I met you." He was sorry now. At the time, he'd thought it was fan-fucking-tastic, heavy on the fan fucking. He now knew quality was better than quantity. Two lovers were plenty for him.

Reagan lifted her head to kiss him. "I shouldn't bitch at you about it. You're so generous with your love. With everyone."

"I think most women would be put off by that."

"You just have so much to give. Enough for me and Ethan." She gave him a hard stare. "That doesn't mean you can go spreading it all over fandom."

"No worries there. I have everything I want right here." Trey hesitated. "Where's Ethan?" he asked again.

"I think he's helping direct traffic or breaking up fights."

"That means I get you all to myself." He stroked her hair from her face and kissed her lips gently.

She closed her eyes tightly and didn't kiss him back. Perplexed, he stared down at her. Maybe she really was just tired. It couldn't possibly be that she'd lost interest.

"Trey?" she whispered.

"Yeah?"

"I need to tell you something."

"I'm listening."

"I think you're going to be mad at me."

"I don't get mad."

"I had sex with Ethan backstage tonight," she blurted. "He just sort of grabbed me and we started kissing. We got carried away and ended up having a quickie up against the wall." She opened her eyes cautiously.

Trey grinned. "Was it exciting?"

"We shouldn't have done it without you there."

Trey stared down into her eyes. He could tell that guilt was eating her alive. "Why not?"

"Because."

"I don't have to be there every time you have sex with Ethan. Just like he doesn't have to be there every time I have sex with you."

"Have you two had sex without me knowing about it?" she asked.

He thought back to all of his encounters with Ethan. Even that first time, Reagan had known. "Well no, but..."

"Why not?"

"Because we like to include you. You feel like you cheated on me, don't you?"

She rubbed her forehead. "This relationship is just so complicated. I get mixed up sometimes. I don't feel like I'm cheating when you're there, but when we went at it behind your back and didn't tell you, it felt wrong."

"So just come right out and tell me when you two go at it."

"You won't be jealous?"

"Will you be jealous when I have sex with Ethan?"

"I'm not sure."

"Do you want to know about it when it happens?"

"Yes, don't hide it from me. No secrets."

He kissed her gently. "There. You found your own solution. You just needed to talk it out."

She wrapped her arms around his neck and snuggled her face against his chest. "I love you so much."

"I love you too."

"I like you like this, Trey. I'm so glad we brought Ethan into our relationship. I was worried at first that I'd feel neglected or you'd love me less, but now I find that when you're happy, you love me even more. I could tell there was something wrong between us when we were touring with Sinners. You were trying too hard to want only me, and now you're just you."

"How do you feel about Ethan?" Trey asked.

She stiffened. "What do you mean?"

"Do you love him?"

"He's my best friend. Well, you are too. You're both my best friends."

"We're also your lovers."

"If I tell you I love him, will you break up with me?"

Trey chuckled softly. "Sweetheart, you're the one who is trying too hard. You can love him. It's not like you can help it, and he's a wonderful man. He treats you well. He'd do anything for you. You've been through a lot together."

"Do you love him?" Reagan asked.

"I like him."

"That's not the same thing."

"I'm well aware of that."

"Do you think you could love a man?"

Trey needed to tell her his deepest remaining secret. He trusted her with it. He wasn't sure if she'd accept it or understand, but if he expected her to be open and honest about everything then he had to treat her with the same respect. "I do love a man."

"Do? Or did?"

"Do. I'll never stop loving him, but he's out of reach."

"What's his name?"

His stomach clenched with apprehension. For a moment, he considered making up some random name. "Brian."

"Brian?" Reagan's eyes widened. "You don't mean Brian Sinclair?"

"Yeah."

Reagan stared up at him in stunned disbelief and then burst out laughing. "Good one, Trey. You had me going there for a minute."

He spilled his guts to her and she thought he was joking? Nice. He rolled off of her and lay beside her on the bed on his back. He pressed against his eyelids with a thumb and middle finger to force all of the hurt and hopelessness back down where it belonged.

Reagan straddled his hips and pulled his hand from his face. "You're serious."

He swallowed, knowing better than to speak, not that he could have around the huge knot in his throat.

"He's married, Trey."

Trey rolled his eyes and grasped at sarcasm. It made it easier to continue. "I know. I was at the wedding."

"Does he know how you feel about him?"

"No."

"You never told him?"

Trey shook his head.

"How long have you felt this way about him?"

Forever. Trey had always felt like they'd known each other before they'd been born. At least spiritually. "For over ten years."

"You have to tell him, Trey."

"What, like he's going to give up Myrna for me?"

She stroked his hair from his forehead. "Is that what you want?"

He bit his lip and shook his head. "No. I want him to be happy. I want to get over him."

"And to do that, you have to tell him. Talk to him about it. See how he reacts."

"I don't want it to ruin our friendship."

Reagan drew her thumb under his eye and collected a tear he didn't realize was there. He wasn't sure how she would respond to her devil-may-care boyfriend getting all emotional and stupid over her favorite guitar hero.

"Brian isn't like that, Trey. You know that."

"He doesn't have time for me anymore, anyway. What does it matter?" He rolled onto his side and unseated her so she tumbled onto the bed beside him.

She rose to sit next to him Indian-style on the bed. "Thanks for the invite."

"Invite?"

"To your pity party."

Trey grimaced. He did this every once in a while. Fell into despair. The problem was instead of dealing with things, he had the tendency to bury his problems and pretend they didn't affect him.

"Are you going to talk to Brian about your feelings?"

"I don't know. I'll think about it."

"Well, I'm in the party mood now. Let's go have some fun."

"I thought you were tired."

"I've just caught my second wind."

She climbed to her feet and found the combat boots she'd been forbidden to wear onstage. They didn't complement her outfit, but they were totally Reagan and brought a smile to Trey's face and his heart.

"Come on, mopey," she said, tugging on his hand until he relented and climbed out of bed. "Let's go party like rock stars."

Chapter 31

REAGAN HELD TREY'S HAND as they entered the hotel's reception hall. She didn't really want to party like a rock star, but Trey was a social creature and he looked like he needed some adulation and excitement. Also, she felt bad for laughing about his love for Brian. It was obviously something that weighed heavily on him. She wasn't sure how to handle that part of Trey. He always seemed to know how to get exactly what he wanted out of life. It must be hard for him to be so close to Brian, yet so far away.

She spotted Dare near the entrance, looking bored, though he was surrounded by enthusiastic admirers. He had this way of answering people in a minimum number of words, yet making them feel like he was imparting the secrets of the universe. Reagan knew Trey depended on his brother for support more than any other person on the planet, unfortunately herself included, so she headed in Dare's direction, hoping that he could bring Trey comfort. Or tell her how to comfort him.

Dare smiled when he noticed them heading in his direction. "Excuse me." Two words and his crowd dispersed as if Dare had erected an impenetrable bubble around himself.

"Back so soon?" He took a sip of his beverage and looked from Reagan to Trey and back to Reagan.

"She wanted to party like a rock star," Trey said. He waved at someone across the room who was waving both arms wildly over her head to get his attention.

"Then you should go get her a drink," Dare said to Trey.

"What do you want?" Trey asked her.

"Something stiff."

"I would have given you something stiff upstairs, but you wanted to come back down to the party."

"If you would have gone down while we were upstairs, I would have come," she countered.

Trey laughed and kissed her on the cheek before hurrying toward the bar. A wave of people followed in his wake. Unlike his brother, he didn't have the skill set to keep them at bay. Or maybe he didn't want to. He seemed to relish the attention of the horde surrounding him.

"Something wrong?" Dare asked. Someone approached them and he lifted one finger from his glass. The man paused in midstride and turned in the opposite direction.

"Trey's a little down. I figured he could use a party."

"So you're here for his sake?"

"Completely. I don't really mingle well."

Dare chuckled. "Me neither. Everyone thinks I'm mysterious and deep. I'm just antisocial."

Reagan grinned up at him. "You're just saying that to make me feel better."

Dare shrugged. "Why is Trey down?" His gaze shifted toward the bar and Reagan followed his line of sight to see Trey talking and laughing with some A-list actor as if they were old friends.

Reagan wondered if Dare knew about Brian. It seemed like he knew everything about Trey, but maybe it was something that Trey hadn't confided to him. She didn't want to toss any bones out of Trey's closet of skeletons without his permission.

"Let me guess," Dare said, lifting his finger at another approaching person to head them off before they got too close. "Brian."

"You know how he feels about Brian?"

"I'm surprised he told you. He thinks it's this huge secret, but anyone with eyes knows how he feels about the guy."

"I didn't know. I always thought there was something different about their relationship, but had no idea Trey's feelings were so strong."

"He must be getting better at hiding it then."

They watched Trey get a bro-slap hug from a professional football player before the guy started acting out passes and touchdowns at Trey's enthusiastic insistence. Trey still hadn't made it to the bar.

"I told him that he should talk to Brian about it," Reagan said. "He didn't seem to think that was a good idea."

"He's made a lot of progress since he met you, Reagan. He's been struggling with this for a long time. Before all he could think about was ways to get Brian to fall for him. Now he's trying to figure out how to let him go. Be patient with him."

"How do you think Brian would react if he knew?"

"I'm sure Brian already knows. He's just too nice to tell my brother to get his head out of his ass." Dare finished his drink and set his empty glass on a nearby table that held a guitar-shaped ice sculpture. "Brian's not stupid, just sort of... non-confrontational. Especially when it comes to those he loves."

"He loves Trey too?"

"Not romantically. Did Trey tell you how they hooked up?"

Reagan's eyes widened. "They hooked up?"

"I guess he didn't tell you. If you want to know, ask him about it." Dare laughed. "Look, he made it to the bar."

Reagan turned her attention back to Trey, who was having beers stuffed into the waistband of his jeans by several women. And men. Squirming, he tried to avoid having additional beverages shoved in his pants, while he placed his order with the bartender. She could tell he was having a great time already.

"What an attention whore," Dare said. He grinned at his brother's antics while shaking his head in disgrace.

"You're not fooling me, Dare Mills. Your kid brother means more to you than any other person on the planet."

"Can't deny it. If it weren't for him, I would have died before my sixth birthday."

Reagan's head whipped up to look at him. "What do you mean?"

"I had acute myeloid leukemia and needed a bone marrow transplant. Trey was a match, so he was my donor."

"He never told me that."

"He knows about it but doesn't remember it. He was only two, but he is still terrified of hospitals, so it had to have some lasting effect on him. Have you seen the size of the needles they use to remove bone marrow? I have." He shuddered.

Reagan wrapped both arms around Dare and gave him a hard squeeze.

He patted her back and asked, "What was that for?"

"For living."

He chuckled. "You should hug Trey, not me. He's the hero."

"Oh, trust me, Trey is going to get a lot of hugs. Do leg hugs count?"

"I'm sure he'd think so."

She gazed across the room to the bar where Trey was trapped between some guy who had a three-foot-tall, lime green mohawk and a Hollywood socialite with a yapping Chihuahua in her purse. Both hands full with stiff drinks, Trey smiled, nodded, and chatted as he inched his way back in their direction. "If he ever escapes his fan club."

"Is this the line for Reagan hugs?" a deep voice said from behind her. She turned and grabbed Steve in a bear hug. He returned her hug enthusiastically. She couldn't help but notice how great those strong drummer arms felt wrapped around her body. Even though the concert had ended two hours before, he still wasn't wearing a shirt with his low-cut leather pants. "Are you two having a guitarist meeting over here?" Steve asked. "I noticed Dare has erected his invisible barrier of cool to ward off the ass-kissers. I hope you don't mind me crashing your private party."

"We're just talking," Reagan said.

"About the show?" Steve asked, giving Reagan one last squeeze before releasing her. "I figured we'd fuck up a lot more than we did. The first show of a new tour is usually the worst. It went well, don't you think?"

She nodded. "Even though I was scared to death."

Steve rubbed her back. "You did great, sweetie. Even Max said so."

"I think he liked being just a front man," Dare said. "He got even more involved with the crowd than usual. He might want to keep this arrangement after his wrist heals." Dare winked at Reagan and she had to remind herself that she was a rock star now and should not be shrieking with enthusiasm.

"He's been trolling the Internet for reviews all night," Steve said. "He won't admit this to anyone, but he really does care what people say about us."

Dare chuckled. "Max? No way. He's too cool to care."

"Sure," Steve said.

"I go off to get the lady a drink and as soon as I turn my back, she starts feeling up her band members," Trey said with an exaggerated scowl.

"Trey, I did not feel up any of my band's members," Reagan said and accepted her drink. "At least not in public."

Steve burst out laughing. "You kill me, Reagan. Really." He pulled a bottle of beer out of the waistband of Trey's pants. "Thanks. I could use a cold one." He twisted off the bottle cap and took a long swallow before flicking the bottle cap at Trey. "What's up, Dare's lil' bro?"

"I thought I might ask my girlfriend to dance, but after seeing the company she keeps, I'm not sure I'm famous enough."

Reagan wrapped both arms around Trey and squeezed. He couldn't reciprocate; his hands were full. "Dare told me what you did."

He stiffened slightly. "What did I do?"

"You saved his life."

"Oh that. I didn't really have a say in the matter. I couldn't even string an entire sentence together then. Trey, do you want to donate some bone marrow? Ba-ba da-da yeah-yeah. They assumed that meant yes."

She snuggled her face into his neck. "I still think it's heroic."

"Did he tell you he almost died last year?" Dare asked, helping himself to one of the beers in Trey's waistband.

Reagan drew away to look up at Trey. "No, he did not. What happened?"

Trey took her hand and directed it to the side of his head. She fingered the narrow scar that arched over his ear.

"Got hit in the head with a ball bat," he said. "Some bleeding on the brain. A couple of grand mal seizures. No big deal."

Dare chuckled. "He says that now."

"I remember when that happened," Reagan said. "It was all over the news. I didn't realize it was so serious." Her throat tightened as she looked up at him. She couldn't imagine not having him in her life and wished she could have been there to help him through all the tough times in his past. Overcome with unexpected emotion, she hugged him tight. She didn't even care that one of the drinks in his hand sloshed onto her back. "I'm finished partying like a rock star for tonight. Let's go find Ethan and go up to the room. I want to be alone with you. Relatively speaking."

"You just got here," Steve complained. "Everyone wants to meet you."

Reagan glanced around the room. All eyes were on her. If her relationship with Trey had been unknown before, it was definitely no secret now.

"One drink," Trey said, handing her one of the glasses he'd carried from the bar. He handed the spare to his brother and kept one for himself. He turned to stand beside Reagan, wrapping his right arm around her waist as he sipped his drink. "Bring on the admirers."

"More like spectators," Reagan murmured.

Before anyone had the chance to approach, Ethan appeared next to Reagan. "There were no deliveries tonight," he said.

"So how did they get in there?" she whispered harshly.

"Someone had to bring them personally."

"They were inside my dressing room?"

"Apparently."

"What are you two talking about?" Trey asked.

"You didn't tell him?" Ethan asked.

"I didn't want him to worry."

"About what?" Trey asked.

"She got another of those threatening messages. On a card in some flowers. I've spent the last hour finding out about any deliveries that were made tonight, but there were no flowers delivered to her dressing room, so whoever it was must have access to the backstage area."

"Reagan, why didn't you tell me?" Trey asked.

"I didn't want you to worry."

"That's kind of my job, babe."

Ethan wrapped a comforting arm around her back and Reagan squirmed away from him. He scowled. "What's your problem?"

"There are people everywhere," she said.

"And?"

"They know I'm with Trey, so I can't get personal with you here."

"Why not?"

Trey laughed unexpectedly and poked Reagan in the ribs. She gave him her frostiest look. He threw a pointed look in the direction of one of the swarms of reporters who were looking their way. "Smile and laugh," he said under his breath. "They can smell drama from a mile away."

Reagan laughed. "You're so hilarious, Trey," she said loudly. "Well, I guess I should call it a night. I'm dead on my feet and I think I've had a little too much to drink." Exactly half of a rum and coke.

"I'll help you find your way," Trey said. "Follow us," he whispered to Ethan. "Like her bodyguard would."

Dare, Steve, and Logan looked entirely perplexed as Trey wrapped an arm around Reagan's back and helped her find the exit. A seething Ethan followed two paces behind—looking every inch the tough bodyguard. Once they were safely on the elevator, they dropped their facades.

"So now I can't touch you in public?" Ethan shouted at Reagan.

Reagan winced at his tone. "No, Ethan. You can't. They know I'm dating Trey and they wouldn't understand this relationship. I'm not sure if I understand it."

"Why didn't you tell me about the message, Reagan?" Trey said. "If this guy—"

"Or girl," Ethan interrupted.

"If this *person* is running around loose backstage, we need to have everyone we trust keep a look out for him." He glanced at Ethan. "Or her," he quickly amended.

"Whoever it is has to be associated with Sinners," Ethan said.

Trey's eyebrows drew together in an angry scowl. "Why do you say that? My crew wouldn't threaten her."

"Because it happened on both tours and the only commonality between the two is *your* band and *your* crew," Ethan said.

The elevator door opened and the three of them fell into an uneasy silence as they passed the eighth floor security guards on their way to their room. As soon as they were safely inside, Ethan wrapped his arms around Reagan and yanked her against his body. "Is it okay if I touch you now? When it serves your purpose?"

Trey grabbed his arm. "Don't talk to her like that."

He shouldn't talk to her harshly, but she understood why he was behaving this way. He was covering up his hurt. "I didn't mean to hurt your feelings, Ethan," Reagan said. "Yes, in private we can be open about our relationship, but Trey and I are in the public eye and we can't—"

"So because Trey is famous, he's the one you're willing to claim in public?" Ethan said.

"She didn't say that," Trey said.

"They saw me with him first, Ethan. That's the only reason."

Ethan shook his head in disbelief. Reagan touched the center of his chest and found his heart was thudding hard and fast. She wrapped both arms around him and held him until he relaxed and lifted his arms to hold her back. "I just couldn't handle the added stress of the press finding out about the three of us, Ethan. I'm so sorry I'm not stronger for you. They'd ruin us all if they knew."

"I understand," he said. "This is enough."

But it wasn't and Reagan knew that. "I should have been more discrete with Trey too. If I can't be open about both of you, I shouldn't be open about either of you."

"We can publicly pretend to break up, if you want," Trey said.

"Don't be stupid," Ethan said. "It's fine. I said I understand. I just hope we're alone as often as possible."

"We're alone right now," Reagan said. She looked up at Ethan and he cupped her face in both hands before kissing her. Trey moved up against her back and wrapped them both in his arms. Ethan released her lips so he could kiss Trey. Pressed between her two loves, she didn't care if the rest of the world disappeared forever. She had everything she could ever want or need right here.

Chapter 32

THEY'D ARRIVED IN SAN Francisco earlier that morning for the second show of the new tour. While Reagan worked through a full dress rehearsal with Exodus End, Trey sat on the edge of his bunk and watched Brian sleep. Reagan was right. He needed to talk to him about his feelings. Trey would never get over him until he knew exactly how Brian felt about him. Somewhere inside, Trey already knew, but he had to hear it from the man himself. Brian's eyes blinked open and he drew a deep breath through his nose before smiling drowsily.

"You're watching me sleep?" he murmured, his voice groggy. He'd gotten in late after skipping the after-party to be with his family and then driving up the coast with Sed and Jessica to meet the tour buses this afternoon. Trey doubted that he'd even slept the night before.

"I need to talk to you about something," Trey said. His heart thudded faster and faster as he tried to think of the best way to broach this subject. How many times had he tried to spill his guts to Brian in the past? A hundred times? A thousand?

"Yes, I'll be your best man." Brian's self-indulgent grin made Trey's heart flutter. Maybe if Brian wasn't so attractive or so lovable or so perfect...

"This isn't about that."

"Need advice about Reagan?"

Trey shook his head.

"Something about the band? Your brother?"

"No, this about you."

Brian scowled. "Did the guys put you up this? Are they going to bust my balls over my family again? I'm here, aren't I?"

"No, it's not the guys. I need to tell you something."

"So tell me."

Trey stared at him for a long moment. "I love you," he said breathlessly before he chickened out.

The tension drained from Brian's face and he grinned. "I love you too, man."

"Not I love you, *man*. I love you. Period."

Brian gnawed on his lower lip and avoided his gaze.

"I thought you should know how I feel," Trey said quietly, his heart twisting unpleasantly within his chest.

"Why?"

Trey wasn't sure what he'd expected Brian to say, but that wasn't it. "Why do I love you?"

"No, *why* are you telling me this? Especially now. What do you expect me to do about it?"

"Nothing. I just thought…"

"That's your problem, Trey. You *don't* think. You just do what you want based on what feels good or what's convenient for you. Did you ever think maybe I don't *want* to know how you feel? Or that I don't *care* how you feel?"

"Brian…"

Brian climbed out of his bunk, grabbed Trey by both arms, and hauled him to his feet.

"Why couldn't you just keep it to yourself? This changes everything, Trey."

"Why?" Trey asked. "I've felt this way since…" He lowered his eyes. Now he just felt stupid. For Trey, the world had revolved around his feelings for Brian and now he realized they meant nothing. They'd never meant anything. Not to the person who mattered.

"Since when?" Brian pressed.

Eyes stinging, Trey shook his head. He wished he'd never brought it up. He placed both hands on Brian's chest and shoved, breaking Brian's grip on his arms. Trey refused to break down in front of him. He wasn't sure what he'd expected Brian to say or do, but he thought Brian would at least be a little understanding. Make him feel better. Show some of that compassionate heart of his. Not be a royal asshole about it.

Brian caught his arm. "How long, Trey?"

"A long fucking time, Brian. Okay? But I'm over it now."

"Liar. I know you."

"You don't know me very well, if this is such a big surprise to you." Trey pulled away from him again. He had to get off the bus. He couldn't breathe. Couldn't think. But he could feel. And it felt like his heart was being ripped out of his chest.

Trey had only taken two steps when Brian grabbed the back of his shirt and tossed him into the corner next to the stereo system in the living area. Brian moved in front of him to block his escape. "Don't run from me. You're the one who brought this up and we're going to have it out now."

Trey glared at him. "Get out of my face or I'm going to fucking punch you."

"So punch me then."

Trey shook his head and lowered his gaze. Brian was right. They needed to get this all out in the open so Trey could find a way to move on. "Did you really not know that I'm in love with you? I thought it was pretty obvious."

"I know that you're attracted to me, but I didn't think you loved me. I didn't think you loved anyone."

"I've loved you since that first time you made love to me."

Brian's body tensed and he took a step backwards. Trey made the mistake of looking at him. Pissed? Why was he pissed?

Jaw set, Brian rubbed a hand over his face. "God, I'm never going to live that down. Look, Trey, I'm sorry about that. I honestly don't know what got into me that night. I was a little drunk and so horny I probably would've fucked just about anyone."

"It didn't mean anything to you?"

Brian tossed his head back as if surprised that Trey was stupid enough to ask such a ridiculous question. "Of course it didn't mean anything. I fucked you, Trey. That's all it was. You should know what sex for the sake of sex means more than anyone."

Trey knew all about meaningless sex, but losing his virginity to Brian had meant everything to him. They'd connected on an emotional level. At least, he'd thought they had. Apparently he couldn't have been more wrong. He'd never meant anything romantic to Brian. Nothing.

Trey stared at him for a long moment, no longer hurt, just kind of numb. "Yeah."

"I'm sorry, Trey. I didn't know you felt that way. If I had, I would have set you straight."

"No reason to be sorry. I'm never sorry for the idiots who fall in love with me just because I fuck them." And if he'd made them all feel this worthless and used, he was the one who was sorry. He'd never meant to hurt anyone. But this… this hurt.

"You should have told me sooner," Brian said.

Why? So Trey could've had his heart shredded before he'd found Reagan? No thanks. He had a powerful need to see her now. Surely, she was almost done rehearsing. He needed her love to fill the gaping hole inside him. "Can I go now? Or would you like to twist the knife in my chest a few more times?"

"This isn't going to affect our music, is it?"

"Give me some credit, Brian. Has it been an issue before? Forget I said anything. Okay?"

This time when Trey forced his body out of the corner and

headed for the exit, Brian let him go. Not that he'd ever wanted to keep him in the first place.

Chapter 33

ETHAN AUTOMATICALLY REACHED FOR his holster when Trey appeared beside him. Ethan didn't carry a gun, but old habits were hard to break and he was on his guard for anyone who looked remotely threatening to Reagan. He hadn't let her out of his sight all day. He even stood outside the door whenever she used the bathroom. Despite his continual questioning of everyone, no one had seen anyone put the flowers in her room and no one had any idea who might want to harm her. Trey wasn't interested in Ethan. He watched Reagan, who was playing through the set again, this time with only Dare. Ethan couldn't read Trey's expression, but something was obviously bothering him and he seemed to think Reagan was required to make things right.

"You okay?" Ethan asked.

"Is she almost done?"

"They just started up again after a little break. She's working so hard to get this right."

"She's already perfect."

Ethan chuckled. "I think so too." Ethan glanced around to make sure no one was watching and then placed a gentle hand in the center of Trey's back. Trey was shaking like a leaf. "What happened?"

"I told Brian," he whispered.

He didn't have to say what he told Brian. The night before, Reagan had pestered Trey about telling Brian his feelings and Ethan had tried to stay out of it. "How did he react?"

Trey leaned against Ethan's side and he knew Reagan didn't want anyone to know that the three of them had something more than friendship together, but Ethan wanted to comfort Trey. He wanted to let his love for him show. Fuck the world and its limited views on acceptable relationships. Why couldn't he love a man? He did. Ethan's arm tightened around Trey's body and drew him closer. He brushed his lips against Trey's ear as he whispered. "You can tell me. I'm here for you too."

Several members of the crew had noticed them and were gawking. Trey glanced up at him but didn't pull away. He didn't seem to care that people knew about them either. If only Reagan were equally unconcerned. Ethan looked up at the stage. Trey followed his line of sight to Reagan. He sighed and pulled away, putting several inches between them.

"I'm going to go wait for Reagan in her dressing room," Trey said.

Ethan nodded. He supposed he shouldn't be surprised that she was the one who Trey would turn to. Trey loved her, after all, and Ethan knew Trey just thought of him as a fuck buddy.

"Will you come with me?" Trey whispered.

Ethan almost didn't hear him over the wail of two guitars. "Alone?"

Trey gave him one of his transform-Ethan-into-a-steaming-kettle-of-lust crooked grins and Ethan knew he would have followed him over a cliff.

"Please," Trey added.

Ethan glanced back at the stage. Surely Reagan was safe here surrounded by the crew and rehearsing on stage with Dare. He'd already alerted everyone to be on the lookout for suspicious characters. Everyone in the stadium had her back. She'd be okay if he let her out of his sight for a few minutes as long as there were a lot of people around. She'd likely be up on stage for another hour and wouldn't even miss him. "Okay." He followed Trey to the corridor behind the stage where there were several dressing rooms. Again,

Reagan had a private dressing room. There were perks to being the only female on an all-male tour.

As soon as they were inside her dressing room, away from prying eyes, Trey turned into Ethan's chest and wrapped both arms around his waist. Ethan locked him in a firm embrace, one hand cradling the back of Trey's head to press his face against his neck. Trey's trembling intensified, but he didn't cry. Ethan was glad because he didn't think he could handle that.

"Brian didn't take it well, I assume," Ethan said quietly.

Trey shook his head. "He thought my feelings for him were friendship and simple attraction. Reagan was wrong. I shouldn't have told him how I feel about him. Now things are going to be awkward between us."

"Maybe he's just covering up his feelings for you. Give him time to think about it." Ethan didn't want Brian to have feelings for Trey, but he wanted Trey to be happy and he knew this had been eating him up inside for a long time. Long before Ethan had even met him.

"He doesn't love me. He never did." Trey's arms tightened around Ethan's waist. "The times we made love didn't mean anything to him. All this time... all this time, I thought..."

"He's an idiot. He has no idea how blessed he is to have your heart. I'd do anything to win it." Ethan touched his cheek and Trey lifted his head to stare up into his eyes. "Anything," Ethan whispered before lowering his head and claiming Trey's mouth in a deep kiss.

When he pulled away, Trey's eyes were no longer sad. They were hungry. "Fuck me senseless," he said.

Can do. Ethan reached for Trey's belt. He didn't have to ask to know what Trey wanted from him. Ethan understood perfectly. Unfortunately, it was not the same thing that Ethan wanted and he wasn't sure how to take this relationship to the next level. Trey leaning on him for emotional support was a start, but here they were back to fulfilling sexual needs. Perhaps Ethan should tell him no. Put some provisions on this relationship. Stop allowing this man to lead him around by the nose. Or the dick. And then Ethan's shirt was off and Trey's mouth was on his throat and Trey's cock was in Ethan's hands and all Ethan could think about was losing himself inside the only man who'd ever touched his heart.

Trey bit his collarbone and sucked a bit of his skin into his mouth, sucking hard enough to leave a mark. Claiming him. Physically.

Fuck!

Trey fumbled with Ethan's fly and released his hard cock. Ethan took it in his hand and pressed his length against Trey's. He stroked their combined cocks together in both hands until Trey moaned. He tugged his head back, releasing the suction on the skin along Ethan's collarbone.

"Take me. Don't be gentle," he said.

Ethan had known that's what Trey wanted, but he'd hoped for something a little more tender. Maybe next time. Trey was hurting emotionally and wanted something physically rough to offset that. This time would be just for Trey.

Ethan kissed him, still stroking their cocks together. When Trey whimpered in his mouth, he decided tenderness would probably upset him more. Ethan pulled away and shoved Trey toward the sofa. He spotted Reagan's purse on the table behind the sofa and knew everything he needed to prepare Trey for penetration would be inside. He adored that woman.

"On your knees with your face in the sofa cushions and hold yourself open for me," Ethan demanded.

Trey smiled sadly. "Thank you for giving me what I need right now."

Trey moved toward the sofa, leaving his pants around his knees. Not bothering to remove his shoes either, he knelt on the floor near one end of the sofa and buried his face in the cushions. Trey gripped both cheeks of his ass to spread them apart. Ethan found a condom and lube in Reagan's purse. He worked quickly to prepare himself and then moved in position behind Trey. He didn't warn him. Just plunged deep and started thrusting. Soon, Trey's body began to move with him, rocking back to meet his thrusts, encouraging him to pound him harder.

"Harder. Please. Drive him away," Trey said, his voice muffled by the cushions.

Ethan stopped moving and grabbed a fistful of Trey's hair. "Are you thinking about him right now? Are you thinking about Brian while I fuck you?"

Trey hesitated. "Not exactly."

Not exactly? Ethan had had enough. He pulled out. "On your back, Mills," he said gruffly.

"Ethan?" Trey's goddamned voice was trembling with emotion. How could Trey expect Ethan to fuck him under these circumstances? Ethan wanted more than a physical connection with Trey and he was going to take what he wanted.

"You heard me, Trey. Lie on the sofa on your back. The floor is hard. It's hurting my knees." Mostly a lie.

Trey looked at him over his shoulder. Ethan somehow managed to keep his expression hard and commanding even though his heart was melting. When Trey climbed up on the sofa and settled down on his back, Ethan finished undressing. "Take off your clothes, Trey."

"But…"

"I can't fuck you in that position with your pants on. Take them off."

He complied.

"Shirt too."

"I don't underst—"

"Just do it, Trey. Why do you always question me after you ask me to take the upper hand?"

He shook his head. "I don't know."

Trey removed his shirt and collapsed against the sofa. He avoided Ethan's eyes and murmured, "Just hurry. Please, hurry." Trey always got what he wanted, but not this time. Ethan wasn't in any hurry at all.

Ethan removed the rest of his clothes and knelt beside the sofa. Gently cupping Trey's balls, he extended his middle finger and rubbed it against Trey's entrance. His other hand directed Trey's cock into his mouth. He sucked hard and bobbed his head vigorously.

"Ethan," he groaned, "don't." Though his hands were pressing against the back of Ethan's head and he was thrusting upward into Ethan's mouth.

Ethan moved his hand to cover Trey's mouth. Ethan lifted his head and stared into Trey's startled eyes. "You'll take what I give you and not complain. Stroke your cock while I suck it, and not in a way that you hurt yourself. So it feels good."

When Trey nodded and wrapped one hand around his cock, Ethan moved his hand from his mouth and trailed it down his chest. He caught Trey's nipple ring with the tip of his finger and tugged it gently in time with the stroke of his fingertip against his ass.

"F-feels so good," Trey gasped.

Ethan kissed a trail down Trey's flat belly, watching Trey's hand to make sure he was stroking himself gently. "Good," he murmured before sucking the head of Trey's cock into his mouth. Trey's entire body jerked. When Trey began to writhe and produce excited gasps of pleasure, Ethan decided he was in a hurry after all.

He released Trey's cock and shifted to look him in the eye. "Are you ready for me?"

"I'm always ready for you."

Ethan climbed onto the sofa, settled between Trey's legs, and possessed him with slow, deep thrusts. He watched Trey's reactions and could tell that physically Trey was enjoying every second of this, but he was still holding back that emotional connection Ethan craved. Mostly because even though they were face to face, Trey refused to look Ethan in the eye.

Ethan kissed Trey's jaw tenderly and then whispered in his ear. "Why won't you look at me? Are you ashamed?"

"Of course not."

"Then why?"

"I never look."

Trey looked Reagan in the eyes when they made love. Ethan had been witness to it. And coveted the same interaction. Ethan lifted his head to stare down into Trey's flushed face. He kissed the freckles on the bridge of Trey's nose and smiled gently. He loved this man. It was about time he knew it.

"Look at me, Trey."

Trey squeezed his eyes shut even more tightly and shook his head.

"You *are* ashamed."

"I'm not. How can you think that?" He opened his eyes and glared at Ethan. That's when Ethan knew he had him. Neither of them could look away as their bodies joined in perfect synchrony and Ethan got his first real look at Trey's emotional side. It was a far greater gift than he'd anticipated.

"I love you," Ethan said. "Trey."

Trey's eyes widened and he shook his head in denial.

Ethan held his gaze and nodded until Trey copied his motion and nodded as well.

"What are you going to do it about?" Ethan asked.

"I don't know. Love you back?"

"Sounds wonderful. Tell me when you get there."

"Almost," Trey whispered with a crooked grin.

The double meaning wasn't lost on Ethan. He rested his weight on one elbow and used his free hand to stroke Trey's cock. Trey's eyelids fluttered as he lost himself to pleasure, but he didn't look away. Even when he let go in Ethan's hand, he continued to stare into Ethan's eyes. Ethan shuddered as he followed Trey to bliss, equally lost in the connection between them as he was in the release offered to his body.

He kissed Trey's lips briefly. "That felt good," he said.

"Of course it did."

"I mean to finally tell you I love you. I've known since our first time together. Now that you know, are you going to make me leave?"

Trey shook his head and touched Ethan's face. He searched his eyes for a moment. "It's gone," he said.

"What's gone?"

"The emptiness. Reagan filled much of it, but there was a part of me I thought only Brian would ever touch. I don't need him to feel loved anymore. I think… I think I need you for that, Ethan."

Ethan smiled, his heart thudding with joy. "Do you mean that?"

"Yeah. I love you. Now cuddle with me for a few minutes and then we'll go tell Reagan."

Ethan reached for a packet of tissues to clean up himself and Trey. He tossed the tissues and his expended condom in the trash. He rejoined Trey on the sofa, squeezing in behind him with his back against the sofa back and Trey wrapped securely in his arms.

Trey snuggled against him. "Nice," he murmured drowsily. "How do you think Reagan will take this?"

"Take what?"

"That her two lovers have fallen in love with each other?"

Ethan smiled and kissed the side of Trey's head. "She can't be too upset seeing as she loves both of us."

"And we both love her."

"Do you think I should be the one to tell her?" Ethan said.

"We'll tell her together."

"In a few minutes…" Ethan's eyes drifted shut.

Chapter 34

"I don't understand what I'm doing wrong," Reagan said to Dare, so frustrated she was nearly in tears.

"You're doing everything right for Max," Dare said. "You're doing nothing right for yourself."

"But I'm supposed to be replacing Max," she said.

"No, you're supposed to be our new rhythm guitarist. Let's play "Bite" again. This time don't try to be exactly like Max. Just play it. How you feel it."

Play it with feeling, Reagan. That's how you win first prize. Not by getting it perfect, but by making the audience part of the music, the advice her father had repeated to her before every competition entered her thoughts. Is that what Dare meant?

She started her part of "Bite" the way Max played it. She glanced at Dare, who yawned exaggeratedly. She made a face at him and then tried to give up on copying Max exactly. She relaxed her stance and let her fingers move with more fluidity.

"Better," Dare said. "Again. Even looser this time."

They played it again. And again, until she finally figured out what everyone had been trying to tell her. She wasn't Max and shouldn't try to be.

Reagan finally felt like she'd found the spark she'd been missing. It felt like the weight of the world had lifted from her shoulders and she loved Dare for helping her. Adored him. She one hundred percent understood why he meant so much to Trey. She supposed

Dare was almost like her big brother too. Her very attractive big brother who made her think incestuous thoughts.

Dare squeezed her shoulder. "You've got it now. Don't lose it again."

She nodded.

"Go rest up for tonight's show," he suggested.

"Thanks, Dare."

"No problem."

She handed her guitar off to some roadie and glanced around backstage for Ethan. She checked behind the equipment cases. In the sound equipment pit at the side of the stage. In the empty stands that would soon be filled with tens of thousands of fans. He was gone. He bitched at her constantly about going off on her own and he was nowhere to be found. Maybe he'd gone to the bathroom. She supposed overprotective bodyguards had to take a piss sometime. She had finished rehearsing much sooner than she'd anticipated, so he'd probably thought he had plenty of time. Maybe she should just wait here for him.

After several fidgety minutes of waiting, she went to ask around. "Have you seen Ethan?" she asked one of Exodus End's stage crew.

"The big, good-looking guy who follows you around?"

"Yeah. Him."

"I think he went that way with Trey Mills." The guy pointed toward the corridor where the dressing rooms were located.

She grinned, hoping they were waiting for her in her dressing room. Naked. "Thanks." She could really use some alone time with her guys before she had to be onstage.

The corridor was blissfully empty. Ethan worried too much. She was perfectly capable of walking twenty feet to her dressing room without a muscle-bound hunk to defend her. When she reached the door labeled with her name, she opened it and paused on the threshold. Well, she couldn't say that she blamed Ethan for wandering off. And they *were* naked, but hadn't bothered to wait for her to join them. Ethan and Trey were tangled in each other's arms, fast asleep on the sofa. They looked cozy and sexually sated. Reagan watched them sleep for a moment, a gentle smile on her lips. She hadn't been sure how seeing them together without her involvement would make her feel. She hadn't expected to feel giddy and full of wonder. In a little while, she'd wake them and demand to become part of their tangle of limbs, but for now she was content to watch them sleep. They seemed so content. Tender. Loving. She wondered what had brought on this change.

She caught her own reflection in the mirror and her heart skipped a beat. It stopped beating for several seconds as the message scrawled in lipstick on the mirror caught her attention.

You took what's mine, Reagan Elliot. I will have it back.

From behind, a hand covered her mouth and nose. Startled, Reagan sucked a deep breath into her lungs. Something chemical accompanied her inrush of air. Her vision blurred. Head swam. "I've come to take back what's mine," a deep voice said in her ear. Familiar. She'd heard it before, but couldn't place where. She managed to bang into the door—hopefully loud enough to wake her snoozing bodyguard—before she totally blacked out.

Chapter 35

ETHAN'S EYES FLIPPED OPEN. Trey flopped from sofa to the floor when Ethan sat up abruptly. Someone had slammed the door shut or something. Reagan would not be happy if someone had caught him in a compromising position with Trey.

Silence greeted his straining ears. It was not comforting.

"I don't hear music," Ethan said and jumped to his feet. He grabbed his pants and hopped into them, still zipping his fly as he darted into the corridor. Except for the bang of a hammer somewhere, the stadium was silent. Sometime between when Ethan had closed his eyes and the door had banged shut, Reagan had finished rehearsing. Some bodyguard he'd turned out to be. He wondered if she'd seen him and Trey together and had stormed off in anger. There was no guarantee that she'd approve of their romantic interest in each other just because she had no problem with their sexual relationship.

"Where is she?" Trey asked. He'd managed his pants and T-shirt but was still barefoot.

"She's probably with the band." Ethan glanced over his shoulder and caught his reflection in the mirror and the message scrawled above his astonished face in red lipstick.

"Do you smell something?" Trey asked.

Ethan took a deep breath through his nose. It was faint, but there was no mistaking the sweet chemical smell. "Ether." He shoved Trey in the direction of the stage. "Go see if she's with the band. I'll go out behind the stadium. He's been in her dressing room again. I'm afraid he's taken her this time."

Trey raced down the corridor while Ethan went in the opposite direction. When Ethan burst through the back doors, it took his eyes a moment to adjust to the bright sunshine. Even when he could actually see what was happening, he blinked several times because he couldn't believe it.

"Get back or I'll kill her. I'll do it." Some wild-eyed guy with bizarre burgundy-and-green-striped bangs had a guitar string wrapped around Reagan's throat. She was unconscious and apparently heavier than she looked. He was having a hard time keeping the wire tight while he tried, rather unsuccessfully, to drag her backwards toward the parking lot. Her heels dragged across the pavement and slowed the wiry-framed guy down. While given time, the wacko could potentially kill her with the guitar string, Sinners' road crew didn't look ready to give him the opportunity. Jake had a guitar cocked like a baseball bat and was slowly inching his way behind the guy. Rebekah had a cymbal in hand and was looking for an opening to practice her discus throwing. Others hopped out of the back of the semitrailer with pieces of equipment and heavy tools.

"You don't really think you're going to get away, do you?" Ethan said. He placed his hands on his hips, trying not to look threatening. He didn't want Reagan to get hurt any more than she already had and he feared if he rushed the guy, he'd do something drastic. "Let her go and you'll only be charged with attempted kidnapping and I won't be charged with homicide."

Brian came out of Sinners' tour bus, a few yards from where the guy was slowly dragging Reagan backward. "What in the hell is going on out here?" He took in Ethan's partial state of undress before his eyes fell on Reagan who'd been dragged another few feet toward the parking lot.

The kidnapper, who was obviously no criminal mastermind,

dropped Reagan on the asphalt. The guitar string went taut and Ethan could see it cut into her skin from a distance. "M-master Sinclair," the man said. "It's a privilege."

"What in the fuck are you doing?" Brian said. "Let her go."

They guy's eyes widened as he realized he'd dropped his cargo. Ethan took a deep breath when the guy bent over and the guitar string around Reagan's throat loosened again. The kidnapper wrapped an arm around her body just beneath her breasts and stood upright, dragging her backward several feet before pausing to catch his breath again. The guy had to be high out of his mind. Otherwise he'd realize there was no way his plan would succeed. Not with this many witnesses. Or maybe he was just crazy and had nothing to lose. Ethan just hoped he didn't do anything even more stupid and hurt Reagan in the process. The sound of approaching sirens drew the guy's attention. "Which one of you called the cops?"

Trey stepped out from behind Ethan and waved a cell phone at the guy. "That would be me. If you put her down now, they might not shoot you when they get here."

"And Jace and I might not take turns punching you in the fucking face," Eric said, coming out of the building to stand beside Trey.

Jace stepped out of the shadows and cracked his knuckles.

"And then there's me," Sed, who rivaled Ethan in build, said from the doorway. "No one messes with a Sinners' girl and gets away with it."

"I wasn't going to hurt her. I just wanted her out of the way." The guy's wild eyes darted from one person to the next.

"Isn't he with one of the opening bands?" Jace asked. "Hell's Crypt?"

"Dim Reaper?" Eric asked.

"No, they stopped touring with us a month ago," Jace said. "Hell's Crypt is the new one. With the movie monster theme. Vampire, werewolf, Frankenstein. Kinda lame."

"Really lame," Eric said.

"Shut up," the guy wailed. "We are not lame."

"I don't even know who you're talking about," Sed said.

"Wait," Trey said. He snapped his fingers and pointed at him. "I know who this guy is. He was at Exodus End's contest audition. The one that Reagan won."

"I never even got the chance to audition," he bellowed. "I was supposed to be the one onstage with Exodus End, not her. She took what was mine."

Reagan moaned and slapped herself in the face with a clumsy hand. "What?" she mumbled.

The guy fumbled with something in his pocket. While he was distracted, Rebekah let the cymbal fly. It bounced off his head with a loud clang. Ethan took the opening and made his move, dashing across the parking lot as fast as his legs would carry him. Brian was closer. He got a hand on Reagan and slid his free hand under the guitar string to protect her throat as he wrenched her out of the kidnapper's grasp. Before the guy could wrestle her away from Brian, Ethan tackled him to the ground. The dark part of Ethan tried to take the upper hand and beat the ever-loving shit out of this crazy bastard, but he breathed through the rage and just held the guy's struggling body down to wait for the police cruisers to arrive. He turned his head to see how Reagan had fared.

Trey held her on his lap and stroked her hair as he spoke to her. She seemed groggy but coherent. "We're going for a ride in an ambulance. Doesn't that sound fun?" Trey asked her.

"I'd rather ride in the limo." She groaned. "Damn, my head hurts."

"How's your neck?"

"I don't know. I feel sort of numb. And tired. And nauseous." She turned her head and stared at the guy who had Ethan's knee in his back and his arms pulled up behind him at a sharp angle. He wasn't going anywhere. Reagan shook her head and laughed. "I can't believe I've been afraid of *Pyre* this whole time. In a fair fight, I could take him down myself."

"I've got him pinned, if you want to take a cheap shot at him," Ethan said.

"Maybe later," she murmured.

"Are you okay, Reagan?" Sed asked, looking from her to Pyre as if he couldn't decide if he'd rather comfort her or kick the shit out of Pyre.

"I'll be fine. I'm just tired." Her eyelids fluttered and Trey gave her a harsh shake.

"Try to stay awake. Okay?" he said. "I'm pretty sure that stuff can kill you if you breathe in too much."

"I didn't mean to hurt her," Pyre said. "Just get her out of the way. So I could have my chance. I never even got a chance. I'm sick of being in the opening band."

Ethan tugged Pyre's arms up another inch, which shut him up immediately. A pair of police cruisers pulled to a halt near the tour buses. Two officers entered the scene with their hands at their gun belts.

"Ethan Conner, professional bodyguard," Ethan identified himself. "I've subdued the perpetrator."

"I'll say," one of the officers said as he removed a pair of handcuffs from his belt and grabbed one of Pyre's wrists.

Pyre was handcuffed and pulled upright to sit on the ground. He didn't look the slightest bit threatening now. More pathetic than anything. The officers started the interview process to get everyone's story straight. Ethan had to talk to one of them while the paramedics looked Reagan over. Besides a severe case of nausea, a headache, and a few small cuts and bruises, she seemed to be fine. That didn't mean Ethan liked to be interviewed for an incident report while Trey got to hold her hand and tell her everything was going to be all right as she recounted her own version of the events to the other officer.

When Ethan finally finished describing all of the details, several of the road crew came over to offer their take on the situation. Ethan went to stand at the end of the ambulance where Reagan sat. "Hey," she said, a delightful blush staining her cheeks.

"I can't begin to tell you how sorry I am that I let him get his hands on you," Ethan said.

She shook her head. "I'm okay."

"That never should have happened. I allowed myself to be distracted and—"

"I did the distracting," Trey said. "I'm as much at fault as he is."

"So while I was being stalked, drugged, and strangled, you two were making love, cuddling, and sharing your feelings."

That made it sound even worse. Ethan's heart twisted with guilt. "Reagan…"

"While I was being dragged across a parking lot, beaten with a rubber hose, and stuffed into the trunk of a car, you two were kissing, touching, and playing hide the salami."

"He beat you?" Trey exclaimed.

Reagan chuckled. "No, I'm just fucking with you. And once I stop feeling like I'm going to hurl, I'd say the two of you have a lot to make up to me."

How could she be so forgiving? He'd put her in danger. She could have been seriously injured. She should be yelling at him, calling him names, firing him for being the worst bodyguard on the planet. Ethan stroked her hair behind her ear and brushed her soft cheek with the pad of his thumb. "I love you."

"I know," she said. "I love you too."

Ethan glanced at Trey. It was the first time Trey had heard Reagan say those words to another man. Ethan wondered how he'd take it. Trey grinned and squeezed Reagan's hand.

"Ethan, I need you to do something for me," Reagan said.

"Anything."

"Tell me how you feel about Trey."

Ethan tried to read her expression to figure out what she wanted to hear, but she was staring down at her hand which was held securely in Trey's.

"I love him," Ethan said breathlessly.

She looked up at him and smiled. "I thought so."

"You're okay with it?" Ethan pressed.

"Under one condition," Reagan said. She glanced at Trey. "Do you love Ethan?"

Trey nodded. "Yeah. I do. I love him."

She smiled. "Good. And who else?"

"You," he said without hesitation.

"And Brian?" she asked.

Trey chuckled and caught Ethan's eye. "Who's Brian?"

Ethan smiled. Trey had let Brian go for real this time. "He's the guy I need to thank for grabbing Reagan so I could take that guy down," Ethan said, glancing over his shoulder. Pyre was in the back of the cruiser now. He had a scrape along the side of his face where he'd hit the asphalt, but Ethan had somehow kept it together and not knocked him around too much.

"Are you going to go back on the force now?" Reagan asked.

Ethan gave her a questioning look. "Why would I do that?"

"Because you loved it and the only reason you left was because you protect the innocent a bit too violently. You were completely in control when you took Pyre down."

"You don't want me as your bodyguard anymore?" Ethan asked.

"You do suck at it," Trey quipped.

Ethan scowled. "Yeah, because I was sucking you instead of guarding her."

"Next time I'll make sure I'm there when you're sucking him so you can keep an eye on me," Reagan said.

"I guess that would be safest," Ethan agreed. He lowered his head and stole a kiss from her.

"What's going on here?" someone said behind Ethan. He turned to find Dare staring at him with a mixture of confusion and anger.

Dare then looked at his brother in question. "You let some other dude kiss your girl right in front of you? No wonder you have relationship problems."

"Ethan's my boyfriend," Trey explained.

"So the thing with Reagan is a front to hide your relationship with him?" Dare pointed at Ethan and looked even more confused. "But he just kissed her." Dare's pointing bounced from Ethan to Reagan.

"That's because he's her boyfriend," Trey said, grinning his orneriest. Ethan figured it wasn't often that Trey got to mess with his brother's head. It was usually the other way around.

"I thought you said he was *your* boyfriend," Dare said.

"He is." Trey nodded.

"And hers?"

"Right."

"And she's your girlfriend?" Dare pointed at Reagan.

Trey pointed at Ethan. "And his."

Realization dawned on Dare's face. He made a circular motion with one finger. "So the three of you? All together?"

"Exactly," Trey said.

Dare smiled and slapped his brother on the arm repeatedly. "That's fantastic!"

Ethan could not imagine telling his brothers about his lifestyle, much less thinking they'd accept it, and they sure as hell wouldn't be enthusiastic about it. Dare just seemed glad that his brother had found happiness, even if it was in an unconventional way.

"Are you feeling okay, Reagan?" Dare asked. "I heard some guy grabbed you."

"I'm fine." She snorted and shook her head. "Worst. Kidnapper. Ever."

Dare squeezed her knee, his concern tangible. "You'll be okay for the show tonight?"

She nodded. "I do think I need to lie down for a little while."

"You should definitely get some rest," Dare agreed.

"I'm bringing these two with me," she said quietly. "Resting will not be on my agenda."

Dare laughed and tousled her hair affectionately. "Rock on, little sister."

Reagan looked into the back of the ambulance to the paramedic who was sitting on a bench along the sidewall. He looked a tad uncomfortable about what he must have overheard. "Can I go now?" she asked him.

"Doc says if you start vomiting uncontrollably you need to come to the hospital."

Reagan made a face of disgust. "I don't think that's going to happen. My nausea is all gone now."

"Then you're free to go. Just make sure someone is around to keep an eye on you."

"Will do," Trey said. He hopped off the back end of the ambulance and lifted Reagan into his arms. "Where to?"

"Take me to bed."

"On the tour bus?"

"I don't think there was enough room on that dressing room sofa for three."

Ethan smiled. Seeing the two of them together warmed his heart almost as much as being with the two of them did. "I'll be right there," Ethan said. "I need to go talk to someone for a second."

"We'll be sure to start without you," Trey said. He nodded a farewell at his brother and headed for the tour bus.

Ethan walked over to Brian Sinclair, who was watching the last police cruiser pull away with a remorseful Pyre in the backseat. Ethan could totally see how Trey could have loved the guy for almost thirteen years. The man was exquisite. He started when he noticed Ethan standing beside him.

"I wanted to thank you for getting Reagan away from that guy," Ethan said. "I wasn't sure how to get him to release her without causing her harm. I was too far away."

Brian smiled. "No problem. I didn't want to see her get hurt either. She means a lot to Trey." His face twisted when he said his name.

"And he means a lot to you."

Brian looked away. "Yeah. He always has."

"And you told him otherwise, why?"

Brian scowled. "How do you know what I told him?"

"He told me. You could have let him down a little easier. Why did you have to hurt him so bad?"

"So he could move on. I should have done it years ago. Having someone like Trey in love with you is hard to give up, you know? He's so…" Brian stared at the darkening sky overhead as he searched for the right word. "…passionate."

"Yeah," Ethan agreed. "So if you cared about him, why not try to make something of it?" Not that he wanted Brian to be with Trey. If Ethan had been in Brian's position, he never could have pushed Trey away.

"Too complicated. And besides, I have Myrna now. She's more than enough for me." He glanced over his shoulder and grinned at Trey's attempts to carry Reagan up the steep bus steps without dropping her or whacking her head on the door. "I just hope Reagan's enough for him."

"She's not, but she knows that and she's okay with it now." Ethan wanted to shout it from the rooftops. *You fucking fool. You gave Trey up and now he's mine—ours—and worth every complication anyone can throw at us.*

Brian shifted his gaze to Ethan's. His expression was a mix of surprise and confusion. "What do you mean?"

Ethan smiled. "You'll figure it out." He slapped Brian on the back and followed his two lovers, his two *loves*, to the bedroom.

Chapter 36

REAGAN HELD ONTO TREY'S neck as he staggered up the bus steps. Maybe she should be upset about Pyre's attempt to kidnap her and strangle her with a guitar string, but she was just so happy that it was over with, she felt like celebrating. And knowing that Trey and Ethan were in love with each other was another reason to celebrate. Trey carried her to the bedroom and dumped her on the bed. "I have a phone call to make," he said.

"A phone call?" At a time like this?

"Yep." He retrieved his cell phone from his pocket and searched for whatever number he needed in his encyclopedic list of contacts. "Hello, this is Trey Mills. I was supposed to call you today about some test results. Yeah, I'll hold."

Reagan grinned. She was willing to wait for him to make this phone call. Sex without condoms. Oh please, oh please, oh please.

"All right, good," he said, giving her a thumbs-up. "And my two partners?" He chuckled. "Yes, two partners." His smile broadened. "Great. Can you hold on for a second?" He covered the phone with his hand. "Do you want her to repeat the results for you, or do you believe me when I say it's time to go all out raw?"

Reagan laughed and threw a pillow at him. "I believe you."

He spoke into his phone again. "That's all then, thanks." He chuckled. "Yes, two partners. And just between you and me, they're both super hot." He laughed again and disconnected.

"We're all set?" Reagan asked.

"All set." He crawled up on the bed beside her and took her hand. He kissed her knuckles as he stared into her eyes. "In a way, this will be like me losing my virginity."

"In a *very* loose interpretation of the definition kind of way," Reagan teased.

Ethan appeared in the doorway. "I figured she'd be halfway to her third orgasm by now. Were you waiting for me?"

"Trey was calling the clinic to find out our test results."

Ethan's eyebrows shot up and he swiveled his head in Trey's direction. "And?"

"I don't have to worry about being caught without a condom ever again. We're all clean."

"That's good," Ethan said, "because we have a lot of unprotected oral sex."

Trey laughed. "That's true."

"Get in here and close the door," Reagan demanded. "Take off your clothes. Take off my clothes. Ravish my body."

Reagan opened her arms wide in invitation. Trey worked on removing her shirt and bra, while Ethan removed her jeans, panties, and sandals. When they had her naked, Trey lowered his head to suckle one breast while he massaged the other. Ethan nibbled trails of fire along the insides of her thighs.

"Has Trey ever told you that he's a virgin?" Reagan asked, stroking Ethan's hair with one hand and Trey's with the other.

Ethan lifted his head and snorted with laughter. "Is today opposite day?"

"He's never had sex without a condom."

Ethan gave Trey a pitying look. "You *are* a virgin. Let me get her ready for you."

Trey smacked him on the back of the head as he lowered it to suck on the heated flesh between Reagan's thighs. Her head was still swimming slightly, so she closed her eyes and concentrated on the sensation of Trey at her breasts, Ethan down lower. She rocked her hips against Ethan's face as her excitement mounted. He lifted his head.

"Come here, Trey." Ethan moved aside and wrapped an arm around Trey's waist to position his hips between Reagan's thighs. "I want to put you inside her. Can I?"

Reagan lifted her head and stared down her body to watch Ethan take Trey's cock in his hand. She lost sight of it as Ethan directed it inside her body, but she felt it, felt Trey, inside of her.

"Oh," Trey groaned as he sank deeper, his belly quivering against hers.

Ethan swatted his ass. "Take her, Trey." He moved to lie next to Reagan on the bed and they both stared up at Trey as he possessed her with deep, rhythmic thrusts. His eyes were closed, mouth open as he gasped in excitement.

Reagan caressed his back with one hand, rocking her hips to meet his strokes. "Look at us, Trey."

His eyes fluttered open and he stared down at Reagan with a look of rapture and love on his gorgeous face.

"How's that feel?" she asked.

"So good. So good," he whispered. "I'm glad I saved myself for you, Reagan." He grinned and winked at her before lowering his head to claim her lips in a deep kiss. He drew away and stared down at her. She got lost in his body. His gaze. "I love you," he said. He then shifted so he could kiss Ethan who was still lying beside Reagan with his head against her shoulder. "I love you," he whispered against Ethan's lips.

He tugged away so he could stare down at both of them. His steady strokes grew more rapid. Reagan's back arched off the bed as her pleasure built to match his urgency.

"Can I come inside you, Reagan?"

"Yes."

He held onto her shoulders as he buried himself deep and

shuddered with release. His mouth dropped open, face twisted in bliss as his gaze shifted from Reagan to Ethan and back to Reagan. His body went slack and he buried his face in Reagan's throat. "I want to do that again," he said.

"Not until I get a turn," Ethan said.

Trey pulled out and rolled over on Reagan's opposite side and Ethan took his place between Reagan's thighs. He plunged into her with one deep thrust.

"Damn, she wet," Ethan said.

"Some of that's mine," Trey said with a teasing grin.

Ethan shuddered. "I can't tell you how much that turns me on. Kiss me, Trey." Trey kissed him. Ethan thrust into Reagan harder and faster. "Let me suck her cum off of you."

"I think he likes this," Trey said to Reagan.

"God, Reagan, you feel so good," Ethan shouted. Trey shifted up the bed so Ethan could bend sideways and suck and lick Reagan's juices from Trey's flaccid cock. Ethan made content noises in the back of his throat. It wasn't long before Trey was hard again.

Ethan rolled onto his side, dragging Reagan with him. "Get in here with me, Trey."

"What?" Reagan said.

"She's so wet. You'll love this."

Ethan pulled out and Trey moved in against her back. Trey thrust into her from behind several times before pulling out to let Ethan take his place. Reagan clung to Ethan's shoulders as her body found release and she cried out. She couldn't tell exactly what they were doing. Didn't care as long as they kept doing it. Their hands were working one cock against another, before one plunged into her, thrust, pulled out, again, again, and then without warning, they were both inside her. Two cocks buried in her sopping wet pussy, working against each other. Together. Against each other. It was a tight fit at first, but her body quickly adjusted to the added girth.

"Fuck, that's amazing," Ethan growled.

"New favorite position," Trey groaned.

Reagan cried out as she came again.

"Reagan, are you okay, honey?" Ethan asked. His hips pounded against her as he kept driving himself deep and rubbing his cock against Trey's which was thrusting into her just as hard and deep.

"Oh yes," she cried. "I'm better than okay. Don't stop. Don't stop."

"I'm gonna come," Ethan said.

"Me too. Me too," Trey chanted breathlessly.

Reagan didn't think she'd ever stopped coming. She felt like she was floating on the ceiling.

Ethan shouted in triumph as his body went rigid. "Keep rubbing against me, Trey. Don't stop."

Trey struggled to keep thrusting while Ethan held perfectly still. And then Trey went rigid. "I can feel you coming, Trey," Ethan whispered, his head tilted back, eyes glazed over in bliss.

They lay in the aftermath for a long time, none of them willing to let go of the other. Reagan had never felt like such an important part of anything before. But she was a part of these two men she loved, just as they were a part of her. And a part of each other. None of them whole without the other two.

Chapter 37

A COUPLE OF DAYS later, Trey stood in the hallway of the tour bus and watched Brian apply his guyliner in the bathroom mirror. They hadn't spoken since Brian had broken his heart in San Francisco. Trey felt he needed to say something to him. He wasn't sure what. Things just felt unfinished between them. Uncomfortable. He'd never felt that way around Brian before and he needed it to go away. It was fucking with his perfect happiness. And he knew without a doubt that it would affect their music on stage that night. Their show in San Francisco had been terse. The flow of music between them had been off all night. He needed to fix that. Somehow.

"Take a picture; it will last longer," Brian said, catching Trey's gaze in the mirror and grinning at him.

Trey laughed. That had been Trey's favorite saying in the fifth grade, when he'd first met Brian. Back before things had gotten complicated. Could they ever get that simple friendship back? Trey wasn't sure, but he had to try.

"How's Malcolm?" Trey asked. Small talk was a start. It would help him find the courage to press forward with more difficult words.

"I guess he's good. I haven't heard from Myrna all day."

Trey scowled. That didn't sound like Myrna. He hoped everything was okay. She wouldn't hide a problem from Brian to keep him from worrying, would she? Of course she would. "Did you call her?"

"Yeah, she texted me and told me her day was entirely full and that she wouldn't have time to talk until tonight."

"So she's okay?"

Brian smiled. "She's fine. Jessica told me to give the woman a moment's peace and sent me a picture of Malcolm in his car seat to assure me he was okay. I guess they're running errands today."

Trey laughed. "Oh. For a minute I thought you'd learned to relax."

Brian met his eyes in the mirror again. "How long have you known me, Trey?"

"Eighteen years." Trey closed his eyes, hoping it would help him find the courage to say what needed to be said. "I forgive you."

"For knowing me?"

"No, for breaking my heart. I kind of needed it actually."

Brian touched Trey's shoulder and he opened his eyes. He stared into Brian's deep, brown eyes and was surprised that the connection between them was still there. It felt different. The horrible aching longing he used to feel when he looked at Brian was gone, but the closeness that can only forge between two people who'd been through everything together was still there. Trey was so relieved his eyes prickled with tears. Brian's fingers clinched in Trey's shirt and he gave him a little shake.

"If you start crying, I'm going to fucking pound you," Brian said. "I just put on my eyeliner and I don't want to have to redo it."

Trey laughed. "I'm not going to cry. I'm just glad we can move forward. I thought maybe I'd ruined our friendship."

Brian's hand relaxed and he smoothed Trey's sleeve. "Does she make you happy?"

"Reagan?" Trey smiled. "Yeah, I love her. And Ethan too."

Brian nodded. "Then we're good." He shoved Trey in the shoulder and brushed past him. "I'm going for a walk." His phone beeped and he paused to check his text message.

"Myrna?" Trey asked.

"Yeah. It says, *Honey, we're home.* I guess that means they're done with errands and I can call her now."

Outside a loud horn sounded. Brian dialed his wife, while Trey looked outside through the large tinted window over the sofa to see what was going on in the parking lot. There was a large RV he'd never seen before parked next to the bus. When Trey recognized its driver, he grabbed Brian by the shirt and pulled him to the window.

"Hey, sweetheart," Trey could hear Myrna's voice coming through Brian's phone. "I've got a surprise for you."

"What are you doing in that RV?" Brian asked her.

"Well, I figured since you can't come home, I'd bring home to you."

"What?"

"Come over and see."

Trey pulled Brian to the front of the bus just as Reagan and Ethan stumbled out of the bedroom at the end of the narrow hall. "What's going on?" Reagan asked.

"Myrna's here," Trey said and hauled Brian down the steps.

Brian finally found the sense to move on his own. He met Myrna at the bottom of the RV's steps and pulled her into his arms. She cupped face in both hands. "Are you surprised?"

"I don't really understand what's going on."

"Come inside and I'll show you."

Myrna took Brian's hand and directed him into the RV. Trey followed them, his curiosity getting the best of him. In one of the captain's chairs sat an unoccupied car seat. In another sat Aggie with a loudly purring black tuxedo cat on her lap. She smiled and waved.

"Aggie is starting up a travelling merchandise shop for her corsets," Myrna said. "Selling them in a merch stand outside of concerts."

"Embedding myself into Jace's life yet again," Aggie said. "I can't seem to stop doing that."

"He'll be ecstatic to have you on tour with us again," Trey said. "Well as ecstatic as Jace can be."

"Where's Malcolm?" Brian asked.

"Jessica is changing his diaper in the nursery," Myrna said.

"Jessica is here too?" Brian asked.

"She's decided she wants to be Malcolm's nanny until she has a baby of her own." Myrna smiled. "In around eight and a half months."

Brian's eyes widened. "Does Sed know?"

"She just found out yesterday. She wants to tell him in person. So keep that to yourself."

"He's going to flip. So all three of you are going to follow us around on tour?" Brian asked, waving a hand in Aggie's direction.

"Four of us. Don't forget your son."

"Myrna, I'm not sure if this is a good idea," Brian said. "Malcolm needs stability in his life. There is no stability in a life on the road. I don't want that for him."

Myrna shook her head at him. "What Malcolm needs is his father. And I need my husband. This will be our home, Brian. Just because it moves doesn't mean it's not a stable environment for him. When we're parked, I can write."

"And I can sew," Aggie said.

"And Malcolm can play and grow up knowing his father," Myrna said.

"What about when we tour Europe?" Brian asked.

"I've been looking into real estate in France. I already ordered my passport. We can follow you there too."

"And South America? Australia? Asia?"

"We'll figure out a way to be together as much as possible. If I didn't know better, I'd think you didn't want us here, Brian," Myrna said.

"It just seems too good to be true."

"I think it's a perfect solution," Trey said. "Myrna, you're brilliant."

"Thank you, Trey." Myrna gave his arm a squeeze and really looked at him for the first time. She smiled. "You look happy, sweetie. Did you just eat a cherry pie?"

"He's in love," Brian said and rolled his eyes.

"Reagan?" Myrna asked, her eyes and smile wide as she nodded enthusiastically.

"And some guy named Ethan," Brian added. "You can ask him for an interview for your book later." He took Myrna's hand and directed her further into the RV. Trey followed. There were several rooms in the back. In addition to the small bathroom and the surprisingly large bedroom with a huge, king-sized bed that was sure to get broken in very soon, a small nursery was connected off to one side. With a crib and changing table, the room was a bit cramped, but not without charm. It had been decorated to look like a regular nursery with primary colors, pictures of musical instruments, mobiles, and stuffed animals. Jessica was blowing raspberries on Malcolm's tummy and he was kicking his feet gleefully. Jessica looked up when she noticed the group of spectators standing in the doorway.

"There's your daddy," Jessica said and lifted Malcolm from the table. She handed him to Brian, who got that wondrous look on his face that he sported every time he held his son.

"Your mother is a genius," Brian said to Malcolm. "The smartest thing I ever did was marry that woman."

Malcolm cooed in agreement.

Someone stomped up the bus steps. Trey turned and caught the look of pure joy on Jace's face, just before he hauled Aggie to her feet and into his arms. "How long are you staying?"

"Forever."

Trey had never seen Jace smile so broadly in all the years he'd known him. Jace kissed Aggie as if he never planned to stop. The man never said many words, but somehow, he never needed to. Jace's cat, Brownie, rubbed up against their legs, meowing for attention.

"Aggie was worried that Jace would think she was being too clingy," Jessica whispered.

"I think he's the one clinging at the moment," Trey said.

Sed appeared in the front stairwell. The RV was spacious, but there wasn't really room for seven adults, a baby, and a cat. Reagan and Ethan were behind Sed, and bringing up the rear were Eric and Rebekah. There definitely wasn't room for four more. Trey started to inch toward the front door. This arrangement would make Brian happy, which was good because Trey knew he wasn't the only one sick of Brian's constant moping.

"You all have to be onstage in thirty minutes," Rebekah announced. She spotted Malcolm and responsibility took the backseat. "Oh, isn't he perfect?" She was down the hall before Eric could stop her. When she got close to Malcolm's face and made a funny expression for him, the baby's eyes lit up and he grabbed a fistful of Rebekah's crimson red hair, ignoring the more boring platinum blond shades that made up the bulk of her hair color. "I think it's time to find us one of these, Eric," she said.

"When we get back from the world tour we'll start looking into adopting," he promised, and placed a protective hand on the base of Rebekah's spine.

Sed had Jessica in his arms. "Wish we had more time to be alone together right now," he said. "We'll have to save our next round of baby-making attempts until later tonight."

"That won't be necessary," Jessica said in a clipped tone.

Trey stifled a laugh. The two of them drove each other nuts on purpose. And they both loved every minute of it.

Sed's face fell. "You haven't already changed your mind, have you?"

She scowled at him. "I hope not. I happen to be pregnant." She dropped her angry ruse, grinning as she waited for his reaction.

It took a moment for her words to register with Sed, because he was apparently expecting her to say something entirely different. When it finally sank in, his eyes lit up and Trey was sure Sed's dimples would cause his face to implode.

"Do you mean it?" he said. "You're pregnant?"

She tilted her head back to smile up at him. "You, Sedric Lionheart, are going to be a father. And I couldn't be happier about it."

"Fucking awesome!" Sed shouted and swung Jessica around in a circle.

When he stopped twirling, Eric smacked him in the head. "Watch your mouth around Malcolm."

Trey squeezed between Reagan and Ethan, wrapping his arms around both of them. "I guess the band's all here now."

"One big, happy family," Reagan murmured, kissing Trey's smiling lips. Ethan's lips brushed his temple. Ethan squeezed Trey and Reagan together, lifting them several inches off the floor in his powerful embrace.

Sinners had always been a family and it still was. Only now it was an extended family. With less beer. And more love.

Read on for a sneak peek at the next from

Sinners on Tour: *Hot Ticket*

by Olivia Cunning

Available February 2013 from Sourcebooks Casablanca

WITHIN SECONDS OF MEETING a man, Aggie could assign him to one of two lists.

List A: *Men Not Worth My Time.*

List B: *Men I'd Like to Fuck.*

List A grew in length every hour she worked at the nightclub, Paradise Found. She couldn't remember the last time a man had landed himself on List B.

That might explain why Aggie dropped her bullwhip when *he* caught her attention. Whoever he was. Potential List B strode across the floor as if he owned the place. He had that stereotypical bad boy look—leather, tattoos, and a giant chip on his shoulder—which was contradicted by the sweetest face she'd ever seen. When he took a seat at the table closest to her stage, he leaned back in his chair and crossed his legs at the ankle, as if he planned to stay for a while.

Interesting. And entirely fuckable.

Sipping his beverage, Angel Face gazed up at her with an odd gleam of challenge in his dark eyes. Something about him had her instantly thinking naughty thoughts. Only half of them involved inflicting pain on his tight body. Oh, the guy was a looker, no denying that, but that wasn't his main appeal. Strange thing was she didn't know what set him apart from the other nightclub patrons. Perhaps she needed a new list just for him.

Temporary List C: *Men I Can't Instantly Label.* She had no doubt that this list's only assignee would quickly land himself on List

A. In no way would she ever consider a customer List B potential. It didn't matter how attractive he was.

Aggie retrieved her bullwhip from the stage floor (how embarrassing) and cracked it next to Hottie's cheek. He didn't flinch. His body tensed, but not with fear. From the slight gasp he emitted and the flutter of his lashes, she could tell her threat turned him on.

Most men liked to watch Aggie's routine from the shadows and think they could take her abuse. Trying to show their toughness, they chose the dominatrix in leather to entertain them at Paradise Found, but few sat within striking distance of her bullwhip. Not that she'd actually hit anyone at the club. If a man wanted her to punish him for being born with a Y chromosome, he had to pay extra.

Aggie drew her arm back and lashed her whip at the new arrival's cheek again. The leather snapped centimeters from his skin. She was satisfied when he didn't flinch this time either. Oh Lord, he'd be fun to break. It had been forever since she'd had a real challenge in her dungeon.

He stared directly into her eyes as she danced closer. He looked quite young—mid-twenties, maybe—but he had eyes wise beyond his years. She'd bet he'd seen a lot of tragedy in his life. Many of those who sought her for release had.

The young man beckoned her closer with a crooked finger. Surprised, she arched a brow at him and glanced at Eli, the bouncer who stood near the stage. She wasn't supposed to discuss her side business at the club. As far as her coworkers were concerned, Aggie's dominatrix routine was entirely an act. Later, when she moved to the floor to interact with customers on a more personal basis, she would slip her card to potential slaves, but her stage set wasn't over yet. She needed to concentrate on her dancing and not daydream about making some tough-looking, übercutie her bitch.

Aggie hooked her leg around a silver pole and twirled around it, her long, black hair flying out behind her. When she stopped, she found the guy had vacated his chair and was standing against the stage at her feet. He pulled a bill from his back pocket and held it out to her between two fingers. *Hello, C-note. Mama needs a new pair of boots.*

Holding onto the pole with one hand, she leaned toward the customer, offering the tops of her full breasts to his view. His gaze shifted to her bare skin, and he drew his tongue over his upper lip. Usually, one guy looked as mundane as another to her, but she took in every inch of this one, from his heavy black boots to his spiked platinum blond hair. Dark eyes. Dark eyebrows. Dark beard stubble. The hint of a tattoo revealed itself above the neckline of his T-shirt. A studded leather band adorned his right wrist. He looked hard and tough, yet saccharine sweet at the same time. A hell's angel, heavy on the angel. She wondered if his beard stubble was an attempt to cover up that undeniably cute face of his.

He slid the bill between Aggie's breasts and into the bodice of her black leather bustier. As his fingertips brushed her skin, her nipples tightened. Totally unusual reaction for her. Customers typically gave her the heebie-jeebies when they touched her. This one had all her systems set to go. The small silver hoop in his earlobe caught a strobe light. Aggie gnawed on her tongue, wanting to nibble on his ear instead. She did have a thing for ears.

Um, wrong answer, Aggie. Customers were never fair game for action in the sack.

"Do you do private dances?" he asked, his chocolate brown eyes locked with hers. His voice was deeper than she'd expected and so quiet, she wouldn't have heard him over the throbbing club music if she hadn't been leaning so close.

"You mean like a lap dance?"

"If that's what you do. How much?"

"Fifty bucks."

He handed her another hundred. The guy must have had a

good day at the casino. He didn't look rich. He wore a plain white T-shirt, worn black leather jacket, and snug blue jeans, which clung to the huge bulge in his pants. *Well, hello there, big guy.* She was glad she wasn't the only one thinking her next dance should be the horizontal mamba.

Aggie, pull yourself together, woman. He's a customer. No can do. Oh, but she so wanted to. Do. Him.

His gaze lowered to the floor, and he flushed. "Do you offer *other* services?"

Whoa, buddy. Brakes engaged. "I'm not a prostitute, if that's what you're asking."

He shook his head. "That's not what I meant. I want you to hurt me." He drew a deep, shuddering breath into his expanding chest. "Hard-core."

Oh yeah. Can do, sugar.

Aggie glanced over at the bouncer again to make sure he wasn't watching her side transaction. Eli's attention was on the far stage, where Paradise Found's newest dancer, Jessica, a.k.a. Feather, was dancing in her white feathers and silk scarf. Men were mesmerized by her. Even though Jessica had a fantastic body and knew how to move it, she simply didn't have the right mind-set to be an exotic dancer. None of the drooling men who surrounded Feather's stage with slightly bulging eyes and excessively bulging flies would agree with Aggie's opinion. All they saw was her beautiful outer package— not the severely broken heart within. Aggie saw it though. She'd recognized it the instant she'd met Jessica and helped her land this job. Poor lamb. So confused and conflicted.

Aggie returned her attention to the guy at her feet. She didn't have the same sympathy for men. "I do indulge for a price," Aggie told him, "but no sex."

"I don't need sex."

She nodded. He wasn't new to this. Which made him so much

more fun than her usual victims. She had a few regulars who visited her dungeon, but most of her customers were guys visiting Vegas, who wanted to explore their darker side for a night. She never saw most of them again, which suited her just fine. Many dommes preferred regulars, but Aggie would rather turn over a quick buck and avoid growing fond of one of her submissives.

Her current interest's body held tension in every line. When he glanced up at her, the deep emotional pain in his gaze made her belly quiver. *Yeah, blondie, you're exactly the challenge I need right now.* "I can work you over, angel, but not here. I'll slip you my card later, and you can call me. If you're lucky, I'll show you my dungeon."

He shuddered, his breath coming out in an excited gasp.

Maybe she should take him backstage and give him a taste of what she had to offer. He looked ready to explode with the strain of containing his pain. He needed the release she could give him. And she needed to see him grovel at her boots so she could dismiss him as not worth her time. The sooner he joined the thousands of men on List A, the better.

Aggie dropped down on her knees on the stage to continue dancing as she talked to him. "When do you need this?"

"As soon as possible."

"I think I have an opening in a few days."

"Tonight. I've got money. Name your price."

Name your price? He was definitely speaking her language, but making him wait would do half her work for her. She ran her blood-red, pointed nails down the side of his neck, leaving light scratches in their wakes. "I'll check my calendar and see if I can squeeze you in. Maybe tomorrow. Or the next day."

She was eager to raise welts on his flesh and hear him cry out in pain. Wanted the ultimate prize he would gift her: begging her for mercy, begging her to stop. That sweet instant he gave her all of his power and she *owned* him. That's what she wanted. What she needed to keep herself elevated from that deep, dark pit she'd once resided in. But it was too soon to indulge him. He'd attain greater fulfillment if she put him off a few days. Let the anticipation settle into his body and his thoughts until he could think of nothing but the delicious agony she promised.

A commotion on the other side of the room drew her attention. Eli, Aggie's bouncer, darted toward Feather's stage. Some big, good-looking customer had captured Jessica in his arms. She was wrapped in a leather jacket with her arms trapped helplessly. Several bouncers were trying to secure her release. Several others were escorting some tall, thin guy out of the club. A third guy standing next to Jessica's captor shook his head in disgrace. All three customers had a similar look to them. Like they were in some rock band or something. Come to think of it, the cute guy at the end of her stage had a similar appearance. A matching set. She looked down to find her potential good time had vanished.

"Motherfuckers!" her blond angel yelled as he launched himself onto the back of one of the bouncers.

When Jace saw that a bouncer was dragging Sinners drummer, Eric, toward the exit, he didn't think, he just acted. All thoughts of the beautiful, black-haired dominatrix and what glorious things she could do to his body fled his mind.

Jace raced across the club, hurdled a chair, and landed on the bouncer's back. He knew he wasn't big enough to take him down, but Jace could fight. If things had turned out differently, he might have become a professional boxer, instead of the bass guitarist for a rock band.

He didn't mind an occasional brawl—he was good at fighting and knew how to knock a man out in one punch—but Jace wasn't even sure why they were engaging with a bunch of bouncers at Brian's bachelor party. They were supposed to be celebrating, not stirring up shit. Eric had better have a good reason for making eight club bouncers pissed enough to hit anything that moved. As the fight moved to the sidewalk outside the club, it escalated. Jace took out a couple of guys with one punch, before pausing to assess the situation.

Tall and wiry, Eric was putting up a fine fight, but was outnumbered four to one. Surrounded on all sides with no way out, Eric unexpectedly pointed to the sky. "Look, the Flying Elvises!"

All four bouncers stared up at the dark sky like turkeys in a hailstorm. When their attention turned skyward, Eric crashed into one of the bouncers at waist level, trying to escape the circle of muscle, but as soon as they realized there were no parachuting icons to entertain them, all four bouncers pounded Eric in rapid succession.

Jace decided to even the odds. Two uppercuts and a couple dozen jabs later, two more bouncers lay on the sidewalk: one out cold, the other attempting to rise, but failing to regain his equilibrium.

Eric wiped the blood out of his eye, his surprised gaze shifting from the human debris at his feet to Jace. "Jesus, little man, you're a one-man wrecking crew."

Distracted by Eric's compliment, Jace found an unexpected fist against his jaw. Pain radiated up the side of his face. His ears rang. Vision blurred. The pain he didn't mind, but the jar to his senses left him unbalanced. He took another hit to the jaw before he could focus well enough to knock his adversary out with one hard punch under the chin.

Breathing hard, Jace spun and saw some guy whack Sinners rhythm guitarist, Trey, in the back of the head with an aluminum bat. Trey hadn't even been in the club when the fight broke out. Why had he been targeted? "Fuckin' queer," the bouncer growled.

Trey dropped to the sidewalk, instantly unconscious. Eric went after the fucktard with the bat, yanking the weapon out of his hands, and tossing it into the road beyond the sidewalk.

Acknowledgments

I'd like to thank the three f's—family, friends, and fans—for keeping me going when the writing got tough. Thanks to the rock and metal musicians who I find to be ever-inspiring. Also, thanks to everyone at Sourcebooks who helped get this book in front of the eyes of readers.

About the Author

Raised on hard rock music from the cradle, Olivia Cunning attended her first Styx concert at age six and fell instantly in love with live music. She's been known to travel over a thousand miles just to see a favorite band in concert. She discovered her second love, romantic fiction, as a teen—first, voraciously reading steamy romance novels and then penning her own. She currently lives in Texas.

The Sinners on Tour series includes:
Backstage Pass
Rock Hard
Double Time
Hot Ticket
Wicked Beat

Sinners on Tour

Rock Hard

by Olivia Cunning

On stage, on tour, in bed, they'll rock your world...

Trapped together on the Sinners tour bus for the summer, Sed and Jessica will rediscover the millions of steamy reasons they never should have called it quits in the first place...

"A full, well rounded romance... another dazzling story of Sinners, love, sex, and rock and roll!"—Night Owl Reviews Reviewer Top Pick

"Wicked, naughty, arousing, and you'll be craving the next page of this book as if you were living it for yourself!"—Dark Divas Reviews

"Hot men, rocking music, and explosive sex? What could be better?"
—Seriously Reviewed

"An erotic romance that is rockin' with action and a plotline that keeps you on your toes."
—Romance Fiction on Suite101.com

For more Olivia Cunning, visit:

www.sourcebooks.com

Backstage Pass

SINNERS ON TOUR

By Olivia Cunning

"Olivia Cunning's erotic romance
debut is phenomenal."
—LOVE ROMANCE PASSION

• •

FOR HIM, LIFE IS ALL MUSIC AND NO PLAY...

When Brian Sinclair, lead songwriter and guitarist of the hottest metal band on the scene, loses his creative spark, it will take nights of downright sinful passion to release his pent-up genius...

SHE'S THE ONE TO CALL THE TUNE...

When sexy psychologist Myrna Evans goes on tour with the Sinners, every boy in the band tries to woo her into his bed. But Brian is the only one she wants to get her hands on...

Then the two lovers' wildly shocking behavior sparks the whole band to new heights of glory... and sin...

• •

"These guys are so sensual, sexual, and yummy.
[T]his series... will give readers another wild ride,
and I can't wait!"
—NIGHT OWL REVIEWS
5/5 STARS
REVIEWER TOP PIC

For more Olivia Cunning, visit:

www.sourcebooks.com